ROSE TREMAIN

Sacred Country

With an Introduction by Peter Tatchell

VINTAGE

1 3 5 7 9 10 8 6 4 2

Vintage
20 Vauxhall Bridge Road,
London SW1V 2SA

Vintage is part of the Penguin Random House group of companies
whose addresses can be found at global.penguinrandomhouse.com.

Penguin
Random House
UK

This edition reissued in Vintage in 2017
First published in Vintage in 2002
First published in hardback by Sinclair-Stevenson in 1992

penguin.co.uk/vintage

A CIP catalogue record for this book is available from the British Library

ISBN 9781784705923

Printed and bound by Clays Ltd, St Ives plc

Penguin Random House is committed to a sustainable future
for our business, our readers and our planet. This book is made
from Forest Stewardship Council® certified paper.

MIX
Paper from
responsible sources
FSC
www.fsc.org   FSC® C018179

Contents

I live without inhabiting
Myself – in such a wise that I
Am dying that I do not die

   – St John of the Cross
   (Tr. ROY CAMPBELL)

'Seems, madam? Nay, it is. I know not "seems".'

   – 'Hamlet' Act I, Scene ii

Between the idea
And the reality
Between the motion
And the act
Falls the Shadow

   – 'The Hollow Men'
   T. S. ELIOT

To the memory
of Bernie Schweid

Introduction

When *Sacred Country* was first published in 1992, it passed me by. Well, not quite. I passed *it* by. I read about its publication and applauded what was, in those days, a rare groundbreaking illumination of transgender life, via a main character no less. This was, however, in the heyday of OutRage!, the LGBT direct-action group that was challenging the homophobia, biphobia and transphobia of the British Establishment. We did dramatic, spectacular protests every couple of weeks and were arrested almost as often. It was non-stop and, for me, full-time activism. I barely had time to eat or sleep, let alone read books – not even really groundbreaking ones like *Sacred Country*.

It has been a great pleasure to rediscover and finally read it decades later. And how moving and relevant it still is. Indeed, perhaps even more relevant than ever, in this era when trans issues are finally crossing over into the mainstream, with Caitlyn Jenner featuring on the cover of *Vanity Fair*, Jack Monroe becoming a celebrity cookery writer, Paris Lees achieving status as a media commentator and Channel 4's *My Transsexual Summer* proving such a ratings success.

The novel begins in February 1952 in the village of Swaithey in Suffolk – a sleepy backwater still steeped in tradition. Six-year-old Mary Ward, the child of an impoverished farming family, imagines sharing her special secret with her pet guinea fowl, Marguerite: 'I am not Mary. That is a mistake. I am not a girl. I'm a boy.' This realisation is the beginning of Mary's arduous, epic striving to become Martin.

Amid the setbacks, including rejection by her own father, Sonny, and neglect by her emotionally fragile and unstable mother, Estelle, there is a touching moment of satisfaction and happiness when Mary/Martin fondly recalls, with discreet pride, being called 'lad' by a boating attendant at the Serpentine. His use of the word lad 'stabbed me with pleasure,' she/he recounted. Stabbed with pleasure? It is a fierce, jolting phrase that evokes an image of painful joy, which is, perhaps, a harsh but true signifier of Mary/Martin's bittersweet personal odyssey.

Traversing three decades, this book is a story of the search for identity and fulfilment, on many different levels and in many different ways, as told through the life of Mary/Martin and from the sometimes contrary and contradictory first-person viewpoints of other characters. It involves several interweaving personal stories of nuanced, layered complexity, which we discover gradually through the slow-burn revelation of their lives as we turn the pages. *Sacred Country* tells not only Mary's journey to become Martin, but a similar searching and self-discovery by all the book's characters for something or someone – occasionally successful, mostly not.

Serious but not without humour and irony, Rose Tremain lightens the narrative with funny, quirky moments, helped by, or because, Swaithey has more than its fair share of oddballs and eccentrics. Many of them, not just Mary, end up facing disappointment or fleeing the village, or both. Mary's father, a stern patriarch, wants his son Timothy to take over the farm, but Timothy deserts the land to become a preacher, while Mary's mother retreats to the security of a mental institution. Walter leaves the family butcher's shop to start a new life in Nashville as a country singer. Gilbert, the gay dentist, runs off to London.

But it isn't all bad for Mary in Swaithey. Although she suffers the hurt of being disowned by many people around her, she is supported by a sympathetic Scottish teacher, her grandfather, who is a fan of Bob Dylan, and a carpenter who believes in reincarnation and wonders whether Mary's dysphoria might be connected to a previous life. It's not as if she is totally alone, and that no one cares about her and the hurdles she faces.

In time and geography, the story spans remote and repressive rural England in the Fifties, London's Swinging Sixties, and the Country and Western capital of Nashville, USA, in the Seventies. Being peppered with topical references to contemporary people and events grounds the storyline in time and place; all the better to relate to the characters and the ins and outs of their lives. The book opens with the death of King George VI in 1952 and is scattered with fleeting references to the English football captain, Bobby Moore, assorted familiar news stories, pop groups, department stores, and much more. It is a careful evocation of an era that older readers will recall and that younger ones may find perplexing.

Sacred Country deservedly won the James Tait Black Memorial Prize in 1992 and, two years later, the Prix Femina étranger. Apart from its undoubted literary merits, the book was ahead of its time in terms of a compassionate, non-sensationalist reflection of the trials and tribulations often faced by people who realise they are not the gender they were told they were. Without sentimentality or a tragic ending, it reflects, through the central protagonist and other characters, the often hurtful but ultimately successful personal struggles of most trans people to make sense of their true gender, find self-acceptance and achieve at least a degree of fulfilment – despite all the obstacles en route. Mary/Martin's striving is waylaid by the many prejudices and pitfalls that are familiar to almost every trans person. During the same period as the book, the former *Vogue* model and 1960s transgender pioneer,

April Ashley, was fighting a very public battle for recognition and rights. It is a battle that is still being fought today by trans men and women.

One of the virtues of *Sacred Country* is that the trans story is not the single overwhelming facet. It is just there, matter-of-factly in the pages, inviting us to accept it as another aspect of the diversity of human existence. Rose Tremain narrates a trans journey, from female to male, and in the process humanises a still-often-misunderstood gender identity; reaching readers who may not be reachable by trans campaigners. There is no anti-trans murder and no trans suicide in this novel. Though such fates befall transgender people disproportionately in a still-ignorant, fearful and prejudiced world, and particularly did so back in the 1950s and '60s when transphobia was far worse than it is today, tragedy was never the universal trans experience. Some people coped. They got through, undefeated. *Sacred Country* reveals the tale of one such ordinary, everyday trans person. Not a remote and privileged celebrity. Just an average Mary who becomes Martin.

Is this the definitive trans story? Of course not. No such single, all-embracing story can possibly exist because there are so many diverse transgender experiences. Although *Sacred Country* embodies only a few fragments of trans life, this does not diminish the insights, power, relevance and lessons of what it highlights in fictional form. Being trans is still a challenge. Leaving aside intolerant attitudes, the typical regime of hormones plus surgery is liberating, but not easy. It can take a physical and emotional toll, staggered over many years of treatment. Speaking of the pain after his first gender-reassignment surgery, a bilateral mastectomy, Martin recalls: 'I remember how, in the past, I had imagined pain was my ally. I had imagined that if I suffered enough, I would become a man, of my body's own accord.'

Martin has more than his fair share of suffering, including heartbreaking disappointment in love. 'The woman I wanted was Pearl. I wanted to be Pearl's universe. For her, I would have re-made myself as often and as completely as she demanded. She could have gone on inventing me until death parted us', Martin avowed, still bleeding from his breast-removal scars. But that is not the emotional end. 'It isn't finished and never can be, really', he later tells his grandfather.

One way you could read this book is as a metaphor for a rapidly changing post-imperial Britain: the decline of the old order, with its cosy certainties, and the rise of new, unexpected and previously ignored, derided and suppressed identities. A transition from a monocultural to multicultural country, with all the upheavals, setbacks, confusions, triumphs and disappointments that personal and social change so frequently involves.

Rose Tremain writes a story that, while it is not the same as mine, is one that I, as a gay man and dissenting critic of the status quo, can relate to. It is the narrative of an outsider in a society of defined expectations and narrow-minded conformism. Mary/Martin faces rejection by much of Swaithey, with its small-village mentality, but still manages to chart a course – with ups and downs – to live as the person he truly is: a man.

This is the account of a life that begins as ordinary, even pedestrian. Then, by dint of Mary's self-awareness of a gender 'mistake', it reaches out to become something that transcends the everyday anticipations of her countryside backwater and beyond; confounding the doubters and antagonists.

Peter Tatchell, 2017

Part One

Part One

I

1952

The Two-Minute Silence

On February 15th 1952 at two o'clock in the afternoon, the nation fell silent for two minutes in honour of the dead King. It was the day of his burial.

Traffic halted. Telephones did not ring. Along the radio airwaves came only hushed white noise. In the street markets, the selling of nylons paused. In the Ritz, the serving of luncheon was temporarily suspended. The waiters stood to attention with napkins folded over their arms.

To some, caught on a stationary bus, at a loom gone suddenly still, or at a brass band rehearsal momentarily soundless, the silence was heavy with eternity. Many people wept and they wept not merely for the King but for themselves and for England: for the long, ghastly passing of time.

On the Suffolk farms, a light wet snow began to fall like salt.

The Ward family stood in a field close together. Sonny Ward had not known – because the minute hand had fallen off his watch – at what precise moment to begin the silence. His wife, Estelle, hadn't wanted them to stand round like this out in the grey cold. She'd suggested they stay indoors with a fire to cheer them and the wireless to tell them what to do, but Sonny had said no, they should be out under the sky, to give their prayers an easier route upwards. He said the people of England owed it to the wretched King to speak out for him so that at least he wouldn't stammer in Heaven.

So there they were, gathered round in a potato field: Sonny and Estelle, their daughter, Mary, and their little son, Tim. Pathetic, Sonny thought they looked, pathetic and poor. And the suspicion that his family's silence was not properly synchronised with that of the nation as a whole annoyed Sonny for a long time afterwards. He'd asked his neighbour, Ernie Loomis, to tell him when to begin it, but Loomis had forgotten. Sonny had wondered whether there wouldn't be some sign – a piece of sky writing or a siren from Lowestoft – to give him the order, but none came, so when the hour hand of his watch covered the two, he put down his hoe and said: 'Right. We'll have the silence now.'

They began it.

The salt snow fell on their shoulders.

It was a silence within a silence already there, but nobody except Mary knew that its memory would last a lifetime.

Mary Ward was six years old. She had small feet and hands and a flat, round face that reminded her mother of a sunflower. Her straight brown hair was held back from her forehead by a tortoiseshell slide. She wore round glasses to correct her faulty vision. The arms of these spectacles pinched the backs of her ears. On the day of the silence she was wearing a tweed coat too short for her, purple mittens, wellingtons and a woollen head scarf patterned with windmills and blue Dutchmen. Her father, glancing at her blinking vacantly in the sleet, thought her a sad sight.

She had been told to think about King George and pray for him. All she could remember of the King was his head, cut off at the neck on the twopenny stamp, so she started to pray for the stamp, but these prayers got dull and flew away and she turned her head this way and that, wondering if she wasn't going to see, at the edge of her hopeless vision, her

4

pet guineafowl, Marguerite, pecking her dainty way over the ploughed earth.

Estelle, that very morning, had inadvertently sewn a hunk of her thick black hair to some parachute silk with her sewing machine. She had screamed when she saw what she'd done. It was grotesque. It was like a crime against herself. And though now, in the silence, Estelle made herself be quiet, she could still hear her voice screaming somewhere far away. Her head was bowed, but she saw Sonny look up, first at Mary and then at her. And so instead of seeing the dead King lying smart in his naval uniform, she saw herself as she was at that precise moment, big in the flat landscape, beautiful in spite of her hacked hair, a mystery, a woman falling and falling through time and the fall endless and icy. She put her palms together, seeking calm. 'At teatime,' she whispered, 'I shall do that new recipe for flapjacks.' She believed her whispering was soundless, but it was not. Estelle's mind often had difficulty distinguishing between thoughts and words said aloud.

Sonny banged his worn flat cap against his thigh. He began to cough. 'Shut you up, Estelle!' he said through the cough. 'Or else we'll have to start the silence again.'

Estelle put her hands against her lips and closed her eyes. When Sonny's cough subsided, he looked down at Tim. Tim, his treasure. Timmy, his boy. The child had sat down on a furrow and was trying to unlace his little boots. Sonny watched as one boot was tugged off, pulling with it a grey sock and revealing Timmy's foot. To Sonny, the soft foot looked boneless. Tim stuck it into the mud, throwing the boot away like a toy.

'Tim!' hissed Mary. 'Don't be bad!'

'Shut you up, girl!' said Sonny.

'I can't hear any silence at all,' said Estelle.

'Begin it again,' ordered Sonny.

So Mary thought, how many minutes is it going to be? Will it get dark with us still standing here?

And then the idea of them waiting there in the field, the snow little by little settling on them and whitening them over, gave Mary a strange feeling of exaltation, as if something were about to happen to her that had never happened to anybody in the history of Suffolk or the world.

She tried another prayer for the King, but the words blew away like paper. She wiped the sleet from her glasses with the back of her mittened hand. She stared at her family, took them in, one, two, three of them, quiet at last but not as still as they were meant to be, not still like the plumed men guarding the King's coffin, not still like bulrushes in a lake. And then, hearing the familiar screech of her guineafowl coming from near the farmhouse, she thought, I have some news for you, Marguerite, I have a secret to tell you, dear, and this is it: I am not Mary. That is a mistake. I am not a girl. I'm a boy.

This was how and when it began, the long journey of Mary Ward.

It began in an unsynchronised silence the duration of which no one could determine, for just as Sonny hadn't known when to begin it, so he couldn't tell when to end it. He just let his family stand out there in the sleet, waiting, and the waiting felt like a long time.

The Beautiful Baby Contest

In April that year, Sonny lost eleven lambs to freezing weather. Anger always made him deaf. The more angry he grew, the louder he shouted.

Part of his left ear had been shot off in the war. He'd seen a small piece of himself floating away on the waters of the Rhine. What remained was a branching bit of cartilege, like soft coral. In his deaf rages, Sonny would gouge at the coral with his thumb, making blood run down his neck.

Sonny took the frozen lambs to his neighbour, Ernie Loomis, to be butchered and stored in his cold room. On Sonny's farm nothing was allowed to go to waste. And he couldn't bear the way Estelle was becoming careless with things in the house, so absent-minded about everything that sometimes she forgot what she was holding in her hands. He wanted to hit her when this happened, hit her head to wake her thoughts up. That day when she'd sewn her hair to the piece of silk, he'd made her unpick the seam, stitch by stitch with a razor blade, until all the hair was out.

In a silver frame on the kitchen mantelpiece Estelle kept a photograph of her mother. She had been a piano teacher. The photograph showed her as she'd been in 1935, a year before her sudden death in a glider. She had belonged to the Women's League of Health and Beauty and this was how she remained in Estelle's mind – healthy, with her hair wavy and gleaming, beautiful with a gentle smile. 'Gliders, you know,' Estelle had once told Mary in the whispery voice she used when she talked about her mother, 'are also, in fact, very beautiful things.' And it was suggested to Mary, even after she began wearing her glasses, that she had some of Grandma Livia's looks. 'I think,' Estelle would murmur, 'that you will grow up to be quite like her.'

Mary was fond of the photograph of her grandmother. She looked quiet and peaceful and Mary was fairly sure she hadn't said thoughts out loud. And when she thought about her death in the glider, she didn't imagine it crashing into a wood or plummeting down onto a village; she dreamed of it just drifting away into a white sky, at first a speck, white on white, then merging into the sky, dissolving and gone. But she had never been able to imagine herself growing up to be like Grandma Livia. She knew she would not become beautiful or join the Women's League, whatever a Women's

League might be. And after the day of the two-minute silence, she knew she would not even be a woman. She didn't tell her mother this and naturally she didn't tell her father because since the age of three she had told him nothing at all. She didn't even tell Miss McRae, her teacher. She decided it was a secret. She just whispered it once to Marguerite and Marguerite opened her beak and screeched.

After the death of the lambs, some warm weather came. In May, the community of Swaithey held its annual fête in a field outside the village, well shaded by a line of chestnut trees. These fêtes always had as their main attraction a competition of some sort: Best Flower Arrangement, Child's Most Original Fancy Dress, Largest Vegetable, Most Obedient Dog, Most Talented Waltzer and Quickstepper. Prizes were generous: a dozen bottles of stout, a year's subscription to *Radio Fun* or *Flix*, a sack of coal. This year there was to be a competition to find Swaithey's Most Beautiful Baby. Entry coupons were threepence, the prize unknown.

Estelle's faulty imagination was tantalised by the idea of an unknown prize. The word 'unknown' seemed to promise something of value: a visit to the Tower of London, a Jacqmar scarf, a meeting with Mr Churchill. She had no baby to enter, yet she refused to let this precious unknown elude her altogether. She bought an entry coupon and took it to her friend, Irene Simmonds.

Irene lived alone with her illegitimate baby, Pearl. The father had been Irish and worked 'in the print' in Dublin. 'He tasted of the dye,' Irene had told Estelle, but the taste quickly faded and was gone and no word, printed or otherwise, came out of Dublin in answer to Irene's letters. She was a practical woman. She had an ample smile and a plump body and a heart of mud. For a long time, she dreamed of the Irish printer but her dreams never showed. All that showed was her devotion to Pearl.

When Estelle came with the threepenny coupon, Irene was

feeding Pearl. Her white breasts were larger than the baby's head. They could have nourished a tribe. Pearl's little life was lived in a sweet, milky oblivion.

Estelle sat down with Irene and put the entry ticket on the kitchen table. 'The unknown,' she said, 'is always likely to be better.'

Irene filled out the coupon, in the careful handwriting she'd perfected to try to win the printer's devotion: *Entrant: Pearl Simmonds, Born April the 22nd, 1951.* While she did this, Estelle took Pearl on her lap and looked at her, trying to imagine herself as a judge of Swaithey's Most Beautiful Baby. Pearl's hair was as pale as lemonade. Her eyes were large and blue and liquid. Her mouth was fine like Irene's, with the same sweetness to it. 'You must win, cherub,' Estelle instructed Pearl, 'our hopes are on you.'

Sonny refused to go to the fête. He had no money to spare on trifles, no time to waste on fancy dress of any kind.

Estelle went in the pony cart with Mary and Tim. It was a hot day, a record for May, the wireless said. The lanes were snowy with Damsel's Lace. Mary wore a new dress made from a remnant and hand-smocked by Estelle. In the pony cart she began to detest the feel of the smocking against her chest and kept clawing at it.

They stopped at Irene's cottage. Pearl was sleeping in a wicker basket, wrapped in her white christening shawl. They laid the basket on some sacks that smelled of barley. After a bit, Pearl began to snore. Mary had never heard anyone snore except her father, let alone a baby.

'Why is she?' Mary asked Irene.

'Oh,' said Irene, 'she's always been a snorer, right from the off.'

Mary knelt down in the cart and looked at Pearl. The snoring entranced her so, it took her mind off the smocking.

The Beautiful Baby Contest was to be held in a large green tent, ex-army. The mothers would line up on hard chairs and hold their babies aloft as the judges passed. From thirty-six entrants, five would be selected for a second round. There would be one winner and four consolation prizes. All the way there in the cart, Estelle thought about the word 'consolation' and how she didn't like it at all. Things which promised to console never did any such thing.

The afternoon grew hotter and hotter, as if all of June and July were being crammed into this single day. At the tombola Estelle won a chocolate cake which began to melt, so she told Mary and Tim to eat it. There was no breeze to make the home-made bunting flutter.

Towards two o'clock, Irene took Pearl to the shade of the chestnuts to give her a drink of rosehip syrup and to change her nappy. Mary asked to go with her. The heat and the smocking had made her chest itch so much she had scratched it raw and now little circles of blood were visible among the silky stitches. She wanted to show Irene these blood beads. Being with Irene was, for Mary, like being inside some kind of shelter that you'd made yourself. It was quiet. Nobody shouted.

Irene examined the blood on the smocking. She undid Mary's dress and bathed the scratches with the damp rags she carried for cleaning up Pearl.

'There's hours of work in smocking, Mary,' Irene said.

'I know,' said Mary.

They said nothing more. Irene fastened the dress again, kneeling by Mary on the cool grass. She held her shoulders and looked at her. Mary's glasses were dirty and misted up, her thin hair lay damp round her head like a cap. Irene understood that she was refusing to cry. 'Right,' she said, 'now we have to get Pearl ready to be beautiful.'

She handed Mary a clean square of white towelling and Mary laid it carefully on the grass. She smoothed it down before she folded it. Irene took off Pearl's wet nappy and laid Pearl on the clean folded square. She took out of her bag a tin of talcum and powdered Pearl's bottom until the shiny flesh was velvety and dry. Mary watched. There was something about Pearl that mesmerised her. It was as if Pearl were a lantern slide and Mary sitting on a chair in the dark. Mary took off her glasses. Without them, it seemed to her that there were two Pearls, or almost two, lying in the chestnut shade, and Mary heard herself say a thought aloud, like her mother did. 'If there were two,' she said to Irene, 'then there would be one for you and one for me.'

'Two what, Mary?'

But Mary stopped. She attached her glasses to her ears. 'Oh,' she said, 'I don't know what I meant. I expect I was thinking about the cake Mother won, because you didn't eat any.'

'It's hot,' said Irene, fastening the safety pin of Pearl's nappy. 'It's going to be sweltering in that tent.'

The mothers crowded in. There were far more mothers than chairs, so some had to stand, faint from the burning afternoon and the weight of the babies. The judges' opening remarks could hardly be heard above the crying. Lady Elliot from Swaithey Hall, neat in her Jacqmar scarf, said she had never seen such a crowd of pretty tots. She said: 'Now I and my fellow judges are going to pass among you and on our second passing we will give out rosettes to the final five.'

There was laughter at the idea of the rosettes. The babies were hushed by this sudden ripple of noise. Estelle, with Mary and Tim, stood by one of the tent flaps, praying for a breeze and for the unknown to arrive in Irene's lap. Mary had her eyes closed. She felt a sudden sorrowful fury. She didn't want there to be a contest after all.

The judges barely looked at Pearl. They walked on with just a glance and the only thing that came to Irene waiting patiently on her chair was a waft of French perfume as Lady Elliot passed.

The competition was won by a Mrs Nora Flynn. The unknown became a trug and trowel, and Mrs Nora Flynn laid her baby, Sally Mahonia, in the trug, like a prize cabbage.

On the way home in the cart, Irene seemed as content as if the day had never been. Timmy was silent, pale from an afternoon like a dream, tugged here and there and seeing nothing but shimmer. Estelle said bitterly that a trug and trowel could not be classified as 'unknown' and she drove the pony at a slow, disappointed pace.

Mary said: 'I didn't clap when that Sally Mahonia won. I didn't clap at all.' And then, tired out from scratching her chest and eating cake and wanting Pearl to be recognised as the Most Beautiful Baby in Swaithey, she fell asleep in Irene's lap.

Pearl, unvisited by any thoughts, slept near her on the barley sacks, softly snoring.

Mary:

I can remember way back, almost to when I was born.

I can remember lying in my parents' bed, jammed between them. It was an iron bed with a sag in the middle. They put me into the sag and gravity made them fall towards me, wedging me in.

Our land was full of stones. As soon as I could walk, I was given a bucket with a picture of a starfish on it and told to pick stones out of the earth. My father would walk ahead with a big pail that was soon so heavy he could barely carry it. I think he thought about stones all the time and he tried to make me think about them all the time. I was supposed to take my starfish bucket with me wherever I went and have my mind on the stones.

I can remember getting lost in a flat field. It was winter and the dark came round me and hid me from everything and swallowed up my voice. The only thing I could see was my bucket, which had a little gleam on it, and the only thing I could hear was the wind in the firs. I began to walk towards the wind, calling to my father. I walked right into the trees. They sighed and sighed. I put my arms round one of the scratchy fir trunks and stayed there, waiting. I thought Jesus might come through the wood holding up a lantern.

My parents came and found me with torches. My mother was sobbing. My father picked me up and wrapped me inside his old coat that smelled of seed. He said: 'Mary, why didn't you stay where you were?' I said: 'My bucket is lost on the field.' My father said: 'Never mind about the bucket. You're the one.'

But when I was three, I was no longer the one. Tim was born and my father kept saying the arrival of Timmy was a miracle. I asked my mother whether I had been a miracle and she said: 'Oh, men are like that, especially farmers. Pay no heed.'

But after Timmy came, everything changed. My mother and father used to put him between them in their sagging bed and fall towards him. When I saw this, I warned them I would kick Timmy to death; I said I would put his pod through the mangle. So my father began to think me evil. I'd go and tell him things and he'd say: 'Don't talk to me, Mary. Don't you talk to me.' So I stopped talking to him at all. When we went stone picking together, we would go up and down the furrows, up and down, up and down, with each of our minds locked away from the other.

My vision began to be faulty soon after Timmy was born. I would see light bouncing at the corner of my eye. Distant things like birds became invisible. People would separate and become two of themselves.

I tried to tell my mother how peculiar everything was

becoming. She was going through a phase of needing to touch surfaces all the time. Her favourite surface was the wheel of the sewing machine and her long, white thumb would go round and round it, like something trapped. When I told her about people becoming two of themselves, she put her hand fiercely over my mouth. 'Ssh!' she said. *'Don't.* I'm superstitious.'

So it was my teacher, Miss McRae at the village school, who discovered my faulty vision. She told my mother: 'Mary cannot see the blackboard, Mrs Ward.' Which was true. The blackboard was like a waterfall to me.

I went with my mother on a bus from Swaithey to Leiston to see an oculist. The bus had to make an extra stop to let some ducks cross the road. I ran to the driver's window so that I could see the ducks, but all I could see were five blobs creeping along like caterpillars.

A week later I got my glasses. Timmy laughed at me with them on, so I hit his ear. I hoped I'd hit him so hard his vision would go faulty too. 'How are they, then?' asked my father crossly, holding Timmy.

'They are a miracle,' I said.

Miss McRae looked like a person made of bark.

Her back was as straight and as thin as a comb. Her nose was fierce. Her long hands were hard and freckled.

Every child in that school was afraid of Miss McRae when they first saw her. They thought, if they went near her, they'd be scratched. But when she spoke, her Scottish voice brought a feeling of peace into the room and everyone was quiet. She began every day with a story of something she'd done when she was a girl, as if she knew she looked to us like a person who had never been a child. The first words I heard her say were: 'When I was a lass, I lived in a lighthouse.' And after that I liked Miss McRae and began to tell her some of the things I refused to tell my father.

That summer, sometime after the Beautiful Baby Contest, Miss McRae said to us: 'Now, class, on Monday, I want you each to bring something to school. I want you to bring in something that is important or precious to you, or just something pretty that you like. And then I want you to tell me and the other children *why* you like it or why it is precious to you. It can be anything you like. No one need be afraid of looking silly. All you have to remember is to be able to say why you've chosen it.'

On the way home from school, I began to think about what I would take as my precious thing. When I'd been born, my mother had given me a silver chain with a silver and glass locket on it. Inside the locket was a piece of Grandmother Livia's hair and my mother had said recently that I should treasure this locket for always and that, if I ever wore it, I should touch it every ten minutes to make certain it was still round my neck. I used to look at it sometimes. It made me wonder what Grandma Livia had been wearing round her neck when she got into the glider. I thought it was the kind of thing Miss McRae would like and I could hear her say approvingly: 'What a pretty wee thing, Mary.' But it wasn't really precious to me. And if a thing isn't precious to you then it isn't and that's it; it won't become precious suddenly between Friday and Monday.

When I got home from school, I looked around my room. I thought I might find something precious I'd forgotten about. But there was hardly anything in my room: just my bed, which had come out of a cottage hospital sale, and a table with a lamp on it and a huge old wardrobe, in which I kept my sweet tin and my spelling book and my boots. The tin had a picture of a Swiss chalet on it. It contained at that time two ounces of sherbert lemons and three Macintoshes toffees. I got it out and put a sherbert lemon into my mouth. I thought the little burst of sherbert might wake me up to the preciousness of something, but it didn't and then I had this thought: no one has ever told me where Grandma Livia was *going* in that glider. Was she just going to Ipswich or was she going to the Tyrrhenian Sea?

By Sunday evening, after looking in my mother's sewing basket and in her button box and in all the crannies of the house where an important thing might have hidden itself and finding nothing, I decided that I couldn't go to school the next day. I would walk a long way from our farm. I would find a hayfield coming to its second cropping and I would sit in it and think about my coming life as a boy. I would examine myself for signs. Or I might climb a tree and stay there out of reach of everyone and everything, including all the stones in the soil.

For my mid-day dinner, my mother made me pickle sandwiches and a thermos of lemon squash. In the winter, the thermos had tea in it and the taste of the tea lingered over into the summer and came into the lemon squash, tepid and strange.

At the bottom of our lane, instead of turning left towards Swaithey and school, I turned right and began to run. I kept running until I was beyond the fields that were ours and then I stopped under a signpost and sat down. It was very hot there, even in that early morning sun. I drank some of my lemon squash. And then after about five minutes I got up and began tearing back the way I had come. I had remembered my precious thing.

I was late for the class. I had had some trouble on the way with Irene, who said: 'What are you thinking of, Mary Ward? Whatever are you like?'

'Please, Irene,' I begged. *'Please.'*

I was in Mr Harker's house, where Irene worked. Mr Harker had turned his cellar into a factory where he made cricket bats. The smell of wood and oil came up into all the rooms. A painted sign on his gate said: *Harker's Bats.*

'It'd only be for half an hour,' I pleaded.

'No,' said Irene. 'Now run along to school.'

But I got her in the end: Pearl, my precious thing.

I carried her like a big vase with both my arms round her. Miss McRae took her glasses off and frowned and said: 'Whatever in the world, Mary?' Lots of children giggled. I opened my desk top and laid Pearl down in my desk with her head on my Arithmetic book. I closed my ears and my mind to everybody laughing.

Pearl gazed at me. She looked frightened. I don't suppose she'd ever been in a desk before. I gave her a little wooden ruler to play with but she hit herself on the nose with it and began to cry.

'My, my,' I heard Miss McRae say, 'this is very irregular, Mary. Will you tell me please what this baby is doing in my lesson?'

I had to pick Pearl up to stop her crying. The boy who sat next to me, Billy Bateman, was laughing so hard he asked to be excused. I looked over to his desk and saw that he'd brought in a stamp album, all mutilated and falling apart, as if it had belonged to Noah. When I'm a boy, I thought, I'll be a more interesting one than him.

'Mary?' said Miss McRae.

I felt my heart jump about inside my aertex blouse. I felt thirsty and very peculiarly sad. I thought I might cry, which was a thing I never did, but sometimes you cry with your face and your mind isn't in it, but somewhere else, watching you. It was like that. It was my face that felt sad.

The thing was, I didn't know what to say about Pearl. I didn't understand why she was important to me, except that I thought she was very beautiful and I still couldn't see why she hadn't won that contest.

I held her awkwardly. When Timmy was born, my mother had tried to show me how to hold a baby, but I'd refused to listen. I thought, I must say something before Pearl slips out of my arms.

'Is this baby your precious thing, Mary?' asked Miss McRae kindly.

I nodded.

'I see, dear,' she said, 'well in that case, perhaps you will be able to tell the class why?'

Pearl, at that moment, let her head fall onto my shoulder, as if she wanted to go to sleep and start snoring. Her hand was still on my cheek, holding on to it. I said: 'Her name's Pearl. I was going to bring this locket with some of my grandmother's hair in it.'

'Yes, dear?'

'But.'

'Yes?'

'It wasn't precious.'

'No?'

'No. It wasn't.'

'But Pearl is?'

'Yes.'

'And I wonder if you can tell us why, Mary?'

'Some things are.'

'That's quite true.'

'But you can't say it properly. Like my mother can't. If you asked her to bring in a thing, she'd have maybe brought in her sewing machine.'

Miss McRae waited. After a bit, she understood that I couldn't say anything more so she nodded gravely. My face was boiling red. I thought I might be going to explode and see my insides splatter out all over my desk and all over Billy Bateman's stamp album. I asked if I could sit down and Miss McRae said yes, so I sat and watched the next child go up with her precious thing. It was my so-called friend, Judy Weaver. She'd brought an ugly little salmon-coloured doll, dressed as a fairy. I'd seen this doll standing on the window sill in her parents' bathroom. It was a toilet-roll cover. You stuffed the doll's thin legs down the cardboard tube and her gauzy skirt went over the paper, hiding it from view.

After that day of the Precious Things, I didn't want Judy Weaver as a friend any more. I didn't want any friends. None.

The Blue Yodeller

For four generations, the Loomis family had lived in Swaithey. Their shop, Arthur Loomis & Son, Family Butchers, had opened in 1861. A faded photograph of old Arthur, wearing a long apron and holding a tray of dressed game, now hung in the shop window above the pork joints and the skinned rabbits and the bowls of tripe. Smiling and plump, with a thick moustache, he looked like a man fattening himself up for eternity. All the generations of sons who followed him and kept the business thriving had heard Arthur Loomis speak to them in their sleep. It was as if every one of them had got to know him in time. Ernie Loomis, the present proprietor, born twelve years after Arthur had died, could describe his voice. 'Nice and slow,' he said it was, 'and nice and gentle.'

Behind the shop was the cold room and behind this, hidden from sight by a high wall, was the slaughtering yard. The animals were strung up by their hind legs on a pulley. Their blood flowed into a gully and from there into a drain which debouched into a soakaway under the very field the heifers grazed in summer.

In one corner of this field lived Ernie Loomis's brother, Pete. His home was a converted trolley bus, its roof pitched and thatched. Between Pete's living room and his cramped kitchen was a sign which read: *Push button once to stop bus.*

Nobody much except the family knew Pete Loomis. He worked in the slaughtering yard or in the fields, never in the shop. The iris of his left eye wandered, so that he could seldom look square at a person, yet at the moment of a slaughter his eyes aligned themselves and he slit with precision. He had no wife or child. He'd spent some time in the American South. There were rumours of a long-ago crime. In the village drapers, where he bought his underwear, the Misses Cunningham referred to him as 'a most uncustomary man'.

Yet he was a boon to Ernie. Ernie had never liked the yard. His art was in dead meat. The gentry of East Suffolk knew him by name, as he knew them. His voice, like his ancestor's, was quiet, his fingers nimble. He was diligent, ordered and clean. Every morning, he got up at five and brought his wife, Grace, a cup of tea and kissed her forehead, moist from her night. By six he was at his block and at eight the shutters of the shop went up. All day long, while Ernie passed between block and counter, Grace sat in a little booth with her cash register and her book of accounts. When there was no one in the shop, Ernie would talk to her through the glass.

Ernie and Grace had one child, Walter. At sixteen, he resembled Pete more than Ernie. He had a dreamy look. His hair was thick and black, like Pete's. His cheeks had a high colour. His spelling was poor and his handwriting laboured. As a child, he'd grown much too fast and the pain of this growing had been felt in every one of his bones. But now it had stopped. He hoped there wouldn't be another spurt of it. He let his limbs relax and get ready for life.

He noticed then, when he could listen to what was outside his pain, that his singing voice was rather fine – so peculiarly fine he felt it couldn't possibly belong to him. He sang as he worked, sometimes helping his parents in the shop, but more often mucking out the pig sties and feeding the hens or working with Pete in the yard. He didn't know the words to many songs, only the things he'd grown up with: old soupy ballads such as 'The Minstrel Boy' and 'Barbara Allen' and some of the wartime favourites his mother loved so, 'Ida, Sweet as Apple Cider', 'Love is the Sweetest Thing', 'When They Sound the Last All-Clear'.

His Uncle Pete taught him to play a banjo. The two of them would sit in Pete's bus, strumming simple chords. And then Walter would sing and they'd both incline their heads towards the *Push button once* sign, as if the song might be coming from there. Sometimes, it got dark on their banjo sessions, and cold, and the grazing heifers would cluster round the bus, flanks tightly packed, drawn to the body of the old trolley by the blueish light of the Tilley lamp and by the melody.

Devotion to things came easily to Walter. Once devoted, he would not be turned aside. In despair about his hopeless schoolwork and the pain of his growing, Ernie and Grace consoled themselves with this devotion of his. Every night before going to his room, he let his mother embrace him and his father give him a comradely pat on the shoulder. He told them he was proud that the name Loomis was known across half the country and that one day the shop would be his. Yet, privately, he had difficulty imagining this. He lacked his father's skill with the knife and his mother's head for sums. And he was happiest outside. 'You and I,' Pete said to him in the bus one evening, 'we're hillbillies, Walter.' And Walter grinned, liking the sound of the word.

On a night of heavy summer rain, Pete got drunk on whisky. He lay on the floor of the bus with his head propped up by a chair. His wall eye meandered about, looking for a memory. He began to talk about Memphis. He said: 'I was a gardener in Memphis in '38. A church gardener.'

'What's a church gardener?' asked Walter.

'Gardener to a church. In this case, Baptist. With three

lawns and two beds of annuals and a lot of roses. And what came out of that church was music.'

'What kind of music?'

'Gospel music. Lovely sound, boy. Used to send me trickles up and down me.'

He told Walter that he never would have left Memphis but for something that happened there. He said happiness was the main condition in Tennessee, despite the Depression and the bad times. Blacks were faithful there. Dogs were faithful. Even the seasons were faithful. Spring came in an afternoon. Winter tore in on an ice storm. 'And the fall, Walter, well, that lets you lie in it an' dream, and out of all the fall-dreaming comes the music.'

He made Walter get up and look for an old record among his collection of 78s in brown-paper sleeves that he kept in a wooden chest with an eiderdown and some mole traps. 'Jimmie Rodgers!' Pete announced. 'The Singing Brakeman, The Blue Yodeller! You put that on the grammy and have a listen . . .'

Walter found the record. He got out Pete's box gramophone and wound it up. The way the heavy, silvery needle arm was moulded to twist over so easily pleased him. He sat down and waited for the scratching of the needle to become song.

It was a jaunty tune. It had a kind of clip-clopping rhythm. It was called 'The Yodelling Cowboy'. Pete made clicking noises with his tongue, keeping time. Walter crouched by the record, watching it go round. The words appealed to him: 'My cowboy life is so happy and free/Out where the law don't bother me.' He liked to think of men on horseback riding about in what Pete called the fall with nothing to interrupt their happiness. He imagined the golden light that fell on them and the faithful dogs at their heels. But it was Jimmie Rodgers's mastery of the yodel that moved him. It was as if the voice had added a second instrument to its own one-note-at-a-time sound. It took the song up into the sky.

'Well?' said Pete, pouring himself the last of the whisky.

'I like the yodel,' said Walter.

'Didn't I tell you? That Rodgers, he could yodel his gizzard off! Play the other side, boy.'

On the other side was 'Frankie and Johnny', a sad number about a man cheating on his love. In this, the yodel was slower and had a sob to it, as if the old singing brakeman were breaking up. The words were easy to remember: 'He was her man/But he done her wrong,' and on the second time of playing it, Pete and Walter joined in. 'He was her man/But he done her wrong!'

Pete shook his whisky-laden head from side to side, as though in despair at Johnny's wrong doing and out of the chaos of his eyes fell slow tears like oil. He looked ready to slump down and sleep, but his mind had a last squeeze of sense in it and he kept talking. 'I saw him sing once, that old yodelling boy,' he said to Walter, 'and I never forgot how he talked in between songs. Just saying things. Whatever was on his mind. He'd say to his people on stage: "Play the tune, Mamma!" and then he'd strum a bit and look at us all out there and say: "Hey, hey, hey, it won't be long now . . ." And he got known for that. That was his trademark: "Hey, hey, hey, it won't be long now." Lord knows what he meant by it, precisely speaking, but when he said that the audience would clap, you see, Walter? You can imagine that, can't you? Everybody clapping? And thinking to themselves, damn it if he isn't right! Because, in all probability, it won't be long, eh?'

Walter put the record back into its charred-looking sleeve. He closed the gramophone. The rain had stopped and he could see a skin of moonlight on the window ledges of the bus. Pete's body had yielded to gravity and his head now lay on the dusty floor. Walter felt light, as if the bulk of his life had gone up into the night sky with the yodel. He thought he should drag Pete onto his bed, but the task seemed to be too heavy for his frame.

He just sat still in his chair and made promises to himself. He would teach himself to yodel. He would practise out in the fields and in the sties where no one could hear. He would save up and buy a guitar. He would sing no more stupid wartime songs. From now on, he would learn hillbilly music. He would try to find the soul of it and lie there, like Pete said you could lie in the Tennessee fall, and dream.

2

1954

In Harker's Cellar

The colour of the light in Edward Harker's cellar was amber. He worked under a row of tilting, parchment-shaded lamps. The only bright spot in the room was a white bubble of illumination at the base of the large magnifying lens with which he examined the grain of the willow wood for his cricket bats.

Harker was exacting about light. A grey or blueish quality vexed him. On days when a pall of flat, shadowless white hung over the village, he would not go out. He sent Irene to do his errands. He refused to look up at the slit of window that gave him air.

The lamps cast long shadows. They were the shadows of ancient evenings, of deckchair and scoreboard, of dead friends. He was a sentimental man. He stood at his workbench as if at an altar to the past.

He was sixty-one. His hair was thick but almost white. His face was narrow, with a long enquiring nose. He sneezed frequently, displacing sawdust never swept from surfaces. His only vanity was the daily wearing of a bow tie. Though he seldom talked about God or the universe, he held an unshakeable belief in the transmigration of souls. He was fairly certain that, three centuries ago, he had been a lutenist at the court of the Danish King, Christian IV. In this incarnation, he had been persecuted in a way that he found both absurd and reprehensible. The story of this persecution he would tell only to people he trusted to understand its significance.

His cricket bats were works of sculpture. He fancifully thought of them as shrouded figures or again sometimes as musical instruments. No two were precisely the same, yet the Harker stamp was on them all. Brand new, they seemed already subtly moulded by usage and time. Their sounds against the ball had a gratifying, recognisable sweetness. An industry of one, the name of Harker was known around the cricketing counties. Players came from as far away as Yorkshire to be measured for a Harker bat.

Married once and long ago divorced, Harker had reached a plateau in his life, what he called 'level ground', from which he could see both forwards and behind. He did not expect to be dislodged from this place. Any significant interruption to his routine was unimaginable to him. He told his few friends that the only event of any importance awaiting him was his death and rebirth. He had an affinity with hunted creatures, with dying breeds. He loved woodland. He wondered whether he might not return as a fox.

And then, in the autumn of 1954, something began to happen to him. Down in the cellar, apparently absorbed at his workbench, among the solid shadows, he noticed in himself a little worm of inattention, minuscule at first, but growing fatter, squirming more uncomfortably inside him with each succeeding day. His mind, his hands, the row of lamps, the wood, the tool bench, the tins of oil – for years these had been as one, a still life. Now, his mind was, almost imperceptibly, leaving the picture, departing upwards and lodging in the rooms above. With Irene.

He was shocked. He reviled himself. He rose earlier and began his work sooner so that he wouldn't see her when she arrived at nine. He locked the cellar door. He turned out all his lamps except one. He got out his calligraphy books and redesigned the Harker trademark. He sat very still at his desk. Being motionless was his way of pretending to Irene and to himself that he wasn't there at all. Only when he heard Irene vacuuming would he allow himself to make a little deliberate noise. He would hum snatches of Bach: 'Pom. Tiddly-tiddly-tiddly pom. Tiddly-tiddly-tiddly-tiddly-tiddly-tiddly pom pom pom . . .' Bach was orderliness and calm. Irene's hoover was anarchy roaring over his carpets.

As winter came on and the skies were draped in the flat, grey blanket he so detested, he decided he would go abroad for a month, to Marseilles, and take a room with a balcony in a quiet hotel. He would sit on this balcony and sip Pernod and in the sunshine cure himself of his wandering thoughts. He telephoned Thomas Cook & Son. He booked himself a ferry passage and a wagon-lit from Boulogne to Marseilles. He bought a panama hat.

Irene came gradually to believe that it was Pearl who was alienating Mr Harker. A man with no children, living like a bachelor, you could understand that he didn't want a three-year-old in his house: the noise of her feet, the things she sang to herself, her fingermarks on the furniture. And yet there was nothing Irene could do. The school would not take Pearl until she was four and she refused to leave her at home by herself. Both her neighbours were elderly and disapproved of Pearl's very existence. Estelle might have cared for her, but the farm was a long way from Swaithey and, besides, Estelle had told Irene she was 'retreating'. She wouldn't say more. She was retreating into the shade was all she'd say. And she said it brightly, in a sing-song voice, as if she were announcing a new malted beverage on the wireless.

Irene lay awake, feeling sorrowful. The announcement of Estelle's retreat and Mr Harker's withdrawal into the cellar made her feel helpless.

She decided she would speak to Mr Harker. She would explain that, although Pearl followed her around the house, she had been forbidden ever to touch anything of his, that she played quietly with her dolls and had been told not to sing to them. She would, if necessary, beg Mr Harker not to sack her and remind him that within a few months Pearl would be going to school. Before the talk, she would polish all his silver and lay it out for him to see on a traycloth, gleaming proof that her work was thorough.

A fortnight before Harker's intended trip to Marseilles (during which he had added to the purchase of the hat some expensive cotton underwear and a copy of *Wisden 1953* to read on his balcony), Irene left a note on his kitchen table. The spelling was weak and Irene, examining her note, marvelled at how difficult writing things down was compared to saying them. Saying something was as easy as laughing; writing caused you grief, as though you were mourning somebody who had abandoned you too soon.

The note read:

> Dear Mr Harker,
>   I would like to talk to you please towmorow. Please will you come up to the kitchen at elevensis time i.e. eleven o'clock. I will make a pot of tea.
>   Yours trully
>
> Irene Simmonds

At home, she baked a pink and yellow Battenberg cake and placed it on a doily to set it off. She washed Pearl's hair and tied it with a blue ribbon. She cut the child's nails and made sure her hands were clean.

As eleven approached, her heart, which she imagined as a thing like a cauliflower, began to thump against the bib of her apron. To lose this job would be like losing the world.

She laid out the tea things. She found a silver cake knife and put it by the Battenberg. She didn't know whether Mr Harker preferred his tea steeped or watery. She sat Pearl at the table with a bib round her neck. She gave her a beaker of lemon squash and told her to be as quiet as a squirrel. She brushed down her apron and patted her home perm. She waited.

Mr Harker came up from the cellar humming. 'Pom. Tiddly-tiddly-tiddly pom.' Irene saw this as a cheerful sign. 'Tiddly-tiddly tiddly tiddly-tiddly-tiddly . . .' Irene smiled her big, dimpled smile and drew Mr Harker's attention to the cake. She saw that he looked relieved, as if he were glad there was something to which his attention could be drawn. He said that no one knew how to make a Battenberg since the war.

Irene poured the tea and they sat down. An electric wall clock let time advance jerkily round its plastic face. Pearl announced to Mr Harker that she was going to be as quiet as a squirrel. He let his eyes move upwards from his own hand stirring his tea and look at the child. She regarded him gravely. Although Harker had seen her many times prior to his self-imposed incarceration in the cellar, he felt now that he had never really noticed her before. He wasn't a connoisseur of infants, he'd encountered so very few, but he could tell straight away that here was a very pretty little girl, pretty beyond telling, with the kind of surprising grace children seem to possess in portraits of them by Gainsborough.

He took a bite of his piece of Battenberg. He saw Irene's plump arm reach out with a handkerchief and wipe a crumb from Pearl's cheek. He looked away. He tried to concentrate on the cake, but there seemed to be a sweet, perfumed taste to it, now soft mush in his mouth, that resembled the smell of Irene and, dare he say it, the taste of her body that his disobedient mind would persist in imagining. He swallowed the last mouthful of cake and washed away the sweetness of it with tea. He wiped his mouth firmly. His decision was made. Harker, he instructed himself, get rid of the woman!

He looked at her then, at her wide, smooth-skinned face, at her huge breasts inside a neat blouse behind the apron bib. He laid a concealing hand on his lap.

'Irene,' he said, 'I wonder whether Pearl could go and play in some other room for a moment . . .'

'Mr Harker – ' Irene began.

'Just for a minute or two, while we get things sorted out.'

Irene undid Pearl's bib and told her to go and sit on the stairs.

As soon as she'd gone, Harker said: 'I've been meaning to talk to you for some time, Irene.'

He said this with such gravity that Irene felt a slippery movement in her heart, like a maggot in it. 'If it's about Pearl . . .' she said.

'Pearl?'

'Yes. If it's about me having to bring her to work, I know this is inconvenient for you, Mr Harker, but I can't rightly do anything about it. There's no one I can trust her with. No one at all. This is why I wrote the note. I know you don't like having her here, disturbing you . . .'

'Oh, it's not exactly that . . .' said Harker.

'She'll be in school springtime, when she's four. Not long to go. And she's a good girl. She does as I say. She plays with her dolls, but quietly. No singing . . .'

'I'm sure.'

'And if I were to have to leave . . . you know my circumstances, Sir. You know how hard it would be for me to – '

'I'm sorry,' said Harker firmly.

'There's no one else in Swaithey would give me work.'

The choke in Irene's voice, her flushed and agitated appearance, these seemed to Harker to expand her presence in the room, so that he felt he was going to be smothered.

Tell her to go and so forth and do it now, Harker, he told himself. The state of his lap was appalling, perilous, even. His face burned with the shame of it and when he tried to speak, his mouth was dry.

'I can't discuss it,' he said. 'I'm sorry. As you know, I'm going to France in a fortnight's time and I will pay you for the four weeks while I'm away and then that will have to be that.'

Irene had not meant to cry. She apologised for herself. She got up and began to clear away the tea things. She let her tears flow onto the doily. She turned and looked at Mr Harker. She was surprised to find him still seated at the table. She thought he would have escaped back to his precious cellar by now.

'Can I ask,' she said through her film of misery, 'if Pearl is the reason?'

Harker blinked. He was distracted, as if his mind had already moved on somewhere else. 'Pearl is the reason?'

'Yes.'

'Oh yes. I'm afraid so,' said Harker, marshalling his thoughts. 'You see, my work is of a solitary kind, requiring great concentration. Any change of atmosphere in the house is damaging. Not your fault, Irene. Not your fault and I'm sorry. But there we are.'

Still, he sat on at the table.

It was most peculiar, Irene thought. He sat there stiffly, as though he were afraid to move.

Irene wrung out the dishcloth and absent-mindedly wiped her face with it. It smelled of cabbage, of carbolic soap, of the wretchedness to come.

Livia's Dictionary

Mary floated in a new vision. The muddy edges of things had become distinct. Released by her new spectacles from a struggle of seeing, her mind found a new curiosity about what there was to understand. Miss McRae's passion for Geography furnished her with words that seemed to come to her from far off: isthmus, glacier, fjord, delta, atoll. She did drawings of cloud formations and knew their names: *cumulus* meaning heap or pile, *stratus* meaning flat, *cirrhus* meaning a lock of curly hair. She learned that a stalactite was a mineral-filled icicle hanging from the roof of a cave and that drips from it built up beneath it and froze into a mound and then into a column, growing on and on upwards and called a stalagmite.

Sometimes stalactites and stalagmites met. Then, it seemed to anyone entering the cave, that pillars had been built there to hold the roof up. 'And this,' said Miss McRae grandly, 'is a quite extraordinary thing! Nature playing a marvellous wee game, children.'

Mary's drawing of atolls and clouds were stuck up on the classroom wall with gummed stars. They were blackly done. The firm lines caused Miss McRae to wonder whether Mary didn't have an artistic talent she should nurture. But then she began to see that Mary loved all her schoolwork so fiercely she was jealous of anyone doing it more competently than her. Even Mathematics. In table tests, her hand would shoot up for every answer. She knew the Dry Measure chart before anyone else. She did sums with exaggerated care, her face very close to the paper.

One day, she brought to school a book that had belonged to her grandmother. She showed it to Miss McRae in the icy playground. It was a *Dictionary of Inventions.* Mary said: 'I always thought the world was finished, didn't you, Miss McRae?'

'Finished, dear?'

'Yes. Long ago. Didn't you?'

'Well . . .'

'But look: Sewing Machine. Thomas Saint. British. 1792. See? Revolver. Samuel Colt. American. 1835. Thermometer. Galileo. Italian. 1597. So before then, those things hadn't been there at all.'

'Well, that's perfectly true, Mary. And this also means, of course, that there is a great deal yet to come, things we might not be able to imagine now.'

'Yes.'

Mary seemed excited for a moment, then suddenly anxious. 'I don't think my mother knows all this, though,' she said.

'I dare say she does, dear.'

'No, she doesn't. I'm sure. Even if she knows there might be new things, she doesn't know that before Thomas Saint, 1792, there wasn't one sewing machine on the earth.'

Miss McRae looked at Mary. Ever since that morning when she brought Irene Simmonds's baby into class, she'd thought her odd, exceptional, one of those whose future you couldn't see. She laid a protective hand inside a grey woollen glove on Mary's head. 'Run and play, dear!' she said. 'It's too cold to stand about.'

So she ran off, clutching her little *Dictionary of Inventions*. Miss McRae saw her wait her turn at the swing. She spoke to none of the children and no one spoke to her. When she got onto the swing, she didn't sit on it as most of the girls did, but stood up and pushed her body out and up into the grey sky. Her expression was blank, unafraid. The chains of the swing ground against the fixings. Mary moved higher and higher.

There was a swing at the farm. It was tied to the limb of a Scots pine. Sonny had made it for Tim from a tractor tyre and a length of rope. He'd tied two superfluous knots in the rope to ensure the boy's safety. Sometimes, in an easterly wind, he glared at the tree, as at a mortal enemy.

Timmy sat in the tyre as though in a bucket, kicking his legs feebly, one by one. He thought the tyre would swing just by being sat in. When this didn't happen, he wanted to be pushed. If no one pushed him, he snivelled. Mary wanted him dead. With his goofy eyes and the way he gulped when he cried and the way his cheeks got slimy with tears, he was like a frog. Every day, Mary prayed he'd go back to being a tadpole and then to a blob of spawn and then to nothing.

There was a gap between the low limb of the pine and its higher branches. When Mary stood in the tyre, it was this gap she was aiming for. The gap was a test. This is what she believed. There would be others, but this was going to be the first test. If she could make the tyre go up into the gap with such speed and power that she and it flew vertically above the pine limb and down again on the other side, completing a circle, well, then anything she prayed for would certainly happen. In particular, becoming a boy would happen. It was just a question of time, a question of waiting until you could invent yourself and surprise everyone with your discovery, like Patrick Miller, British, 1788, who had invented the paddle wheel. Before, no one had dreamed of a boat with wheels, just as now, no one could dream of Mary Ward not being a girl. But, as Miss McRae had said: 'There is a great deal yet to come, things we might not be able to imagine now.' One day, she would be in a dictionary. But the tyre wouldn't go high enough to reach the gap. It wouldn't even get to the vertical point where Mary was upside-down.

Mary asked herself if she was afraid. 'You're not afraid,' she answered. 'You need more practice.'

On a Saturday morning, with the gap between the pine branches full of blue sky, Mary sat on the grass, stroking Marguerite's neck with her finger. She was waiting for Timmy to get off the swing. It was December, yet the meadow looked shiny. Mary's head ached with the brightness of everything. She yelled at Timmy to let her have a turn on the tyre. 'It's mine,' he said.

He sat in it, feebly rocking, like in a hammock.

'One day soon, he'll be frogspawn,' Mary said to Marguerite. The bird opened its stubby wings and flapped them and Mary could feel a kind of shiver go through its body. Timmy sat up higher in the tyre and began his feeble swinging. Marguerite walked away from Mary's hand, then made a little scuttling run towards the tyre. Timmy kicked out at the guineafowl and one of his wellingtons flew off and landed near it. Marguerite screeched. Timmy threw his head back and gave a foolish laughing scream. Then Marguerite did a thing Mary had never seen her do before: she flew up into the tree.

Timmy went on with his shrieking laugh. He was more interested in annoying Mary's bird now, than he was in sitting in the swing like a princeling. He climbed out and stood on the grass, looking up at Marguerite. Then he started running round in a circle, windmilling his arms and making bird noises.

Mary got up and began to walk towards the swing. From somewhere beyond the field, she could hear her father call to them to come in for their dinner. Timmy didn't hear. Mary thought, he's in a world of stupidity. In that sagging space in the big bed, his brain is turning to dough.

Mary stood on the swing. She called to Marguerite. She worked the tyre lazily backwards and forwards, calling. The bird looked peculiar up there. It was one of those creatures that forgot, most of the time, that it could fly and so never practised. 'Come down, Marguerite,' Mary said.

The creature was agitated. It moved restlessly about. Then it ran along the branch and took off. It screeched as it swooped down. In a corner of her new vision, Mary saw Sonny arrive, shouting. Marguerite landed on Timmy's head and pecked viciously at his ear. Mary drew in a breath so deep, it coloured

red everything that she could see. The momentum of the swing died. She saw Sonny run like a bullet to his son and hit out at Marguerite with his cap. Marguerite flapped off, landing awkwardly on a mole hill, then scuttling towards the farmyard like a hen. Sonny picked up Timmy and held him, binding his ear with a handkerchief and swearing. Timmy screamed and screamed. Mary breathed her red breaths. He's screaming himself to death, she thought. He's returning to pre-invention, to before the paddle wheel and the gun.

Mary:

My father caught Marguerite. He held her under his arm and put her in a sack. He tied the sack with bailing string.

He said she was bewitched. He said that, out of my jealousy, I had made fierce a normally docile bird. He said God would punish me in ways I could not imagine.

God was punishing me already in a way I could imagine because my father gave Marguerite to the Loomises to be killed and plucked for somebody's dinner.

What he wanted was for me to cry. When his rages made him go deaf, this was the thing that brought his hearing back.

I refused to bring his hearing back. I ate my dinner, then I walked out into the yard and vomited it up. My mother watched me through the kitchen window. Her look was all in tatters. That morning, she'd begun on a patchwork and her sewing table was covered with cardboard shapes and bits of old curtains. Somebody, I thought, is soon going to have to mend her.

I turned away from the yard and the puddle of sick and from my mother's look. I went out into the lane and began to walk towards Swaithey. I didn't dare think about Marguerite, her little wizened legs and her speckled sides. I put her into the past. Some of the past is visible and some of it isn't and I hoped the bit of it with Marguerite in it would stay hidden. But I had this thought about suffering: I thought, if I suffer a lot, I will grow a man's skin. If I suffer and refuse to cry, a penis will grow out of all that is locked away inside. It needs only time.

After that bright blue day we'd had, the air got as cold as a knife. I could see the tower of Swaithey Church and the sun going down behind it, sliding away fast and letting the dark come on without any fight. In Geography, Miss McRae had told us that in Australia our night was their day. Australia has two tips to its shape like mountains. As I tramped on towards Swaithey, I imagined the sun arriving there and the bears in the gum trees blinking as it woke them.

I was going to Irene. I wanted her to hide me away in a shelter of my own making. I hoped Pearl would be awake, doing a jigsaw. I hoped Irene would know why I had come without my having to tell her.

The word Marguerite was beyond my saying.

It felt like night by the time I got there. There were stars above the lane. I remembered Miss McRae saying: 'This is what we call the universe, children,' but I still had not understood whether the universe went away in the daytime altogether, or whether it just left us and floated over Australia like an airship. My mother could not look at the stars. They made her remember being a girl, lying in her bed.

The light was on in Irene's hall. When I knocked, I heard Pearl run to the letter box and try to open it and look out. Not many people came to see them, my mother said. People in Swaithey couldn't bring themselves to show compassion. Only Mr Harker.

Irene took me into the kitchen. I sat Pearl on my knee and helped her do her Knitting Nancy. She was using yellow and pink wool and there were quite a few holes in the little snakey rope where stitches had fallen off the nails in the cotton reel.

Irene waited. She poured me a cup of tea and put a flapjack on a plate for me, tempting me to speak, like someone trying to tempt a bear out of a gum tree.

After a long while of not speaking, she said she would make up a bed for me on the floor in Pearl's room. I said: 'Thank you, Irene,' in a very clear voice and then when she came down I told her, in a quick rush to get it over with, that my bird had dived on Timmy and now it was in a sack, waiting to die. I didn't cry. I only felt freezing cold. I held on to Pearl to keep warm.

Irene came and squatted by my chair and stroked my hair.

She told me my father's rages were not his fault. Losing half his ear in Germany had damaged him, just like thousands of men had been damaged in the war. 'At heart,' she said, 'he's a good man.'

'He's good to Timmy,' I said. 'That's all.'

'Shall I take Pearl,' she said, 'while you drink your tea?'

'No,' I said, 'don't take her. We're doing the Knitting Nancy.'

Pearl's room was very small. My bed was three settee cushions laid out next to the old cot she still slept in. Irene gave me a green eiderdown to cover me and a proper pillow. My supper was a marmalade sandwich.

I had a kind of waking dream that my father came with the pony and cart and drove me home through the freezing dark. I kept listening for the sound of the wheels of the cart, but it only came in my mind and not in reality.

I liked being there on the floor. I wanted to stay a long time and not go home. To get Pearl to lie down and be quiet and go to sleep, I told her a story about Joseph Montgolfier, French, 1782, inventor of the hot-air balloon. In my story, Montgolfier ballooned around the sky, looking for the universe and never finding it because his balloon travelled as fast as the sun. He found Australia instead and decided to stay there and then on his first night in an Australian jungle, surrounded by parrots and kangaroos all chattering and jabbering in a language he couldn't understand, he looked up at the sky and saw it there, the universe, and thought, oh bother it, oh sacrébleu, it's too far away to find. Australia's better.

There was quite a lot in this story that Pearl didn't understand, but it sent her to sleep and that was the idea of it, to get her to sleep and start snoring, so that I could just lie there and listen to her, like you listen to the sea, not thinking of anything at all except the sound.

In the morning, Irene told me about Mr Harker giving her the sack and going off to France. She said: 'I don't know why I'm telling you this, Mary.'

I told her I would take Pearl to school with me. She could do her Knitting Nancy under Miss McRae's desk. She could look after our silkworms.

Irene said Miss McRae would never allow this, but I said: 'Miss McRae looks like a fir tree, but inside she's kind.'

Irene kept shaking her head and saying no, no, so I told Irene a thing I never told my mother or father, that I was Miss McRae's best pupil, with my drawings of clouds on the wall and thirteen stars against my name on the star chart and that I had no friends at all.

'Well,' said Irene, 'it'd only be for the mornings . . .'

So I began it the following day, taking Pearl to school with me while Irene went to Mr Harker's and set to work polishing everything for his return from France. I told Miss McRae this was a temporary arrangement, that Pearl could be a silkworm monitor and that if she wasn't allowed to be there, I wouldn't be able to come to school. She shook her head, just like Irene had done, turning it from side to side, so that little thin hairpins fell out of her grey bun, but then she found a small chair and desk and put it by hers and sat Pearl in it.

'Luckily for you, Mary,' she said, 'I was born in a lighthouse, or I would not be the kind of person I am.'

I stayed at Irene's for a week. My father came while I was at school and told her this would be best and gave her ten shillings for my food.

In my life to come, I would sometimes remember it, my week at Irene's when I couldn't say the syllables of Marguerite's name.

I remember the feel of my body, trying to grow its man's skin between the settee cushions and the green eiderdown.

I remember Pearl's love of the silkworms.

I remember the marmalade sandwiches.

I remember Irene at the bedroom door, saying: 'Goodnight, my doves, and dream of princes.'

3

1955

'The Last Loomis'

Learning to yodel was far more terrible than Walter had imagined.

Pete said it was a sound born in the mountains, where a man could hear his own echo. He said it was a shame there were no mountains in Suffolk.

Walter tried to teach himself by copying Jimmie Rodgers. Then, on his parents' wireless, he heard a Canadian singer named Hank Snow, known as 'The Yodelling Ranger', making that same easy, high-spilling sound and he said to Pete: 'This confirms me in what I'm doing.' Snow sang a song so sad, it made Walter's spine ache. The song was called 'I Don't Hurt Anymore'.

Customers to the Loomis shop sometimes caught an unexpected burst of Walter's yodel-practice coming from the yard and the Misses Cunningham, in particular, were not at ease with it. 'You know, Amy,' said one sister to the other, 'I think Loomis must be killing things more slowly, in a way that makes them sound human.'

The task was so hard. Perhaps it would kill him? It was like trying to put fizz into something still. It was difficult for Pete to believe that all this struggle had arisen from a night of rain and booze. He warned Walter not to push himself. He became aware that the boy was running a fever that refused to abate. In the cow-sheds, he could see Walter's head steaming. His neck, above the collarless shirt, was plum red.

'Give that yodel a rest,' Pete advised, 'or it'll burst your brains.'

But he had forgotten Walter's devotion to things. 'Of course I can't give it a rest,' Walter said, 'not till I've got it.'

But he couldn't get it. Not quite. He could master a kind of warble, a little trill at the back of the throat. The great swoop up to a falsetto that Rodgers and Snow achieved so effortlessly remained beyond him. He could hear it inside him. In his fever, he sometimes felt that he could even *see* it, as a bouncing light above the trees.

Then he heard a new song on the radio, Slim Whitman singing 'Rose Marie'.

Pete told Ernie: 'That's going to be the death of your boy, that "Rose Marie".'

Grace advised her son: 'We've all of us got only one voice, Walter, and you're hurting yours.'

But he'd bought the record now. He wore out four gramophone needles, playing it over and over. The ease with which old Slim Whitman sang it reminded him of a waterfall. He had dreams of mountains. The word 'whippoorwill' (its meaning unclear to him) kept patterning and punctuating his thoughts. He remembered Pete's tales of ice storms and prayed for one to come and cool him. The morning arrived when his fever was so thick and deep that he couldn't move.

And he couldn't speak. In answer to the doctor's questions, nothing came out. The pain in Walter's throat was so spectacular, he thought an ice-pick must have lodged there. He tried to ask his mother to remove it, but realised he was incapable of the least sound.

He was put into the doctor's Morris Minor. A blanket was laid round him. On the way to the hospital, he lost track of the seasons and thought autumn had come – autumn known as fall. You lay in the fall, Pete had said, and dreamed. Something came out of that dreaming, but Walter couldn't remember what. He feared death might come out of it, and silence, for ever. He fought with his blanket, as if death and silence were in that. The doctor's Morri's kept swerving. Having Walter in the back of the car was like having a sick bull there.

It wasn't autumn. It was still early spring, grey and chill at its heart.

In the cold hospital ward Walter, clamped to the bed by a damp sheet, saw old Arthur Loomis come to his side and sit down. He was wearing his apron. His face was pink with vitality and health and his beard was crisp and shiny. 'Walter,' he said, 'I'm glad we've got this opportunity to talk.'

He seemed to wait for Walter to speak, but Walter could say nothing.

Arthur stroked his moustache. His eyes were brown and gentle, like the eyes of a doe. 'I think,' he continued, 'that this is the right time to remind you that you are alone in your generation, the only Loomis.'

Walter tried to turn his head towards Arthur, but it seemed to him that his ancestor was holding the handle of the ice-pick, pinning him down.

He slept a hot sleep. The words of 'Rose Marie' filled it up. 'No matter how I try, I can't forget you/Sometimes I wish that I had never met you!' These words were the narrow bridge to a future life, and everything else – his mother, the yard, the blood gulley, the animals and the sky – belonged to the dead past. When he woke, he thought he would try to tell Arthur that all of this was gone, but he found that Arthur's voice, so often described by Ernie as 'nice and gentle, nice and slow', was speaking to him firmly and could not be interrupted.

'. . . known across East Suffolk, boy. Purveyors of fine

meats to some of the best houses. A family business. And the name Loomis on it. On the window in gold and blue letters. On the awning, also in gold and blue. On the bills of sale. On the minds of hostesses. Large on shopping lists . . .'

'I know,' Walter tried to say.

'So there's the picture,' said Arthur, 'you can see it, can't you, as plain as death. You are the last Loomis and you mustn't desert the meat.'

Arthur stood up and went away then, without another word.

For the first time in a long while Walter felt cold, and from this moment his fever began to die down.

It was convenient, after that, not to be able to speak. He wanted no questions to be asked and no promises to be demanded. In silence, he looked at his future and saw that he might not be able to become a hillbilly singer. Yodelling was beyond him. He had almost died trying to do it. And without a yodel, there would only be an imaginary America, not a real Tennessee with its faithful darkies and its faithful dogs. All of that was shimmer.

He came home and his mother made him broth from marrowbones. The red in his cheeks had faded to a grey mottling; his forehead was a slab of white. He lay in his bedroom and heard the business of the shop going on beneath him, the scratch and thud of the cleaver, the ping of the cash till.

In time, as if oiled by the real coming of spring, the pain in his vocal chords lessened and his voice began to return, a minute thing at first, with no power to disturb his breath and no will to be heard.

The first time it came louder was on a late afternoon at the river, under a fish-scale sky. His mother had sent him there to gather watercress for tea. The river flowed through the fields owned by Sonny Ward into the Loomis pastures.

Estelle was there. She was sitting on the plank bridge Sonny had made on his own in a day. Beside her was a pail of watercress. Her feet were in the water and she was holding on to her shoes.

Walter waved at her. She looked up at him, but didn't move or make any greeting. So he called out and heard his voice quite strong again, as it had been in the days before 'Rose Marie'. He called: 'Good afternoon, Mrs Ward!' but Estelle didn't reply and Walter wondered whether the strength he heard in his voice had, after all, been an illusion. He was about to try calling out again when he saw Estelle stand up and walk away, leaving her pail of cress behind.

At tea, Grace said: 'You don't surprise us, Walter. But you've been ill a longish while, dear, and haven't heard the things they're saying in the village.'

Estelle:

They say: Sonny is a good man.

They say: England is a good place.

They say: I don't know what frightens you so, Estelle.

I can tell them. When I was fourteen, Livia took me to a play. Near the end, the man peels an onion. He is trying to find the onion after all the layers of peel. He gets to the heart of it and there is nothing. How absurd, he says, there is nothing there at all.

Irene thinks she has found the onion. The onion is the old man, Harker. You could die laughing at this.

He comes up from the cellar. Hard as an armadillo, she says. Surprising for his years. She switches off the Hoover. 'It's wonderful, Estelle,' she says, 'I'd forgotten how wonderful.'

You could die laughing.

If dying were easy. If you could just say, goodnight etcetera. I tried it one night. Sonny lay on his side, facing me. I put my face close to his mouth and breathed his breath, like mustard gas. For I had often thought, the breath of a person you no longer love or respect could be a poison to kill you, and it does. But it kills you slowly. So slowly that it isn't often you notice you are dying.

I try to tell Irene, I used to caress his coral ear, with my fingers and with my lips. I try to remind her, in her onion bliss, these things are like sunlight and vanish. It can happen at mid-day or happen late. And then, what was possible no longer is or ever will be again.

'I never met,' she says, 'anyone so full of bad-weather forecasts as you, Estelle.'

And I say, well Irene, wait and watch and see if from one split second to the next, it doesn't go. Watch and see. You might be on the stairs in just your slip, or you might be somewhere else, lying in the dark. You can't predict the place or time. Only afterwards will you be able to say, for always, it was then; that was the moment.

'I know I'm alive again now,' she says, 'that's the point.'

'Well, *that*,' I say. And I laugh.

But she's right that this is what we look for. Despite all the evidence. A desperate search. Grabbing any old thing; even a cricket bat. God's thigh must have bruises and welts on it from so much slapping. His ribs surely ache. My mother found life in a silent plane, held aloft by currents of air. The things we dream up! She searched in her house for it, at the piano, at her mirror, in my father's bed, but not a trace of it remained where it once was. She said: 'It's not just being alive we seek. It's the *experience* of being alive.'

'You're everything to me, Estelle,' Sonny still sometimes says. It's then that I know his breath is killing me. You cannot be everything to a person and still survive. I go to my sewing machine. To me, it is a flawless thing, designed by a mind that did not lie to itself. Its handle is polished by my touch. I let my hair fall round it, blocking Sonny from my sight. Mary will come and stare at me. Her stare is changing. Getting harder and harder. Because it is her that he punishes. You can't punish the thing that is everything to you; you punish something else. And so her stare says, aren't you sorry, even? Aren't you ashamed? And I hide from her more and more. I let her go to Irene or wherever she needs to go to survive. I don't look. Sometimes, I walk out of the house and pretend I'm going for ever, carrying an empty bucket, as if it were a suitcase crammed with all that I need.

I go to the river. I reconstruct what is past: cause and effect. Cause so swift and foolish; effect so endless.

I was born in a tidy village. Fences round everything; Albertine growing over the porches; a flint church. When I was a child, my mother played the church organ. Odd for those days, a female organist.

I met Sonny in church. For weeks, he came and stared at me, never speaking. He held his cap in his hands. He behaved like someone in a queue, waiting his turn.

I had had another fiancé before the war, a young man who thought staring was rude and common. He was a naturalist who dressed in green corduroy and yellow cashmere and bought his wellingtons in London. His passion was for moths. His kiss was a faint and weak thing. He used to say: 'I will never take advantage of you, Estelle. That is out of the question.' And I would reply: 'Thank you. That is very considerate of you and most reassuring.'

His name was Miles, but he like to be called Milo. Some people do this: they make themselves ridiculous by one small thing of their own choosing. He was killed in the Ardennes and buried in Belgium somewhere. I used to imagine him turning to dust like a moth. To me, moths seem to be *made* of dust, but Milo was made of England and couldn't have wanted to die where he did. I never mourned him. He had smelled like a Gentleman's Outfitters. You could have done invisible mending with his thin, silky hair.

When Sonny had stood in his queue long enough and when I stared back at him and he came close to me, I understood that nothing was out of the question. He took me out in his old pony-cart and pulled up in some shade and explored the shape of me with his hands. He said: 'I've been waiting for a beautiful woman all my life.' I was his onion. He did not know there is nothing at its centre.

Because I came from a smart village, he thought I didn't understand the countryside. He thought I was as blind and deaf to it as the people who drove out in their Austins to have picnics on family rugs and grab armfuls of wild flowers to stick in vases. The idea of flowers in a vase was repugnant to him. He said women loved too many of the wrong things. He said: 'To live in the country, you have to have your heart in it. You have to have knowledge.' I did not say that Livia had had a talent for arranging flowers.

He showed me some of the hidden things the Austin drivers did not know existed: edible puff balls, chanterelles, bullaces, fennel roots and wild garlic. He had never been in an Austin. He could recognise the footprint of a badger and the call of the nuthatch. He had no particular interest in moths.

He climbed into my bedroom through the dormer window, while my father sat alone by the fire, sipping Wincarnis. What he had sampled in the cart he now used and I used him back. And, I remind Irene, usage of this kind is a drug. You want and want and your brain turns to slush and your cunt to a velvet river and your limbs to willow, bending to the least touch. You want and want. Until the day when you do not want any more. And then you are cured and free, but are a prisoner and have nothing.

In one month, I was pregnant with Mary. Sonny and I got married in the flint church. My bouquet was lilies and smelled of the past. Rose petals were flung at us. Even in church, the feeling of wanting was there, as we knelt down.

I moved to Sonny's farm, leaving my father quite alone with his bottle of Wincarnis and the *Daily Telegraph*.

In bed, Sonny laid his damaged ear on my belly. He said: 'Pray it's a boy. Pray and pray.'

And so I wonder now, as I walk by the river, what, among all the lost or strange or disappearing things, does an unborn child know? What can it hear through the womb wall? Did Mary understand that it was not her that I was made to long for, but somebody else, a child of Sonny's imaginings?

I remember, she got lost once. Almost before her life had started, she got lost in it. She wandered off into a wood and held on to a tree, as if the tree were what would save her and what she sought.

We didn't find her for a long time. I thought she was drowned in a ditch and I began to cry. Sonny said: 'All your looks go, Estelle, when you start weeping. Any resemblance you ever had to Ava Gardner disappears absolutely.'

So I go to the river and stare at myself. I look down at my face, at the ripples of water ignoring it and moving on. The river has a goal, to get past the weeds and the rushes and on to the salt sea, and I have none and all my wanting of things is over. And on glittering days, I have the following thought: sadly, I think, for that girl in *Hamlet,* she did not return home, as I do from the river, to wash her hair in Drene.

'Light, light . . .'

It was near to Christmas when Mary was enrolled in Miss Vista's Saturday-morning dancing class. This class was held in the Swaithey Girl Guide hut, a building that looked like a settler's cabin, with creosoted plank sides and an iron roof. The floor was linoleum, waxed once a week. Miss Vista's dancers squeaked around on it, eager but mortified. The squeaks were like farts, funny and yet awful.

It was Sonny's idea. He said to Estelle: 'That child is never still. Look at her.'

She'd found an old tennis ball in a ditch, electric green with algae stain. She'd dried it on the stove till it was crisp and bouncy and now she had it as a companion. She threw it and ran after it, hurled it and caught it, flung it at trees, kicked it and bounced it and rolled it. It wore her out. She slept with it in her hand.

Estelle watched. Mary's movements were jerky and wild. More disconcerting seemed to be her aims. She'd pitch the ball in an arc and then try to outrun it. She'd try this again and again and again, refusing to see that it couldn't be done. It was as if she wanted to *be* the green tennis ball hurled in the air, flung at trees to bound back.

'At her age,' said Sonny, 'she should have some grace.'

'I know,' said Estelle. 'But grace is not in the air, is it? It's not something you can breathe.'

'You don't breathe it, you learn it.'

'Yes. But I wonder how?'

'By example.'

So they enrolled Mary with Miss Vista.

Estelle remembered her own childhood dancing lessons in the library of a private house. She remembered ribbons and glancing sunlight, a piano played with the soft pedal down, Livia on a hard chair, watching. Estelle thought she was giving Mary something of value – a compartment of her own past.

Mary asked if there would be boys as well as girls in the dancing class. Estelle said she thought there might be; they might be taught to dance hornpipes.

But there were no boys. And the girls were rehearsing for a Christmas show Miss Vista had entitled *Meadowsweet.* The dancers had been divided into three groups; one group were buttercups, another scarlet pimpernels, the third thistledowns. 'Welcome in, Mary,' said Miss Vista, 'you can join the thistledowns. Just follow what they do.'

It was cold in the Girl Guide hut. Miss Vista danced in her overcoat, with coils of knitting round her calves. The children wore only their chill proof vests and knickers and over these their flimsy meadow costumes: scarlet and yellow shifts for the pimpernels and the buttercups, and for the thistledowns skirts of white net that stuck out stiffly like fans. Miss Vista had a fervent mouth, lips ticked orange. Out of it poured her passionate instructions as she moved, squeaking on her blocks, about the room, her arms lifting and swaying under the weight of her coat. *'Bend,* buttercups! The wind is coming. Yield! Yield to the wind. You can do no other. But you, thistledowns. Up you go! You're aloft. The wind is carrying you. You're light, *light!* In a bunch, all together at first. Puff, puff! Then off and away singly. That's right, Mary, off on your own. Riding on the wind. Light, light, light!'

Mary had thought there would be rules to dancing. Miss McRae often said that everything in life had rules, even if sometimes you couldn't see what they were. 'In these cases, they're internal rules, Mary, hidden completely, but present nevertheless, dear.' Yet in Miss Vista's class you just skipped about, pretending to be weeds. You were not told what your feet should do or how to make a circle with your arms. You could tell from Miss Vista's legs that she had once learned some rules. She had just decided not to pass them on. If boys had come to the lesson, she would not have taught them how to do a hornpipe.

Mary was repelled. She despised Miss Vista. She wanted to hurl her green tennis ball at her face. She wanted a real wind to come and swoop her up into the black universe.

When she told her parents that Miss Vista was not teaching her how to dance, they said she could learn to 'move better'. Estelle said: 'When I was your age, we made beautiful patterns with ribbons.'

They'd spent money on ballet shoes. Wearing them was like wearing gloves on your feet. You could feel every bit of ground underneath you, every stone. Mary looked at her pink legs with these pink shoes on the end of them and pitied them, as if they belonged to some other girl, fooled into believing she could dance. With her thistledown skirt on, she reminded herself of the toilet roll cover doll Judy Weaver had brought to school as her 'precious thing'. She tore off the shoes and the fan of net and put them out of sight. She lay down on her bed, balancing her tennis ball on her chest. She formed a plan.

As the day of the Christmas show neared, Miss Vista grew more attentive to unity. She urged the buttercups to bend in unison, the pimpernels to crouch down together. Only the thistledowns were allowed to scatter and fly, because this was their nature, this was what they did. But she urged on them the need to become insubstantial, to pretend they had no bodies, no feet on the earth. 'Light, light, girls!' Miss Vista implored. 'Feathers! Dreams! Particles of dust!' So they tore round the hall squeaking and jumping, sometimes falling over or accidently bumping into the walls.

Miss Vista grew hot in her efforts to alchemise them into windblown seeds and removed her overcoat, under which she wore an orange roman tunic and a fairisle cardigan. Mary moved with big, fast strides. She turned the near-chaos in the hut into an absolute, dreamlike chaos by removing her glasses. Now, Miss Vista was not only parted from her coat, but from herself. Mary felt laughter rising inside her: laughter like a scream.

The parents arrived for the show and sat in two rows on hard chairs. Estelle's hair was greasy from the oil baths she kept giving it to restore its lustre. Sonny sat with his head bowed, like a penitent. Estelle looked at the lino and remembered the yellowy parquet of the library.

While the thistledowns clustered behind a thin curtain waiting to come on, Mary left the group and returned to the cloakroom where her coat hung on a peg. She took off her pink ballet shoes and put on her wellingtons. She imagined each of them as a cardboard cylinder and her legs as the salmon-coloured plastic legs of Judy Weaver's doll. She puffed up her net skirt round the boots. Now, she thought, I am a living toilet roll cover.

She returned to the group, shivering by the curtain. You cannot walk lightly in a wellington. The thistledowns turned, as if in one, synchronised movement, to stare at Mary. They drew in an anxious breath. They held on to each other. Their shivering intensified. The strongest of them put their hands to their mouths, stifling laughter.

The thistledown music came. Out they streamed, puff, puff, up and away, things of no substance, chaff and prayers. Mary followed, striding and leaping. The squeak of the wellingtons was louder than anything the class had heard. The buttercups gaped. The pimpernels huddled down in shame. From the two rows of parents came a muttering and whispering like voices in a dream. Then Mary felt Miss Vista's hand on her arm. She stopped dancing. She smiled as she was led away. She couldn't see her parents. The parents were a blur. What she saw were two Miss Vistas, both of them fragile and neither of them a dancer.

Sonny said, after this incident: 'We must watch her all the

time, Estelle. Day and night. Now, there's no knowing what she can do.'

There *was* no knowing. Mary did not know.

When they got home after the thistledown show, Sonny hit Mary on the ear eight times with the flat of his hand.

She covered her ear with a grey mitten. She thought it would turn to coral. Without speaking, she said to her father: When I'm a man, I will kill you.

Estelle did not protect her or comfort her. Estelle went out and stared at her bantams in their compound, trying to hear contentment somewhere. Timmy followed her and put his hand in hers.

On Christmas afternoon, Sonny and Estelle went to the sagging bed. They smelled of the cheap port they'd drunk with the pudding. Sonny had his arm round his wife's neck and his hand on her breast, fondling it like money. He told Mary and Timmy to go out and play and not to come in until dark.

Mary threw the green ball at Timmy. She threw it several times but not once could he catch it. She thought, this is why Estelle is in despair, because Timmy can't catch a ball, because he walks about with his fingers over his eyes, because he has no stars on his class star-chart at school. 'You're barely human,' she said as he dropped the ball yet again, 'you're killing our mother.'

He began to cry and run towards the house but Mary remembered the smell of port on her parents' breath and the skewed look in their eyes so she ran after him and picked him up. He struggled in her arms and she hated the feel of his limbs. She dumped him in the tyre swing and pushed him till the sun went down behind the hedge and a green twilight hung over them. And all the time she was pushing she counted the things that Timmy could not do for himself and which were driving Estelle into her own unreachable world. He couldn't tie his bootlaces; he couldn't read a simple word like 'thing'; he couldn't get through three consecutive nights without wetting his bed; he couldn't learn his tables; he couldn't remember the words of 'In the Bleak Mid-Winter'; he couldn't eat a meal without spilling it; he couldn't feed the bantams without throwing the grain up into the air. He was beyond hope. It would be better if, one morning in his saturated bed, he did not wake up. He would be buried in a little grave, nice and neat with a stone angel kneeling above him making sure he stayed where he was. Estelle would mourn. She would take flowers. She would go and stare at the angel. Then she would recover. She would no longer say thoughts out loud or sit in a trance, stroking her sewing machine. She would abandon her walks to the river. She would come back from wherever it was she'd been.

Mary decided to kill him that night, Christmas night, 1955.

She kept herself awake by hitting her ear, still bruised from Sonny's slapping.

Her head ached. She wanted everything to be over. She thought, I know now why Grandma Livia went up in her glider; she was tired of every single thing except the sky.

When she heard Sonny's snoring start, she went barefoot down the stairs and into the cold kitchen. She opened the door of the larder and took down the insect spray kept there for the summer flies. It was called Flit. She liked the word. She thought, this is how you kill: you have a weapon and a word you say. You use both. Flit. 'Flit.'

She came back up the stairs. She didn't feel afraid, only tired, so that her legs were heavy.

She knelt by the door to Timmy's little room and opened it only wide enough to put her arm in and point the Flit gun at the bed. As a precaution against her own death she'd brought a handkerchief and she held this over her nose and mouth.

She began to pump. The nozzle of the gun bubbled and

fizzed. There was no sound from inside the room. A Flit death was a peaceful one. You breathed the sweet-smelling poison and you slept. And in the morning you didn't wake.

Sonny had woken at midnight with a drink headache and a thirst. On his way to the bathroom, he'd found Mary crouching by Timmy's door.

'What are you doing?' he said.

'Nothing,' said Mary.

But Sonny could smell the Flit. He pushed Mary aside and went into Timmy's room and saw his son sleeping peacefully under a cloud of poison.

He shouted for Estelle and she came running, in her stained nightdress, and gathered Timmy up and put him by the window of her room and made him breathe the freezing air of Christmas night. She didn't look at Mary, nor at Sonny. She closed her door.

Sonny went to work with his hands. He took down Mary's pyjamas and hit her buttocks and the backs of her thighs.

When she didn't cry out or make any sound, he punched her ear, the same ear he had slapped after Miss Vista's show. The force of this blow knocked Mary to the floor. Sonny pulled her up by the arms and hit her head again and then again and again until he had no more strength to haul her to her feet.

He left her lying and walked away. He stood in the cold bathroom, drinking a quart of water.

Mary remembered no morning or returning day. She lay in a pit. She knew she was deep down in the earth, where no one could find her.

Sounds came and then passed, came and passed. One of the sounds that came was the voice of Miss Vista. 'Light, children!' it whispered. 'Light, light!'

4
1957

Mary:

My grandfather – Livia's husband – was called Thomas Cord. We knew him as Grandpa Cord. He was sallow and small and fond of history. He was addicted to Wincarnis. When he talked, he closed his eyes, as if seeing and speaking at the same time were too difficult for him. He loved four things in the world. One of these was his remembered Livia. Another was the face and voice of an actress called Mary Martin.

He wrote sayings out in green ink on little cards and pinned them up over door lintels. Some of these were in Latin. His favourite one was *Ama et fac quod vis*. He would stop at this one sometimes and say: 'True, true. All too true.' Some of the sayings were faded. Grandpa Cord said: 'Green ink perishes, Mary. As can wisdom. When a saying is faded, it might be time to take it down. Or it might not.'

He lived eleven miles from our farm, in a village called Gresham Tears. His house was flint and brick and square and dark. This was the home where my mother had lived as a child. There were twin holly trees at the gate, their heads shaped into cones by Grandpa Cord's shears. His address was Holly House, Gresham Tears, Suffolk and he thought this address very marvellous and cheering. It was the third thing that he loved in his life.

I had thought that I would never really know Grandpa Cord. I had thought I would always see him on short visits and he would pour me ginger beer and tell me about King Ethelred the Redeless, and then he would die. But I was wrong about that. In the summer of 1957 I was sent to live with him. I left the farm and my address became Holly House, Gresham Tears, Suffolk. I took all my clothes and my school books and my *Dictionary of Inventions* and my green tennis ball. My father said: 'We're sending you for the coaching. Grandpa Cord will get you through the Eleven-plus.'

On my first night, Grandpa Cord showed me a theatre programme for a show called *South Pacific*. It had a picture of Mary Martin in it and Grandpa Cord said: 'What do you think of that?' I thought people looked dead in photographs, like they were ancestors of themselves, long departed, but I said the name Mary Martin was a good name and that I would call myself that from now on. And this amused Grandpa Cord. He slapped his old corduroy knee. He said: 'No one told me you were a good sport, but I can see that you are!'

So I began to live there and to be called Mary Martin. After a week I said: 'Much as I like Mary Martin as a name, it is rather long, Grandpa Cord. So I think you can just call me Martin.'

'Plain old Martin?' he asked.

'Yes.'

'Very well. A bit peculiar, but who cares? And you call me Cord, Martin. "Grandpa" makes me feel I should have lumbago. Is that a deal?'

I said it was a deal. We shook hands. The skin on Cord's hands had the feel of medal ribbon, ribbed and silky. He closed his eyes and said: 'Scouts honour, as they say.'

So then I thought of us as a firm, Martin and Cord, Limited. We were a firm of dreamers. Cord specialised in the past, the long-ago past of Ethelred the Redeless and the middle past of the Battle of Marston Moor and the near past of Livia wearing a shawl from Madagascar and playing Liszt. My department was the future, the future spinning towards me, of Weston Grammar School and the loss of Miss McRae, and the future that sat still, waiting for time to get to it, the future of Martin Ward. Cord supplied me with green ink – the only kind he bought – and in it I wrote out my new name hundreds of times in different writing.

No one told me the real reason for my leaving the farm, but I knew it.

Irene, who now lived with Pearl in Mr Harker's house, had said to me twice: 'The day may come, Mary, when your mother will have to go away for a bit. Just Until.' So I understood. I was being sent to Cord's because Just Until was coming. Because I couldn't stay alone at the farm with my father and Timmy.

I didn't want to think about where Estelle was going. On the other side of Leiston there was a place called Mountview Asylum which we had sometimes passed on the way to the sea in Sonny's van. I whispered once to Timmy that this was a loony bin where boys got sent if they couldn't learn multiplication. Instead of cringing with fear as I'd hoped, he looked at the place, which was a converted stately home with red walls and flying turrets, and said: 'Which bit of it is the actual bin?' And we all laughed. Even Estelle. This is the only time that I can remember us all laughing together – like a proper family in an Austin with a picnic hamper – when Timmy asked the question about the Actual Bin.

But now I had dreams about Estelle in a metal bin, being hurled about and hurt as the bin spun round. In the dreams, I was a knight. I had armour. I jousted with the bin and stopped it turning. I put my mother on my grey charger and rode away. The dream never said where I rode to or where or if I set my mother down. I just rode out of the dream and woke up in Cord's house in my room that was wallpapered with scenes of boating. I said to the boaters: 'I refuse to think about what's happening.' And then I'd put on my glasses and open one of the History books Cord had given me and read a thing like 'Thomas Wolsey was the son of a butcher and cattle dealer of Ipswich' or 'Early death was common in medieval times' and wait for my day to begin.

Cord started his day with Yoga. His mat was a bath mat with all its thickness worn away by time and the mangle and Livia's wet feet long ago. Yoga was the fourth thing he loved in his life. He'd learnt it in Ceylon, in the house of a man called Varindra. He said Varindra had taught him how to put the world away and how to move inwards instead of out all the time and that this 'moving inwards' had kept him breathing and alive when the news came of the glider crash. I didn't understand what 'moving inwards' meant and Cord said: 'Well, no, I don't expect you to, Martin, not at your age, but later when you're in your proper life, you will.'

I said: 'Do you mean, when I'm Martin Ward?'

'You *are* Martin Ward,' said Cord.

I thought, I shall tell him one day soon. He will be saying something like 'John Davis made three further attempts to find the North-West Passage, but he failed to notice the Hudson Strait and was driven back by ice,' and I will say: 'I have made three attempts to tell somebody that I am not a real girl,' or he will say: 'Life on board a carrack was full of hardship,' and I will say: 'Life as Mary is full of confusion.' And then, once this is said, we won't just be a firm of dreamers but a firm of surveyors and planners.

I trusted Cord. I began to like being with him, old as he was. I thought he would agree with me when I said I was a boy inside.

I thought a lot that was wrong. I thought the whole summer would pass at Holly House without any word about Estelle coming to disturb us. I thought we would just go on doing our history and listening to *The Brains Trust* and drinking Wincarnis and ginger beer. I thought we were being *allowed* to step out of the world, being given the knack of it, like old Varindra in Ceylon in 1924. But then one morning, after Cord had made us bacon and fried bread and we were listening to Brenda Lee he said: 'Listen to me, Martin, we're going to see your mother today and I suppose we're also going to have to be brave about what we find.'

'Is she at Mountview?' I asked.

'Yes. That's it. But not for long, I don't expect.'

'Only Just Until.'

'Yes. Just Until. And it won't be long coming.'

I thought of my dream of the bin and the jousting. 'I'm sorry!' sang Brenda, 'so *sorry!*'

It was a bright August morning in Gresham Tears. The flints of the houses opposite looked polished. Cord's Hillman Minx sat waiting in the sun to take us to Mountview. I thought, names are often wrong: Minx for a little slow car; Mountview for a place not near any mountain. I thought, people just decide things without giving them any attention and Miss McRae would not approve.

Then I went up to my bedroom to get ready. I stood and looked at the boaters and decided that I would not be capable of going into a room full of mad people and finding my mother there. I tore a page out of my History exercise book opposite a very bad drawing of Vasco da Gama and wrote her a letter:

> Dear Mother,
>   I am writing this very quickly, as we have to leave in five minutes to come and see you.
>   I hope you are getting better. I hope everyone is kind to you. I hope you can have your sewing machine.

I am having a nice time with Grandpa Cord. I
am learning about explorers, including Hakluyt. He
went to Russia. He said, 'their streets and ways are
not paved with stone as ours are'. In the evenings,
I have Ginger Beer.

I hope you are getting better. I want you to get
better now, this moment, and not be there when
we arrive.

love from Mary

I did not put Martin. Miss McRae once said to me: 'Living
in a lighthouse taught me that not all wisdom comes from
others, Mary. Some comes from oneself, if one can but hear
it.' But I had on my Martin clothes, my aertex shirt and
my grey shorts and my plimsolls, Blanco'd white. I stuffed
my letter into the pocket of my shorts and we got into the
Minx and drove away. We sang all the way. We sang 'I'm
sorry' and 'Bye bye, love'. Someone had told us a rumour
that Brenda Lee was a child of my age or younger than me,
but we didn't believe it.

When we turned into the drive of Mountview, Cord said:
'Rum show, Martin, eh?'

I said: 'Was this once a house?'

'Oh, yes,' said Cord, 'Jacobean, 1618. Peacocks on the lawn,
cold woodcock for breakfast, that kind of nonsense. Became
a hospital in the '14–'18 war. A lot of shrieking then, I dare
say, soldiers and peacocks all screaming.'

Now, you could tell it was a bin and not a house because
of a huge chimney, like a factory chimney, they'd built behind
it and some little huts like pre-fabs they'd put on the lawn
and signs that said *Car Park* and *Laundry* and *No Visitors
Beyond this Point*.

Cord was trembling. He kept saying: 'Rum show, damn
bad show.' I could tell he didn't want to be there but back

in Gresham Tears pouring himself another glass of Wincarnis. His sallow face looked a kind of custard colour and his eyes bruised and heavy, like prunes in the custard. He held my hand. I thought, this is more than we can stand.

We went in and stood on a polished floor, waiting. There was a smell of Dettol and of something sweet and living but terrible, like brains. People passed us but didn't seem to see us or else saw us and looked away. We didn't know where to go or how to be. I thought we should go back to the Minx and sit in it and think and then maybe drive away and pretend we'd never tried to come there at all. But then Cord went up to one of the people, a person in a white overall, and spoke in a firm voice, as if he were Hakluyt asking the way to Moscow. So we followed the man through an enormous room with a ceiling moulded into square roses and upside-down pinnacles that looked like stalactites about to form. Men and women sat about under the stalactites all silent and grave, waiting for the first icy drips to fall on them, and it was their brains that were smelling and their plastic chairs that were swabbed with Dettol.

The man in the white coat walked very fast, so Cord and I had to run and Cord detested running more than almost anything in life.

We dashed down a long corridor made of something like stone and then up some stairs covered in coconut matting. Out of the windows on the stairs you could see the chimney, with black smoke coming out of it. And then we were on a landing, a shadowy place with lots of doors with numbers on them and I knew my mother was going to be there, behind one of these doors, so I got out my note, ready to give it to Cord to give to her. But Cord still held my hand clenched in his. I tried to pull it free but it was difficult to get my hand out, and then Cord farted twice, out of fear and exhaustion, and I thought, I can't abandon him while he's farting, I must be Martin and strong.

My mother was sitting in a chair. Her hair was tied back in a rubber band. She had a simpering expression on her face, like someone behind a counter trying to sell liberty bodices. She was doing some knitting. Her ball of wool trailed away across the room and under the bed made of pine slats. When she saw us, she smiled and held her knitting to her breasts, covering them with it and smoothing it down over them, as if she thought they should be hidden.

Her room had orange curtains. The floor was lino and her chair was plastic. There was nowhere for us to sit except on her bed, which was very narrow, so we sat there side by side smiling at Estelle and she smiled back and Cord took out a handkerchief and wiped his face and rubbed his eyes.

'How are you feeling, Est?' Cord said after a moment. He usually called her 'Est', or sometimes 'Stelle' or sometimes 'My Girl'.

She said: 'I'm right as rain, Daddy, as you can see. I am receiving a great deal of help, in particular with my shadows that I used to see and with my worry about the onion.'

'Good,' said Cord. 'That's what we want to hear. Eh, Martin?'

I nodded. 'What are you knitting, Mother?' I asked.

She looked down at the knitting, a grey slab, on her breasts.

'Oh,' she said, 'I forget what it is. What things are is of no importance, is it?'

'No, no,' said Cord, 'absolutely none.'

We kept on smiling. I was glad we were alone with Estelle and not with those other people under the stalactites.

'Food all right?' asked Cord.

Estelle shrugged. The smile left her face. 'Meals are a farce,' she said.

'What, no good, eh? Nursery food, is it?'

'People.'

'Say again, Stelle?'

'A farce. Utter. But I don't look. I close my eyes.'

'Not a pretty sight, I dare say?'

'I don't see them. I close my eyes. I do this knitting. Far better to do that.'

I thought, it's like that Nativity Play we did at school, where I was the Angel Gabriel and Billy Bateman was the First Shepherd, wearing a teatowel on his head with a rubber quoit round it. He got all his lines mixed up. I said: 'Don't be afraid, oh ye shepherds,' and he should have said: 'What have you come to tell us, good angel?' But he said: 'How far is it to Bethlehem?' Then I said: 'I bring you wonderful tidings,' and Billy should have asked: 'What are they?' And instead he said: 'I fear some of our sheep will die of cold,' so I had to depart from the script and say: 'Shut up about your sheep. I repeat that I am bringing you tidings.' At the play, though, there was an audience to laugh and clap, and here there was only the play and no audience.

I found a toffee in the pocket of my shorts with my note and I unwrapped it slowly and my mother watched me as I put it into my mouth.

'I'm sorry, Mary,' she said suddenly, 'I am.' Then she tugged the rubber band out of her hair and spread the hair across her face, rubbing it over her nose and mouth.

'Don't, Est,' said Cord.

The knitting fell onto the floor and Estelle began to rock backwards and forwards and you could tell she was crying into her hair.

Cord was weeping, too. Tears were streaming down him.

'Oh heavens, Stelle,' he said. Then he got up and tried to push back the hair from my mother's face. He kept saying: 'It won't be for long, Stelle. Only till you're better, my girl,' and I thought, I am not coming here again, ever! I am never going to set foot in this Mountview place ever again in my whole life.

I ran out of the horrible little room and along the corridor. I ran like a sprinter, faster than a boy. I didn't stop running until I got to the car and I stood holding on to the Minx that was burning hot from the sun until Cord arrived and we drove home.

We couldn't find much to say on the way back.

I stuck my head into the fresh air, and it smelled of hay and mustard flowers.

When we were nearly at Gresham Tears, Cord said: 'What about a song, then?' and so we tried 'Wake Up, Little Susie', but we didn't know very many of the words.

Oh, Sandra

That summer, Walter Loomis fell in love for the first time.

He met his love at the farmworkers' cinema, held in the Girl Guide hut. The film was *Captain Horatio Hornblower,* starring Gregory Peck and Virginia Mayo. His love's name was Sandra. Walter, on catching sight of Sandra, yearned to be Gregory Peck and to be able to raise one eyebrow without moving the other.

She wore a felt skirt and a webbing belt. Her hair was the colour of marmalade. She told Walter that she had ambitions to become a stenographer, but meanwhile worked at Cunningham's, selling bias binding and rick-rack and knicker elastic. She said her hobby was boating.

Walter had had no practice at loving anybody except his parents and Pete. He didn't know whether what he felt was what he was supposed to feel. He wondered whether he should write to a magazine for advice, but he didn't know which magazine to choose. He said to Pete: 'I feel as if I'm full of something that isn't mine, as if I was the whale that swallowed a man.' Pete yawned and then made an effort to align his eyes. 'I'd better warn you, Walter,' he said, 'women can be the death of you and that's just the start.'

A summer fair came to Leiston. Walter went into Cunningham's and found Sandra reorganising the trays of Sylko into a rainbow spectrum of notable precision. She was a girl who loved order. She plucked her eyebrows to a perfectly even arch. Her father was a spinner and weaver who made tassels and fringes for Harrods in London and for the Queen at Sandringham. Sandra had his long, careful hands and his liking for things done with care. Walter was not her type. When he stood in front of her, wearing his collarless shirt, and invited her to go with him to the Leiston fair, she looked up from the cotton reels and smiled and said: 'No, thank you. I don't think I will, thank you.'

He walked to Leiston and went to the fair on his own. He got into a bumper car and knocked into some girls and laughed but they didn't laugh back, they stuck their fingers up and said: 'Buzz off, Curly!' He sat on a carousel horse and went up and down and round and round and thought of Sandra's marmalade hair lifting into the wind and her feet in their white shoes and socks dangling down.

He found a fortune teller. She put on her glasses that had spangled frames and stared at Walter's big red hands. She said: 'I see a quest. Very long and difficult. And I see a river.'

'The person I love is fond of boating,' Walter said. 'Could that be it?'

The fortune teller frowned. She had no eyebrows at all, only a line of dusty pencil where they used to be. Before she could reply Walter said: 'Can you do spells?'

She was called Madame Cleo. She had paid twenty-nine pounds, seven shillings for a set of perfect teeth. She liked to smile and show them off. She smiled at Walter and told him that she only did good spells, beautiful spells, never bad ones and that a spell cost two guineas.

Walter fumbled for his money and began to count it out.

Madame Cleo took off her spangled glasses and let her shawl slip off her shoulders revealing the tops of her breasts bunched up above her pearly bodice. Walter understood. He took a deep, terrified breath. The feeling of having swallowed a man became so profound that he thought he might choke and die. He let Madame Cleo caress his cheek with her scarlet nail. He watched as she got up and put the *Closed* sign on her caravan door. He did not protest or move or ask himself whether he wanted to protest or move. He let her lead him like a lamb to her boudoir that was painted pink, with old blackout material at the window and two candles burning on saucers.

The bed was soft and smelled of scorched rayon. Madame Cleo had a jewel in her navel and a rose tattoo on her thigh. She said all the spells were inside her, as many as he could dream of.

Walter told Pete what he'd done at the fair.

Pete laughed a roaring laugh. 'You know what that Cleo's real name is?' he said. 'Gladys.'

'I don't mind,' said Walter.

'Gladys Higgins.'

'I still don't mind.'

Pete gave him some ointment that smelled of tar. 'If you've caught a spell, rub that on!' he said.

Anointing himself nightly, Walter returned to his dreams of Sandra. He put a jewel into her navel and a rose tattoo onto her white thigh. He lay with her under the counter at Cunningham's.

Then in the soft summer dawns, before going to work in the slaughtering yard, he wrote her a song. He didn't have the tune for it yet, but he knew that it would come and when it came, his hopes for a distant future in Tennessee might come back with it. Even without a yodel. Because now Sandra would be his inspiration. With her in his heart, he would manufacture music.

His song was sad. Most country songs were, he realised: sad and simple, because that's how life is on the land, especially if your work is over a blood gulley. Days come and then they go and in all this repetition there is a sorrow somewhere, even when you can't quite see it. He wrote the song on a bill of sale pad printed with the familiar words, *Arthur Loomis & Son, Family Butchers*. It was called, 'Oh, Sandra'. So far, it had one verse and then a chorus.

> I am a boy of twenty-one
> Before we met I thought my days were done
> I thought my life had been and gone
> I thought I'd always be alone
> Until I saw you I was just a stone
>
> Oh, Sandra,
> For you I'd ride across the tundra,
> For you I'd journey far and yonder
> If I could make you happy I'd be glad
> Oh, Sandra, do I need to feel so sad?

He was proud of it. He recited it to Pete. Pete smiled. 'Difficult word to rhyme with, Sandra,' he said. 'But it's not a bad start.'

In the bus, just like in the old days of the yodel, they sat up late, searching for a tune. The summer was beginning to be over. The dark enveloped them earlier and earlier. Walter stared out at it and thought of Sandra taking off her webbing belt and circular skirt and standing alone in her room, brushing her hair.

When the tune arrived at last and Pete wrote it down, note by note, counting on his fingers, Walter began work on more verses. He wanted his song to be endless. He wanted it to take the place of ordinary time. He didn't know which he loved more now, the song or the girl, 'Oh, Sandra' or Sandra. He was so pleased with himself his mouth hung open in a perpetual half-smile.

Pete noted the boy's pleasure and understood it. He said: 'I felt like that in Memphis one summer. It had been cold and then there was this one hot night that came and the next day it was Sunday and all my roses had come out, bang, and the Minister said to me, "You have created a fine beauty here, Pete." That's how they spoke down there then: "You have created a fine beauty, Pete. Yes, *Sir.*" And that's how I felt. Full of grin.'

Walter went back to Cunningham's. Amy Cunningham was unpacking a box of 2-ply wool. She fixed Walter with the stare she was famous for, hard as the tundra.

Walter nodded to her politely, ignoring the stare. He'd put on a tie that day. He approached Sandra. She was inserting a plastic display hand into a black leather glove. He executed a little foolish bow. That part of his body that had probed for spells inside Madame Cleo he covered with his tweed cap.

He suggested a boating outing on the River Alde. He said summer would be over soon. Sandra did not look at him. Once, with her father, she had rowed down the Alde as far as Orford Ness and the sea, and she had often dreamed of doing it again. She said: 'Very well, Walter. On Sunday, then.'

He collected her in the Loomis delivery van. He'd brought his banjo and a little hamper of cold meats and bottles of Tizer. He'd hoped for sun, but what he got was a white, unearthly day with no shadows and no wind.

The boat hire firm was called Wheatcroft's. The boats sat heavy in the water under layers of varnish. No cushions were provided. You sat on hard plank seats. Water collected between the slats under your feet. You could not lie your girl down with a parasol, like in an oil painting.

Sandra did not talk. She watched the river banks going past and the cows standing still in low meadows. Her eyes were blue and lively.

To initiate the subject of 'Oh, Sandra', Walter started to tell Sandra the life story of Hank Williams who had overcome his poor beginnings as the son of a log-train engineer to become a great singer-songwriter of hillbilly music.

Sandra had never heard of Hank Williams. She said she couldn't think what a log-train engineer could possibly be. Walter hurried past this hurdle. He told her that Williams had died in a car crash aged thirty but his songs carried on.

'The reason they carry on,' he said, 'was because Hank understood the *foundation* of Country Music and that is sincerity. Hillbillies don't pretend. They sing what they feel. And Hank said the reason they're more sincere than most entertainers is because they know about hard work.'

'Why are you telling me this?' asked Sandra.

Walter paused in his rowing. He was sweating. He let the boat drift slowly on the current.

'Because,' said Walter, 'I thought it was something you might like to know. You know his famous number, "Your Cheatin' Heart"?'

'No.'

' "I Don't Care If Tomorrow Never Comes"?'

'What?'

'That's another song title.'

'No.'

'He had a spine defect, you know. He had to walk with a stoop, but he didn't let this stop him.'

'Oh well. Shall we turn round now? I think it's going to rain.'

Turn round? They had hardly started out. There was the Tizer yet to be drunk and the hazlet, wrapped in greaseproof, to be eaten and, when the moment was right, the song to be sung. In Walter's mind, the afternoon had had no end, dusk never fell, the hired boat was never returned.

'Let's go on a bit,' he said. 'If it rains, I'll take you back.'

She said nothing. She pulled the skirt of her pink dress further down over her knees and tucked it in behind her calves. And Walter saw in this gesture a love utterly unrequited.

He steered them on. They saw moorhens busy at the river's edge and the first willow leaves falling in showers, like petals. He thought, loving Sandra is like being the moon and trying to warm the sky.

In the Surgery

Margaret Blakey lived within sight and sound of the sea. She was fifty-seven. Her house stood on the soft sandstone cliffs above Minsmere. In her lifetime, vast pieces of the cliffs had fallen away, bringing the abyss nearer to her door by some twenty-two yards.

She had one son whose name was Gilbert. He was a dentist. He was thirty and unmarried. Margaret liked to keep him by her. She had calculated that, if the sandstone continued to crumble and fall at its present rate, her house would drop into the sea when Gilbert reached the age of sixty-eight. Having Gilbert at home somehow prolonged his youth and so kept at a safe distance the loss of her own life and of the bit of earth on which it rested.

Gilbert resembled a young Anthony Eden. His hair was pale, his upper canines and incisors prominent, his eyes dreamy. He kept his little moustache fastidiously trimmed. His hands were long and white. Margaret who had wept after Suez – for England and for Eden – took pride in Gilbert's affinity with greatness, even with a greatness that was past.

She cherished him like a baby. He slept between sheets of Irish linen and here dreamed, so Margaret assumed, of an imaginary surgery in Harley Street and the caries of famous mouths.

He did not dream of these things. He dreamed of boys and young men. They waited for him on hard chairs, reading magazines. He summoned them one by one. He shone his 12-volt Miralux lamp on their soft mouths. 'Open,' he said sweetly. 'Please.'

On a day in October, two people sat in Gilbert Blakey's waiting room. Neither of them was reading a magazine. Both were in pain. The two were Mary Ward and Walter Loomis. Neither had been to a dentist before.

They talked. Fear had misted up Mary's glasses and, to her, Walter looked damp, like a person sitting in a Turkish bath. His face was red, as if from all the steam. She said: 'Are you frightened, Walter?'

He ran his big hands through his thick curly hair. 'Shouldn't be,' he said, 'not at my age. Should I?'

'I'm frightened,' said Mary. 'Boys are, sometimes.'

Next door they could hear the whine of Gilbert's drill, a whine like a gnat. Often, pain had no sound, but today it did. It was better to talk of anything than listen to it.

'I heard your mother was away, poorly,' said Walter.

Mary rubbed her misty glasses with her fist. 'Yes,' she said.

'We were all sorry for that. We were all sorry in the village.'

'Do you live in that trolley bus, Walter?' asked Mary.

Walter smiled. Smiling seemed to add to his pain and to his fear. 'I like that old bus,' he said. 'It's Pete's, not mine. He's got a kitchen where the driver used to sit.'

'When were trolley buses invented?' asked Mary.

'Invented?'

'Yes. 1892, for instance.'

'You're a strange one. Who'd know a thing like that?'

'Someone would. Everything had a time when it wasn't there.'

'Except the land.'

'What?'

'Except the earth: Swaithey. That's always been there. It's in the Domesday Book.'

'You still can't say "always". There's a time before "always", even.'

Walter nodded. At home, his parents referred to Mary Ward as 'that poor plain little mite'. 'I heard you're going to Weston Grammar School, Mary,' he said.

'If I pass the exam.'

'You will, I reckon.'

'I'd like it to be over.'

'The exam?'

'No. The drilling.'

Mary was the first to go in. She felt guilty to be leaving Walter alone with his fear. She thought of him sitting there and hearing her pain through the wall. She wondered whether he would pick up a copy of *Needlework for Beginners* and try to read it.

Gilbert Blakey was drying his hands when Mary came into the surgery. He smiled his charming, toothy smile. He wore a white gown tied at the back with tape. Mary was surprised by how gentle he looked.

He told her to sit down in the complicated chair and tilt her head back. Her head was meant to come to rest on a hard leather pad, but she was too short for the chair, so her head rested on nothing. She wished Cord were here. Cord would say: 'This doesn't look right to me, Martin.'

There was a nurse standing by. She put a pink pellet into a white enamel mug of water, where it began to dissolve, staining the water mauve. The nurse was old and didn't smile.

She wore a starched thing on her head, fastened to her hair with kirbygrips. She didn't look at Mary, but kept her eyes on some distant point in the room, and this distant point stared back at her, hardening up her look. Mary thought, if all the nurses at Mountview are like this one, my mother will die.

Gilbert finished drying his hands and came to the chair. He lowered the leather pad and Mary felt it arrive behind her head and give her courage. The Miralux lamp shone in her eyes. She thought, this is a complicated kind of light, showing up things that no one noticed were there.

'Well?' said Gilbert. 'Let's have a look, shall we?'

The nurse passed him a tray of metal instruments, like somebody offering a selection of biscuits. He chose two and the nurse put the tray down. Then the two faces bent over her and stared at her: Gilbert's face, with its sweetness, and the nurse's, as unforgiving as time. Mary held on to the metal arms of the chair and wished one of them was Cord's hand. 'Steady as we go,' Cord said in her mind.

Gilbert, helped by the clever light, found the source of Mary's pain and probed it, and the probing, for Mary, was like an electrocution and all memory of no-pain vanished and became the past, to which there was no return. And then, beyond the two faces and beyond the light, beyond the lost past and beyond the absence of Cord, Mary rediscovered her old ally – suffering. She had forgotten its power. In her fear, she had obliterated her belief in its magic. But now, once again in its company, she let herself yield to its transforming properties. She let go her grip on the chair. She stopped wishing for the touch of Cord's medal-ribboned hand. Her thoughts were clear and hard. As Gilbert began to drill into her decaying tooth, she felt Mary annihilated a little more each second, Mary becoming fragments, pulp. Martin reaffirming himself.

'Amalgam,' said Gilbert to the nurse.

The nurse disappeared from Mary's vision. Gilbert's face, near to Mary's, smelled of Eau de Cologne and his breath of sweetcorn. Behind him, at a great distance from him and from the centre of her pain, she could hear the nurse grinding some substance in a mortar and she thought, this substance is new and is part of Martin Ward.

By the time Walter was called into the surgery, he was dazed with fright. He sat down in the leather and metal chair and held onto it. His large hands were wet and limp.

Gilbert turned from washing his white hands for the eighth time that day and saw steam rising from his patient's head. Beneath the steam, there were wiry black curls, the soft eyes of an animal, a fleshy mouth very pink and moist. The infinitesimally small but telltale feeling of bruising on the inner thighs that accompanied desire made Gilbert turn quickly back to his little sink.

Gilbert Blakey's dreams of young men remained dreams. He never touched them, except in his mind. He believed that by touching them he would make his life fall away bit by bit, like the cliffs of Minsmere into the sea.

As Gilbert finished drying his hands and approached Walter, the telephone in his small office began to ring and the nurse slipped away to answer it, leaving Gilbert and Walter alone face to face.

Gilbert smiled. He asked Walter to describe his pain and point to where it was. He selected a probe and a dental mirror from the tray. He heard Walter say that his pain was everywhere, filling his whole face. He adjusted the head-rest until Walter's head seemed comfortable on it. Then he put down the probe and touched Walter's lips with his fingers. 'Open, please,' he said.

Walter closed his eyes. Behind his closed eyes everything was getting dark, everything was in front and becoming small and retreating . . .

Gilbert's face was close to the thick hair, to the curled lashes on the wet cheek. He steadied his hand. He thought of his mother's house safe and sound and far, yet, from the advancing precipice. The probe lighted unerringly on an occlusal cavity in the lower right pre-molar five, visible lesion and surrounding opacity . . .

Gilbert saw the pallor come into Walter's face.

He shouted for the nurse. He let the instruments drop. He pulled Walter towards him, into his arms, for a moment so brief he was able to deny to himself that it had ever existed, then tipped his head down to his feet where he noticed for the first time the heaviness of Walter's shoes. He crouched by Walter. His hand was on Walter's neck, one thumb just beneath the frayed collar of his woollen shirt.

The nurse strode back into the surgery. She was too old to run. Her measured step gave her authority, she thought. It was her firm, measured step, more than her hard look, which said to the world, I am to be relied upon; I am always here watching everything that happens.

Unbaptised Children

Edward Harker's house had never been cleaner. The leaves of plants were polished. Every morning, as soon as Harker had gone down to the cellar and Pearl had left for school, Irene put on her flowered apron and took the Min Cream down from its shelf and a clean duster from its drawer and went to work.

Harker had told the village: 'I am taking Mrs Simmonds in as my housekeeper.' The term had a respectability about it that moved Irene. She had been taken in. Now, she would keep the house. The house was not hers and never would be, but because she lived there, everything in it became precious to Irene. Harker was a person of taste. He knew how furniture should look. He knew that the feet of a table should have claws, that a wooden washstand could be a thing of value. Irene knelt by the Carolean day bed in the sitting room. She polished the wicker. She took down the china dogs from the mantelpiece and looked at them. Blessed with sudden good fortune, she was able to see some beauty in almost everything. She wrote to her sister in Ipswich: 'I am learning the names of things and where they come from. Mr Harker is an excellent teacher.'

In the daytime, as instructed, she addressed him as Mr Harker. 'Simply out of prudence, my dear,' he said, 'to ensure against malicious gossip.' And, really, it was as Mr Harker that she still thought of him, but at night-time she had a different set of instructions; in bed, she was to call him Edward. 'Say Edward,' he would whisper neatly packing himself inside the billowing firmament of her body. 'Say Edward, I want you.'

Sometimes the names escaped their boundaries. In Loomis's one Saturday morning, she let an Edward slip loose. She saw it arrive in Mr Loomis's startled eyes. Then, in the night, now and again, moved by the fervour with which her breasts were being caressed, she would murmur: 'Go on, Mr Harker. Don't stop, don't stop.'

Pearl's father, the printer from Dublin, was being obliterated from Irene's consciousness. She could no longer recall the taste of dye on his hand, his hard, bony back, his moustache as thin as a line of writing. She was in love. Her desire for her elderly lover grew. Sometimes she went down to the cellar in broad daylight and sat in the amber shadows watching him work. The atmosphere in the oil-scented room would become charged. Often she would leave with just a glancing kiss on his white head. Occasionally, when she felt brazen and as syrupy as a bee, she would remove her knickers.

She had her own room. Harker had insisted on this. He

did not want Pearl to tell the children at school that her mother slept in her employer's bed. But sometimes after Harker had made love to Irene, he went instantly to sleep. He was getting on, after all. Sleep came to him as easily as a leaf falling and settling on the earth. And now he did not know whether Pearl might not have seen him there like that, sleeping with his arm across Irene's breast. He did not know that she hadn't come into the room and stood there staring at him, before tip-toeing away. He thought, meticulous as I am, I have become careless in this one regard.

They were careless in other ways. On a night of soundless snow Irene said: 'Did you know, Edward, that I am going to have your child?' She had rehearsed this line. She thought it sounded beautiful, as if it were being spoken by Celia Johnson. She waited for the shock that it was going to cause. She hoped Edward did not have a faulty heart he had not been honest about. He was silent for some minutes. Irene listened to the quiet that was the snow falling. Eventually Harker said: 'Well. There it is.'

Harker considered leaving Swaithey. He had a night of pessimism. During his night of pessimism he mourned the loss of his solitary, orderly life. Respectability, too, had been important to him. Now, he had put himself among the outcasts. His standing in the village would drop. Orders for his bats would decline. He had a dream of himself as an ancient Bedouin, pricked by sandstorms, with no shelter and no destination.

He woke early and went to his cellar. A new shipment of willow had recently arrived. He sat down at his desk and took out a sheet of the thick vellum on which his drawings were made. He designed a crib.

At noon, with the drawings finished, he went upstairs. He found Irene brushing the carpet under the Carolean day bed. He sat her down on the polished wicker and asked her to marry him. He showed her the design for the crib. She put her arms round his neck. 'Edward,' she said, 'I don't know whether to laugh or cry.'

They were married in Swaithey Church. Irene wore a blue costume and a blue hat with a veil.

Estelle was driven over from Mountview. Her hair was turning grey. The hymn they had to sing made her weep.

Sonny wore a black suit like a mourner.

Most of the village came out of respect for Harker. Ernie Loomis's gift was a crown of lamb decorated with cutlet frills. The Misses Cunningham smiled the apology they felt should have been on other faces.

Estelle got drunk in what seemed to her to be a matter of moments. She felt vomit rise in her throat. She let Mary lead her to the waiting car. She said to Mary: 'They're hiding something. Even from me. It's probably in the cellar.'

The sight of her mother had destroyed Mary's happiness for Irene. She had looked forward to seeing Estelle, but when she did see her, she wished she hadn't. Estelle had been wearing a polka-dot dress, too young for her, the material too thin for the cold December day. Mary had never seen this dress before. She knew that it must belong to one of the women sitting under the stalactites. This woman would have said: 'You can't go to a wedding in your old skirt, Estelle. You'd better wear my lovely polka dot dress.'

After her mother had been driven away, Mary didn't want to go back to the party. She found the door to the cellar. She had never been down there. She knew this was where Harker worked and that his work made him famous in places Swaithey people never thought about. It was peculiar to imagine fame, which seemed like something made of air, coming from an old cellar with its feet in the dark.

Mary switched on the row of parchment-shaded lamps and looked at what their yellowy light revealed. The place was so crowded with machinery and tools and wood and paper and dust that there seemed to be no room in it to make anything. It smelled of glue and resin and linseed oil, and the smell was so thick it made breathing peculiar.

Mary moved cautiously. She wondered if her mother was right about something being hidden here. It seemed to her a place of infinite confusion where it would be difficult to distinguish between one thing hidden deliberately and another hidden by mistake. You couldn't tell whether what you saw was what you were allowed to see or whether one small thing in your line of vision was supposed to be invisible to you. At school, at Easter, coloured eggs were concealed around the playground for the infants to find. The playground was grey and the eggs bright so the infants found them without any difficulty. But this was not like that. Here, everything was different and everything the same. You could hold a hidden thing in your hand and not know it.

Mary inspected Harker's workbench. She picked up a chisel and was surprised by the weight of it. Above the bench was a brass plate screwed to the brick wall. On the plate were the words *Harker's Bats. Estb.* 1947. She stared at it and smiled. It made Harker heroic to her, to be placed in the ranks of Montgolfier and Galileo.

She moved to Harker's desk and sat down on his stool. She switched on another lamp. On the desk were Harker's designs for cribs. There were standing cribs and cribs on rockers and cribs that swung from a bar. There were solid cribs like mangers and open cribs like cages. Mary took a breath and covered her mouth with her hand. Dear Mother, she wrote in her mind, I have found out the secret. You were quite right, it is in the cellar. It is a baby.

She heard the door open and she turned. Harker was standing there. His nose was a little red, his white hair a little wild. He said: 'Well, now, Mary.'

'I'm not meant to come in here, am I?' she said.

'It's not holy ground, only a place of work. I heard somebody go down.'

'I saw the cribs, Mr Harker.'

'So you did.'

'I won't tell anyone.'

Harker sat down on a wooden chair he was half-way through mending. He remembered the chair's precarious state and stood up again. He took out a red handkerchief and blew his nose.

'I promise,' said Mary.

'Let me sit down a minute,' said Harker.

She made way for him at the desk. He sat down gratefully. He felt like a runner who needed to catch his breath. Mary thought how terrible it would be if he suddenly died right there near the sign that said *Estb. 1947* and took all Irene's happiness away with him into the grave.

'I promise I won't tell,' she said, 'not even my mother.'

'Very considerate of you,' said Harker, 'but after today it doesn't much matter any more. And people will know soon enough.'

'They're very beautiful cribs,' said Mary.

'Thank you,' said Harker.

'I like the rocking one best.'

'You do?'

'Is it going to be a boy or a girl?'

Harker had recovered his breath. He looked up at Mary. His face had a serene smile on it, like the smile of an angel bringing tidings.

'A more pertinent question to ask,' he said, 'is, "Who has it *been*?" '

'What?' asked Mary.

'Well, we've all been here before, you know. As Voltaire said – though you won't know Voltaire of course – "Everything in nature is resurrection." '

'I haven't been here before.'

'Yes, you have. Not as you, of course. As someone else. Even *something* else.'

'Have I? What as?'

'You may discover. Something may give you a clue. Or you may die not knowing.'

'Were you here before?'

'Oh yes.'

'Who as?'

Harker sighed. 'I've had a few goes at it, but I still don't feel positive that I know. I am fascinated by hidden places, cloistered places, so I think I may have been a nun. Good at knitting, probably. Very tidy with my food.'

'Nuns are women.'

'Yes.'

'So?'

'Souls have no gender. You could have been a man, Mary. Or again, you may have been a marmoset.'

Mary's round face behind her glasses regarded Harker as gravely as the moon.

People tell anything to children, she thought. They think you know nothing about the world and have never heard of Hakluyt.

'You don't believe me, do you?' said Harker.

'No,' said Mary.

'Well, there is no certain, incontrovertible proof; only signs, things which fit too well or don't fit at all. And many different people, all over the earth, believe in this kind of resurrection. The Chang-Nagas of Assam believed that those with good voices returned as cicadas and those who couldn't sing as dung-beetles.'

Harker thought Mary would smile at the mention of dung-beetles, but she didn't. He went on. 'In parts of Brittany, do you know what they believe, Mary?'

'No.'

'That if a child dies unbaptised, it will return again and again as a sparrow, again and again, until judgement day.'

Mary was quiet, still staring at Harker.

'Who else believes this?' she asked.

'Well, even in the Bible, you know, in Ecclesiastes, it says: "there is no new thing under the sun".'

'Does Irene think her baby has been someone else?'

'She understands that it is very likely.'

'When you die, do you become your next person or next thing straight away, or is there a gap?'

Harker smiled. He sounded pleased with this question when he said: 'There's a fascinating story to come out of Cornwall on the subject of gap. A certain Parson Jupp died in the vicarage of St Cleer. He was a very good man, loved by everyone and especially by his staff who mourned him for a long time. A year or so passed. And then one morning, one of the housemaids, who had been particularly fond of Parson Jupp, found a spider in her broom cupboard. She was afraid of spiders and was about to kill it with a broom. And then she stopped. She was filled with a feeling of peace and joy – the same feeling she used to get kneeling in Parson Jupp's parlour for evening prayers – and she felt certain that here was her old master, in the body of this spider. And after that no one in the household could kill a spider, in case they were killing Jupp. But the odd thing was a year had gone in which there was no sign of the parson. So here there does seem to have been a gap, and of course there are hundreds of other stories where there seem to be gaps, too.'

Mary looked down at her feet. She was wearing white ankle socks and brown sandals. One of the things she was hating about this day was how stupid her feet looked.

She was about to say: If I was anything before, I wasn't a girl, when she heard Irene call down the steps: 'Edward, are you there?'

Harker stood up. He smoothed his white hair. He told

Mary she could stay and mooch around in the cellar, but he had to return to the party. He said: 'It's *my* party, in this new life of mine.'

That night, Mary began to construct her previous life.

She had been a magician, known as 'The Great Camillo'. His hair had been black and shiny. He had been clever and good-looking. His speciality had been cutting and restoring rope. He'd had a brilliant future, but it had never arrived. A jealous rival called Timothy had strangled him with a line of knotted silks.

He had been born again as Mary. Someone had decided that to be the grandchild of a person who had died in a glider would be suitable. No thought had been given to anything but that. Not even to lack of height and short-sightedness. It was like the Charge of the Light Brigade. There had been a blunder.

5
1958

Estelle:

They came and told me, You are a great deal better, Estelle. We think you can go home.

I said goodbye.

Goodbye, they said, and take care of yourself, dear.

I said goodbye to Alice, the Chicken Woman.

She said, Oh, no, oh no . . .

Sonny collected me in the muddy van, with its old smell of sacking and seed. As we drove away, I turned round and saw Alice running behind the van, calling to me.

'That is Alice,' I told Sonny, 'and she is happier as a hen than as a woman.'

He said: 'You'd best make an effort to be yourself again, Estelle. Unless you want to fetch back here.'

Sonny's face was purple-red. His damaged ear looked very dark and inflamed. I thought of him sitting alone at the kitchen table with bottles of stout lined up in front of him like skittles. England is full of men who drink alone.

I didn't want to go home. At Mountview, my room was high up and I could look down on the world. I could see the gardens and the tarmac paths, nice and neat. I had beautiful dreams.

In the evenings, we did not stare at a candle or stare at the dark; we watched television. We sat in the day room with the lights turned out and our chairs in two rows and the light from the television flickered over us like snow. The programme we liked most was *What's My Line?* People come on and perform a little mime of the job they do in life: glass-blower, lamplighter, taxidermist, deckchair attendant, bailiff, Keeper of the Queen's Purse. Then a panel of famous people asks the person questions such as, Does your job require water? or, Are you mainly sitting down? until they've guessed the answer and everybody claps and the person says, You are quite correct, panel: my line is I am a brush salesman.

Who invented this *What's My Line?* How did it come into his mind?

The staff at Mountview decided that we would all play our own *What's My Line?* I said, You can't have a panel, there is no one famous here. And they said, No, there is no need of a panel, everyone can ask the questions.

A man called Fred Tulley, who used to be a jockey until he fell on his head at Chepstow, said, You can't call this game *What's My Line?*, because at Mountview no one has a line any more; you've got to call it *What Was My Line?* But they said, Oh no, Fred, Mountview is a refuge and you will all of you one day go back into the world and take up your lines again. Fred said, Excuse the language but bullocks, Doctor, I'll never get on a horse no more, if I live to be ninety. We all, except Alice, laughed. Alice made her chicken noise and Fred Tulley started to cry. On the wall of his room, he had a photograph of himself in the winners' enclosure at Newbury. The horse he had ridden was called Never Say Never.

We began the game. A lot of people at Mountview did not understand the meaning of the word 'mime'. When it was the turn of a man who had been a tram conductor he began to say, Hold tight, hold tight now. I thought, it is odd, after my beautiful childhood in Gresham Tears, that I am in a place with people who believe themselves to be birds and who do not know the meaning of the word 'mime'.

We were not good at *What Was My Line?* The only person we guessed was a tap dancer because you cannot mime tap dancing. On the other hand tap dancing *is* a kind of mime, a mime of an internal music no one hears but you.

Another thing. None of the women, including me, had ever been anything. We'd never had a line. Being a mother and a wife is not a line. You cannot mime those thing. Only Alice. She had been a cleaner at the Stock Exchange. The floor of the Stock Exchange measures eighteen thousand five hundred square feet and all these thousands of feet have to be cleaned every night and Alice told me it was the vastness of this floor that had made her long not to be human any more.

I explained to her the idea of mime. So she had a go at it. She got down on her knees and mimed a bucket and then a rag and people shouted out straight away, 'Cleaner!' 'Skivvy!' 'Mrs Mopp!' 'Cinderella!' Then she started picking up imaginary things from the floor and examining them and nobody knew what this could be, so they gave up. On the real *What's My Line?* the panel do not give up. They are famous. If you are famous, you cannot say, I give up.

I said later, What were you picking up, Alice? First she said, Straw, seed, pellets, worms, all her chicken things. Then she had one of her memories as a human being and she said, Oh you wouldn't believe, Estelle, what was dropped there, what was brought in or fell from the roof. She said, I used to find silk handkerchiefs and casino chips. I found a cowrie shell and a sparking plug and a dead pigeon. I found a diamond bracelet and a crocodile card-case and quite a few rubber johnnies, used and un.

I said, No, I would not believe, Alice.

The tap dancer's name was Joseph. One night, after the television was turned off and we sat in our two rows blinking as the lights were switched on, Joseph got up and began to dance. He'd put on his tap shoes which were black and shiny like Fred Astaire's. Everybody went silent.

Alice put a claw over her beak.

He shut us all up, even the nurses and doctors. Snickety-snick, clickety-click. On he went. It was the best moment ever to happen at Mountview. When he stopped for breath, we clapped and stamped and screamed and knocked over all the hard utility chairs.

Now I am home.

Dear Alice, [I write.]

How are you? I am at home now and my father has come to stay. He is teaching Mary how to do marbling on sugar paper. All the walls of her room are covered with the sheets of marbling. There are at least thirty. In the bottom righthand corner of each one she has written the name, Martin W.

Sonny is saving to buy a combine harvester. He showed me something in a farming magazine, a photograph of a man called Roland Dudley on his farm called Linkenholt Manor Farm, near Andover. He said, Roland Dudley has been using combines since before the war, Estelle, and look at what he says: 'When the engineer rules the harvest there are no sheaves to be set up in the field, no pitching into wagons, no threshing in the autumn.' And I said, Well Sonny, don't drink the combine harvester money away . . .

Timmy is nine now. He has started singing in the church choir. His voice is so high and sweet you could cry. He is very thin. His little shoulder blades stick out under the white lace thing he wears for service. He asked me the other night, Is

Jesus everywhere or are there some places where
He isn't? I wanted to say, There are a thousand
places where He isn't. He's not in the dark with
me when I lie beside Sonny; He's not at the river
gathering watercress; He has never been seen on
What's My Line? But all I said was, I really do not
know, Tim.

Did I tell you, Alice, my mother was a glider
pilot? She liked to see England from above, neat
and flat, like a map of itself. And this is how
everything seemed to be, in the end, at Mountview,
once I got used to it: far away below me and quiet
as summer.

I hope you are well and still enjoying *Dixon of
Dock Green.*

I didn't like it when you ran behind the car,
calling out Estelle.

With best wishes from
                Estelle Ward

Elm Farm
Swaithey
Suffolk
England
The World

March 1958

Mary:

I was the only boy at Weston Grammar.

There were ninety-seven girls and me.

On the first day, we had to announce our names to the

class. The teacher said: 'If any of you has a nickname by which you like to be called, then tell us what it is.' She said: 'My name is Miss Gaul, but I believe I am known as Gallus,' and everybody laughed except me because I had never learned a word of Latin. I felt stupid and sad. I imagined Miss McRae saying: If you live in a lighthouse, Mary, there are certain things that may never reach you.

Almost every girl had a nickname. They blushed in turn as they said them. It was embarrassing. The girl next to me said: 'My name is Belinda Mulholland, but I am quite often actually called Binky,' and I saw her blush spread right up into the roots of her pale hair and down her scalp and into her neck and I thought, saying a thing you didn't really mean to say could be like poliomyelitis entering your veins and you could be crippled by it for ever.

When it came to my turn, I did not blush. I said: 'My name is Mary Ward. but I've never been Mary, I have always been Martin, and I would like to be called Martin, please.'

Miss Gaul wore her hair in a long plait, fastened around her head like a rope and when I said my name was Martin the rope sprang loose from its kirbygrip and unwound itself.

She said: 'Marty? Very well, dear. We shall call you Marty.'

And because of the jumping plait, I didn't feel able to contradict her.

The school was a large, grey building, built in Victorian times. When you opened your desk lid, you could breathe history. The inkwells were made of porcelain. In the corridors there were rows and rows of photographs of Old Girls wearing long skirts and the sweet smiles of the dead. At dinner time, the gravy tasted old, as though some mildewed wine had been poured into it. The kitchen staff were Portuguese, descendants of Vasco da Gama.

I liked the school uniform, especially the tie which was red and white and like a man's tie. I looked nicer in my uniform than I'd ever looked in any other clothes and the only bit of

myself that I couldn't stand to see were my bare legs between
my grey skirt and my grey socks. So I began to walk with my
head held very high and my eyes behind my glasses looking
out hungrily. And this new way of conducting myself (as
Cord might have put it) was mistaken for an invitation to
friendship. On the first morning, three girls came up to me
at different times and offered to share their sweets with me.
But I refused. I said: 'No thanks. I don't like sweets,' and I
walked away. I didn't know how to be anybody's friend.

Then I saw Lindsey Stevens.

She was the tallest person in our class. She had long, heavy
hair, tied back in a ribbon. Her eyes were sleepy and kind.
You could tell that there had never been a moment in her
life when she had not been beautiful. I stared at her until I
was worn out and I remembered Miss McRae once saying
that beauty can be tiring.

I closed my eyes. A teacher called Miss Whyte with a
y was giving us our first physics lesson on earth. She was
describing to us the principles of the thermos flask. She said:
'The areas of contact between the inner and the outer wall
are minimised to limit conduction of heat and the inner
surfaces are silvered . . .' and I thought, I will get Lindsey
Stevens to be my friend, or I will die.

I had begun to teach myself conjuring. My imaginary former
life as The Great Camillo had given me the idea. Cord had
found me a book called *Black's Book of Magic*. It was old and
heavy and illustrated with woodcuts of men in tail coats
who all looked as if they couldn't move but were waxworks
of themselves. In the introduction, the writer put: 'He who
learns to be a magician makes himself master of the seemingly
impossible. In his world, the laws of nature appear to be
defied. He puts before one's very eyes that which one never
dreamt to behold.' I thought, my life has been full of things
that I never dreamt to behold: Marguerite flying out of the

tree and landing on Timmy's head; steam rising from Walter Loomis in the dentist's waiting room; the stalactite ceiling at Mountview; Irene in blue silk getting married to Mr Harker; and, now, the exhausting beauty of Lindsey Stevens.

I practised my first two tricks at home in front of a mirror and then on Cord and on my mother. The tricks had names. They were called the Initial Transfer and the Classic Palm Vanish. 'The real art of magic,' said *Black's Book,* 'lies in the way a trick is presented.' It explained that you had to learn all the ways of distracting your audience, of making them look where you want them to look and not at the place where you are making your secret move. This technique is known as Misdirection.

Cord was a good audience and my mother a bad one. Her look wandered about. You couldn't rely on her eyes to be where you wanted them to be. It was as if, all the time, day after day, she was searching for something that wasn't there.

Cord noticed this. When I started my patter, when I said: 'Ladies and Gentlemen, you now see a two-shilling bit in the palm of my hand,' and my mother did not look at it but up at the ceiling, Cord said: 'Come on, Est, pay attention. Watch Martin's hand.' I stopped and waited for her to look at me and then I began again: 'Ladies and Gentlemen, please observe this two-shilling piece . . .'

My mother said: 'Why do you call her Martin?'

Cord said: 'Hush, Stelle. It's only a nickname.'

I started a third time and now she watched me very intently, as someone might have watched The Great Camillo, and for a small moment – for the seconds that it took to open the fingers of my left hand to reveal it empty of the coin assumed to be in it – I felt warmed by her look.

I had practised the Classic Palm Vanish in front of the mirror so many times that I could do it quite well. I could amaze. I saw this amazement for the first time on the faces of Cord and my mother. The trick succeeded. They smiled and clapped. And this is what I thought about when I saw Lindsey Stevens; I thought, now I must use my power to make extraordinary things happen.

She had a friend already. The friend's name was Jennifer. They went around together, arm in arm. Jennifer had a head full of curls. They did not notice me.

I went up to Lindsey's desk at the end of morning lessons. I said: 'Would you like to see a trick?'

Lindsey had very beautiful skin. There was no freckle or mark of any kind on it. She said: 'I've got to go, really.'

I took a halfpenny out of my blazer pocket and I did the Palm Vanish very quickly before she had put her books away. I waited for her look of amazement and it came and I thought, this is the beginning, then.

She said: 'Can you do other tricks?'

I said: 'Yes. I can. Would you like to see another?'

She didn't reply. She turned to Jennifer who had come up to her. She said: 'Marty does conjuring.'

'Do you?' said Jennifer.

'My grandfather was a famous magician,' I said.

'What was his name?' asked Lindsey.

'He called himself The Great Camillo.'

'I've never heard of him,' said Jennifer.

'No. He died quite young. He was strangled by a rival.'

'Strangled?'

'Yes. With a line of knotted silks, all colours.'

'Weren't you sad?'

'I didn't know him. He died when I was in the womb.'

Other girls had clustered round us. I had become a small centre of attention.

I said: 'If someone could go down to the kitchens and get me a sugar lump and a glass of water, I'll show you some real magic.'

One of them went of it. It may have been Binky. I stood

94

at Lindsey's desk and didn't move. She and the others asked me questions about The Great Camillo and I invented things about him on the spot. I said that he always travelled in London by taxi and paid his fare with money plucked out of the air; I said when he dined with friends at the Savoy Hotel he could make their champagne glasses disappear and reappear any number of times.

When the glass of water came, I put it down by Lindsey's porcelain inkwell. I gave her a lump of sugar and one of the soft pencils I kept in my blazer pocket. I thought, I'll do my patter and they will laugh, so I said: 'Very well, Miss Stevens, now if you would kindly and clearly and for everyone to see write your initials on the sugar lump.'

'My initials?'

'Yes. Write them boldly and blackly on the sugar. L.S.'

She wrote them and I asked her to show them around and then return the sugar lump to me. She did this and I dropped the sugar lump into the glass with the little flourish *Black's Book* advises you to use when performing the movements you want your audience to see. Then I took her hand. I guided it towards the glass. I said: 'Now, Miss Stevens, I want you to concentrate very hard on the sugar. In a moment it will start to dissolve and I want you to watch it until it has gone, keeping your hand absolutely still above the glass. And then I shall reveal to you something that will astound you.'

She looked at me and smiled. The ribbon that tied her hair that day was black velvet. I looked down at my hand holding hers. My fingers were stubby like my father's and hers were long and white.

We were all silent, watching the sugar. I thought, when the spring comes I will invite her to the farm and we will climb trees together and play French Cricket on the grass with Timmy and Cord, and at night she will sleep in my bed and I will sleep by her on the floor, and I will tell her what I used to imagine about the universe.

When the sugar had gone I said: 'Very well. The moment is here! If, when I let go of your hand, Miss Stevens, you would turn it over, you will find, I believe, that the initials you wrote on the sugar have transferred themselves – through my powers of magic – to your palm.'

I released Lindsey's hand and she turned it round. The initials L.S. were faint but clearly visible on her palm, and she laughed with pleasure.

The other girls, including Jennifer, applauded. Then they began to question me about how it was done, but *Black's* had warned me that 'The wise young illusionist does not reveal the tricks of his magic,' and so I said: 'I can't explain it. It isn't like Physics with set laws. It's something else.'

I kept myself awake most of that night, perfecting a new trick to show Lindsey the next day. By the time dawn broke, I could pass a plastic beaker through the surface of a table.

Then I lay down on my bed and went to sleep in a second, like Cord could do when he turned off *The Brains Trust*.

I had a dream about Miss McRae. She stood in my room looking at my sheets of marbling. She turned to me and said: 'Oil upon water. So simple. Yet look what can be done, Mary.'

The Good Man

On a Sunday morning in April, Ernie Loomis woke up very early and looked at the soft light in the bedroom and at Grace sleeping peacefully beside him.

He could hear pigeons murmuring in the yard and other birds singing somewhere in the high beeches behind the barns.

He felt contented, as he could never remember feeling before. He looked at his life and admired it. He thought, everything is good: the acres of land and the acres of sky; Grace in her little booth with her cash register; the grazing animals; Pete safe in his bus; the smart shop with its blue and gold awning; the name Loomis travelling further and wider across Suffolk; even Walter, his sweet nature and his bull's head and his songs.

Easter was coming. Ernie had an order of two dozen ducks to dress for Swaithey Hall.

After he'd admired his life for ten or fifteen minutes, Ernie got up and, without waking Grace, found his clothes and tip-toed downstairs with them and put them on.

He let himself into the shop. He saw the sun coming up behind the pink colourwashed cottages opposite and knew that the day was going to be fine.

He put on his apron. He sharpened a paring knife and a cleaver. He prepared a clean tray. He went to the cold room and took half a dozen mallard off their hooks. They had been plucked and drawn by Pete and Walter, but their sleek heads were still on, and their webbed feet. He set them down on his block and began work, slicing off the heads and the feet with the cleaver, paring out the tail skin, trimming and tidying and then, with deft, effortless movements, tying the birds up and plumping their breasts before laying them on the tray.

The sun climbed higher and shone yellow on the empty shop-window. Ernie turned and looked at it. He thought of Easter Sunday, of daffodils and forsythia in the church and bowls of primroses picked by the children. He thought, everything is at peace.

He stood very still as he worked. He was forty-nine years old. Since the end of the war he had been entirely happy.

He looked up from the block for a split second. He fancied

he had heard, in the midst of the dawn quiet, the shop bell jingle.

His right hand should have paused half-way from his shoulder but it did not. It brought the cleaver down on his three fingers resting on the duck's neck and sliced them off, just above the knuckles.

He saw what had happened. He saw his three ends of fingers lying on the block and thought, I have done a fatal thing, I have done something that has no ending and no resolution. But then, when the pain came flying at him, he said to himself: It's perfectly all right: I've armed myself against it. This is why I woke when it was barely light with my vision of a beautiful life – it was to arm myself against this. Because these things conquer: the spring sky with no clouds, the Easter bells, the shine on the grass and the innocent pride of the gold and blue lettering, *Arthur Loomis & Son, Family Butchers*. They conquer. This is what they do.

So he didn't move. He saw his blood soak into the green feathers of the duck's head and stain them brown. He noticed, after a moment or two, that the duck was lying in a puddle of blood that was spreading across the block and oozing into his apron like warm oil.

His right hand lost all its strength and the cleaver fell out of it and clattered to the floor.

This little noise might have woken Grace, far above, but it did not. Sunday morning sleep was precious and she turned over and sighed and went back to her dreams.

Ernie tried to move now because he looked at the window and saw that there was no sun there. The shadow of his adversary was so great, it was taking away all the light, and for the first time he thought, perhaps I'm not going to win the fight. So he tried to move to Grace's little booth where, in a wooden drawer, bandages were kept.

He was down. He couldn't walk. It's all right, he thought, I am down but that's all and I can crawl now or slither across the tiles like an eel and what matters is not only a bandage but all that was in my head or in my mind . . .

But he had forgotten what was in his mind. His mind was a hollow and dark. He knew that what had been in it still existed, still lay beyond it somewhere, was still out there in the silent morning.

'It *is* there!' he said aloud. And then a question, a last one, flared like a thin flame in the blackness: 'Does it no longer belong to me?'

His blood had been flowing for almost an hour when Grace found him at half-past seven. He had been dead for nine minutes.

She screamed. Walter came flying down the stairs in his flannel pyjamas. They knelt in the blood puddle, clinging together. 'It *can't* be. It *can't* be. It *can't* be!' they said.

Later that morning, Pete laid out his brother's body in the cold room. He removed the saturated clothes. Ernie's body was waxy and white, the colour of tripe. Pete washed it and dried it and bound the mutilated fingers with muslin. He said to himself, Ernie was a good man.

He covered him with a sheet.

It was Easter Week. The Rev. Geddis could not fit in a funeral. There would be a wait, just a short one, of eight days.

In the lanes and ditches and woods outside Swaithey, the village children went to gather primroses, to make posies for the church.

In the wait for the funeral, while Grace lay in bed and couldn't be consoled, not even by her dreams which were all of her wedding, Walter went out to Pete's bus and sat in it alone, playing records on the wind-up. It was the year of the Everly Brothers' 'All I Have to Do is Dream'.

At night, in his bed next to his mother's room, he lay awake. He felt thirsty, not for liquid, but for something he couldn't put any name to. And the moment he slept, the thing he dreaded most started to happen: Arthur Loomis began talking to him.

In his dreams, Walter tried to hide from Arthur. He tried hiding in the pig-sties and underneath the bus and in a barrel of rain, but Arthur was all-knowing and all-seeing and could find him anywhere. He smiled at Walter. His eyes were gentle and kind. He said, 'I'm only here, boy, to tell you what you already know. Your future is in the shop. It is the only future you possess.'

'I know,' Walter replied. 'I know.'

The shop was closed for a while. The blinds were drawn down. A notice was taped to the glass. It was Pete who scrubbed Ernie's blood from the floor and from the block. He cleaned the cleaver with steel wool and put it away.

Relations arrived to comfort Grace. Somehow it was she, only, who was considered to be in need of comfort and they did not try to console Walter or Pete. They were mostly women, Grace's sisters and cousins. They discussed the floral tributes they would order and the hymns that were to be sung at the funeral service. They sat by Grace's fireside and did their knitting and patted their hair and looked at their clean hands. They repeated old stories about war-time. They baked scones and made strong tea.

Walter left them sitting there. They appeared not to notice his going, yet they did, and felt more at ease, more ready with their small comforts and their plans, after he'd gone. For one thing, his Aunt Josephine remarked to herself, he's too large for the chairs.

There was nowhere for him to go except the bus. Wandering in the sunshine hurt his eyes and his heart.

He and Pete cooked sausages on the primus stove and wore out two gramophone needles on the Everly Brothers.

They had a lot to say, but couldn't say it. Then, in the space of one evening, they composed one verse and the chorus of a song and Walter's thirst for something he couldn't name abated.

He owned a guitar now and could play it well. The song had a two-part accompaniment on guitar and banjo. Proud of it, Walter's thoughts drifted away from death and away from his future in the shop and back to Sandra who had sent him a card of condolence. The card had a poem in it. It was the kind of poem that seemed to have been written by a factory of poems, Walter thought, and Sandra's own little message – 'With deepest sympathy for Your Recent Loss' – seemed made, too, in a message factory. But this didn't diminish her. It made Walter all the more determined to sit her down in an empty green field and sing her his own songs that came only from inside him and not from a song-making machine.

He was going bald. He thought of Sandra running her fingers through his curly hair and coming across the thin patch on his crown and caressing it sweetly.

The song was called 'Cold as Winter in the Spring'. It was a song for Ernie. It would describe his dying. The words, all except one or two, were Walter's and the tune mainly Pete's. The bit of it they wrote in a single evening went like this:

> They say the snow falls at the turning of the year,
> They say in April come the meadow flowers,
> They say the short days are the ones to fear,
> They say that life gets sweeter in the longer hours.
>
> But oh I don't believe them any more.
> I don't believe in April blackbirds sing.
> The worst came later and the best before.
> For me it's cold as winter in the spring.

They wanted to finish it in time for the funeral. They

wanted to ask Grace and the Rev. Geddis if they could sing it in the church, like the relatives of the dead sang at funeral services in the Southern Baptist churches. But the next verse wouldn't come. Ernie's death had been so ugly and so swift, there seemed to be no words stern enough to describe it. They attempted some lines in which they rhymed 'cleaver' with 'never', and then felt embarrassed by them. They had the tune and the thing about winter and spring which Pete called 'a pretty idea, Walt' but this was all.

They stayed up late, struggling with the song. It was the night of Easter Sunday. The funeral was two days away. All the floral tributes had been designed and ordered and a black veil sewn onto Grace's hat.

In the dark, Aunt Josephine was sent out with a torch to bring Walter home. As she made her way carefully across the meadow she heard the sound of singing and said under her breath: 'A good man has left us and this is what they do.'

Magic Boxes

Mary was trying to grow.

Her head barely came up to Lindsey Stevens's shoulders and she wanted it to reach much higher, to her eyes.

Someone had told her you could grow by stretching yourself. In the school gym, she hung by her hands from the wall bars. At home, she swung from door lintels.

She reminded herself of a pupa, suspended by a thread in its interim life. She imagined that, as she grew, her man's skin was hardening on her.

She liked vaulting. The gym teacher noted her agility and her lack of fear. She hit the springboard hard, and flew. Her landings were neat. She won a place in the Junior Gym Team and with it a yellow sash. She examined the sash which was like sacred ribbon. She wondered whether brilliance at vaulting could lead to fame and glory.

When the summer term began she returned to school with seven new conjuring tricks. She told Lindsey: 'I'm working on a very big, difficult trick at home and if you'd like to come and stay with me in the summer holidays, I'll have it ready to show you.' Lindsey said she didn't know whether she would be able to come and stay. At Easter she'd met a boy from a public school. His name was Ranulf Morrit. He was sixteen. He had taught her how to French-kiss. He understood Greek. He had minute handwriting. He was going to write a letter from Haileybury once a week.

Mary thought, one day I will be like Ranulf Morrit. I will be tall enough to bend down and kiss Lindsey's mouth. I will not be able to show off with Greek, but I will care for her.

In History, the class was studying the Arthurian legend. Miss Gaul said: 'It may be that the Round Table did not exist, but of course it has existed down the centuries in people's minds, so you could say that it has an existence of a certain kind.' Mary said: 'Are there other things in History that only had one kind of existence and not another?'

Miss Gaul said: 'Well, Marty, History is full of myths, legends and superstitions. For one person a myth may be a truth and for another just a foolish story.'

'Who is right, though? The person who believes in it or the person who doesn't?'

Miss Gaul smiled. It was a thing that seldom happened to her features. She said: 'Neither is right. Neither is wrong.'

So Mary decided, Arthur was not a legend. Not for me. For me, he existed and Sir Galahad and Sir Lancelot. And I will be like them. I will acquire an armour and I will be afraid of nothing. And in this way I will protect the people who could come to harm. I will protect Lindsey, who signs herself 'Mrs Ranulf Morrit' in her Geography Book, and I will protect Pearl, who refuses to learn to swim and could drown in Swaithey pond, and most of all I will protect Estelle: from Sonny's rages; from forgetfulness; from being sent back to Mountview.

Mary's big, difficult trick was called The Incredible Sword Box. She had bribed Timmy with Smarties to be her assistant. She had written a letter to the Magic Circle in London asking where or how she could come by ten swords. They wrote back: 'Dear Martin Ward, It always gives us great pleasure to hear from budding magicians,' but they hadn't been helpful on the subject of the swords. They said: 'Equipment of this kind is very expensive and we suggest you invite your friends to help you make swords of papier maché, which can look extremely effective.'

She didn't want papier maché swords. She wanted real danger to be in this trick, so that her audience would first be frightened and then stunned with relief. If there was no danger, there would be no real fear.

She wrote to Cord, now returned to Gresham Tears. He wrote back: 'I say, Martin, swords are a tall order. Not used much, you see, since the Charge of the Light Brigade. But here's a thought: fencing rapiers! Do they do fencing at Weston? I used to fence as a boy. Makes you sharp and quick.'

But they did not teach fencing at Weston Grammar. Miss Gaul, when consulted, suggested the wardrobe department of the Maddermarket Theatre in Norwich. She had a friend who worked in it in her spare time. The friend's name was Miss Lyle. Miss Lyle wrote: 'Dear Marty, What a fascinating request! Alas, we are an amateur company, and I am not at liberty to put Maddermarket property out to hire.'

Mary had built her box out of cardboard. She had made the holes where the swords would go in and where they would come out the other side. She had put Timmy inside the box. She fed him Smarties through the holes. *Black's* advised: 'Find the correct line of trajectory for each sword by practising with lengths of dowelling.' Mary had never heard of the word 'dowelling'. She unscrewed the iron rods from the head and end of her bed and practised with those.

To get Timmy to crouch absolutely still in the recommended position she played a game with him. She said: 'What comes through the hole will either be a Smartie, or it will be an iron bar. If you move a single muscle I will know and no more Smarties will come, only the iron bars, and then you will be locked in.'

She loved the thought of Timmy waiting in the box, hoping for Smarties, with only the smallest pin-pricks of light to see by and no way of escape once the first five rods were through. When she performed the trick, using real swords, she was going to get him to sing in his sweet soprano to show the audience he hadn't escaped and, then, when the first sword went in, the singing would cease and everyone would be afraid.

It was a cold, windy summer. As it passed and the holidays got nearer, Mary began lying to Lindsey. She told her there was a pony to ride at the farm. Lindsey said: 'Great.'

Lindsey showed her some of her letters from Ranulf Morrit. His parents lived in a manor. A trout stream ran through their garden. They employed a Spanish cook called Ramona.

Mary said: 'He's very boastful, isn't he?'

Then in June, it was agreed: Lindsey would come to stay in the first week of the holidays for three nights. She was looking forward to the riding. She was curious to see Mary perform her 'big, difficult trick'.

And it was in June that Estelle began to beg Sonny to hire a television. She said they were not a luxury any more. She said: 'This is nearly 1960, Sonny.' But he refused. He said it could not be afforded but this wasn't his reason. He saw televisions as things which belonged in cities. The blueish light they gave out reminded him of the light of a city, its restlessness and its flicker. He didn't want a square of city in his front room.

So Estelle wrote to Cord. She said: 'The thing that helped me recover when I was at Mountview was *What's My Line?*'

Cord sat in his chair and wondered about this. He remembered his own fondness for *The Brains Trust* and how it calmed him and reminded him that he was safe and that his country was safe. He wrote back to Estelle. He told her to hire a television and he would pay for it.

It arrived one afternoon. The first programme Estelle watched on it was *Muffin the Mule*. 'Hello children,' said Muffin.

The installers had climbed up onto the roof and attached a large aerial to the chimney, but the picture was indistinct, not clear and bright as it had been at Mountview and Estelle complained. She was told that a tree was interfering with the signal from London. The installers said: 'If I were you and paying this kind of money I'd chop the tree down.'

Sonny, out in a wheatfield looking at the ears blown flat by the wind, saw the aerial go up. He guessed what had happened. Thomas Cord had always spoiled Estelle, always given in to her and pretended to her that she led a charmed life. And now she was in the middle of life, she saw it wasn't charmed. She saw that no life was charmed, except at the pictures. So this was what she wanted now, her own little picture screen. Sonny spat at the wheat. He thought, now, with that television, *my* life won't be the same. Every evening, it will do me some harm.

But there was a change in Estelle.

Instead of going out and staring at the river, instead of walking alone in the brown dusk, she sat quietly in the darkened room waiting for the programmes to come on. She no longer cried in her sleep but talked. Her voice was girlish and happy. 'Hello, Pop-pickers,' she said one night.

Her suppers were on time. She prepared them in the early afternoon before the programmes started. Some of her forgotten neatness returned. And now and then, her forgotten ravishing smile.

She said to Sonny: 'There's only one thing, and that's the tree.'

'Sonny said: 'That tree is a hundred years old.'

She said: 'Trees are cut down all the time.'

'Not by me,' he replied. 'Not on my land.'

The night Lindsey arrived to stay was the night which decided the fate of the tree. It was a beech tree. The tops of its grey roots spread out in a perfect fan.

Mary's preparations for Lindsey's visit had been arduous. She felt ready to lie down and sleep and let a dream of Lindsey replace the reality. In a dream, there would be no lie about the pony.

She had gone to the Loomis's slaughtering yard in search of swords for the box tricks. Knives, she decided, would create greater fear in her audience than swords. Swords caused an old-fashioned kind of death, knives a modern one without any chivalry.

She had hoped to find Walter and begin a conversation by enquiring about his teeth but only Pete was there, swabbing out the blood gulley in the sunshine. In so bright a light, Pete's wall eye moved about crazily, the way living cells move about under a microscope lens. When he found Mary in his vision, he looked perplexed. 'What d'you want, then?' he said.

She asked for Walter and was told he was working in the shop. She explained that she was an apprentice magician who needed ten lethal knives for the most ambitious trick in her brief conjuring life. Pete took out a red and white rag and wiped his face.

He said that as a slaughterer he'd had some queer requests but none so odd as this. Then he said: 'How old are you, Mary Ward?'

'Twelve,' said Mary.

'Twelve,' said Pete, 'and you want me to furnish you with not one but ten knives sharp enough to cut off a man's head?'

'Yes,' said Mary. 'Only for one night.'

He laughed. He rubbed his neck with the rag and then his forearms and his hands. He said some people in Swaithey thought he was daft on account of his eye but he wasn't daft enough to do a thing like that. Then he said: 'I saw a conjuror once. He read minds. But he was no good. All he knew were telephone numbers.'

Mary stood there waiting for Pete to change his mind. He put his rag into his pocket and walked away.

She went home through the village and she heard the sound of lawnmowers and this gave her an idea. And it was this idea – the transformation of lawnmower blades into knives – that cost a night and a half of sleep. She worked by torchlight in the machinery shed. There were six blades, not ten, and she had to remove each one and make a wooden handle for it and fix the wooden handle to the blade. Only the thought of the fear she would create kept her from lying down on the earth of the shed and sleeping like a soldier.

And then, the manufacured knives were not as long as the bedpost irons. She had to make a smaller box. The space for Timmy's body in it grew less. She had to explain to him that if he moved a single inch he would be cut. So he sat like a stone mannequin in the dark. On Mary's orders he sang: *'Agnus Dei, qui tollis peccata mundi/miserere nobis pacem/Agnus Dei, dona nobis pacem . . .'*

*

Lindsey arrived in the afternoon. Her father drove her to the farm in his Humber Super Snipe. There was no one to greet her except Mary. Estelle was watching television with the curtains drawn and Sonny and Timmy were out in the harvest fields where the air was dusty and bright.

Mary showed Lindsey her room. In a corner of it, covered by a dust sheet, were the magic box and the six knives made from the mower blades.

Mary said: 'You can have my bed and I'm going to sleep on cushions.'

Lindsey said: 'Okay. But you look ill, Marty. You look awful.'

Mary said: 'Yes. I'm sorry, Lindsey, but I've had some sad news. My pony died.'

Lindsey was unpacking a framed photograph of Ranulf Morrit. She set it gently on the bedside table. She crossed to Mary and put her arms round her. Mary's face was pressed against her chest that was no longer quite flat. 'Bad luck,' said Lindsey. 'Horrible luck. Cry if you want to. What was his name?'

With her face buried in Lindsey's angora jersey, Mary couldn't think of any ponies' names so she said nothing, knowing that Lindsey would interpret her silence as grief. After a while, Lindsey moved away and began to unpack some brand-new riding clothes. Mary watched her and waited but she did not know for what.

Later, she waited for the evening to come, for the moment of performance of the Incredible Sword Box Trick.

She lined up three chairs. She wished her audience were larger. She sat her mother down and then Lindsey and Sonny. The ribbon on Lindsey's hair was green. She thought, I will have absolute power over the three of them for as long as it takes to put the six knives in and take them out again, and then it will be gone.

She produced the box which she had covered in gold and

silver stars. She turned it round to show them its six sides. She called to Timmy, and said: 'Ladies and Gentlemen, my assistant in this amazing trick is a chorister and he is going to sing the *Agnus Dei* for you to show you that he is still inside the box. Now, Timmy, it's time to go into the box.'

He forgot the bow Mary had taught him to make to the audience. His mouth hung open. Mary wondered if he was afraid, if he knew she had once tried to kill him with Flit.

She closed the door of the box. Hidden behind an armchair were the knives. *Black's Book* had advised her: 'Reveal your swords with a flourish. Try to hold them in one hand and fan them out,' but the mower blades with their wooden handles were heavy and couldn't possibly be fanned. It was much as Mary could do to lift them.

She showed them clumsily. At her signal (a kick on the side of the box) Timmy started to sing his *Agnus Dei*. His voice sounded thin and frightened. The audience began to look afraid. Mary smiled to herself. She walked forward.

'Now, Ladies and Gentlemen,' she began, 'you see here some of the most lethal knives ever sharpened – sharper than swords, sharper than scimitars . . .'

'Wait a minute!' Sonny barked. He stood up.

Mary went on as if nothing were happening.

'This I can promise you,' she said, 'that my assistant the chorister is going to come to no harm!'

'Stop!' said Sonny.

'Let her finish the trick,' said Estelle.

'Oh gosh . . .' said Lindsey.

Sonny came to Mary. He grabbed her wrist, holding the swords. Timmy's *Agnus Dei* petered out. 'What are these?' said Sonny.

'You're spoiling the trick,' said Estelle.

'Shut up!' shouted Sonny. 'What are these, Mary?'

'Blades . . .' said Mary.

Sonny snatched them out of Mary's hand. Mary noticed how light they seemed to him.

'*And?*' he said.

'They're part of the trick.'

'No, they're not. They're not part of any trick. I'm not fooled. You've been trying to make an idiot out of me ever since you could walk, but you haven't succeeded. These are part of my mower and you've stolen them and if you think any of us are going to sit here like monkeys and watch your so-called trick you're stupider than I already thought.'

Timmy had crawled out of the back of the box and stood gaping at Sonny.

Sonny cuffed Mary's head and she fell backwards onto the box which collapsed under her. Timmy let out a shriek of frightened laugher.

Estelle covered her eyes with her hands.

Mary and Lindsey lay side by side in Mary's room in the dark.

'I'm sorry the trick was such a failure,' said Mary.

'It's okay,' said Lindsey. 'I'm not that fond of conjuring really.'

It was more or less as Mary had imagined it would be: Lindsey in the bed, Mary on the floor on sofa cushions.

But she'd also imagined a colossal silence, a silence like the end of the world falling upon everything, except the two of them in the room, as if they were the only people alive. And it wasn't silent at all.

Next door, in their bedroom, Sonny and Estelle were arguing about the tree. It was embarrassing. Mary had to apologise to Lindsey. She had to say: 'Don't listen.'

But there they lay, listening.

Estelle accused Sonny of caring more about a tree than he cared about a person's sanity. He said she cared more about a flickering box than she did about a beech that had been growing for a hundred years.

Estelle began to cry. She said: 'A tree does nothing, tells you nothing, never makes you laugh.'

Sonny banged on the bed-end with his fist. He said he would fell the tree in the morning, but that was the last thing he was going to do for her, the very last thing of all.

It was quiet after that.

Mary heard an owl calling out in the empty dark, and she thought, it's like my childhood, near and yet far, stopping for a moment to call and then flying away, who knows where.

Part Two

Part Two

6

1961

A Storm

On a May morning and in silence Gilbert Blakey's nurse fell down on the surgery floor and died. Gilbert and his patient heard a thud. He paused in his drilling of an upper pre-molar five and turned round, and the patient turned, and they saw Nurse Anstruther fallen to the lino like a waxwork with a smile on her face.

Gilbert set the drill down. He went to a cupboard to search for sal volatile.

The patient was a trout farmer. The trout farmer noticed that there was a cloudy look to the nurse's eyes. In his shocked, half-drilled condition, he saw her body float to the surface of some imaginary water. He said to Gilbert: 'I don't reckon this is a faint, Mr Blakey.'

That night the storm came. In ten hours it rained seven inches. The apple trees were stripped of their blossom by the wind. The telephone lines and the power lines fell onto the lanes and fields. The shoulders of the ocean hurled themselves at the undefended shore and the cliffs at Minsmere began once again to slip and fall away.

Waking to this storm, finding his room in darkness, Gilbert Blakey's thoughts went to the precipice. He tried to gauge how near it might have come. His room faced out to sea. He lay quiet and listened for cracks underneath him. He wasn't afraid. He stroked his moustache. He felt ready for a thunderbolt, for a cataclysm. The death of Nurse Anstruther had elated him, its suddenness and its swiftness, its glorious finality. He had thought, if this can happen, then so can anything. So can anything at all.

His mother came tapping on his door. She had lit a candle in a jam jar. Her hair was in yellow rollers. 'There's no electricity,' she said.

She was worried about her pear trees. She didn't mention the cliff. She said she hoped the fishing fleet wasn't out.

Gilbert put on his silk dressing gown. They went down to the kitchen and Margaret Blakey got out her wartime primus stove and boiled water for tea. Gilbert smoked a du Maurier. In his silk robe and in the candlelight and with his elegant hands he could have been at some exclusive London club, playing a little Baccarat.

Margaret thought, he shouldn't be here and with me but far away and with women his age.

After a while, when she'd made the tea, she said: 'Did they forecast this storm, Gilbert?'

'I don't know,' he said, 'but in any case what they forecast is never to be believed.'

Margaret offered her son a biscuit, but he refused. He wished she wouldn't put her biscuits into a tin that smelled of lard. The death of Nurse Anstruther had made him suddenly impatient with pathetic routines.

The storm woke everyone in Swaithey.

Edward Harker's cellar had been flooded in a deluge in 1950 and, when he found himself awake, he thought about everything left lying on his workshop floor, the piles of willow planks, the sawdust and shavings, the oily rags, the ends of string. He saw the water pouring in through the ventilator brick and through the hinged edges of the street-level window. He sighed. He hated water. He had never been out on the Broads or travelled to the Lake District. Until his meeting with Irene, he would have described his entire life as dry.

It felt cold in his room. He woke Irene on the pretext of comforting her. He wanted them to lie together and chat about cricket or sputniks till the storm passed. But she was up and tugging on her housecoat and searching for night lights the moment he touched her. Her first thought was for Billy, to snatch him up from his little cot and keep him with her so that he wouldn't be afraid.

'Is he crying yet?' she said to Harker, as she lit a night light. 'Can you hear him crying?'

'No,' said Harker. 'Billy sleeps like a lead soldier.'

'Lead soldier?' said Irene. 'What a thing to say!'

Then she opened their bedroom door. 'Edward,' she said, 'I can hear water indoors somewhere.'

'Yes,' he answered. 'In the cellar. Will you fetch the Tilley lamp and I'll go down?'

'You fetch it,' said Irene. And she was gone. Her role as Harker's servant was in the past.

They came back a few moments later, a ghostly trio, casting enormous shadows: Irene carrying Billy asleep on her shoulder; Pearl in a white nightdress holding on to her brother's foot.

'Edward,' said Pearl, 'what if the roof gets blown off?'

'Well,' he said gently, 'we'll get a good view of the sky.'

Pearl got into the large bed. Her long, lemon hair spread out on Irene's pillow. People in the village had expected Pearl's baby prettiness to vanish as she grew, but it hadn't. She was ten now and she knew she was beautiful.

Billy woke up. He looked at his mother and at the flickering light. He sneezed. Irene stroked his hair and told him not to be afraid of the storm. He smiled and waved at his family like a little fat emperor. Fear wasn't a thing he often felt.

'Aren't you going down?' asked Irene.

'Yes,' said Harker. 'I'm going down.'

Billy trampled his way out of Irene's arms and ran to him and held on to his leg. 'I can find the cellar,' he announced.

'No, Billy,' said Harker. 'Stay with Mum and Pearl.'

'No,' said Billy.

He was holding Harker's leg so tightly that Harker couldn't move it.

'It's cold in the cellar,' said Irene. 'You'll catch cold.'

'I can find the cellar,' repeated Billy.

'I'll take him with me,' said Harker.

Irene lit another night light and gave it to Harker. He carried his son in one arm and held the small light out in front of them. Together, they moved through the dark house and heard what the storm was doing to the street, making the lids of dustbins fly and milk bottles fall over and sending pantiles sliding off the roofs.

In the kitchen, Harker lit the Tilley lamp.

He opened the door to the cellar. It felt cold. It sounded as if there were a burn down there rushing down a hillside.

'Water,' said Billy.

Harker sat Billy down on the steps and told him not to move. Not moving was an unbearable condition for Billy Harker. He saw his father wade out into the black lake. He saw twists of wood-shaving bobbing on the water like boats. He began to laugh.

'It's not funny, Billy,' said Harker, 'it's a flood.'

But then he thought, well, perhaps it is. Perhaps it is funny. Not just this river coming into my workroom, but all of it. Because here I used to be, a quiet person with passion for nothing except bats, a former nun, fond of silence and order. And now there is not only Irene. There is not only that. There is Billy. He rampages through the house pretending he's a car. He uses his cot as a trampoline. He does somersaults on the landing.

*

Pete Loomis had smelt the storm long before it came. He made coffee and sat in the bus and waited for it.

The bus rocked. After all its years of service on the trolley route and then as his home, was it going to get blown into the sky?

Pete sipped the scalding coffee and decided to remember Memphis. He hummed a Gospel tune, 'Dust on the Bible'. He sat himself at the bar in his favourite honky-tonk called Jo Ann's Lounge. Outside in the night beyond the bar, a storm was coming. The lights kept flickering out. He hadn't known it then, but in this night of the Memphis storm Pete Loomis was going to meet the girl who would bring to an end his lovely life in Tennessee.

She came into the honky-tonk. She sat down by Pete and ordered a chocolate milk. She was shivering. She wore a cotton dress with short sleeves.

Pete was drinking coffee and chatting to Jo Ann. Tennessee was a dry state back then. Jo Ann said she didn't have any candles but she had a ton of soap. Could you burn soap if the lights went out? Pete said, Yes, if you had a lamp, you might be able to burn it. If you melted it down and put it in a lamp and lit the wick. The girl on the stool next to him in her cotton dress said: 'That's baloney, mister. Why y'all talking baloney about soap?'

He laughed. He had noticed the girl had a pretty face. He said that seventy-eight per cent of what human beings talked about was baloney, but it kept them alive.

She looked at him hard. She had a thin moustache of chocolate milk. Pete could feel his wall eye wandering round like a compass needle, searching for a contact with her hard stare. He knew what she was going to say and he didn't want her to say it. If he let her speak, she was going to make a comment on his ugliness and this was – at that moment, in that bar with a storm creeping on and there being no candles to burn – more than he could stand. So he said: 'I know what you're thinking, miss. But you're wrong in your thoughts. My name's Pete and I'm from England and I can tell you there's plenty of goodness and beauty in me, it's just that the beauty don't show.'

She turned away and smiled.

The smile was embarrassed and mocking. Jo Ann laughed. The musicians standing by laughed. Pete thought, well, I made them laugh and it's late and now I should go home before the storm gets here.

But he knew that he wouldn't go home. He knew that he had to bring this girl around to his way of seeing himself. He had to stay with her and be with her till she recognised his inner beauty. He had to.

The rain had begun now. The wind whipped it sideways so that it stung the windows of the bus like a shower of pins.

Pete's coffee was cold. His Memphis thoughts had held him so still, he'd forgotten to drink it. Only his heart and his eye were jumping everywhere.

It was raining in Mary's room. When the lightning came, the rain had a shine on it.

Mary lay and stared at it. She thought, this is not meant to happen. Rain in a room is all wrong.

But it was of no vast significance. She was fifteen and she could see and feel damage all around. It had begun in her. Her flesh had refused to harden as she believed it would. It had disobeyed her mind. In her mind, she was Martin Ward, a lean boy.

She touched her breasts. The skin of them was very white, their texture indescribable, like no other part of her. They seemed like sacs enveloping the embryos of other things, as if something had laid two eggs under her skin and now these parasites were growing on her.

She always touched them when she woke, hoping vainly to find them shrunk or burst or sliced away. She touched them under the bedclothes in the dark, where she couldn't see them. She couldn't stand to look at them. In the day, she wound a crepe bandage round and round them seven times and fastened it with a safety pin. She was Martin in her mind and she hoped that, with the bandages on, it would be her mind that showed.

They were still there, hard yet squashy under her pyjamas. It was raining in her room but nothing else extraordinary had occurred, like the disappearance of her breasts. Mary had studied the monsoon in Geography. Rain could bring change. There could be rivers where streets were, with dry goods and silk tassels floating on the water. Some people could be saved from starvation and others ruined. It might be the same in Swaithey, but nothing had happened to her.

Mary got up and went to the window. The next time the lightning came, she could see something large and metal lying on the grass. It was the television aerial. It had lost its original shape. Now, there would be nothing on the television screen for Estelle except a white storm. She would sit down in front of it and there would be no picture and no voices, so she would get up again and go looking for her pills that she carried round with her and put down anywhere and lost.

Mary listened for sounds of her family awake, but nobody seemed to be moving about and she thought this typical of them – a tempest comes and they all stay asleep in their own useless dreams and never hear it. Then, in the morning, they'll be amazed: Oh look, the roofs blown away, the cows have gone mad with fear and reared up in their stalls like stallions, the chickens are swimming! Sonny will swear and shout. Estelle will sit down with her pills and pull grey hairs from her head. Timmy will dry the chickens, one by one, in a tea towel and they will peck his knees.

Mary put on her dressing gown and fetched her torch from her night table. She liked her room. She didn't want it ruined by rain.

The house was silent. Mary tip-toed like a thief. In the kitchen she found Sonny asleep with his head on the table in a puddle of stout. The room smelled of his stout breath. Mary shone her torch on his face. There were bubbles like spittle in his coral ear. Since he'd bought his combine harvester and gone into debt for it, his drinking had got bad. Mary thought, one day, he will fall over on the earth and his ear will hit a stone – a stone that was never picked up and put into a starfish pail – and he will die.

She went to a cupboard and found some bowls. She decided she would set them out in a line under the eaves of her room and watch over them, like a person watching over saucers of spice in a Bombay market. The big monsoon drops would clank into them, making a peculiar kind of music.

Timmy's Angle (1)

Timmy Ward hadn't passed the Eleven-Plus exam. Long division he saw as a queue of numbers at a gate. You had to open the gate and make them go through, but they would not. And then there was his spelling. He thought the first two letters of 'world' were w and r; he thought 'America' must have a y in it.

He was sent to the Secondary Modern School in Leiston. He struggled to understand what a cross-section was. He set his hair alight with the flame from a Bunsen burner. He thought, the air they give you to breathe here in this school is old. It's been breathed before. You can't see anything clearly in it.

On Friday afternoons, his class went swimming at the Leiston baths. Pale, greenish light fell on the water and on the white limbs of the children. Those who couldn't swim were towed up and down, like barges by their horses, held by a strap on a long pole. Some of them were afraid of the water but Timmy wasn't. Here, at the baths, the air was luminous and when Timmy's feet kicked off from the slippery tiles to launch him, weightless, on a width of breaststroke, he felt as happy as a frog.

From widths, he progressed to lengths. The swimming master was surprised by his speed. He was small for his age and a dreamy-seeming boy. He would look peculiar in a team. The swimming master told his wife: 'We've got this little lad from Leiston Secondary and I've never seen a boy swim quite like that.'

The only other time Timmy felt anything like his swimming-happiness was on Sundays in church. He still sang in the choir. He knew grown-ups cried at the sound of his high voice. The air above the choir stalls did not smell as if it had been breathed before and the light from the stained glass had the clarity of water.

When he swam, his body followed an imaginary horizontal line that pulled him on. Singing the Psalms, he sent his voice up an invisible vertical wire.

These two lines made a 90° angle in his mind. A 90° angle was a simple thing and this gave him hope that all the other more complicated sums he couldn't understand at school would, in some future time, turn out to be superfluous. But he wondered where the two arms of his 90° angle were going. Did they stop in blank space or go on until they collided with something?

He began to search, while lessons went on around him – while meals at home were eaten in silence in front of Estelle's television – for the thing with which they might collide, but he couldn't see anything at all, only the two lines going on and on and up and up.

He wanted to tell Estelle about his angle. He asked her to come and sit down in his room. He closed the door.

Estelle couldn't bear to be told important things. She wanted nothing to be important and nothing to matter. She stood up and walked around Timmy's room, looking at the things he'd pinned up on the walls, one of which was a list of the winners in the men's swimming events in the Olympics of 1960 and Estelle began to read out: 'J. Devitt (Australia) 100 metres freestyle, 55.2 sec. M. Rose (Australia) 400 metres freestyle, 4 min. 18.3 sec . . .'

'Please sit down,' said Timmy.

'Yes, Tim,' she said. But she didn't sit. She examined a dusty palm cross, a set of instructions for life-saving with drawings of a drowning person who could have been boy or girl, child or man, it was hard to say, and a photograph of herself and Sonny standing in front of the combine, neither of them smiling.

She said: 'I'm no good at secrets. I always forget to keep them. Better not to tell me one.'

So Timmy changed his mind about the angle. He said: 'It isn't a secret. I wanted to ask you, can you come to the swimming gala at Ipswich?'

She laughed. 'Gala!' she said. 'What a word!'

'Can you?'

She looked amazed. 'Will there be diving?' she enquired.

'Yes,' said Timmy.

'High diving?'

'Yes.'

'I like to watch that.'

'So will you come? I might win the under-13s boys' butterfly.'

'Of course,' she said, 'if it's not too *grand,* as long as no one has to pretend it's grand.'

And then she told Timmy that she had to go, that it was time for *Hancock's Half-Hour* and that she didn't like to miss any of her favourite shows.

*

Timmy knew that his father wouldn't understand about the horizontal and vertical lines, but he needed someone else to think about where they were going and whether they were likely to end. So he went into Mary's room late at night and shone his Woolworth's torch onto her sleeping head. She didn't move, but just opened her eyes and looked at the light. Her pillow was bunched up. Underneath it Timmy saw a pile of bandages. Still not moving, Mary said: 'Timmy, fuck off out of my room.'

He turned round and went back to his bed. He thought about the bandages and how the sight of them had been revolting. He had gone to talk about a secret thing, his angle, and instead he had seen the bandages, which he knew from the way they'd been pushed under the pillow, were part of some awful secret of Mary's.

He said a God Bless prayer and left her out of it. He thought how stupid he'd been to imagine that his sister, who cared for nothing and no one except herself and her school and Cord and the Harker family, would tell him anything helpful about an imaginary thing with a measurement of 90°.

And he decided that when he went out with Sonny after school to feed the hens he would tell him what he'd seen in Mary's room in the night. Then, Sonny would do something about it. He would do something about Mary.

The Forest of Long Ago

Sonny did something.

He crooked his left arm round Mary's neck and pinioned her against his chest. With his right hand he pulled off her school tie and opened her shirt. She screamed. She tried to push his hand away. She kicked his shin.

The crepe bandages were exposed. They were grey by now. They could have been secretly washed and hung to dry out of Mary's window, but part of her had refused to believe that she would keep on needing them.

Sonny pushed her in front of him towards the kitchen table. She clawed at his arm. He pulled open a drawer and took out the kitchen scissors. His wrist was against her windpipe, beginning to choke her. She felt blood go streaming to her eyes. She felt her legs weaken.

Sonny cut into the wad of bandage in the cleft between Mary's breasts. The scissors were blunt and the bandages wound round her seven times. One arm of the scissors dug into her breast bone, bruising her.

She hauled her neck free of the choking wrist, pushing her head against Sonny's chest. His breath began to mist up her glasses. He was breathing hard from his exertions. She could smell his body which had never touched hers since she was a little girl in his arms. She felt a sickly sorrow, like a dose of poison going into her and spreading all through her.

She started to cry. This was a thing she never wanted to do and never wanted him to see as long as she lived. Not crying was what had given her hope. Now she was sobbing and she couldn't stop. She begged him to let go of her. Screamed and begged.

When he'd cut through the wedge of bandage, he pulled back her shirt. He held her breasts in his hands. He pushed them up, showing them to her. He said: 'Look at them. Go on. You look at them!'

She had her eyes closed. The tears came out and ran down her face and fell onto Sonny's hands. She thought, this is the worst moment of my life. This is worse than my mother at Mountview.

Sonny pushed her away and she fell onto the gritty paments of the kitchen floor. She struggled to find the two sides of her shirt and close it. Sonny kicked her thigh. 'You're an abomination,' he said. 'That's what you are.'

He kicked out again with his boot, then Mary heard him walk out of the kitchen and slam the door behind him. She thought, now it's over. Except that it isn't. It's now that it all begins.

She packed her suitcase.

She had more to put in it than the time she'd gone to live at Cord's. She had books on the English Civil War and a copy of *King Lear*. She had her magic props and her favourite sheets of marbling. She had a hockey stick and a Baby Ben alarm clock and a box camera.

She trembled. She took out her photographs of Lindsey. She wanted Lindsey to walk out of the little black and white snaps wearing an angora jersey and to put her arms round her.

She washed her face. Her cheek was grazed and her eyes stung. She threw away the cut bandages. They stank of fear. She threw away the shirt that Sonny had torn. It was five o'clock in the afternoon and a smell of Irish stew came up into her room. She thought, I will never sit round the kitchen table with them again and eat what they're eating. There will be just the three of them for always.

The suitcase was a cheap thing. Grandmother Livia had owned bottle-green luggage trimmed with pigskin and with her initials, L.C., engraved between the clasps, but this case seemed made of metal and board. Mary thought, if you know who you are, if you have a name you love, you can travel with green luggage and shout for a porter over the heads of other people. If you are Martin Ward and you have white breasts, you pack your life up in cardboard and carry it away, always away, always on and never knowing where.

The sight of her room made her pause as she was about to leave it. It was the only thing she didn't want to abandon.

She felt sorry for the room. Nobody would go into it to turn on a light or draw the curtains against the dark. When it rained through the holes in the lath and plaster roof no one would set out a line of bowls.

It was an autumn evening, full of the scent of fires. From the sitting room came the sound of television laughter. 'Laughter,' Edward Harker once said, 'is our postponement of death.'

When Mary walked out into the yard, two shadows went in front of her – her own shadow and the shadow of the suitcase. They kept on going and Mary followed them and they did not look behind and no one called to them to stop.

She had no plan.

The money she possessed was five shillings and eight pence.

She remembered when she'd run away to Irene's and told Pearl stories about Montgolfier and the universe. She didn't think there would be any time for her in Harker's house at the moment. And this was what she wanted, for somebody to give her time.

Her first thought was that somehow, by changing buses, she would get to Gresham Tears. Cord wouldn't comment on her heavy suitcase. The Albertine roses round the door would still be in bloom. Cord would say: 'Room's ready. Bed's made up. Ginger beer's in the larder.' But then what? They would sit by the wireless. She would try to tell Cord things that he would not be able to believe. She would do him harm. He would blow his nose to conceal his shock and his sadness. He would murmur: 'Damn rum show,' into his hankie.

She reached the end of the lane. She put the case down and took out the hockey stick, which was making it heavier than she could bear. She carried the stick like a rifle over her left shoulder. She thought how comforting it must be to be a soldier and to have a regiment you could be proud of and which was proud of you.

She abandoned the idea of going to Gresham Tears. She knew that before it was dark, and before the suitcase got too heavy to be borne, she would arrive somewhere else, and she did.

She arrived at Miss McRae's.

Miss McRae was eating a lone supper of kippers. She had retired from teaching. She was growing old in the brown darkness of her cottage. When she saw Mary with her suitcase, she thought, now I can be of use again. Good.

She removed her half-eaten kippers and made a pot of tea. She handed Mary a fine china cup and saucer and Mary asked: 'Did you have this china in the lighthouse?'

'I don't remember, dear,' said Miss McRae, 'and that is the most vexing thing about getting old – not remembering.'

Mary found it difficult to drink the tea. She wondered if Sonny had made a dent in her gullet.

Miss McRae said: 'Take your time, Mary. Take your time.'

Mary said: 'Now that I'm here, I'm afraid to tell you. I'm afraid to tell anyone.'

Miss McRae said: 'Well, I see from the stick that you've been playing hockey. Would you like to talk about that? What position on the field do you take?'

'I'm a winger,' said Mary. 'I can run very fast.'

'You always could. That I can remember.'

Mary looked round the room. The ceiling was very low, too low for Miss McRae, who didn't diminish like some elderly people, but kept on being upright and tall like a fir. And she looked, now, as if she were unable to bend, as if she were petrified inside her clothes. When she sat, her body made a stiff but perfect right-angle in the chair.

After a while, when she'd drunk a little of the tea, Mary said: 'I'm never going home again.'

'No,' said Miss McRae.

Then Mary said: 'Someone has to help me.'

There was a long silence. Mary took off her glasses and cleaned them on the sleeve of her blazer. Miss McRae sat perfectly still and straight, waiting.

Mary thought, perhaps after all it was Lindsey I should have told. That night in my room, or after that. Perhaps, after all, she wouldn't have hated me and would have helped me somehow. But now here she was face to face with Miss McRae, in a low space that smelled of kippers.

A sense of such shame began to grow in her that she could feel herself aching to disappear, to be dead and forgotten.

The silence went on. Mary replaced her glasses on her nose. She thought, in a minute I'll get up and leave and go nowhere, just sleep out in a beanfield or under a stack.

'Mary,' said Miss McRae, 'do you know what my name is?'

'What?' said Mary.

'My name is Margaret. Margaret McRae. And perhaps you never knew what it was and thought it must be a secret. But it isn't. It's no secret from anybody. I am Margaret McRae. So you see, sometimes we consider to be secret certain things which need not be . . .'

'This is secret. My thing is a secret.'

'Then, if it's not too heavy to bear, you must keep it. It's only if – '

'It *is* too heavy to bear!'

'Then, that's why you're here, Mary. Because it's got too heavy. That's all. It's like your suitcase. Too heavy. There comes a moment when you have to lay it down.'

The silence crept back. Mary didn't want it back, but back it came.

Then she had an idea. She thought, if I get up and go to the window and turn my back on her, I might be able to say it. I might. If I don't look at her, but out at her front gate and her bird bath and at night coming on, then it might be easier.

She went to the window. She tried to imagine that Miss McRae was an actual fir, without sight or hearing, sighing gently behind her.

But this didn't work. Nothing could, now. Miss McRae had told her her name. You couldn't reveal to a person who had been kind to you and who told you her name out of sympathy for you that you were an abomination.

Mary held on to the window. She saw a bird fly through the dusk and settle on the rim of the bird bath. 'I'm here because of my father,' she said. 'He hits me and knocks me down.'

'I was afraid that might be it,' said Miss McRae.

'I don't want to go back. Ever.'

'No.'

'Can I stay here?'

'Naturally, you can, Mary.'

She continued to look out at Miss McRae's front garden. Silence came again. Or not-quite-silence. Trees in a wood, long ago, swaying, sighing. Then somebody, far off, calling Mary's name, her old name Mary.

She turned.

'Someone has to help me, Miss McRae,' she said again.

Miss McRae nodded. 'Yes, dear,' she said. 'Well, as you know, I am a person of some limitations. I have never visited the shrines of Ancient Greece. I have never walked arm in arm down the Champs-Elysées. The music of Elvis Presley is entirely lost on me. But I shall try to be the one.'

7
1962

The Hired Man

After the death of Ernie Loomis, irrevocable change had come to Walter's life.

He had been warned. His ancestor, Arthur, had begun to smell. He had sat by Walter's bed, stinking the room out. He had said: 'I'd better mention, in passing, Walter, that your dreams for your future were very inaccurate.'

Walter worked in the shop now. Grace stared at him critically through the glass of her booth. Pete struggled on by himself in the yard. Grace had said: 'This is a family business and that's how it's going to stay. I'm not taking on a hired man.'

But this wasn't all. The other thing was the loss of Sandra. She got married to a young vet. Every attempt that Walter had made to arrange more boating outings with her had failed. The card of condolence containing the factory-made words, 'With deepest sympathy for Your Recent Loss' was the last and only communication he received from her. She had never sat down under a tree and listened to his songs.

He was going bald at the crown. His head felt cold where once it had steamed. He lay in bed with one hand on the area of white scalp and remembered Sandra's lively eyes and the way she had covered her knees with her skirt. He could understand why a girl of her kind might want to marry a man who nursed animals in preference to one who slaughtered them. The vet was handsome and showed no sign of baldness and in every respect Walter thought Sandra's choice a sensible one. What he couldn't seem to dispense with was his own devotion to her and the peculiar habit of imagining that one day she would somehow be his.

She still worked at Cunningham's. Nobody said what had happened to her ambition to be a stenographer.

Walter would go into the shop and pretend to examine woollen scarves, but not really look at them. He would be braced for the sight of the marmalade hair and if it came he would send Sandra an anxious smile. She would look away, as if Walter were a stranger, as if she had no memory of the varnished boat and the bottle of Tizer.

One day, Amy Cunningham said to him: 'I'd be very obliged, Walter, if you would make up your mind about which scarf you want and then leave this display in peace.' The display she referred to was a line of plastic heads and necks on which hats were placed and scarves tied. They were male heads. They regarded Sandra working two counters away, fitting ladies' gloves onto smooth severed hands.

He didn't spend his days with Pete any more. Nor could he spend his evenings singing songs in the bus because Grace didn't like to be alone for long, it made her feel 'fidgety'. But sometimes late at night, when Grace was asleep, he would go and drink whisky with Pete and tell him about the stench that had begun to come from Arthur's ghost, and about his love for Sandra that refused to lie down and die.

Pete was getting older. His nose was very purple and thick. He said he had dreams about a Memphis storm. He said to Walter: 'I've seen your precious Sandra. She's a dry pole. Forget her. When June comes, go and see Gladys and you'll feel better.'

It was a bond between them, this referring to Madame Cleo by her real name, Gladys. It made Walter feel mannish and proud. Every June when the fair came to Leiston he spent a single afternoon (always a Wednesday, half-day closing at the shop) in Gladys's caravan, tangled in pink rayon sheets, hearing himself pant and gasp like a runner in the murky candlelight, eating lipstick, while the fairgoers shrieked and screamed outside. Her price went up. The skin on her thighs felt loose, as though she had taken to wearing thigh gloves. Otherwise the experience didn't change from one year to the next.

In June of 1962 word went round the village that Sandra was expecting a child. She left Cunningham's. The vet's house was called 'Meadows'. Sandra stayed at home at 'Meadows' and baked thin-crusted pies and ironed her husband's Viyella shirts. Walter walked by the house and saw her inside, her back turned, standing absolutely still. Her name was now Mrs David Cartwright.

He went off to the Leiston fair. Cleo's caravan was always parked in the same place, at the end of a line of vans behind the big wheel. Sometimes there was a little queue at it. The sign *Fortunes Told* seemed to be one that people couldn't easily pass.

The caravan wasn't there. Walter walked up and down the line several times. Then he wandered the whole fairground in search of it. He noted how swiftly a year had passed.

He stopped at a little rifle range. The targets were tin swans. He told the stallholder that he was looking for Madame Cleo and the stallholder said: 'Sorry mate. Cleo's passed on.'

Walter paid a shilling to have six hits at the swans. His father had been a good shot, but Walter wasn't. He said: 'Do you mean passed on somewhere else?'

'Two hits. No prize,' said the stallholder. 'I mean passed on into the sky.'

Walter drove the van home. He avoided going past 'Meadows'. He wondered whether Cleo's spangled spectacles had been put on her face in the coffin and what had become of the rayon sheets. He thought of her real name, Gladys, and how this somehow suited her better now, lying in a graveyard swept by the east wind, than it had when she was alive and selling spells at rising prices. Then he parked the van and put his head on the steering wheel. He thought, someone keeps drawing a line through bits of my life, cancelling me out.

In his imagined life with Sandra, he abandoned everything to live with her on a moving barge. He sang to her as she hung out her personal washing.

Now, he was in the shop for eight hours a day and seven hours on Saturdays. His mother stared at his clumsy hands as he worked. He had to wear a white overall and a straw hat. He had to make decorations out of fat for saddles of lamb. He hated the sight of himself. He was twenty-six and he had no future except the present. Life had hired him and that was all.

He listened to the first Beatles songs. They were not songs about log-train engineers or honky-tonk women. Someone had drawn a line through hillbilly music as well as through everything else.

Pete had a favourite saying: 'If life gives you a lemon, make lemonade.' Walter thought hard about this, but found that he couldn't remember what the ingredients of lemonade were. He assumed that sugar would be one. He looked all round his life for something sweet and all he could find was that feeling of sliding away from the world of hard things that drinking whisky gave him.

His late-night visits to Pete increased. Some nights he got so drunk that he passed out on the floor of the bus or fell over in the field as he tried to stagger back to the house. The next day, his hands would tremble as he cut and weighed the meat and his head hurt and he couldn't look his mother in the eye.

She was ashamed of him. Snivelling, she said: 'People are starting to notice, Walter. I see them watching you.'

He wanted to say, Well, my life is a lemon. It's bitter. But all he said was: 'I'm twenty-six and I'll take a drink sometimes if I want to.' Her life was bitter, too. She'd loved Ernie and relied on him and every morning for thirty years he had made a cup of tea and brought it up to her.

But Walter shared her shame. He saw how awful his drinking was, how repulsive he was becoming. He thought of the clean, sober vet and his wife smelling of talcum powder. He was putting himself further and further from them, changing himself, making their kind of future an impossibility for him. And he was searching now, sometimes unconsciously, sometimes with all the power of his muddled brain, for one thing, one single act of degradation, that would put them and everybody like them beyond him forever. He knew that soon enough he would find it and it would be committed and then he would be lost to Sandra forever and headed to another place entirely.

In Walter's dreams, Arthur began to divest himself of his clothes. He appeared first without his apron, then minus his bow tie, then wearing no shoes. The buttons of his shirt were undone and wisps of grey chest hair poked through. He was also losing weight and the stench of him was becoming so terrible that the dreaming Walter had taken to wearing a balaclava made of oiled wool, such as he imagined mountaineers to wear on their arduous, pointless journeys.

Mary:

There were two bedrooms in Miss McRae's cottage. The one I slept in felt as if it had never been inhabited by any living thing ever before. The floor of it was stone and the bed was as narrow as a tomb. The only decoration was a collection of cowrie shells in a green saucer. It was downstairs and looked out at a hedge and the hedge took away all the light.

For a long time, I had nightmares in that room. They were dreams of killing. Miss McRae told me I screamed, 'screamed like a banshee, Mary'. The word 'banshee' was new to me. After the screaming, I would sit up in the tomb and let Miss McRae put a crocheted shawl round my shoulders. Sometimes she made Horlicks in coronation mugs and we'd sip this and discuss Miss McRae's life-long desire to visit the great chestnut forests of Corsica, and the murders I'd committed in my sleep would vanish.

I discovered that Miss McRae was a person who hardly slept at all. She would take the pins out of her bun and let her grey hair down in preparation for her night and then seem to forget that night had come. She listened to the World Service. She read *Little Dorrit* and a book about butterflies. In the morning, I would find her in her chair, dozing a little, with her arms folded. When I asked her whether she was tired, she would reply: 'No, no. Certainly not.'

After that night of my arrival with my hockey stick, she told me I could stay as long as I needed to. The phrase she used was: 'Until better times come, Mary,' and I told her better times would never arrive while my father was alive. And this was one of the things I was waiting for in the depths of my mind: for my father to die and for the farm to fall into ruin with Martin Ward the only person capable of saving it.

At school, we had a debate entitled 'What Makes a Good Leader'. Everyone in our class – including Lindsey, who was secretly engaged to Ranulf Morrit and had entirely given up studying in order to dream about him full time – was expected to contribute to it and so I asked Miss McRae what her views on the subject were.

Miss McRae cooked plain and tidy meals, mushroom pie cut into squares, toad-in-the-hole with the sausages in a line, and while we ate these we talked about Leaders. Miss McRae put a lot of salt on her plate. She said: 'In this kind of discussion, Mary, there is the literal response and the acceptable response and it is important for you to understand the difference.'

I went to the debate armed with all her wisdom. I told no one that my thoughts weren't mine. When I asked to put forward my choice of person in the category of Good Leader I said: 'Hitler', and the whole room fell silent and Miss Gaul began pushing kirbygrips violently into her plait to stop it jumping away from her head. She said: 'As chairman of this debate, I have to remind you that certain conclusions have already been reached and agreed: namely, a Good Leader is a man who acts for the public good, a Good Leader is one who shows far-sightedness and mercy, a Good Leader has respect for his enemies.'

Lindsey was sitting next to me. She wore pink nail varnish to school. She smelled of flowers and milk. Her hair was tied in a tartan ribbon. I didn't let her nearness to me distract me or make me faint-hearted. I stood up. I said: 'There is another definition of "Good Leader" and this is the one we haven't talked about and this is why I mentioned Hitler. And this definition is a literal definition.'

'That's enough, Marty. Thank you. You may sit down.'

'I'm just pointing out, Miss Gaul, that – '

'Sit down, dear. You have taken this discussion off at a tangent and it is very important to learn, in debate, that tangential excursions serve only to waste time and confuse your listeners. Now. Lindsey, we have not heard very much from you. Perhaps you would like to give us your choice of Good Leader and then we can proceed to a summing up.'

I sat down. My feet were burning where I had stood on them. Lindsey did not look at me, nor did anyone in the room. Lindsey said: 'Well, I would choose Sir Winston Churchill,' and Miss Gaul nodded and put her hands together in a kind of prayer position and a little applause clattered out very softly from around the class.

That night, I thought about the great silence that had fallen when the word 'Hitler' had come out of my mouth. Miss McRae hadn't reminded me that literal answers – if they are the ones not expected – can evoke fear and loathing. She expected me to remember that for myself.

I remembered it now and it helped me to see something else. My own literal answer to the debate entitled 'Who Am I?' was: 'Martin Ward. A boy.' The set answer, the one that everybody knew and expected, was: 'Mary Ward. A girl.' I had never ever in sixteen years dared to give the literal answer because I was afraid to be loathed. I'd tried to tell Miss McRae and then at the last moment I'd run away from the words. To be hated by my father was enough for me. I was too cowardly to risk being hated by the whole world and to hear only silence falling all round me and then a voice of authority telling me to sit down.

Some subjects are not supposed to be debated, and this was one. I thought of Miss Gaul's jumping plait. I thought of Lindsey looking up from the ornate initials, R.M., she was drawing on her debating notes and giving me a stare of horror. And then I thought, perhaps the one person I could tell would be a stranger, someone who didn't resemble a tree, who didn't smell of flowers, who did not make cricket bats, who did not sit in the darkness watching Fanny Cradock. Someone impartial. Someone whose loathing and fear were of no consequence to me.

The person I chose as my tellee was the vicar of Swaithey, the Rev. Geddis. He was someone I had refused to get to know and so he qualified for the category of stranger. Also, he was a man who reminded me of a woman. He had a soft voice and he held his white hands very still.

I chose a Friday evening. I hoped there'd be no choir practice. Miss McRae and I had eaten a supper of mince and boiled carrots, followed by baked apples. It was early May. Miss McRae had finished *Little Dorrit* and started on *Bleak House*. That morning, she'd seen a swallow swoop over the bird bath. She said: 'A. E. Housman was fond of swallows. They gave him hope.'

I went into the church and sat down in a pew. I remembered Ernie Loomis's funeral and all his sisters weeping and Walter looking lost, like a panda in a zoo. I stared at the chunks of different-coloured light coming through the window known as the Sower Window because it depicted the parable of the sower, with his words falling on stone.

I didn't want to talk to Geddis at the rectory, sitting in a proper room with a three-piece suite and anti-macassars on the chairs. I wanted to be in a place which felt as though extraordinary things could happen in it, like Wembley Arena or the Cheddar Gorge, a place where someone could go and say things he'd never said before and listen to the echo of them.

Swaithey Church, with its one stained-glass window and all its rafters being eaten away by Death Watch beetle, wasn't an ideal location, but odd things had happened there, like a sighting of the first Sir John Elliot, ancestor of the present Sir John, kneeling at the altar with his arms around a willow sapling. And in church – this is what I thought – Geddis wouldn't be able to turn me away. I was part of his flock.

I waited a long time. The sun went down and the Sower started to fade. I'd imagined that the Rev. Geddis did the rounds of his church every evening to make sure that no one was swiping the hymn books or playing 'Heartbreak Hotel' on a portable gramophone by the bell ropes. But he didn't come.

I thought, I'll wait until I can't see any light at all behind the Sower and then I'll go. I had waited sixteen years to tell somebody my secret. I could wait another day or even until Monday, a slack day for vicars.

Then the church door opened. I picked up a hymn book and held on to it like a float made of cork. I didn't turn round. I thought, have I confused the words 'literal' and 'imaginary'? Am I deluded? Is there a tempest in my mind or a tumour in my brain?

A voice said: 'Mary?'

I turned. In the dingy light, I saw a halo of bright hair. I thought, I have met an angel unexpectedly.

The angel was carrying a bucket of lilac. It was Pearl.

She put the bucket down. She said: 'What are you doing here all alone?'

I didn't tell her that I was waiting for the vicar to come. I said I'd come here to think.

'Think about what?' asked Pearl.

'I don't know,' I said. 'What are you doing with that mass of lilac?'

'Mum sent me. It's for the church flowers.'

'I thought you were an angel.'

Pearl giggled. Her laughter had always been a light and bright thing. I began to ask her about her swimming lessons. I had rescued her from drowning so many times in my dreams that it had exhausted me. I'd begun to worry I wouldn't have any strength left for the real thing.

She came and sat down in the pew beside me. She was eleven. She must have been the most beautiful eleven-year-old girl on earth. She said she dreaded the swimming lessons. She said when she got into the water she went cross-eyed. She said being frightened could do this, make your eyes go wonky.

She put her thin little arm through mine. She said: 'You don't come to see us so often, now, Mary.'

'I know,' I said.

'Why don't you?'

I told her that I had a lot of homework. I warned her that if she went to Weston Grammar she would have to work very hard, too. She said that she didn't want to go to Weston. She said that when she grew up she wanted to be a dentist's nurse. She wanted to wear a white, starchy hat and put the dissolving purple pellet into the mug of water. I said: 'That's a very peculiar thing for an angel to want to do,' and we both laughed and then I looked up and saw that the Sower had turned to blank, empty lead and that we were sitting there in the pitch darkness.

I had to wait a week before Geddis came into the church. I went there every evening, except on Sunday, after supper. I took a roll of sugar paper and some black crayons. I started to do a brass rubbing of the first Sir John Elliot, Knight of the Garter, 1620–1672.

When I saw Geddis come in at last, I said: 'You don't come here very often, do you?' as if we were guests at a posh party, at the kind of party Ranulf Morrit would give, with food cooked by Ramona the Spanish cook.

Geddis said: 'Mary Ward, isn't it?'

He said if I wanted to talk to him privately, we could go into the vestry, where we wouldn't be overheard. I looked round the church and there was no one in it but us. I thought, this is a farce. And I remembered my mother saying this word at Mountview. 'Meals are a farce,' she'd said and Cord had knelt down and said: 'Don't, Est!'

I told Geddis that I'd changed my mind. I didn't want to talk to him after all. He looked relieved. Behind his wispy head, the flower arrangement of lilac and tulips was wilting from lack of fresh water. In the vestry, I knew that I would see Timmy's surplice hanging on its peg. I knew that there would be no echo.

I showed the Rev. Geddis my brass rubbing of Sir John, only half-completed. I said: 'There's just one question before I go.'

He put his white hands into a knot. 'Always happy . . .' he said.

'Do you think that men ever, you for instance, ever believe that . . . inside them they're not men, but women?'

Geddis's mouth went very slack. I imagined him putting a Communion wafer into it.

He fumbled for a handkerchief and put his whole face into it, pretending to blow his nose. Through the handkerchief he said that questions like this come from the sewers of the mind. He said: 'All I can think is that you have had access to the *News of the World*.'

'I don't mean it literally,' I said. 'I don't want a literal answer. All I meant was, could a man ever feel this, like saints used to feel peculiar things, in a kind of vision?'

He shook his head violently. Side to side. Side to side. He said there was a fee for brass rubbing. Five shillings per rubbing. To go towards the Roof Fund.

In One Place

On a late September evening, Thomas Cord saw a flock of geese pass in perfect V-formation over Gresham Tears. The sight of them first moved him (this faultless alignment in the air) and then confused him (were they coming or going, arriving or departing, he could not remember).

That night he couldn't sleep. He felt a trembling in his left eye. He had a memory of his honeymoon in Brighton:

Livia in a taffeta dress, dancing at the Grand; a walk with Livia along the shingle, their feet slipping and sliding and the surf rattling the stones like change. He tried to console himself with his remembered love.

He woke up at seven. He had thought he hadn't slept at all and then that he had woken from something which must have been sleep. The trembling in his eye had not gone away, it had spread down the left side of his face and into his jaw bone. He put his hand up to his cheek. He knew that something peculiar had happened to him. As he put on his woollen dressing gown and walked to the bathroom, he whispered aloud: 'I've stayed in one bloody place too long, that's why. And now I'm too old to leave it.'

In the grey, northerly light of the bathroom Cord saw that the left side of his face, the trembling side, had been incomprehensibly altered. It had been pulled downwards, or else had suddenly refused to hold up any longer. Whatever the cause, it had fallen. His eyelid was rolled down like a collapsed awning. One side of his mouth tilted away from the other. His own image, in the glass of the medicine cabinet, was now an unrecognisable thing. He thought, the geese came and went and are now miles away, feeding among wheat stubble somewhere, and I'm left in ruins.

He felt shocked and sick. He sat down on the bathroom stool which doubled as a washing basket and into which, years ago, Livia used to drop her silk cami-knickers and her insubstantial brassieres. He put his altered face in his hands. He wasn't normally a vain man.

After a while, he went downstairs and telephoned the doctor. He was told to come to the doctor's surgery. He informed the receptionist that for reasons he couldn't describe he was unable to leave his house. He said the matter was urgent. He said that otherwise he would not have bothered the doctor at all. He was told to wait. He was glad that, while he waited, no one was looking at him. The receptionist returned and informed him curtly that the doctor would come at mid-day, after morning surgery.

The doctor examined him. It was a bright morning by now, the sky a bird's-egg blue. Normally, Cord might have been out in the garden, raking the first leaves.

The doctor listened to his heart. He pinched Cord's cheek for evidence of feeling. He rolled up the fallen eyelid and shone a torch into the eye. Cord disliked having the doctor's face so close to his. He thought how nauseating and smug doctors were. He longed to be left alone, to begin on his horrible changed life without any prying or interference. He knew he had had a stroke.

But then the doctor surprised him. The doctor said he had at first suspected a stroke but was now inclined to believe, from the normal aspect of the pupil, that Cord had been struck by what he called 'a reactive palsy'. This, he said, was in some cases an irreversible condition and in some others a temporary syndrome. It was impossible to say which.

Cord stared at the doctor with his one alert eye. Even as a child, he had not liked having his hopes raised. He said: 'Are you telling me I could get back to normal?'

'I'm telling you,' said the doctor, 'that in some cases the palsy is temporary and in some others it is not.'

'And you can't say which this is?'

'No. I can't. I'll send you to Ipswich for tests.'

After the doctor had gone, Cord remembered the word 'reactive'. He had meant to ask about this. What had the left side of his face reacted to? Was there a single case, in all of medical history, where a man had been paralysed by a passing flock of birds?

Winter came on, ferocious in the vicinity of Gresham Tears, giving the retired residents dreams of tea in Le Touquet.

Every morning, Cord got up and put on his cherry woollen dressing gown and went to the bathroom and looked at himself in the mirror of the medicine cabinet. And every morning, finding his face unchanged, he returned to his bedroom and took off the dressing gown again and went back to bed and lay there, just lay there, trying not to think and not to be.

He had bought a second wireless. He was told it was called a transistor. It was as small as a box of Edinburgh rock and fitted easily onto his night table. He would reach out and turn it on. Instead of listening to the Home Service, as he always used to do, he would move the dial about, so that he got different stations broadcasting illegally from ships in the channel or reaching him from Luxembourg and Monte Carlo. All these stations played Beatles songs. Cord knew the words to several of them.

He saw no one at all. Bridge and chess no longer interested him. His palsied eye wept for itself on its own. When he went shopping in the village he put on his reading glasses. Now, he could read the prices on tins and packets in the grocery shop, but couldn't see the grocer himself, and so sustained the illusion that the grocer couldn't see him either. In this way, he did not starve.

Snow fell in early December. Cord had let his moustache grow very long. He had got the idea from a photograph of the Beatles in the *Radio Times*. The moustache almost covered the corner of his mouth that had collapsed. He looked out onto the snow and decided he would do one thing, just the one, to lessen his loneliness: he would invite Martin to stay with him for Christmas.

There had been letters from an address in Swaithey. 'Dear Cord, I'm staying with my old teacher, Miss McRae, for the time being. She is helping me a lot with my A-level work.' 'Dear Cord, I'm still at Miss McRae's and I'm getting a lot of work done. Have you read *Bleak House*?' 'Dear Cord, I miss you. Here I am still with Miss McRae and we often read *King Lear* aloud in the evenings. I am Lear. Miss McRae is

Regan and Goneril. I'm Edmund. Miss McRae is Gloucester. Neither of us likes being Cordelia.' 'Dear Cord, Thank you for the money to buy a transistor. I'm going to get one immediately that is as small as a box of rock. Yes, I like the Beatles in a way. I'd like to come from Liverpool and be a star. Instead, I have merely taken up brass rubbing.' So now Cord sat down and wrote:

> Dear old Martin,
>   With all this snow, I've been thinking about Christmas. Did you know that your Grandmother, Livia, used to make tree decorations out of horsehair? I still have some horsehair angels somewhere.
>   Are you going home for Christmas? Or spending it with Goneril? It would cheer me if you would come to G. Tears. And how.
>   I've been in a terrible funk. Never seeing a soul. Will you come? We could stuff a capon with chestnuts, make some paper chains, play some Rummy. We could read *Hamlet* aloud, if that would please you, and I would let you be he.
>   Do geese go away in winter, or return? You'd know a thing like this. Write to me with your answers to a) Christmas and b) the migration of water-birds.
>   From your loving Grandfather,
>   Cord.

Cord made a shopping list. When the snow thawed, he drove the Hillman Minx to Norwich and parked it by the market and walked about blindly, wearing his reading glasses, peering into shop windows, looking for something to buy Martin that would be precious to her. Beatles music was coming out of some of the shops. Nobody stared at him

– or not that he could see. He felt some of his old self return.

He went into a sports shop and looked at a ski-ing anorak trimmed with fur. He said to the shop assistant: 'My granddaughter's good at all sports.' And he thought, this might be a thing Martin Ward would like more than anything she's liked in her life – to take a cable car up a mountain and come flying down it on skis, scorning danger. And he wished that this was what he could give her, the chance to fly down a mountain very fast and the chance to look out and away from England into another world. Because staying in one place disfigured you. Your eyelid wearied of the view and refused to admit it any longer to your sight. Your mouth went down in a sulk. It was obvious now.

Livia had understood this. She spent her money on clothes and luggage. On a walk, she would throw her head back and stare longingly at the sky. And she would do this even on grey days when there was no sign of the sun.

8

1963

Estelle:

The world reached Christmas.

We did not seem to have died. The bomb did not seem to have fallen.

Alice, the Chicken Lady, sent me a postcard showing the sands at Whitby. 'Phew,' she put, underlined three times, 'I think my yard is safe.'

I watched everything happen on the television. I'd never realised Cuba was near America. I thought it was miles from anywhere, out in a sea of its own.

For a month we thought the end of the world was coming. No one knew where the first bomb would fall or how long anything would survive after it had fallen. We had no idea if wheat would die. We imagined a cloud expanding. I said to Irene: 'I've never known what was in ordinary clouds or why they're there, or why they don't fall.' Irene said: 'Men have a better grasp of these things.'

I tried to add up everything that was in England. I began with churches. Then the stones that the churches were built from. Then the timber that made the roofs and choir stalls and the pews. Then the trees that had been cut down to provide the timber. Then the number of years that the trees had been growing. And then, last of all, everything inside the churches such as hymn books and the hassocks and the fonts and the bell ropes and the crosses and the candlesticks and the handwritten flower rosters pinned up in all the porches. I did not try to count prayers or singing or breaths. I concentrated on things and on time. And the answers I got were so enormous that my brain stopped being able to imagine stone quarries and forests and seasons and started only to see numbers. So then I thought, this is probably what Khrushchev is doing now, he is stopping seeing or imagining America. He is deliberately forgetting that there are cars called Oldsmobiles, that on days of rejoicing people hurl pieces of paper out of high windows, that Doris Day is a lovely woman. He is looking at maps, perhaps, at lines and names and symbols and altitude figures. Or maybe someone has told him that in the city of Los Angeles alone there are more than half a million lawn sprinklers and this is what he has chosen to see in his mind. He stands at a window in the Kremlin, a window I have seen on the television news, and he says aloud in Russian: 'I am only going to bomb a number of lawn sprinklers.'

But it didn't happen.

Sonny hired a digger. He said he would build us a fallout shelter. He told me to buy rations – dried pears and packets of raisins. The beets stayed in the ground and their tops went to seed like spinach while he concentrated on the shelter.

It was Timmy that he wanted to save.

He wasn't clever with the digger and he had no one to help him. He dug an oblong pit like a swimming pool or a mass grave. I thought of us lying in it and being set alight. He knew it was no good. He'd done drawings of an underground home with a portable toilet and a gas cooker and bunk beds, but it bore no resemblance to these.

On the television news, they showed us the great grey American fleet sailing towards Cuba and then, later on, sailing away from it. Ships and the sea and Cuba have no colour in my mind. And I thought at the time, I'm pleased this is all black and white, as if it were already part of history.

When it was actually over, Sonny was more relieved about not having to finish his fallout shelter than about the saving of the world. Since the loss of half his ear, he and the world have not been happy together. If the world had had to choose between an empty fallout shelter and Sonny, it would have chosen the shelter.

There were three bunks in Sonny's drawing. Not four.

I go into Mary's room and look at what has been left behind. I try to guess her line from the little that is there. She was a cloud artist, once. Then she began to manufacture weapons against us. She became the enemy.

I tear down her pictures of clouds. In a dusty cupboard are a pair of wellingtons which may have been the ones she wore to the ballet show. There is a tennis ball, ditchwater green, split at the seam. There is a *Dictionary of Inventions* which belonged to Livia. There is a kitchen knife, missing for a year. It makes me shiver to touch things that were lost.

Since she left, I've begun to dream of her. We can't choose our dreams. They choose us. We are always at a railway station, Mary and I. I am younger. My hair is black and thick. I get onto the train and I'm relieved to be going, to be leaving Mary behind on the platform – her flat face so unlike mine, her peculiar body.

But she makes me lean out of the train window to say goodbye. She makes me lean down, out of the open window, to kiss her. And then my hair falls round her neck like a noose and, at that moment, the train starts to move and I try to push her away, but she's held in the noose of my hair and she has to start running along the platform to keep up with the train, to stop her head from being pulled off.

I scream for someone to help us but there is no one on the carriage and no one on the platform. And then the platform ends and Mary hangs by her neck from my hair and her weight pulls me half-out of the train, but I hold on, keep holding on, knowing that soon she will fall and be left by the line and then I will be free of her and ready to sit down and get out my sandwiches and my thermos of tea and enjoy my journey. But I don't enjoy my journey. I wake up. I cannot survive this dream without waking.

I say to Sonny: 'I had my dream about Mary.' He says: 'She's gone now. Forget her.'

I'm trying to find a way to forget her.

I have distempered the walls of her room grey and painted the windows white. I have put it all into the past. Like Cuba.

Now, in this New Year, something new has come into my mind.

It started to come in when Irene brought Billy to the farm. I hadn't seen Irene since our discussion about the H-Bomb cloud, because there's a big difference between us now. Irene is happy.

But then she wrote to me and said: 'You're becomming a strannger, Estelle.' Edward Harker has taught her a lot of things, but spelling isn't one of them. She said: 'Billy loves all annimals, small and large.'

Billy Harker is five. He wants to be a fireman. He owns a tortoise called Tarzan. He is trying to teach it to jump. He has brown eyes and thick brown hair, cut in slabs. Most of the time, he pretends he's an engine. After teatime, says Irene, his engine blows a gasket and Billy comes to a halt and falls asleep on the stairs.

They came and spent a day here, Billy and Irene. He arrived wearing a little muffler. His face is quite round and his cheeks dimpled, like Irene's. It was a sunny February day.

We showed him the combine, covered in old sacks against the damp. We had to take the sacks off so that Billy could climb up onto it and pretend he was cutting a cornfield.

Irene and I stood in our winter coats while he harvested a whole imaginary field.

Irene started to talk about Mary, but I said: 'Irene, I am not discussing that subject.'

When we got to the meadow where the hens are, we gave Billy a basin of grain and he ran about, scattering it everywhere and the hens squawked and tried to fly away. He began chasing them. I was glad Sonny was nowhere in sight. Billy dropped the basin and threw himself on one of the hens, like a rugby player doing a flying tackle. It fell over and Billy held on to it. I hoped its legs hadn't snapped. He stood up and the hen pecked his hands, but he didn't cry. He tucked it under his arm and stroked the feathers on its neck.

In the afternoon, we sat in the winter dark and watched *Andy Pandy*. Billy had never seen television before. He didn't know what to do except stare. He became very quiet and still. I put him on my knee. He was much heavier than my children had been. He lay back with his head against my shoulder and for the first time in years and years I felt entirely comfortable and warm. I wanted to hold Billy on my lap for ever. My envy of Irene was a well inside me, black and deep.

So that night I decided: I want another child. Why not? I'm still young, not yet forty. I still catch sight of my old resemblance to Ava Gardner. I will hold the baby to me safe and warm and this will be my new reason for living.

And I have a room for him: Mary's room. On the grey walls I will pin up some brightly coloured pictures of tortoises and fire engines. I will ask Edward to make a crib.

This is my new idea for the New Year. All through *Z-Cars*, I smile.

Calculus

The ghost of Arthur Loomis was behaving badly.

He walked into Walter's dreams naked, still smelling of the grave. His penis was red and stiff. He waved it in Walter's face. 'Go away,' Walter told his dreaming self to say. 'Stop persecuting me. I've done everything you've asked.'

He told Pete what he had to put up with now: Arthur's flesh hanging in tatters, his erect prick. But Pete only laughed. 'Usually ghosts wear white,' he said.

And another thing: when Walter woke up from his dreams, some of the stench of Arthur was on his pillow. It was as if he had sat down right there by Walter's head all night. Grace, when she came in with a cup of tea for him at six, would screw up her thin nose and say: 'It stinks in here, Walter. You'd better open a window and give the place an airing.'

Even in the shop he'd catch it now and again, that whiff of the dead. It wore off after dinnertime and by the evening had almost gone, only to return while he slept.

It took Walter many weeks to realise that it came from his own mouth.

He felt afraid. He was twenty-seven and his breath smelled like a corpse and he didn't know why.

He met Sandra in the street one lunchtime. She was wheeling a navy blue pram. Inside the pram was her baby, Judy. Sandra stopped and smiled at Walter and invited him to look at Judy, as though this were a special privilege given only to a few. Walter had no interest in babies, but felt he couldn't refuse, out of politeness. He bent over the pram. He filtered his breath with his fingers. The baby wore a salmon-coloured bonnet. She looked ugly to Walter, like a prawn. 'Isn't she lovely?' said Sandra. 'She's yours,' said Walter. 'She would be.'

Sandra was wearing blue and white – blue dress, white collar and cuffs, like a nurse. Her breasts were large. Her long marmalade hair had been cut short. The Sandra for whom he had written the song no longer existed. He hated the new smile she wore, so smart and smug. He wondered what he could do to wipe it away. As he talked to her he tasted blood on his gums. He said: 'Goodbye, Mrs Cartwright. It's been a pleasure to run into you.'

That night, the ghost of Arthur didn't appear. A nurse with a starched hat shone a torch into Walter's throat. He remembered the old pain of yodelling and his dreams of writing songs and going to Tennessee. He remembered his visit to Gilbert Blakey and Blakey's nurse kneeling by him with a look of stone.

When he was woken at six his mouth was so full of blood, he couldn't say good morning to his mother. She put his tea down. She said: 'This dreadful odour, Walter. Could it be your teeth?'

He opened his mouth and stared into the cavern of it in the little plastic mirror on the bathroom wall. He curled back his lips. Poor Cleo, examining his face through her spangled glasses, had once told him his mouth was very sweet. 'So pink, ducky.'

Now, it wasn't sweet. His gums were the colour of Arthur's prick. They oozed. It was as if, while the rest of him lived, his mouth was dying. It had never kissed Sandra. It had given up.

He asked Grace to telephone Blakey. She sat in her booth and dialled the number, watching Walter all the time.

He was dressing duck. He thought, of course she doesn't want me to slice off my fingers, but what *is* it that she wants? A grandchild like a boiled shrimp? The name Loomis going forward into the silent future?

Global crisis had altered the landscape of Gilbert Blakey's mind.

After Cuba, after he had understood that his nature could

allow him to die long before it had allowed him to love, he began to feel the pathos of his own reticence.

He'd believed that if he gave in to desire a fissure would open up in the earth, that the ground would no longer have permanence. Now, he realised that there was no permanence in anything, not even in the sky. So he allowed his dreams to increase. His behaviour towards his male patients changed by a degree so small that his new nurse noticed nothing different. Merely, his fingers lingered longer in their mouths. He talked to them reassuringly.

He told his mother that he thought change might be arriving in one form or another. He said this idly, as though he were making an imprecise weather forecast. Margaret Blakey didn't pay much attention. She noticed only that her son had taken to staring out of the window in a determined way. She said: 'I hope you haven't been over-working, Gilbert. You look tired.'

Gilbert had no idea when the alteration to his life would begin. He was unable to make plans, he hadn't the courage. He had faith in the arrival of something. He thought, if the world can seem to embrace its end with so few regrets, then I can meet a man I can embrace and not die for it. And he knew that when he saw the man, he would recognise him; he would know.

Walter cycled to his appointment with Gilbert Blakey. The field beans were in flower. It was an early evening of extraordinary sweetness. Since his mouth had begun to taste of death, Walter had become more sensitive than usual to the scent of the earth.

He wasn't afraid. He believed that a cure existed for the thing he had, whatever it was. He whistled as he pedalled. He had faith.

Gilbert remembered him as soon as he saw him – the young man who had fainted. He remembered the fleshy lips and the heat of the heavy head. He dried his long-fingered hands. He noticed that Walter again looked very hot. He smiled at him, his Eden smile, canines prominent. He asked him why he had come.

Walter didn't know how to put it. Being there under the Miralux lamp made him feel confused. He was on the point of telling the dentist about Arthur's naked ghost or even about Sandra and her vet and her prawn baby, because he knew that these things were somehow connected to his arrival in the leather chair that could be pumped up and down. He stopped himself in time. The presence of a different nurse, very plump and crackly with starch, prevented him from babbling about his hauntings. All he described was his bleeding.

Gilbert selected a periodontal probe. He tipped back the headrest of the chair. The look in Walter's eyes was resigned and pleading. He laid a caressing finger on Walter's lower lip. 'Open,' he said.

It was only then that he became aware of Walter's Devilish breath.

He talked gently and slowly, as if to a foreigner who might not understand him. He explained how, if a mouth was neglected, food stagnation occurred in the minute space between the gum margin and the tooth surface called the gingival crevice. This stagnation began a cycle of decay. Calculus formed to irritate and inflame the gum, loosening its grip on the teeth, and so creating a 'pocket' in which more food could collect and decay. Calculus was a gritty substance. Its scales were jagged. This, combined with bacterial poisons, ulcerated the gum and caused bleeding at the least touch. If treatment wasn't given swiftly, gingival disease would destroy sections of the jaw or alveolar bone and teeth would first become loose and subsequently be lost . . .

Walter listened. He was relieved there were nouns and verbs to describe his condition. And he thought, this is why

I liked writing songs: I could make the words describe things I hadn't known about until they did.

He looked up at Gilbert, at his white coat and his pale hair and his reassuring smile. He asked him what had to be done. He was told that his teeth would be scaled and polished to get rid of the calculus. He would be given a mouthwash to bathe the gums. He would be shown some principles of dental hygiene. The process of healing would be closely monitored. Three or four more appointments would have to be made . . .

Gilbert exchanged the periodontal probe for a scaler. He held Walter's mouth open with his left hand, the chin resting in his palm. His thumb grew sticky with Walter's blood.

Gilbert thought, this is what I am going to do: I am going to buy an expensive car. I am going to take the Devil for a ride. I will have one hand on the wheel and the other on the Devil's thigh. I will feel the heat of hell coming into my fingers and spreading down my wrist and all along my heavy arm. That will be the beginning. And by my calculation, there will be no end, once it has begun. There will be no returning, ever.

Mary:

I spent Christmas of 1962 with Cord. He had an altered appearance. He said a flock of geese had flown over Gresham Tears in a V-formation and the V was the arrow of time, wounding everything in its path. His consumption of Wincarnis had gone up. He said: 'Martin, I'm becoming a damn drunk.'

I got drunk with him. The days of ginger beer were past. We sat on the hearth rug getting sloshed and making paper

chains. There was meant to be a colour order in the chains –
red, blue, green, yellow, violet – but we were reckless with it.
Our chains looked as if they had been made by chimpanzees.

The doctors had told Cord that there was no specific name
for what had happened to him. He said: 'There's a name
for every damn thing in the world but not for this.' I said,
thinking of Mary Martin: 'Names are no comfort, Cord.'
He said: 'I don't agree with you there. Remember the three
syllables of Livia.'

I wanted to console Cord with a nice Christmas present. My
mother had sent me a postal order for twenty-five shillings. It
was tucked inside a card that said Seasons Greetings with no
apostrophe. The word 'home' was not written on it anywhere,
nor the word 'father'.

I decided that Cord would be cheered up by my brass
rubbing of Sir John Elliot 1620–1672, so I had it framed and
wrapped it with six sheets of wrapping paper.

Cord hung it in the downstairs lavatory. He said it was
capital. He said brass rubbings were ghostly things in two
senses and everything important in life was dual, like being
and not being, male and female, and that there was no country
in between. I sat on the toilet and looked at Sir John and
he looked at me with his empty eyes and I thought, Cord
is wrong, there is a country in between, a country that no
one sees, and I am in it.

Cord gave me a ski-ing anorak with a hood trimmed with
white fur. I put it on. Cord said I looked like the Snow Queen,
so in the night I unpicked the fur and folded it away to give
to Lindsey, if ever I should see her again.

And that is all I remember of Christmas. For the rest of
everything, I was out of my mind.

I began a new year with Miss McRae. She said: 'Are you
making any resolutions, dear?'

The resolution I made was to forget Lindsey. She had

left Weston Grammar. She had become engaged to Ranulf Morrit. She behaved as though she had become twenty-five overnight. She said, 'Darling Ranulf is going to become a chartered accountant.'

Darling Ranulf made love to Lindsey in a forgotten maids' room at his parents' house. Ramona the cook slept next door. Spanish people were not supposed to have ears.

When Lindsey began describing all this to me, I wanted to say 'please desist', but she held on to me and laughed in my ear and her hair touched my face and all the breath in me seemed to collect at the top of my lungs and become heavier than stone.

She said: 'I never knew about *giving* myself before, Marty. About, you know, absolutely *submitting*. But this is what's so fantastic about it. I mean, to have Ranulf on top of me and making me do whatever he wants . . . and I *want* to, that's the thing, I mean do whatever he wants, not what I want and when he comes – you know about coming, don't you? – he always tells me, he says God I'm coming Lindsey, I'm coming and I think God's he's coming and I feel so . . . . *privileged*. Do you know what I mean?'

I had to go far away. I walked across the frozen hockey field. I let myself into one of the tennis courts and sat down on the grit and pressed my back into the wire. I could see myself, as if from above, as if I were God or a navigator. I looked like a sack of coal. I could feel my lungs turning black.

I tried to think of tennis and summer. There were no nets on the courts. The lines needed repainting. I thought, I'm seventeen and it will always be winter. My knees were violet with cold. My hatred of Ranulf Morrit had made me a petrified thing. By the time it got dark, I couldn't even move my eyes.

Miss Gaul found me. A drip from her long nose plopped onto my hand like a waking spell. She made me stand and try to slap myself but I couldn't straighten up. I walked back across the hockey field bent over, with my arms hanging down, like Neanderthal Man. I thought it would be nice to go back in time, to an era when no one could talk.

I was taken to the Staff Common Room which was the only room at Weston with an electric fire. It was the end of the school day and the teachers were making coffee and lighting up cigarettes – activities you never thought them capable of. They smiled at me kindly, as if they were a family and I were part of it for half an hour.

That was before my Christmas with Cord. When I got back to school, Lindsey was no longer there. I tried not to imagine where she was or what she was doing. I did not send her the fur from my anorak hood. I was glad I was not Ramona, the Spanish cook. I made my resolution to forget her.

I couldn't forget her.

I would look in my thoughts for an equilateral triangle and I would find Lindsey instead. She lay in wait for me all the time.

I had been a chaste person. Now, at night, in my coffin bed, I became Martin Ward, Lindsey's lover. I couldn't help it. She should not have told me what Ranulf did to her. She made me want it. I laid her underneath me. My breasts become hers. I closed my eyes. She begged me to go deeper into her, to hurt her. She said: 'Destroy me, Martin.' And when I was finished, she was bruised, she was crying. I licked her tears. I whispered to the wet pillow: 'Lindsey, it's your own fault.' Before I slept I would think, tomorrow this will be over. Tomorrow I will be able to forget her and get on with my essay on *Hamlet*. And then tomorrow would come and she was not forgotten.

And my longing to confide in somebody came back. I wasn't little Martin any more. I was a young man in my mind.

I sat in silence by Miss McRae's fire. She believed I was mourning my home and family. She was knitting an arran jumper for her sister in Oban. She said: 'Time changes everything, Mary, and not always for the worse.'

I said: 'I'm ill, Miss McRae. I can't work. It's something internal.'

Miss McRae put down her knitting. 'That's serious, dear,' she said.

So I found myself in the doctor's surgery. I had no memory of walking there.

I sat alone with a line of others all alone on hard chairs. The waiting room was a passage with no light to read by. The others fidgeted and coughed. I was afraid to look round the faces and find my father there, clawing at his ear.

When I went in, the doctor pulled his chair very close to his desk and said: 'Well?' He was a doctor I had never seen before. The old one had been called Hodgkin and he'd lived in Swaithey for twenty-seven years. I thought, he could be dead. Even my father could be dead. Because it feels as if a lot of time has passed . . .

I found an unexpectedly strong voice. It was as if my breath had been saved by history for this moment, ever since the death of Hakluyt. I said: 'You won't believe what I'm going to say.'

I held myself very straight and still. I spoke clearly and fluently, like I'd tried to speak on the subject of Hitler in the school debate. I told the doctor that I was seventeen years old.

He said: 'Yes. Well?'

I felt a silence coming on. I knew that I couldn't allow this, that my words would fall into it and drown.

I said: 'I've tried to tell people. Twice. But I changed my mind.'

'Tell them what?' said the doctor. He seemed in a hurry.

'Tell them that I'm not really a girl. I never have been. When I was very small maybe, but not since the age of six when the King died. Since then – '

'Wait a minute,' said the doctor. 'What are you saying?'

'I'm saying that although in some respects I've got a girl's body, I have never felt, I mean not for one hour or one day or one minute, that I was a proper girl or that I'd grow up to be a woman. I have always felt male. And the older I get – '

'You have breasts.'

'Yes.'

'Presumably you menstruate?'

'No.'

'You know what menstruation is?'

'Yes.' I thought about Lindsey. Lindsey used to bleed and bleed. She used to swoon from her loss of blood.

'You have no menstrual cycle?'

'No.'

'And because of this, you've come to believe you're not a girl?'

'No. Not because of this. I've always believed it. Always. Since I was six. Since the King – '

'What does the King have to do with it?'

I stopped and looked at this doctor. If we'd had a debate entitled 'What Makes a Good Doctor?' I would have said: 'Patience is one thing.'

The doctor had a smile on his lips that he was trying to hide. I thought, when I am a man, I will not resemble him in any way; he is a loathsome person.

He wrote down a few words on a pad. He said the most important thing to establish was why my periods had not begun. I told him it was because I had no womb. He shook his head again.

He took a sample of blood from my arm. He asked me to show him my breasts, which I still kept bandaged up. I unwound the crepe. It felt icy in his room. Lindsey had told me that at the mere sight of her bosoms Darling Ranulf lost control of himself, but this doctor did not lose control of himself at the sight of mine. He looked away and I was glad. All I wanted then was to get out of there.

I was about to leave when the doctor said: 'Wait a minute. I'm going to give you a prescription.'

'A prescription for what?' I asked.

'Some tablets. They should bring on your bleeding. Your delusion is probably allied to hormone deficiency. Once your cycle is established, I'm sure it will disappear.'

I took the prescription and walked out. I did not say, Thank you, Doctor. I just left without a word.

I sat down in the main street of Swaithey, on a bench by the horse trough. I tore up the prescription and scattered the pieces onto the water, where they floated like white petals. I thought, the medical profession has turned me into a litter lout.

Later in the year, after the summer had come and I had received an invitation to Lindsey's wedding, I went to see Edward Harker. It was the day of the village gymkhana. Pearl sometimes liked to pretend she was a pony. She sneezed and whinnied and tossed her lemon mane. She let Billy sit on her shoulders and slap her arm with a willow wand. So I knew that Pearl and Billy and Irene would be at the gymkhana and that Edward, who suffered from hay fever, would probably be alone in his cellar.

I realised after my visit to the doctor that telling somebody about myself wasn't as hard as I'd imagined. I just said some words and there it was, over. Except that it wasn't, because the words had not been believed. I might as well have said, 'I am the Virgin Mary.' I was thought to be suffering from a delusion. My mother told me she had a friend at Mountview who thought she was a chicken. And this was why this person was locked up there. No one examined her for feathers. No one offered her a worm. I thought of writing to her: 'This country is afraid of the unusual,' but then I found that I didn't relish the idea of writing a letter to a hen. I was as narrow-minded as everyone else.

So the question of belief began to torment me. I made a parade in my mind, like an identity parade, of everyone I knew and I passed slowly down it, telling them one by one. Only my father was absent. I told Cord and he began staring at the sky. I told Timmy and he said: 'I have to go to a swimming lesson now.' I told Lindsey and she laughed. She said: 'Does this mean you can't be one of my bridesmaids?' I told my mother, but she wasn't listening. She was trying to remember the words of a Perry Como song. I dismissed the parade and they all walked away without a backward glance.

And it was after this that I remembered Edward Harker saying to me on the day of his wedding: 'Everything in nature is resurrection,' and I thought, a person who believes in previous lives is the person to tell, and he has been there all the time . . .

He was oiling a bat. He wore a grocer's apron. The arrangement of light in his cellar hadn't changed since I was a child. The smell of linseed oil was heavy, like incense. He caressed the bat with his oil-soaked hand. He said: 'I hope I'm not losing my touch, Mary.'

I said: 'You can keep a secret, Edward, can't you?'

I used the same kind of words I'd used in the doctor's surgery. I said: 'There has been a mistake somewhere, Edward, and it won't ever be put right or made more bearable if no one believes what I'm saying.'

'I believe you,' he said quickly.

And we both sat down where we happened to be standing. I sat on the iron head of a belt-driven lathe and Harker sat on his desk and knocked over one of his lamps. Neither of us spoke for quite a while and the silence marked the passing of something: it marked the passing of my isolation.

I watched Harker's hand go towards the lamp and right it and set it down again exactly in the place that it had been.

9

1964

Marshall Street

Every Thursday morning, Timmy Ward was driven to Saxmundham Station in Sonny's van and put on the early train to London.

His destination was the Olympic swimming pool at the Marshall Street baths. He was fifteen. His voice had broken and he could no longer sing in Swaithey Choir. He missed his singing. He missed the purity of his own sound. Swimming seemed to be the only beautiful thing he had left.

A talent scout, a former member of the British Olympic Swimming Team of 1956, had been invited to Timmy's school. He had worn his Olympic track suit, very faded with eight years' washing.

The sports teacher had said to him: 'That's the one to watch, the thin lad with the silly smile in Lane 2.' Timmy had swum three lengths of butterfly and the talent scout had been so impressed he'd felt his heartbeat quicken. He said to Timmy: 'I'm going to pluck you from Fenland obscurity, Timothy.' Timmy said: 'This isn't Fen country, Sir. That's over above Cambridge.'

'Wherever it is,' said the scout, 'I'm plucking you from it.'

The group Timmy joined was called The Otters. They had three hours of intensive swimming coaching from ten o'clock till one. They had to bring their own lunch. From two till three they were taught diving. Every week, they were told that their country would be proud of them one day.

Timmy was the smallest member of The Otters. His fear of the high board was acute and his dread of the day when he would have to dive from it intensified as the weeks passed. To make a long vertical line downwards with his body was, in his spiritual imagination, a fearful thing to do. He thought it unfair that, when swimming was what he excelled at, this other, terrible endeavour was expected of him. Even Estelle kept saying: 'I hope you'll learn diving, Tim. That's the thing I'm waiting to come and see.'

He hoped she would have to wait a long time. He said: 'All I'm good at is butterfly.' She smiled her far-away smile and said: 'Strokes have such funny names – crawl, butterfly. Who thought them up?' Timmy told her he didn't know. He didn't know the answer to any of Estelle's questions. Can you mime tap dancing? What are dreams? When did history begin? The questions just floated away, unanswered, into the air.

The Marshall Street pool seemed vast. There was a steep bank of seats for spectators on one side. Light fell onto the water from a long way up. The shouts of Mr McKenzie, the Olympic coach, echoed, as in a cathedral. If it had not been for the high diving board, Timmy would have found it a marvellous place. At the start of a butterfly race, three lengths, one hundred metres, when he stood, ready to spring, on his starting block waiting for Mr McKenzie's gun, he felt more fond of existence than at any other time. The way the surface of the pool (no matter how much it had been disturbed by previous swimmers) returned to a glassy calm seconds before the race began never failed to impress him. He loved this about swimming: you left no trace of yourself, no footprint, no track. You described a horizontal line. It moved ahead of you, always ahead, with nothing remaining behind.

Mr McKenzie reminded The Otters quite regularly of the pride England could one day feel on their account if they exerted themselves. 'Timothy,' he would say, 'we have to strengthen your legs or the Union Jack will never be run up for you.'

On the long journeys to and from Marshall Street, Timmy would examine the idea of future glory. He found that he wanted it not so much for himself as for Sonny. Sonny's life was going down, it was a runaway thing, on a falling curve, like a dive. The combine was rusty. Parts for it were ordered on credit and never paid for. Fields were left fallow because Sonny didn't have the will to plough them and drill them. Thistles seeded themselves everywhere. The whole farm was blighted with thistles and Sonny did nothing. Timmy hated the sight of all the thistledown blowing like cotton above the ground.

He had a recurring dream: Sonny came to Marshall Street, wearing a suit and tie. He saw Timmy win two butterfly races. He stood up and cheered and waved a handkerchief with joy. They went home together on the train, father and son. As the fields began to move past the carriage windows, Sonny said: 'That's how everything's going to look from now on, flat and tidy and neat. And it will be because of you.'

But then there was the wretched question of the diving. Both his parents would keep on mentioning that. It was as though they saw all the swimming as an apprenticeship for this other, greater thing, this moment when Timmy would put his body into the air and they would watch it fall.

One Sunday

Gilbert Blakey had taken delivery of his new car, an MGB Convertible with wire wheels, on the day Kennedy was murdered. He heard about the assassination on the car radio. He felt so shocked that he had to pull over into a lay-by and sit still. The black, leather-scented interior of the car, until a moment ago an entirely marvellous thing, now seemed to Gilbert like a soft chamber of death. He had difficulty breathing. He wound down the window to let in the sharp November air. He laid his head on the steering wheel.

The car frightened him from then on, just enough to make him drive more sedately than he would have liked. The winter was bitter and the Suffolk roads icy. Gilbert dreaded turning the MG over onto its vulnerable soft top. He imagined his own head turned to pulp, like Kennedy's. He longed for spring. He wanted to believe that all he had to do was survive the winter and then everything would become gentle again: the weather, the behaviour of the world, the beat of his own heart. And part of him knew that this was a fond expectation. No moment in time can ever be revisited.

He'd continued to treat Walter's gum disease. He told Walter that he wished to see him regularly until every manifestation of decay had been eradicated. He said that if his teeth weren't saved now, he would have none left by the time he was thirty-five. He said: 'It was profoundly important, Walter, that you came to see me when you did.' By January, Walter's mouth was pink and clean again, his breath sweet. He said: 'So is that it, Mr Blakey, for now?'

'No,' said Gilbert. 'Monthly check-ups must continue, until the spring.'

He told Walter he'd bought a new car, an MGB. He didn't say that it made him afraid. Walter said: 'I'm envious, Mr Blakey. If there's one thing certain about my life, it's that

I'll never own a sports car.' Gilbert replied that nothing was certain in any life and they laughed and Walter noticed for the first time Gilbert's resemblance to Anthony Eden and felt flattered by it, peculiarly flattered to have seen it.

From this moment they told each other odd details of their lives. Because Walter couldn't speak for most of the time he spent in Gilbert's adjustable chair and because Gilbert preferred not to talk while he was drilling or scaling, small details were all they had time for. So Gilbert learned that Walter's uncle lived in a trolley bus in a field. So Walter found out that twelve times a year Gilbert's mother went out with an eighteen-foot measure and measured the distance between her front door and the Minsmere cliffs. They found these details strange and absorbing. Walter was surprised to discover that he was not the only person in Suffolk living a solitary life in his mother's house. Gilbert thought, the uncle in the bus is unconventional and this makes Walter less ordinary than I'd presumed.

Walter was pleased with the change in himself. He hadn't enjoyed smelling like Arthur Loomis's corpse. When he opened his mouth, now, and saw his pink gums and white, shining teeth, he had the thought that he had been saved from something, perhaps even from dying. One man had saved him: Gilbert Blakey. And not only from his own decay – from his nightmares also. Because Arthur began to leave him alone. When he did appear, he didn't stink any more, he wasn't naked or waving his prick about, he was wearing clothes and his butcher's apron.

Walter felt a grateful relief and an admiration for Gilbert that bordered on worship. Eden had stepped forward into the present and smiled on him. In exchange, the ghost of Arthur had returned to a pre-Suez state of quietude. The next bit of Walter's life could now begin.

But what next bit? There was no change to any part of his

daily routine. There was only spring slowly unfolding around everything and light coming and showing white on the marble counter and on the cold room floor. Grace celebrated her fifty-third birthday. Her sisters came to stay for a weekend and talked in whispers as they had done after Ernie's death. In their soft voices, they congratulated Walter on doing well in the shop. He poured sherry for them and nodded but didn't thank them.

He was sent out to buy Eccles cakes and at the baker's there was Sandra with the prawn. And the prawn wasn't lying down asleep but kneeling up in the pram, pink and squeaking, and Walter thought, the prawn will soon be walking and starting to have its own human life, and still nothing will have happened to me. Then Sandra will have another of the vet's babies, a second horrible shrimp in a salmon bonnet, and all that will have been given to me will be the passing of time.

He brought the cakes home and put them on a plate. He took them into the front room where the sisters were. Their voices reminded him of the wind blowing along the river and lifting the skirts of the willows. He saw Sandra in the varnished boat. He rowed. She covered her knees with her skirt. He helped himself to a cake and ate it quickly and greedily. He thought, everything good is in the past. Even things that were only half-good – they're in the past too. Things like that day with the bottle of Tizer, never drunk. And all my songs. And my half-yodel. Everything.

A hot Sunday came.

Walter told his mother: 'Mr Blakey has invited me to go for a ride in his car.'

'Go for a ride?' said Grace. 'Why would you want to do that, dear?'

'It's a sports car,' said Walter. 'Convertible.'

'Convertible?' said Grace. 'What does it convert to?'

'It's a term,' said Walter. 'Convertible is a term for something.'

He wished he'd told Grace nothing about it. She made it seem like a babyish thing to want to do. Little boys went for rides in cars, not men in their late twenties. But he didn't care. He was looking forward to it, to moving along familiar roads very fast. And then arriving at the sea. Because the sea was their destination. Mr Blakey had said: 'I'm conservative in this way, Walter. I like every trip to have some purpose to it.'

It was the first hot day of the year, a Sunday in May. Gilbert had washed and polished the car and the wheels shone. The black canvas hood was folded down. As Walter got into his warm leather seat, Gilbert smiled at him, his Eden smile, and Walter felt pleased with this, as if he had been sent a greetings card with an authentic message inside it.

The sun caught Gilbert's teeth and made them glisten. He wore a blue shirt with a sleeveless fairisle jersey like a little waistcoat and a red silk tie. Walter had never seen him in anything but his white coat. And he had never been alone with him before. He felt suddenly breathless. He thought, it's like being alone with someone famous. There's a difference between them and you which makes breathing awkward. They drove towards Aldeburgh. There was a brightness in the air that Walter couldn't remember seeing ever before.

They talked about the murder of Kennedy. Gilbert told Walter how he had had to stop the car in a lay-by and put his head on the steering wheel. Walter told Gilbert that he had heard about the assassination from Pete, who had come into the shop, crying. Talking about Kennedy seemed to create a bond between them. They were silent for a bit and the sound of the car's marvellous engine was the only thing to be heard. And then Gilbert took his left hand from the metal steering wheel and laid it gently on Walter's knee.

Walter didn't move. He looked down at the hand as though it were a thing that had landed on him from outer space. He saw that it was a pale hand, lightly freckled with soft blond hairs on the back of it. The fingers were very long and the nails perfect and shiny.

Walter wondered whether he should say something. He wanted to ask, Do you want me to say anything, Mr Blakey? He turned his head, just fractionally, so that he could see Gilbert's face and his expression. Gilbert was staring ahead at the road. It was as though the hand that he'd put on Walter's knee didn't belong to him, as though he hadn't noticed that it was there. Walter thought, in a moment or two, he'll take his hand away and we'll start a new conversation about some ordinary thing, not Kennedy, and this moment will not have happened. It will be like everything else; in the past and not there.

He had an erection. He didn't often get them. Not since Sandra and the death of Cleo and the sight of the prawn. He wanted Gilbert's hand to stay and the erection to stay. He didn't want these things to disappear into time. So he put his own wide, cumbersome hand on Gilbert's slim one. Touching it was like touching a meteorite, just as extraordinary. He moved the hand up his thigh. He felt a wild, hot happiness.

The light changed. They were driving along the edge of Tunstall Forest. The sound of the engine changed. They were slowing down. Gilbert took away his hand to shift into third gear. He turned the car into a track in the forest and the tall trees leant over it, curtaining out the sun.

Walter waited. He felt as if he wanted to scream something out, a word or a sound he'd never made before but which everyone – his mother, Sandra, the vet and the prawn – would hear and be so frightened by they would turn white and open their mouths in disbelief.

Then he felt Gilbert's mouth on his. The little moustache

brushed his top lip. He thought, once again Mr Blakey has put me in a position where I can't speak, but now this is probably best. This is the future, but it's a future without words. Things will be done and never spoken about.

What Is There?

Sonny was having difficulty remembering.

He thought, there are holes in the years gone. Spaces with nothing.

Irene said to him: 'Is drink turning your brain to soup, Sonny, or what?'

He couldn't stop drinking. Drink was almost all that was left to him of pleasure. He'd lost half an ear for England. England owed him something, a few glasses of something every night. Darn right, as John Wayne would say. Old John Wayne drinking his Black and White whisky, with his black and white horses to ride through the black and white scenery; Sonny was sure John Wayne didn't have holes in his past, but then he always had some black and white woman to kiss and to ride with into the future. Darn right.

He went out one morning to feed the hens. He was alone. Timmy wasn't interested in feeding the hens any more. Sonny saw all the hens standing about in their field, standing absolutely still and not moving. They looked like decoys. Sonny thought, is this a real sight?

He stood still and didn't move. He set down the pail of grain. It was early and the sun was low and the shadows cast by the chicken coops were long. Sonny's head ached. He had a longing to lie down where he was on the stubble.

He sat instead. The ground was hard and prickly under him. He put one hand into the pail, to reassure himself that the grain was still there. The hens were in shod, that was how it seemed.

Sonny wondered whether a fox had come in the night and terrorised them. But there was no smell of fox.

Then he knew what had happened. A spell had been cast on the hens. He saw it clearly. He saw Mary, in the dark cottage where she lived with the Scottish teacher, practising witchcraft. She had progressed from conjuring to real, deadly magic. She was taking her revenge on him. It was Mary who was bringing ruin to the farm.

Sonny got up. He felt stiff in his knee-joints. He lifted the pail and scattered some handfuls of corn, but the hens didn't seem to notice and remained stock still, looking at their surroundings, like hens in a painting.

He knew there were certain steps he should take, certain things that a man with a proper memory would do, but he couldn't think what they were. He craved, then and there, a long swill of black beer, its sweet-bitterness, its quenching of a thirst which, with the dry winds as his enemy, seemed perpetual.

His next thought was, I'd better go to that hole of a cottage and see her, that witch-child, and tell her I know her game; tell her if she doesn't stop putting spells on my land, I'll lock her up. I'd better frighten her. She'd better remember that I'm her father. She owes me her life and I still have power – power to take her life away.

Darn right.

He didn't go that day. He did nothing that day, and he didn't tell Estelle about the hens or about the witchcraft. Because for some time now, Estelle had been behaving differently towards him and he wanted this different behaviour to continue. He wasn't imagining this: her behaviour towards him had changed.

She asked him to make love to her. She lifted up her nightdress. She wouldn't let him kiss her. He longed to kiss her mouth and she wouldn't let him. But she allowed him to stroke her hair and then to lie on top of her and release himself inside her. She took no pleasure herself. She lay there with her eyes closed and her mouth turned away, but at least she let him do this, *invited* him to do this. 'Tonight is a good time,' she'd say, 'so you can do it, Sonny. I want you to do it.'

So his old desire for her crept back. As long as he didn't look at her feet, which used to be beautiful and now looked ugly to him, gnarled by time, he could summon up his old passion for her. Not too much though, he told himself. Don't let it come back like a flood because then when Estelle gets another crazy spell and starts wandering the fields and won't let you come near her, you'll drown.

He didn't know, from night to night, what she would do. He'd wait in the big iron bed, hollowed out by all the years. When she had her period she'd move herself to the far bit of her side of the bed and curl up like a child, like someone wounded. Then, when this was past, she would either lie on her belly, turned away from him, or she would take his hand from wherever it was and no matter how much he had drunk that night and push her nightdress up with it and say: 'You can do it, Sonny. I want you to do it.'

On the night after he had seen the hens standing still in the field, Estelle turned to Sonny. He thought she was going to take his hand and push her nightdress up, but she didn't. She lay very still and said to him: 'Sonny, you know I've painted Mary's room.'

'Yes,' he said. 'You did it grey.'

'Since then,' she said, 'I've painted it again.'

He thought, she thinks she can paint Mary out. He was tempted to say, paint isn't enough, Estelle. It needs something far more terrible than paint because she's casting spells now. But he kept quiet.

Estelle said: 'Will you go and look at the room?'

'All right,' said Sonny. 'Tomorrow, I will. What colour have you done it this time?'

She said: 'Go and look at it now.'

He didn't want to go there and then. He was hoping that what he would do there and then was make love to Estelle, even force her to look at him and let him kiss her mouth. In the long-ago days, before Mary was born, she used to say to him: 'Kissing is beautiful. Don't you agree, Sonny?'

He got out of bed. He'd been drinking stout, quite a few bottles. He would rather not have had to walk.

He went along the passage. He couldn't remember the last time he'd been in Mary's room. And he realised now that he no longer believed that there was a room there. What he believed was that there was just a door and that the door was a piece of decoration in the wall with nothing behind it.

He opened the door and switched on the light. There was a room there. It felt chill. It smelled of new paint. Sonny stared at it. The colour of the walls was pale blue like a May sky. Then he saw that everything in it, everything that had remained behind when Mary went, the wooden chest of drawers, the bed, the night table and the chair, had also been painted blue.

He blinked. He thought, Estelle's playing tricks on my eyes. She's laughing at me.

Then he heard an unfamiliar sound. It was pleasing and delicate. It seemed to come from far away but Sonny knew that it wasn't far away but in the room somewhere. He looked up and saw that there was something suspended from the ceiling. It was a wooden crossbar, like the wooden handle of a string puppet. Hanging from the bar were pieces of thread and attached to the thread were little oval shapes like honesty made of thin glass. The shapes moved in the current of air made by the opening of the door and when they touched each other they made this tinkling, far-away sound.

Sonny couldn't imagine where this thing had come from

or why it had been made. He moved the door backwards and forwards, backwards and forwards. He stood there for quite a long while, staring and listening.

When he returned to his room, he said to Estelle: 'What is that? That thing that makes a sound?' But she didn't answer. She lay on the far side of the bed. She was asleep or pretending to be, Sonny didn't know which.

Mary:

Lindsey and Ranulf had an autumn wedding. They thought a golden light, like the light in a painting by Samuel Palmer, would bathe the wonderful scene. They forgot that it pours with rain in October and that the east wind comes and slices you in half.

I went to the wedding by bus. I had to change buses three times. The rain was falling so hard it was putting out the stubble fires. The buses stank of cigarettes and soaking tweed. On the second bus I thought, I'm only enduring all this because I want to see how beautiful Lindsey looks in her dress; in other words, I only want to catch sight of her for a split second and then I will get back on some more buses and go home to my coffin room. It was the stupidest journey I had ever made.

When I arrived, I looked like a pot-holer just up from a hole. My hair stuck to my head like a bathing cap. My shoes were full of water. There was a smell on my skin of wet earth. I was wearing a long green coat that was Miss McRae's best coat and it came down to my feet. In the pocket was a packet of confetti. It was called 'Big Day Genuine Confetti', made in High Wycombe. I could not remember whether there had been an entry for confetti in my *Dictionary of Inventions*, so I had made one up to pass the time on the slow bus: 'Confetti. Rinaldo Confetti. Italian. 1920.' And this is what I decided: he was a ticket puncher in Naples Station. All the little bits of the punched tickets collected at his leet, multicoloured and weighing nothing. He found them oddly beautiful. He stooped and picked up a handful. He was feeling happy that day. He had just got engaged to Luminata, the girl of his dreams. He decided: from now until the wedding I am going to stand on a blanket at the ticket barrier. At the end of each of my shifts, I'm going to collect up the ticket bits, which will be clean and not spoiled by the dust and dirt from people's boots. Then on the day of the marriage, when we walk out from the cool church into the hot sun, I'm going to shower my bride with them. She will say: 'What is all this, Rinaldo mio?' And I will say: 'It is the future, Luminata. It is a thousand pieces of love.'

On the third bus, I saw some lightning far away beyond the flat, dark fields and I remembered who had invented the lightning conductor: Benjamin Franklin. American. 1752. And then I remembered something else, something awful: in the whole of the *Dictionary of Inventions,* which spanned nine centuries, there was only one woman inventor. Only one! Even the wool-combing machine and the stocking frame had been invented by men. It made me feel terrible, sad as the wind. I thought, when I've had my split-second glimpse of Lindsey, I'm going to go home and suggest that we make a little shrine to the one woman who invented something in a thousand years. She was called Miss Glover. Her Christian name wasn't even mentioned. She made her invention in the year 1841. It was the Tonic Sol-fa.

In one of my nightmares or waking dreams, I had been a bridesmaid at Lindsey's wedding, but of course she had never asked me. I didn't resemble a bridesmaid. She had her sister, Miranda, and her friend, Jennifer, as her maids. They had to dress up in pink satin frocks and carry nosegays and wear floral bonnets on their heads. They looked completely ridiculous. They looked like toilet roll covers. I could imagine their pink-satin feet being stuffed down into cardboard tubes.

I arrived at the church late. I was the last person to arrive before the bride. Darling Ranulf was already up by the altar, waiting. The toilet roll covers were huddled in the freezing porch, trying to warm their gooseflesh arms with their flowers. Jennifer glowered at me. She had always been jealous of my love for Lindsey. She said: 'What are you wearing, Marty? It's frightful.' I said: 'It's what I always put on for pot-holing,' and went into the church.

People turned and stared at me. All the women wore hats and lipstick. You could tell none of them had ever dreamed of rain falling on this day. Nor had they dreamed that someone like me would be invited. One of the ushers came up to me and said: 'Bride or bridegroom?' I said: 'What?' He said: 'Which side do you belong to?' He looked smart, despite the rain. I thought, the elements destroy women faster. They do. I said: 'I'm on Lindsey's side. Despite everything.'

He smirked. He sat me down at the very back and walked away from me as fast as he could. I had a stab of envy for his long, smart legs and for what he carried between them. The bells of the church were pealing like mad, pealing for this joining of the two sides – woman and man. I thought, they're ringing like they ring at the end of all the wars. They think all the soldiers have come home. They don't know I'm still out there in the mud, in no-man's-land.

When the bells stopped, I knew Lindsey was about to arrive, that I was about to get my glimpse. She came in. She stood by the door for a moment, arm in arm with her father, Mr Stevens. She was trembling. Her long hair was sculpted up into a kind of diamond crown, as if she were a royal princess, and a veil fell from the crown, covering her face. I'd forgotten about veils. I'd thought I'd be able to see her face and etch it on my memory for ever and I couldn't.

I put my hand in my pocket and opened my packet of 'Big Day Genuine Confetti'. I decided I would wait until I could throw some of this over her – my thousand pieces of love – and then I would walk away and catch my bus.

I couldn't hear much of the ceremony. There were only echoes, far away. I wanted to take off my shoes and empty out the water. I didn't like the squelch sound I could hear every time I moved my feet. I thought, this is the kind of noise Lindsey and Ranulf make together in their ecstasy. This is what Ramona, the Spanish cook, had to hear through the flimsy wall.

Steam began to come off the shoulders of my coat. And I had a ravenous hunger. I knew that at the reception there would be shrimp vol-au-vents and bits of cheddar cheese and pineapple on cocktail sticks and I thought, this is how life is: we are tempted from our chosen paths by the smallest things. We deserve to die.

When I looked up again from my squelching shoes, Lindsey and Ranulf were coming down the aisle, smiling. The organ was playing a march. I could see her face now and every one of her brilliant teeth and the bright bloom on her skin. But I could also see Ranulf's face – for the first time – his beaming face going along next to Lindsey's, the face of the man she had married seven times in her Geography book at the age of sixteen. And I was shocked. It wasn't a handsome face. It was white like suet with narrow eyes and big jowls. It was almost fat. Lindsey had described him as a god. She'd said: 'That's how I think of him, Mary, as a Greek god.' And I had never been in a position to contradict her. I had never been able to say: 'On the whole, Lindsey, the Greeks did not have double chins.' So I thought now, did she means Romans? Roman Emperors? Because she was never good at History. She thought Michelangelo had lived in the days of the Bible. She thought Queen Boadicea was an invented person, like Mrs Danvers.

Well, I had had my glimpse. The sight of Ranulf's stodgy face had taken away my appetite for the shrimp vol-au-vents. I wanted to leave. I took out my packet of confetti and shook a big fistful into my hand. I thought, in the rain, this stuff will turn to pink and yellow slush, to a mess resembling vomit. What Rinaldo the ticket puncher had to do was keep it dry. And so he could, because above him was the glass dome of the station roof and the only thing to fall on him and his invention was light.

On that day of Lindsey's wedding my life was going to change. I didn't know it yet.

On the last of the returning buses, I began thinking, not about Ranulf, but about Edward Harker's theories about my previous life. I felt a great longing to be sitting on the lathe head in Harker's cellar and listening to him quote from the Talmud or from Aristotle or from his favourite writer, Sholem Asch. In the Talmud, it says that the niggardly man is punished by being reincarnated as a woman in his next life. Aristotle believes in the immortality of every soul. He describes the soul's sojourn in the body as an illness. And Sholem Asch says: 'If the law of the transmigration of souls is a true one, then these, between their exchange of bodies, must pass through a sea of forgetfulness.' Harker had come to believe that all my suffering was caused by the Angel of Forgetfulness, who presides over the supposed sea. He said: 'What has happened, Mary, is this. The Angel of Forgetfulness – every now and again – is himself forgetful. He forgets to remove from our memories every fragment of our previous lives. And when this happens – as it has happened to you – the person is haunted by a belief that he or she is in the wrong life. It makes complete sense, doesn't it?'

I said that it made sense. But I said that the sense it made to me did not feel complete somehow. And I could tell that Harker was a bit disappointed. He wanted to help me. He thought that an explanation might be enough. I said: 'Edward, it's explained to prisoners how they came to be locked up in a cell with an iron bed and a grey blanket and a bucket. This isn't enough to make them enjoy prison.'

But talking to Harker, sitting in a pool of lamplight and telling him about my loathing of my body and my passion for Lindsey Stevens (now Mrs Ranulf Morrit and lost to me for all time) had become the thing that was most consoling to me. Harker was a good listener. Nothing that I said surprised or shocked him. He would work away on some piece of willow and nod and sigh and occasionally sigh and nod both at once and then say to me: 'Yes, well it all fits, Mary. It all fits.' And on the bus I thought, Edward Harker has probably saved my sanity. Without him, I might have been sent to Mountview. I might have shared a room with a chicken.

He told no one else. He swore this to me with his gnarled old hand on the sign that said *Harker's Bats. Estb. 1947.* He said Irene knew nothing, not a syllable of any of it, and nor did Billy.

'What about Pearl?' I asked.

'Nor Pearl,' he said.

'So,' I said, 'what do they think we're discussing down here?'

'Reincarnation, of course. My belief in it, not yours.'

Then he told me he knew, as much as one could ever know for certain, what Billy had been before: he had been a wrestler. He had died of his own weight. In seconds. He had fallen down and his contact with the earth had killed him. He said: 'I didn't really want Billy. But Billy wanted me and Irene. He was hungry to be reborn.'

When I got back to Swaithey, it was dark. I'd lost track of time. I thought, those Morrits could be in bed already, squelching together. The rain had stopped, but you could still feel the wind and winter right behind it, impatient to arrive.

My hunger had come back. I hoped Miss McRae had made some parsnip soup. And I hoped she had lit a fire, so that I could get dry and warm after my stupid day.

But I went into the cottage and there was a terrible smell and on her knees in the little entrance hall was Miss McRae scrubbing at the lino with a bucket of Dettol. There was no smell of a fire or of soup simmering, only the Dettol smell and this other stench that was unendurable.

'Ah, Mary,' said Miss McRae.

'What's happened?' I asked.

'You look a wee bit bedraggled, dear. What about a good hot bath?'

'What's this smell?'

'You go along and have your bath, while I just finish off here. Then I'll tell you what happened.'

I did what she instructed. This was part of my life with Miss McRae: obeying her.

But I lay in the bath too long. I let it get cold. My skin was bright pink, but I was cold again and while I tried to warm myself with the towel, I started to feel afraid. I thought, something horrible has happened. I can feel it now.

We sat in the dark parlour with the one-bar electric fire on. I wore an old dressing-gown of Cord's with eiderdown pockets. Miss McRae held a lace hankie to her nose. The smell of Dettol was so powerful, it felt more comfortable not to breathe at all.

Miss McRae spoke in a grave, frightened voice. She told me my father had come to the cottage. He was blind drunk. He wore no coat. He had a three-day beard. He had forced his way in, to try to find me. He began bawling out my name. He said he'd come to get me because I was a witch. I was putting spells on his land. I was poisoning his hens. He'd come to deal with me, once and for all.

He pushed Miss McRae against the wall and shook her. He accused her of hiding an evil person, a black magician.

She was afraid, but she remembered her upbringing in the lighthouse and all the storms she'd endured and she stayed calm. She said: 'Mr Ward, you are utterly mistaken. Mary is an ordinary girl.'

'Ordinary!' he screamed. 'Ordinary is what she is not! She's a perverted witch and I've come to put an end to it all!'

I asked whether he had a weapon, a knife or a hammer or something. Miss McRae said: 'No, Mary. Just his hands.' She made two fists at the ends of her thin arms and held them up like a shadow-boxer. One of them still clutched the hankie. She was almost seventy years old. I thought, I will never forget her. Never.

She told me what occurred next: Sonny vomited all over the hall. That was the stench: the mess in my father's stomach. Then he left. He just turned and walked away into the night. If I had returned ten minutes earlier, he would have been there. The slowness of the country buses had saved me from him. This once. Or, when you thought about it, it was Lindsey who had saved me by getting married to the podge on this particular day. I imagined her laughing and saying: 'Well, just this once I did. Lucky for you, Mary.'

I was trembling very violently. My teeth were clicking. I wanted to put my arms round the electric fire.

Miss McRae got up. She said she would go and make us some Horlicks. I told her I felt a bit sick, it was probably the Dettol.

Then when Miss McRae had gone to make the hot drink, I felt it arrive in my mind: the feeling of an ending. I'd planned to stay one more year in Swaithey, to retake the A-levels I had failed because of my insane love for Lindsey and then to try for a university far away from Suffolk and far away from everyone I'd ever known. And now I saw that I had to leave straight away. Not that actual night, wearing Cord's old camelhair dressing gown, but as soon as I could, as soon as something could be found for me – a place to live and a job with the post office or in a shop or in a factory making gliders, it didn't matter what. I had to transmigrate. Not my soul, which I knew would probably stay behind, hiding in the Suffolk lanes or in a ditch like my old tennis ball, but my body. I had to move it, or it would die right here. Not even Miss McRae would be able to save it.

Part Three

Part Three

10

1966

'Far from Crep'

The last feature in the old landscape that Mary saw was Cord's face at the train window. He was weeping from one eye, his palsied one. His Beatles moustache looked yellow, but his mouth was trying to smile. Then the train took her away towards London and Mary closed her eyes.

She got a job in a coffee bar, washing cups. The sink she had to use was old and deep, like Estelle's sink at the farm. The cups were made of glass. It was the era of ice-pale lipstick. Hundreds of cups had this little half-moon frill of candy pink near the rim. Mary had dreams of beautiful pale-lipped girls in short skirts and white boots.

Cord had said: 'Earl's Court used to be the place to find a room, Martin. Try there, old chap.'

The room she found was at the back of a six-storey mansion block. It was described as a bed-sitter. It looked out onto a tiled well of windows and fire-escapes on which the sun never fell. Remnants and echoes of other lives came up into the airwell, things that were not meant to be heard. And Mary liked this. She liked it when people screamed and cried and swore. It made her feel less lonely – as though she'd found herself on a great shipful of people, a ship of fools, and they were all together, safe and alive, out on a big ocean.

The walls of her bed-sitter were green. It wasn't Mary's favourite colour. She wished she had some brass rubbings to cover them with or some of her old sheets of marbling. She wondered whether she would be thrown out of the room if she painted it white and grey.

The bed in it was quite large, big enough for two people. It had polished mahogany ends and a mattress with a sag in the middle. In the first month she lay on one side of it. Then she moved over and occupied the sag. She thought, from now on, I will take possession of things and make them mine.

She bought two tins of paint, one grey and one white. She knocked on the door of her nearest neighbour across the landing and asked whether he owned a ladder. He said: 'No, girl, I don't.' He was South African, but his face was whiter than the sky. He enquired: 'What do you need a bleddy ladder for?' Mary told him about the painting she planned to do. He told her his name was Rob. He was young and thin with sandy hair. Mary said: 'What are you doing in London?' Rob said: 'I live here.' The word 'live' sounded like 'luf'. He said: 'Right now I'm running a poetry mag.'

Mary said: 'Oh that's good.' She thought the only person in Swaithey ever to have heard the words 'poetry mag' would be Miss McRae.

Rob said: 'Sorry about the no ladder.'

Mary said: 'That's all right. When I've painted my room I'll invite you for coffee. We get free packets of coffee sometimes where I work.'

She did the room standing on a pile of books on a chair. She painted two walls white and two walls grey. When she'd finished, all four walls looked the same. It was the sombre quality of the light.

Mary bought a pair of jeans. She put them on. She hurled all the skirts she owned out of her window into the sooty airwell. She could see them lying there, yards below: suicided skirts.

She bought the jeans from a shop in the King's Road. It was filled with hot light and music. In the communal changing room, long-legged girls pouted at their reflections. No make or style of jeans was right for Mary: she was too short. But the hard feel of the denim in her crutch was potent. She felt bigger than she was. She chopped off six inches from the legs of the jeans. She had seen people wearing them like this, with the ends frayed. When they needed washing, she lay in the bath with them on, soaping them all over. While doing this, she let herself dream of the pale-lipped black-eyed girls in their sleeveless sack dresses and with their sculpted, scented hair. They gave her their dark nipples to suck. They said: 'Let's have fun, Martin.'

She still hadn't seen the Tower of London. Only parts of the city were known to her. The rest was there somewhere, waiting for time to bring her to it. She bought postcards of the places she hadn't been: the Royal Mint, the Greenwich Observatory, Carnaby Street, Petticoat Lane, and stuck them up on the grey-white walls. She supposed you could live in London a whole lifetime and never go to these places.

She wrote letters to Miss McRae and to Cord. She thought, it's odd that the only two people who care for me are both aged seventy-one. In two of these letters she said: 'The main thing I first noticed about London is that the people here are mostly young. I don't know where all the older people have gone. I expect they may have moved to Suffolk or to High Wycombe. The only old one I see every day is the newspaper seller at Earl's Court tube station. He's been calling out a two-syllable word for so long that it's become another completely different two-syllable word, like in a game of Chinese Whispers. What the word was that he started with I don't know, but when I get more courage, I might ask him. Then he could return to it. And sometimes the things you first say have more meaning than things you think up later.'

Cord wrote back: 'At a fair guess, Martin, your paper chap

was originally saying *News* and *Standard* – so you see, four syllables can become two without anyone doing anything: it's called the Americanisation of the English language.'

Miss McRae wrote back: 'I was very struck by your thoughts on the paper man, Mary. Why not try to write a poem about him that your South African friend might publish?'

She began to hate her job, its repetitiousness, the futility of it, the smell of the water, being alone all day except for the coming and going of the waitresses with their trays of crockery. And one night, mainly out of her habit of obedience to Miss McRae, she sat at her table and wrote a poem about this – not about the paperman's Chinese Whisper, but about all her endless days and evenings spent at the deep sink. She called it 'Prisoner of Brown'. It was not until the next morning that she saw that what she had written, quite by mistake, was a protest poem.

A few days later, she ran into Rob, the South African, on the stairs. He was carrying a plastic wardrobe. She said: 'Would you like to come for coffee one evening?'

He balanced the plastic wardrobe on the last but one step. He looked round it at Mary. She could see him assessing her: flat face, short hair, short body, spectacles . . . She said: 'I'm not trying to get you to like me. I don't like men. I wrote a bad poem, that's all.'

She could see it was the word 'bad' that interested him. If you tell someone a thing's bad, they want to see it, to decide for themselves.

He said: 'What's it about?'

She said: 'It's about being trapped in things.'

He said: 'I'd better warn you, I don't like much poetry. Most of what we get sent is crep.'

She said: 'This is crap.'

And that made him smile. He said he would come for coffee on Wednesday at nine.

*

The poetry magazine was call *Liberty.*

Rob said: 'It's meant to be a consciousness-raising mag. All the material in it is meant to have something to say about political repression, but the trouble is there just aren't enough good poems on this subject, so we sometimes have to fill in with stuff about graveyards or Kafka or Leeds.'

Mary's poem, 'Prisoner of Brown', was never published in *Liberty.* 'It's far from crep, Martin,' Rob said when he'd read it and when he'd learned her name, 'but you can tell it's a first-time thing, hey? You're not at ease with the genre, not yet.'

Mary didn't mind. She'd only written the poem for Miss McRae, and as a kind of protest against the monotony of her job in the coffee bar. She didn't want to become a poet.

But she became, as she had somehow predicted, Rob's friend. She repainted his room. The colour he chose was red. They ate supper together occasionally in a Greek café. She told him about her love for Lindsey. He told her about his love for his country, to which he might never return. She described Lindsey's wedding. He described the summer sky above Cape Town. They sat opposite each other in the Greek café, staring at their separate pasts, and then one night Rob said: 'Give up the coffee bar. Come and work on *Liberty.* We need someone to help out. And we'll let you *make* the coffee, not just wash up the bleddy cups!'

Liberty was housed in a two-room office above a hairdressers. The hairdressers played music all day long: the Hollies, Marvin Gaye, Dionne Warwick, the Beatles. The stairs above stank of peroxide. Sometimes there were shrieks, whether of delight or horror, it was hard to tell. A sign on the hairdressers' door read: *This is the entrance to* 'Comme il Faut' *Salon.* Liberty *is on the first floor.*

In letters to Cord and Miss McRae, Mary described the *Liberty* office and her role in it. She wrote:

> I work with Rob and his partner, Tony, who is Australian. The magazine is international but not many nations have heard of it. I think we have more contributors or would-be contributors than readers. I am in charge of subscriptions. My desk is a drinks trolley that was here when Rob rented the office. I have taken off its wheels. I have been told to have a subscriptions drive.
>
> Rob and Tony are very nice to me. They call me Mart. Tony has yellow hair in a pony tail. He would rather be a poet than a poetry editor and sometimes we publish poems of his. They are about 'Abos' and lost land. The 'Abos' of Australia and the blacks of South Africa are the two groups *Liberty* is trying to help. Rob and Tony say the middle classes in England have to be woken up to the plight of these people. And I needed to be woken up to it, too. I knew about South Africa, but I didn't know – for all the years I lived in Swaithey – that the Abos were in a plight.
>
> I wouldn't say this to Rob or Tony, but I think the magazine is in a plight. I found a printer's bill for £197.3s on Monday and past contributors write letters all the time demanding the £5 we pay for every poem published. I said to Tony: 'What are we going to do about all these bills and demands?' He didn't seem flustered. He said: 'Stay cool, Mart. Sit down and knock off a few stalling letters, okay?'
>
> I like working here. I like coming in in the morning and opening the window near my trolley and watering the weeping fig plant and putting on the kettle for coffee. I like the smell of paper

that is with us all the time because of the piles of unsold past editions of *Liberty* that wait in my corner of the room for new international readers. I like learning to type. I like opening the brown envelopes containing the poems of hopeful contributors and trying to decide, before I pass them on to Rob or Tony, whether they are any good. One came last week that I enjoyed very much. It was about an elephant trapped in a concrete pit in the middle of the Serengeti plain. It raised my consciousness of what elephants need to live their lives. But Tony said it was sentimental and Rob said it was crep. So it was sent back, with quite a few others we received between Monday and Friday. *Liberty* is too poor to put stamps on its rejection letters.

It is also too poor to pay me very much. I get £11 a week and three of this is my rent for my room. What I eat is mostly tins of tomato soup, but we still go to the Greek café. And it's a strange thing, but it's in the Greek café, which is called Zorba's, that I have this strong sense of being in London and not just in it any more but becoming part of it.

Mary lay in bed, hearing the fragments of other lives in the dark well outside the window and she thought, I am as near as I have ever been to happiness. She knelt up on the bed and opened her window and leant out into the well and looked down. Long ago the dead skirts had been cleared away but she thought now that the start of her happiness had been there, when her skirts had thrown themselves out into the void.

One evening, when Mary got home from the *Liberty* offices, she found a letter from Cord. It said: 'There's good and bad news to tell you, old thing.' The handwriting was small and shaky. There were brown blobs on the paper, stains of tea or Wincarnis.

Cord wrote:

> The good thing is my eye has stopped blubbing on its own and seems to be back in line with its partner. No one has a clue why. Not the doctor. Not me. But that's the way of the times. No one has a clue about anything. Do you listen to that Bob Dylan chap? He has a whining voice but sometimes a whine can be just the thing you want to hear. He says all the answers are blowing in the wind and he's damn right.

> Now the bad. Your mother is back inside Mountview. She took herself there. It is called a voluntary admission. I went to see her of course (and selfishly wished you had been with me) and she seemed calm and quiet. We took a walk round the gardens, which she admires. I said, Est, tell me why you put yourself in here, and she said, this is home, my second home.

> I had a word with a person in a white overall. He looked like a senior type. He told me that your mother's kind of depression is like an illness, no different from Beri-Beri or measles. And they are going to try ECT as a cure. You know what this is, don't you? Electric business. So I said, I'd rather you didn't do that. I lost my wife in a glider; I don't want to lose my only child. But he said, It's nothing to be afraid of. It's the best answer. I refrained from mentioning the Bob Dylan fellow. I came away, because there was nothing else to do.

*

Mary folded Cord's letter and put it away. She walked out into the evening traffic. She had no idea where she was walking to. She was glad of the noise and the fumes and the neon light.

She went into a basement bar. She'd passed its sign hundreds of times. It was called Ethel's. The steps down to it smelled of seaweed. She sat down on a high plastic stool and looked around. The place was painted black, but lit brightly with thin pencil-beams of white light. Music was playing: Joan Baez singing 'Copper Kettle'.

Smoke collected in the light-beams and hung suspended in them. The faces Mary could see beyond the smoke were all women's faces. She ordered a half-pint of Guinness and drank it quickly, like Sonny drank it. And then she began to stare at her surroundings, letting the place fill her mind so that there was no room in it for a vision of Mountview or for any vision of the past. And the women stared back.

She ordered another drink. She saw how the black and white of Guinness matched the black and white of the place. She thought, no one in Swaithey could imagine that a bar like this exists, not even Edward Harker.

At the end of the bar was a woman on her own, older, smartly dressed in a lime-green suit. She was watching Mary like a lioness watching her prey. When Mary caught her eye, she got down from her stool and picked up her drink, which was a cocktail of some kind, and sat down next to Mary. She smelled of perfume. Her hand, holding the cocktail glass, had long, pearly nails. She said: 'My name's Georgia.'

They sat very still, side by side. They breathed the scented air. Mary thought, Georgia is a beautiful name, more beautiful even than Pearl. She said: 'I'm called Marty or sometimes "Mart", as in *Exchange and Mart*.' Georgia said: 'I'll call you Marty, can I?' Mary said: 'Names are important. Don't you think so?' Then she looked intently at Georgia and saw that the name was more beautiful than the woman.

Georgia said she would take Mary to dinner in Soho. They rode in a taxi. Georgia took Mary's hand and put it on her left breast. The restaurant she chose was Russian. There were flickering red candles on the tables and gold icons on the walls. Georgia and Mary sat on two velvet banquettes and Georgia leaned towards Mary and smiled, showing her large teeth. She said: 'Don't look now, but in that far corner over there is Darryl Zanuck.'

They drank vodka in small glasses. Mary felt the anxious part of her mind – the part affected by Cord's letter – fall in on itself and vanish, like a Black Hole.

She stared and stared at Georgia. She didn't resemble the ice-lipped girls of her dreams. She had no real grace. But it was enough that she wanted Mary. Quite enough. No one had wanted her before, but Georgia did. She was flirting with her eyes. Her foot touched Mary's under the table.

Mary thought, being wanted gives you power – just for a while. And this feeling of power is something magnificent. As Rob would put it, it is far from crep.

Estelle:

Sonny gave me a dog. He couldn't give me the baby I'd longed for ever since I held Billy Harker on my lap, so he thought I would be capable of loving a dog instead. It was an Alsatian puppy. Sonny put it into my arms and said: 'It's called Wolf.' I suppose he expected me to swoon with happiness and cradle the dog's head against my breast. But I felt nothing for it, zero, as they say on *Top of the Pops*. I let it drop out of my arms. Sonny swore. He's forgotten he ever had any manners and once held his cap in his hands and stood with his head bowed. I walked away. Then I turned and watched him. He picked up Wolf and sat down and put him on his knee.

He is the one capable of loving a dog, not I.

I came to Mountview because I was about to commit a crime. I planned it. In my dreams and out. I was going to take the train to Lowestoft and take a suitcase full of the things I'd need . . . But I see the magnitude of it now. I see the terror and pain I was going to cause. I saw all of this just in time.

And I have been rewarded. I am in love. My love is far away and never speaks to me but this is the way of the world. He is Bobby Moore, the captain of England. His hair, on the TV screen, is white. He has a dimpled smile. All that I care about now is his destiny and the destiny of what he calls the 'squad'. And that is all any of us at Mountview cares about: football. We have forgotten our lives and what was in them. They are filled up with dreams of England's glory. We sit in the dark and chant with the crowd: 'England! – England! England! – England!' And we have new enemies: their names are Pelé and Jairzinho and Eusebio and de Michele and Weber and Beckenbauer. It is summer outside but we hardly notice it. And even the nurses, with nothing to be cured of and with nothing to try to forget, you see them sidling into the room and standing still and watching and you know their heads are emptying themselves of everything but football. They forget time. They forget to remind you to go to Ops Wing for your treatments. They're sliding away. We're all sliding away fast. And we don't want it to end.

England are in Group One. We drew nil-nil with Uruguay. We beat Mexico two-nil and France two-nil. My love and my hero, Moore, is a visionary captain, so the commentators say. He knows how to read the game, how to turn defence into attack. Only his head is suspect, so they say. He is suspect in the air. So I want to write a girlish letter: 'Dear Bobby,

We have this one and only thing in common: our heads are not to be relied upon . . .'

My head took me to a caravan site. I could see it clearly: old caravans with peeling paint waiting in the hot sun. I could see the families occupying their little bits of ground and all the things they left lying about, tricycles, blankets and anoraks. And prams. Sometimes the prams were empty and sometimes they were not. Sometimes they were parked in the square of caravan shade, with a stretched white net over them, and under the net there was a baby, sleeping.

I know, that if I had gone there, this place would have been exactly as I'd seen it in my mind. My head is not suspect in this way; I can see things in advance of seeing them and know precisely how they are going to be. I was going to steal a child. I was going to buy tins of milk for it and nappies and castor-oil cream. I was going to take it to Scotland, to a wilderness where I would not be found. I knew this was a criminal act, but I also knew that I was going to do it. I didn't think about what would come after.

The quarter-finals are coming. Oh God. If Bobby and the squad lose, there is going to be weeping here. Even among the nurses. So I say to Sister Matthews: 'Have ready all the medication. Have stuff that will send us to sleep for four years until the next World Cup. And in this way, you will save on time and on tea and on the cost of laundry.' I laugh and Sister Matthews laughs. She looks at me approvingly. The staff at Mountview think if you can make a joke, you are almost well again, almost ready to be sent back to wherever you came from.

The place I came from has changed, changed. Even Grace Loomis has started to complain that the weeds on our land seed themselves in her fields. It is harvest time and Sonny and Tim and the combine and the dog, Wolf, are alone with it and it is beyond what they can manage. I said to Sonny, on the morning he drove me here: 'Sell the land. That's the

best hope. Sell to the Loomises and then we can all rest.'
He drove and said nothing. He's fifty, but he looks like an
old man. At the gates of Mountview, he said: 'Never.' Then
we stopped and he got out and handed me my suitcase and
he said it again: 'Never, Estelle.'

We are playing Argentina. They have beaten Spain, West
Germany and Switzerland. We are told they are football-mad.
In all the slums and back alleys of their cities, day and
night, winter and summer, their lunacy goes on. When they
line up on the Wembley turf and their national anthem is
played, they cross themselves. Like Timmy, they believe in a
Creator. But their Creator doesn't save them from a header
by Hurst. Their goalkeeper kneels on the ground. He wishes
he was not here but far away in his own country, in some
hot street hung with familiar washing.

On the day of the final, England v. West Germany, I
was due for one of my treatments, but I didn't want to go.
Because, after a treatment, you wake and you feel nothing,
no anger, no joy, no longing, no sadness, nothing. All the
love you had for anything has gone. You are still and empty
and white. You have no desire. You cannot believe you ever
stood up in the TV room and shouted: 'England! – England!'

I went into one of the greenhouses and hid. Tomatoes were
being grown in it and they scented the moist air. I sat in a
sliver of shade by the water tank. I felt afraid for England
and for Bobby Moore and his smile. My mother was a person
who dreamed of glory and she passed those dreams to me.
I'd wanted Tim to be a high-diver. I never noticed he was
afraid. And now I was waiting in a greenhouse for the hour
of England's trial to arrive. I thought, the worst thing to
happen would be a power cut. Not to see this, not to suffer
it, would be worse than seeing it and seeing it lost. For it is
only infrequently that I am able to care, one way or another,
about something in my life.

I had cared about the child. I had the room waiting – Mary's old room – painted blue and hung with mobiles made out of balsa-wood and glass. For two years, I endured Sonny's attempts at impregnation, until I saw they were futile. Then I planned my crime. The only thing that stopped me from committing it was a memory. It concerned Mary. It was a memory so distant, it seemed to belong in another life, not mine. It was a memory of losing Mary in a field, in darkness. She was lost for three hours – one hour for every year of her life – and Sonny and I were in despair.

So I remembered how it was going to be for the mother of the stolen baby. I saw her come to the pram and find it empty. I saw her snatch up the little pram quilt and hold it to her mouth. I saw the ugliness of it all and the terror. I sat down and picked up our black telephone. I dialled the doctor's number. I said: 'I want to go to Mountview. I want to have my old room, please, with its view of the garden.'

They came and found me in the greenhouse. They were understanding. They said I could have my treatment another day. They asked me kindly whether I had eaten many tomatoes. I replied that I'd eaten none because I was so sick with fear for the squad. And they said: 'Well, come along, Estelle. It's nearly time.'

Now, we're into 'extra time'. The score is two-all. 'Extra time' is a different quality of time, hung with doom, as if the whole world were about to end. There is suffering in the room. There are no more cries of 'England – England!' There is a smell of urine and sorrow. An old man who used to be a postman says: 'They're finished. Look at them.'

But I can see that Bobby is still urging them on. He shouts at them. His face is streaming with sweat, his socks are down, but he still wants them to attack. And they haven't given up: Jackie Charlton, Bobby Charlton, Nobby Stiles, Martin Peters, Ray Wilson . . .

I turn round to say to the man from the GPO: 'They're not finished. Not yet.' And in that second, while I have turned away, Geoff Hurst scores. His shot has hit the bar and dropped behind the line. A cheer goes up, round Wembley and round the room. A cheer and then a hush. The goal is disputed. The Germans appeal against it. On the faces of Haller and Weber and Beckenbauer there is a petrified look. The goal is allowed. Another, mightier cheer goes up. In the room, Sister Matthews is weeping. The postman has climbed onto his chair and is waving his arms in the air. And we see it come towards us again: glory.

We are at the end of what we can endure. 'Extra time' passes more slowly than ordinary time. Extra is short for extraordinary. I say aloud: 'They should resume normal time.' Someone screams at me not to speak. I put my fingers over my eyes exactly as I remember doing when I was told that Livia had died in the sky.

Then it's over. In the dying seconds of it Hurst scores again. It is won. It is safe. My love, Bobby, and his England are at the pinnacle of the world and all the mad of the shires and the counties and the cities are shouting and weeping their hearts dry.

I want to hurl myself, like Livia, into the clouds. I want to dissolve and become suspect in the air.

A Nose for It

Walter felt confused. His own feelings confused him. They weren't what he'd expected.

He'd thought, on that Sunday in Tunstall Forest when Gilbert Blakey had first touched him, and then later in the room next to the surgery, the room with a sign on it saying *Waiting Room*, he'd thought, I'm letting all this happen only in order to become an outcast, to separate myself from the world of polite front rooms and babies in salmon bonnets. He waited to feel the self-loathing that would follow.

What followed wasn't loathing, but elation and a feeling, at last, of being grown up. And here was the confusion: Walter felt happy. He hadn't expected happiness.

When he looked at Gilbert – every single time he looked at him – he found him entirely beautiful. Compared to him, Sandra had been pretty only, pretty like a gift-box of assorted marmalades, never for one instant beautiful, not even on the day in the boat with the bottle of Tizer.

He now saw his feelings for Sandra and his afternoons with Cleo as maladies of his late adolescence. He'd known nothing, only craved romance and then mistaken it for love. But it wasn't love. *This* was love: Gilbert. This was Eden.

But then – and this was why the happiness he felt began to slip away – he began to realise that his love for Gilbert wasn't returned. Something was returned, but it wasn't love. And so his confusion was compounded. Gilbert had started it all: he'd bought the convertible car, he'd talked about Kennedy in a personal way, he'd put his slim hand on Walter's thigh, he'd leaned over and kissed his mouth. These things Walter recognised as a kind of courtship, a carefully planned prelude to a love affair. And the affair was of long duration. Gilbert referred to it, after a while, as 'necessary'. But there was no love in it. Only what Walter felt. And now when Gilbert kissed him, Walter had a feeling of choking.

One evening, he tried to describe this to his lover. Gilbert was lying naked on the waiting room couch with his head turned away. Walter was kneeling beside him. Without moving his head, Gilbert said: 'It's because you let yourself *feel* things. Try not to feel. Try just to *be*.'

Walter couldn't not feel. He could slaughter a heifer without feeling or empty a chicken of its bowel and heart. But just to *see* Gilbert was to feel. He ached with him everywhere, behind his eyes, in the stoop of his shoulders, in his heavy feet. What he lived for was to be touched by him. It was not logical. He'd expected revulsion and an ending and neither came. Passion came and stayed. It wouldn't leave. A new summer started and passed. There were no drives in the MGB. There were only the meetings in the waiting room and Walter's obstinate, confusing love.

And he could tell no one about it. Not even Pete. Once, he would have tried to write a song about it, but a country song didn't seem appropriate to someone of Gilbert's class and sophistication. And lately, Gilbert had even started to complain about life in the country. He said Suffolk people were narrow in their hopes, he said they had no vision, he said it might soon be time for him to be moving on.

Walter's thirtieth birthday was coming. Sandra Cartwright had two children now. A hired man, with the word 'Mother' tattooed on his neck, had been taken on to help Pete in the slaughtering yard. Aunt Josephine came to stay in the house for long periods of time, scenting it with talcum powder, boiling milk in the middle of the night. Walter endured these things, but felt the awfulness of them.

He said to Gilbert: 'Couldn't we go away somewhere?'

Gilbert said: 'Where?'

Walter said: 'I don't know. I don't know the world.'

Gilbert said: 'No, you don't. If you did, you wouldn't have asked the question.'

Once every six months, Walter had to have his teeth scaled and polished by Gilbert. He sat, tilted backwards, under the Miralux lamp. The nurse crackled and sighed somewhere to the left of him. Gilbert's face was near to his, yet upside down, unrecognisable, as though Gilbert were wearing a mask. The touch of his fingers was familiar enough, though, and his clipped, lisping voice criticising the way Walter neglected his mouth. And these quarter-hours in the dentist's chair confirmed to Walter that he was at the mercy of something he would never fully understand.

Meanwhile, the ghost of old Arthur had stopped visiting him. Walter was grateful for this. The sight and smell of him had been grotesque. Yet sometimes Walter found himself thinking that it might have been possible to confide in his ancestor and that this ghost, with its rude behaviour, would not have died a second, astounded death from shock. The need to confess his love to someone was growing very strong.

Margaret Blakey noticed changes in her son's behaviour and in his habits. She thoughts he was attempting to conceal change from her and that he'd forgotten she had a nose for such things. They'd lived together a long time. Forty-seven feet of cliff had fallen in that mass of years. A woman who lived on a precipice was sensitive to alteration. But Gilbert seemed to have let this slip from his memory.

He was restless. He stayed at his surgery very late some evenings. He talked condescendingly to her, like someone returned from a far place that she would never visit. He appeared to her as a person on the edge of catastrophe. He had begun to dye his hair and his moustache. They were a brighter yellow, like sherbet.

She said to him one evening: 'I know you don't like me to say things like this.'

'What things?' he said wearily.

'I'm worried about you,' she said. 'I can't put my finger on it, but you're not your old self.'

He couldn't bear the way his mother so often spoke in cliches, as though she had never really learned how to use the English language.

'I don't know what you mean by my "old self",' he said.

'Yes, you do,' said Margaret. 'When you were calm and content.'

'I don't know when that was,' said Gilbert.

Margaret sniffed. 'If something's happened,' she said, 'I think you owe it to me to tell me what it is.'

Gilbert was silent. He let the silence last. In it, they could both hear the sound of the sea. Gilbert allowed himself to imagine the silence that would arrive when he finally left the house and began his life again somewhere else. It made him feel both exhilarated and afraid.

'Nothing's happened, Mother,' he said. 'Only time passing.'

On a November evening, after their hour in the surgery waiting room, Gilbert said to Walter: 'I'd better tell you, I'm winding up everything here in Swaithey. I should have done it years ago. I was too cowardly. But this decade is different.'

Walter felt as though he'd swallowed a stone. It was about the size of a potato. Its surface was smooth but its weight enormous. It was lodged above his heart.

He dressed himself. He watched Gilbert put on his trousers. He thought, the real Eden died from failure and shame, but this one is alive and sailing forwards. He will never give this moment another glance.

'Where are you going?' he asked. His voice was faint, impeded by the stone.

'London,' said Gilbert. 'I'm joining a practice in Flood Street.'

'Where's Flood Street?'

'In Chelsea. The swinging part of London.' Then he smiled his dreamy smile. 'It's time to swing before I'm too old. Don't you think?'

Walter had never been to London. He thought of it as a red and black place: red buses, black churches, red guardsmen, black gates, red telephone boxes, black water. He knew this image was inadequate, childlike. He said: 'What I think isn't of any importance.'

Gilbert took out a comb and began combing his hair, that he now wore much longer than before. He said: 'Perhaps it's better if we put an end to these meetings, is it? It's you I'm thinking of, mainly.'

Walter sat still, without blinking or moving any part of him. The stone was weighing him down. And he felt half-blind, as if there were murk behind his eyes or in his head; smog somewhere. After what seemed to him a long time, he said something. He said: 'What will happen to my teeth?'

He heard Gilbert laugh. Then the laughter died. Walter imagined it re-surfacing again in London, on the top of a red bus. Gilbert stood beside him, very tall-seeming, and touched the bald space at his crown with one of his long caressing fingers. He said: 'All of that is up to you, Walter. Everything is up to you.'

Walter dragged his stone-weighted body out of the chair and then out of Gilbert's waiting room and out into the black evening. The air hurt him. He felt his windpipe freeze. He wished he had had the final word. He wished the final word had been a curse. He cursed now, silently, yet knowing that Gilbert was far beyond reach: beyond reach of his words and beyond reach of his power – such as it had ever been – to touch or wound.

When he got home, he told Grace he was feeling poorly, with a pain in his chest. She threw him a fearful glance. 'It's not that thing you had before, Walter, is it?' she asked.

'What thing I had before?'

'That vocal thing. In your throat, after that Rose Marie business?'

'No,' said Walter. 'No.'

He said he didn't want anybody to fuss. Grace put her hand on his forehead. It felt cool, cold even. She said she would bring up a hot-water bottle.

Walter got into his pyjamas. He could still smell Gilbert's body on his hands. He lay on his back in his bed like a corpse, with his arms crossed over his chest.

Grace brought the bottle and gave it to him. She kissed his

head. She said: 'At least you can sleep late, love. Tomorrow's Sunday.'

He lay in the dark, weeping. He heard his mother and Aunt Josephine come upstairs and go into their bedrooms and then later he heard Aunt Josephine get up again and go down to the kitchen to boil her milk. She had told him that night starvation could kill you when you were old. You could wake and find yourself on the ceiling, looking down at your own corpse.

His weeping dried up and he closed his eyes. He felt faint with tiredness. He waited for sleep to enfold him, like a lover.

The following evening, he went to see Pete. He didn't mention Gilbert. He said: 'I'm in a life I don't understand. Nothing makes sense to me.'

Pete made strong coffee. The night outside the bus was silent. The white whisper of the Tilley lamp was the only noise.

Pete said: 'Anything in particular?'

'No,' said Walter. 'Only everything. I don't know where I'm going or why.'

'You're not alone there,' said Pete.

'I'm serious,' said Walter.

'So am I,' said Pete. 'Shall we put on some early Elvis?'

These days, the old gramophone looked like something that belonged in a museum. The sound it was capable of getting was old sound; it felt thin, night-starved. Walter wanted to give Pete a proper record player, but there was no electricity in the bus and Pete said he was happy without it. He said it was a mistake to believe you needed something only because others did.

They listened to a song called 'Workin' on the Building'. It was a Spiritual. Elvis had hired a backing group of gospel singers. Pete knew the words and sang along:

> I'm workin' on the building,
> It's a true foundation,
> I'm holdin' up the bloodstained
> Banner for my Lord.

Pete shook one of his wide, grimed hands in time to the beat, as if he were holding an imaginary tambourine.

> Well, I'll never get tired of
> Workin' on the building.
> I'm goin' up to my Heaven,
> Getting my reward!

It was while Pete was singing, when he leaned forward nearer to the gramophone and his features were harshly illuminated by the lamp, that Walter noticed for the first time the change to Pete's nose. One side of it had put on flesh. The flesh was pocked and fat. It looked stuffed, like a chicken's arse. Walter stared at it. It horrified him. It looked as if it contained something that was going to burst out.

Pete stopped singing and Elvis began a melodic number.

> In the early morning rain
> With a dollar in my hand,
> And an aching in my heart,
> And my pockets full of sand . . .

Walter said to Pete: 'What's happening to your nose, Pete?'

'Oh, nothing,' Pete said. 'Nothing.'

'One side of it's grown bigger.'

'Yes.'

'Well?'

'That's what a nose can do, grow irregularly. It's the only bit of us that doesn't stop growing. Knew that, didn't you?

The rest of us shrivels but the nose expands – even in the grave.'

'Someone ought to look at it, Pete.'

'Why?'

'In case there's something wrong.'

Pete began singing again: 'Out on runway number nine/ Big 707 set to go . . .'

'Are you listening to me?' asked Walter.

'Yes,' said Pete, 'I'm listening, Walt. But there's nothing wrong. It's just my nose doing what it's doing.'

Walter felt moody, defeated. He'd come to the bus to talk, not specifically about Gilbert, but about the way things confused and astounded him, about his inability to predict how anything was going to turn out. And now, with this fat nose of Pete's visible above the Tilley flame, he found himself confronting yet another mystery. He drank his coffee and was silent and Pete sang on, ignoring his sulking. Walter thought, it's *cause* I never understand. Cause and effect. I haven't the least idea why I wanted to marry Sandra. I have no answer to why I feel love for Gilbert and not loathing. And if I can't understand cause, then of course I don't understand effect.

Then he said suddenly to Pete: 'I want to write a song. I want to go back to that. Can you help me?'

Pete nodded. He stood up stiffly and went to his small kitchen to fetch some whisky. He had the feeling that this was going to be a long night.

II

1967

Mary:

My lover, Georgia Dickins, was thirty-nine. She worked for a weekly magazine called *Woman's Domain*. She ran the Problem Page. Her nom de plume on the Problem Page was D'Esté Defoe. She thought this a wonderful name, far superior to Georgia Dickins. And her readers liked it. Especially the barren readers. They sometimes put, as a kind of footnote to their Problem: 'I hope you do not mind my saying that if God is good enough to give me a beautiful baby daughter I shall christen her D'Esté.'

I thought it a ridiculous name. It sounded like a corrupted word, short for Destitute. But I didn't say this. I had to say enough hurtful things already. I had to say: 'I don't know whether I love you, Georgia. I would like what I feel to be love, but I have a feeling that it isn't.'

She would cry sometimes and her mascara tears would make her face stripy. And then she would catch sight of herself and say: 'My God, I'm a wreck. I look like a badger. No wonder no one fucking loves me!'

She taught me to swear and to drink Campari. She showed me St James's Park and Heal's department store. She tried to get me to love my breasts. She invited me to live with her in her flat in Notting Hill Gate, but I refused. I'd become fond of my building and of my grey room. And I didn't want to wake up somewhere else, in a Heal's bed, lying with Georgia.

She was proud of the Problem Page. She said: 'D'Esté Defoe is a woman with empathy. Her readers trust her. And she's a professional. She has a team of doctors and psychiatrists advising her. She offers genuine solutions.' She talked like this, Georgia. As if she were always advertising something. She told me her flat was nicely situated. She said London was the toast of the world.

I was going to be twenty-one. I was still small. Sometimes I made myself hang from a door lintel, like in the old days. I wanted to reach 5 foot 4 inches. I hadn't given up on any possibility, not even on growing. And now I saw that a moment had arrived for action. I remembered Cord saying: 'Without action, Martin, nothing can be begun, what!' He said this sitting beside me on the hearth rug making a paper chain. We were both of us drunk. Drunken words sometimes get remembered because they're unexpectedly wise.

I wrote a letter to the Problem Page. Every letter had to begin 'Dear D'Esté Defoe'. I made several drafts of my letter and then I typed it out in the *Liberty* offices, during a lull in rejections. This is how it went:

Dear D'Esté Defoe,

You may feel shocked by the contents of this letter. My problem is not one shared by any of your other readers, as far as I can tell.

I am a woman of twenty-one. Or rather, my body is a woman's body, but I have never felt like a woman or colluded with my body's deceit. In my mind, I am, and have been from childhood, male. This belief is an ineradicable thing. I am in the wrong gender.

I dress as a man. I loathe my breasts and all that is female about me. I have never been sexually attracted to a man. I do not even dream of Sean Connery.

Please help me. Please tell whether anyone else has ever felt this? Please tell me whether it could ever be possible to alter my body to fit my mind. Since the age of six, I have suffered very much and I want, at last, to take some action. I have no friends in whom I can confide.

I signed myself 'Divided, Devon'. I thought D'Esté Defoe would be attracted by the letter D. I had no faith in Georgia, but it was the team of doctors and counsellors she had mentioned that gave me hope.

The following evening I spent in the nicely situated flat. Georgia showed me a new kind of grapefruit she had discovered, with pink flesh. She loved new things. As she cut my half of the pink grapefruit she said: 'D'Esté had an extraordinary letter today. From a transsexual.'

I had never heard this word before. I thought, if there's a word for this, then it exists outside me, it exists in other people. I'm not alone.

Then I thought, is the time actually coming, is the date actually coming at last for the invention of Martin Ward?

It was difficult to concentrate on anything, on the grapefruit and then on Georgia's lips, tasting of Revlon. I wished I was in my grey room, sitting absolutely still.

Two weeks later, an answer to my letter appeared in *Woman's Domain*:

Dear Divided, Devon,
I have given a great deal of thought to your problem, and no, you are not unique. Others have suffered as you are suffering and have been helped

by counselling and, in some cases, by surgery. The first male-to-female sex change operation was performed on an American GI, George Jorgensen, in 1952 and he/she is now living happily as Christine Jorgensen. In 1958 it was revealed that ship's Doctor, Michael Dillon, had been born Laura Maude Dillon and had changed herself surgically.

But a word of warning, Divided, Devon. The route to surgery is long. And it is not a route that all can take. Your first step must be to see your GP and ask him to refer you to a psychiatrist specialising in sex counselling. Only he will be able to ascertain what path is the right one for you. Only he will be able to discover whether you could adapt to life as a member of the opposite sex. Put yourself in his hands and he will help you towards your future.

Good luck and *bon voyage*!

D'Esté Defoe

The person in whose hands I put myself was called Dr Beales. The teams of experts at *Woman's Domain* found him for me.

I had thought all people like him had consulting rooms in Harley Street, but Dr Beales did not. He had his consulting room in Twickenham and the journey there from Earl's Court took an hour and a half. Twickenham isn't really even in London, but in Middlesex. By the side of Dr Beales's house flowed a slow bit of the Thames, brown as tea. The smell of it was rank. It reminded me of the smell of the Suffolk ditch where I'd found my green tennis ball. And after my first visit to Beales, I had a dream of my childhood on the old farm. I was picking stones and dusk was falling.

Dr Beales had a face like a kitten, squashed and small but with bright eyes. He was about forty. His hair was black. He had a habit of pinching the slack skin under his chin. He dressed like a school teacher, in brown corduroy. He sat me down, within sight of the water, on a leather chair. He stared at me. He said: 'You're very small. There aren't many men of your height.'

I said: 'Growing is something I've been trying to do for years and years.'

He smiled. He had one of those smiles that vanishes the moment it's there, like English spring sunlight. He began to write notes on a pad. I imagined he was describing me to himself – the open-neck shirt I wore, my jeans and my jeans jacket, my heavy-frame glasses, my brown hair cut in a Beatles style by Rob, my look of dread.

He invited me to relax, to make myself comfortable in the chair, to look out at the water. I felt tired and far away from anywhere that I knew. The dirty river wasn't a consoling sight. I thought, if Rob were here he would say: 'It's a bleddy cesspit, Mart. Nothing can stay alive in it.'

Dr Beales began asking me questions. He asked me whether I could mend an electric fuse and whether I knew the rules of cricket. He said: 'Do you enjoy or repudiate domestic tasks, such as hoovering?' He said: 'Are you jealous of men's superior strength?' He said: 'Have you ever been train spotting?'

I kept one eye on the water, imagining shrimps and water snakes trying to have an existence there and drowning in sewage and floating to the surface, like feathers and like rope. I said that I had never possessed a Hoover. I said that I thought men used their strength to annihilate women, as my father had tried to annihilate me. I said: 'If I'd let myself be a true girl in my childhood, I would have been destroyed.'

Then Dr Beales said: 'I'd like you to tell me about your parents.'

I turned from the river and stared at his kitten face. I was about to say that I still had dreams of being Sir Galahad and going to rescue my mother from Mountview and from Sonny when Dr Beales gave me one of his fleeting smiles and said:

'You know that they're going to have to be brought into this, don't you? Family support for what you're attempting to do is vital. Patients whose families are opposed have to fight an almost impossible battle.'

So then I saw them arriving here: Sonny in his farm clothes, smelling of beer; Estelle in a polka-dot dress with her grey hair in a tangle.

I said: 'They're dead.'

'Ah,' said Dr Beales and he wrote this down – parents dead.

I was going to tell him that my father had been killed on the Rhine, but I realised in time that if he had died in the war I wouldn't have been born. So I thought then, I won't tell him about my life as it's been, but as it might have been. I'll tell him a story.

I said: 'I was six years old when they died. They died in a plane going from Southampton to Cherbourg. The airline was called Silver City. You could put cars into those planes and fly them to France. My parents' car was a Humber Super Snipe and it died in the plane also.'

Dr Beales wrote this down, too – car dead.

'What happened to you then?' he asked.

I thought of Cord and Miss McRae and I knew that neither of them would want to come to Twickenharn. I said: 'I went to live with a family called Harker. They had been friends of my mother's. Edward Harker is a very wise person and he knows about my predicament and he would come and see you if this was necessary.'

'And your adoptive mother?'

'Irene. I've never talked to Irene. Irene is very simple and good.'

'If she's "good", then she might be in sympathy with you?'

'No. It'd be beyond her. Beyond her understanding.'

'You can't be sure of this.'

'Yes, I can.'

'But she'll have to know, in the end.'

'You mean, in the end when I'm a man?'

'You will never be a man. Not a true biological male. It's important that you understand this. Do you understand this?'

'Yes.'

'You will – if you proceed, if I recommend that you proceed with hormone treatment and eventually surgery – be able to pass as a man in ninety-nine per cent of social situations. But you will not be a man. Nor will you any longer *be* a woman. Have you heard me? Are you keeping relaxed? Stay looking at the water while you answer.'

I looked at the water. A barge was passing. Its cargo appeared to be stones. 'What *will* I be?' I said.

Dr Beales pinched and pulled his bit of neck skin. I imagined him old, looking like a turkey. 'You will be a partially constructed male. The world will take you for a man and you will look like a man – to yourself. And so your internal conviction of your essential maleness will receive confirmation when you look in the mirror – and your anguish will cease, or so it is hoped.'

The barge had gone by and was out of sight. The river banks were washed with the brown waves of its wake. I thought, by the time the water is quite still again, my fifty minutes here will be over.

I said: 'Is this what has happened in the past?'

'What do you mean?'

'To other people like me – that their anguish ceased?'

'It is assumed,' said Dr Beales, 'from what they told me. But we are running ahead of ourselves in any assumption about you. Because for all I know at the moment your idea of your maleness could be a delusion or you could be lying. I know nothing yet.'

I said: 'I lied about one thing.'

'Yes?'

'About cricket. I do know its basic rules. My adoptive

father, Edward Harker, makes cricket bats and he taught the rules to me and I used to practise bowling in his backyard.'

'Oh yes?' said Beales. 'What did you bowl, spinners or bouncers?'

'Spinners,' I said. 'I was a spinner and by the time I was twelve Edward was afraid to face me at the crease.'

There was no way of getting to or from Twickenham by any means of transport, as far as I could see. There was no tube station. It was beyond the end of the line. I never saw a bus pass.

I had taken the tube from Earl's Court to Richmond and walked from there, following a map, like a lost tourist.

When I left Dr Beales's house, I decided to walk along the river on the old towpath where the horses used to go up and down long ago. I felt like a horse, trying to pull something, trying to pull along the idea that a surgeon could transform me and I would become Martin. The odd thing was that all my life I had thought this would happen one day, I had believed in it without knowing of any means by which it could happen. And now that I knew the means, I had trouble believing it. I think this happens to the human mind: it sometimes finds it easier to believe in the dream of something than in the something itself.

And I felt afraid. I thought, will Mary be gone utterly? Do I want her gone utterly, or only parts of her? Is there anything about Mary I should remember to save?

I came to some steps that went down to the dishwater river and I sat on them, watching boats pass. Not far from the steps was an old houseboat slung with tractor tyres as fenders and flying a Union Jack from a metal pole. An area of water between the boat and the bank had been fenced off with chicken wire. In the water, several families of ducks swam in little circles. Duck ladders went up from their pond to the dilapidated deck of the boat. There didn't seem to be anyone on the boat and I thought, well, maybe no one lives there, only these patriotic ducks. We always think a person must be there, at the centre of everything, and sometimes we're wrong.

The sun came out and the water was fingered by an unexpected sparkle. I didn't know what place I was in. It could have been somewhere called Ham. I put my arms round my knees and held on to them. The shine on everything had made me wonder about love. I thought, will Pearl for instance still be fond of me after Mary has gone?

The Sorrow Party

A letter came from Mary to Edward Harker. It was marked 'Confidential'. Irene recognised Mary's handwriting on the envelope and said: 'Is she in trouble, Edward? Is that going to be it?'

Edward took the letter down to his cellar and read it by the light of the parchment lamps. It asked him whether he would come to London and talk to Dr Beales. It asked him whether he would pretend to be Mary's adopted father.

'Well?' said Irene, when he came up.

'Well what?' he said stubbornly.

'What's happened to her, Edward? I deserve to know. I used to house that girl when she was little. I was like a mother to her once.'

'I never break a confidence,' said Edward.

Later, at supper, Pearl said: 'Is Mary really in trouble, Edward?'

He looked at her and at Irene, at their sweet faces. He wanted no harm ever to come to them.

He spoke gently. He said: 'Mary has asked for my help,

so that she can make some changes to her life. That's all I can say. She isn't "in trouble" as you put it, Pearl. She's just trying to find the best way through her life.'

That night Irene had a dream about Mary on the hot day of the Beautiful Baby Competition; it was a dream about smocking and beads of blood. She found Edward awake, reading *Gulliver's Travels*. She said: 'If there's anything *I* can do for poor Mary will you be sure to tell me?'

'Not *poor* Mary,' he said.

'Will you tell me, though?'

'Yes, Irene. Now go back to sleep.'

'I had a terrible dream. Read me some of your book, will you?'

He began, without comment, to read from Chapter VII of the voyage to Brobdingnag. 'The learning of this people is very defective, consisting only in morality, history, poetry, and mathematics, wherein they must be allowed to excel. But the last of these is wholly applied to what may be useful in life, to the improvement of agriculture, and all mechanical arts; so that among us it would be little esteemed. And as to ideas, entities, abstractions and transcendentals, I could never drive the least conception into their heads . . .'

He didn't have to read aloud for long before Irene had returned to her silent sleep. He knew she hadn't understood a word.

He put his book down and removed his spectacles. He switched out his light and sat there in the dark, as if waiting for someone or something to arrive.

He couldn't get Mary's letter out of his mind. It enthralled him. He was a quiet man with a secret passion for the unexpected, the miraculous. His need for Irene, the birth of Billy – these had been minor miracles. But what Mary was proposing to do was exceptional, quite outside most human experience. He thought, no one here will understand it, perhaps not even Irene, who loves her. Or Pearl.

He lay down and closed his eyes. What remained of Edward Harker's vanity was flattered to be chosen to impersonate a father. He thought, before I met Irene, I couldn't have played this part, but now I've had these years of practice with Pearl and with Billy. I know what kind of person a father has to try to be.

In her small room next to Edward's and Irene's, Pearl was doing Biology revision by torchlight. She was a person who liked to remember things by heart, word for word.

She was memorising the description of an insect called the Brown Water Beetle. In her Biology exercise book, she had written in her round, clear writing: 'The Brown Water Beetle has a brown, oval body and a yellow line just above the horny wings. It swims quite rapidly about the pond, in search of small flies, which are its preferred meal.' So now she was reciting this to herself with her eyes closed. She tried to make it sound like poetry or like a song. These things were easier to remember than sentences:

The *Brown* Water Beetle
Has a *brown* oval body . . .

When she got to the end of it, she tried to imagine eating a meal of flies. She thought of them alive in her mouth, trying to move, trying to buzz, then being swallowed and dying. Biology was peculiar. It was her favourite subject.

She was fifteen. Her lemonade hair had never darkened. People stared at it and at her, but she was indifferent to them. With her clear blue eyes she kept them away. She wanted to choose, not be chosen. And she wasn't ready to choose. Not yet.

She loved her room, the white curtains Irene had made for her, the pale green walls, her old dolls sitting in a line, her books in a precise order. From it she could see Swaithey church where, every fourth Saturday, she arranged the altar flowers. She was far better at this than Irene had ever been. She could look at a bucketful of greenery and flowers of differing colours and lengths and know straight away the order in which they should go into the vase. She told Irene: 'Flower arrangement has rules. Everything does.'

Pearl switched off her torch and lay down. Every night, after her revision, she memorised her future. She was going to be a dental nurse. She had already applied to the college in Ipswich where she would train. She was going to wear a brilliant white uniform and fold her long hair into a pleat and attach a nurse's hat to her head by means of kirbygrips. She was going to be the person who put the mauve mouthwash pellet into the glass of water, who placed a little bib round the patients' necks, who cleaned them up and kept them calm. She was looking forward to her life. She knew that every life should have a plan and hers did.

But tonight, she found herself thinking about Mary. Edward had said she was 'trying to find the best way through her life'. And she thought, perhaps Mary, even though she was always clever, has never had a *plan*. And now she's lost. Her mind's gone into a black place like a forest and she can't find any way out again.

The next day, Pearl decided to talk to Edward alone. She waited until Irene had taken Billy upstairs for his bath.

She said: 'Edward, is Mary lost?'

'Lost?'

'Yes.'

'What do you mean – lost?'

'I don't know. Can I see her? Can she come here?'

'No. I don't think so. But I shall be going to London. You could write her a letter or a card and I'll take it.'

'Can't I come to London?'

'No, Pearl.'

'Why not?'

'You can't.'

'Is she ill?'

'No.'

'*Tell* me, Edward!'

'I can't tell you. I've promised.'

'Break your promise. Tell me, just me.'

'No.'

'Is she hurt?'

'No.'

'I think she is. I think something bad has happened, after all the other bad things that happened to her when she was small. And I don't *want* this to happen!'

Pearl began sobbing. She thought, I've been sobbing all day really but it's just come out now.

Edward put his arms round her. He found a red handkerchief in his pocket that smelled of linseed oil and he gave it to her. He said gently: 'Listen. Write a letter to Mary and I'll take it. And I will tell her that you'd like to see her and then, perhaps, in her reply to you she'll invite you to London, for the day. If she invites you, you can go. She might take you to see the Natural History Museum.'

'She's had a horrible life!' said Pearl.

Irene heard Pearl's crying and came running down the stairs. Billy came after her, steaming pink like a pudding and trailing a custard-yellow towel.

Pearl felt herself transferred from Edward's embrace to Irene's. She was crying so hard, she couldn't speak and her chest had begun to hurt. She heard Billy begin to howl in sympathy and then she could tell that Irene, too, was weeping. She thought, we're having a sorrow party. There *are* such things.

She felt calmer then. She decided she would write a letter to Mary and she knew how she was going to begin it. 'Dear Mary, we had a sorrow party for you on Friday. We all stood at the bottom of the stairs, crying. I expect, if you had come in and seen us, you would have laughed.'

Timmy's Angle (2)

Timmy thought, what is to be done?

He was eighteen. He had not become an Olympic swimmer. He worked twelve hours a day on the farm and all around him the farm was in decline. He was in a race with ruin. Ruin didn't keep to its lane, it wore no number, it never tired.

There was no one else in the race. Sonny and the dog, Wolf, spent most days in the barn where the combine sat, covered in sacking against frost and rust. Wolf lay on the earth floor and slept. Sonny patched and mended old broken machinery. He put handles on things. He made plumblines. He sat on a straw bale and talked to the dog.

He was very thin. He hardly ate any more, only drank. In the clothes he wore and with his white stubble coming through, he looked mangy. He said to Timmy: 'The farm's yours, every square foot of it. You know that, don't you? I've kept it all going for you.'

Timmy got rid of the hens. Grace Loomis now had three hundred birds laying round the clock in an aluminium shed under bright lamps. Timmy told his father: 'We can't compete any more, not at this new low price of eggs,' and Sonny had stroked Wolf's head and said: 'They're a barmy lot, hens, anyway. Remember the day I saw them all standing still?' He had forgotten his accusations of witchcraft. At times, he seemed to have forgotten Mary's existence.

Nothing replaced the hens in their field. Sonny said: 'Put rape in. That's the coming crop.' But the field was simply abandoned. Nettles and horseradish sprang up around the vacant hen houses. Timmy stared at it all. One of his earliest memories was feeding the hens. He and Mary. Mary carrying the heavy pail of grain. The hens running towards them and clustering round their legs. Mary saying: 'Imagine if they were people and we were the Shah of Persia.'

One night Timmy remembered how he'd once seen his life as a 90° angle, made by the vertical line of his devotional singing and the horizontal line of his swimming practice. He had never been able to see what filled the 90° between the two arms of the angle, but now he did: he saw it was his imprisonment on the failing farm.

It was late. The house was silent and damp-feeling, as if autumn were seeping into it through the plaster. Timmy put on his dressing gown. He found an old school exercise book and a blunt pencil and a ruler. He made a drawing of his existence.

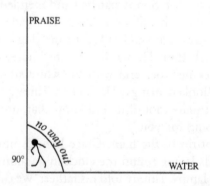

The sight of himself, a minute pin-man in a one-sided tunnel, choked him. He thought, I'm here because I was afraid to dive. If I could have dared to be a high-diver and not just a swimmer, then my mother would have been enraptured and she would have gone on paying for the lessons at Marshall Street. But swimming wasn't enough. It didn't interest her enough. She once said: 'Butterfly is an ugly stroke, Timmy.'

So she let my father step in and put an end to Marshall Street. I'd seen the horizontal line as infinite, but it has turned out to be short.

He sat there, looking at the angle. He could hear Sonny snoring next door in Mary's old room where he slept now, the room his mother had made ready for a new child that never arrived. Sonny snored beneath the baby things, a paper frieze of tigers, the balsa-wood mobile that tinkled like mountain bells. Estelle had offered to take them down. Sonny had told her not to bother. He told her he liked them.

Pity for his parents and rage against them alternated in Timmy. Now, face to face with his angle, he saw *them* as the two lines that held him trapped: Estelle the vertical line with her head in the sky somewhere. Sonny the horizontal, flat as the fields, going nowhere but hopelessly on.

It was the time of the sugar-beet harvest. There was good money in beet. People wanted their food sweet and sugary now. Beet and rape, this was where the money was these days – and in the poultry factories. But Timmy loathed lifting beet. The crop stank, it sat heavy in the soil. It was like gouging up something dead. And the machinery often broke. The conveyor that carried the beets aloft and tipped them into the lorry was a cranky thing. Belts snapped. Individual rollers worked loose and stopped turning despite Sonny's hours of tinkering and mending. The wheels of the lifter sank into the mud. The November rain had an icy feel.

Estelle was at home. She had entered a period of calm. She never cried or shouted. She spoke politely. She said: 'It is my intention to watch *Match of the Day* at 10.10.' No one knew how long this period of calm would last.

Sonny seldom went into the house at dinnertime. He sat on his bale in the barn, scratching the dog's ears and drinking Guinness from bottles. But Timmy always came and sat by the Rayburn and Estelle put food in front of him. Since

Mountview, she no longer baked bread or made meat stews. She liked tinned things and soft sliced white loaves in plastic bags. She was fond of Salad Cream.

On the day following Timmy's drawing of his angle, Estelle served him a plate of tinned spaghetti. It was too hot to eat. The slimy sauce had a skin on it. Timmy put his spoon down and waited. Estelle was eating radishes. She had spread a slice of bread with Primula. Her grey hair was in a bun. All her beauty had disappeared and Timmy thought, where is anything beautiful to be found?

His mind returned to Sundays in Swaithey church. He saw and heard the choir and saw the light coming through the Sower Window. And he realised in that moment that his original vertical line might still be in place. He could no longer sing like a girl, but he could pray. It didn't matter how prayer sounded. It could even not sound at all.

'What are you thinking about?' asked Estelle. 'The hens' field? Those little houses all still there?'

'No,' said Timmy.

That night, Timmy rummaged in the cupboard where all his childhood seemed to have been flung, item by item. He found a little leatherbound book, given to him by the Rev. Geddis when his voice broke and he had to leave the choir. It was called the *Daily Light on the Daily Path*. It described itself as 'a devotional text book for every day in the year in the very words of the Scripture, with additional readings for special occasions'. One special occasion was headed 'Disappointed Hopes'. Timmy turned to this and read: 'Although the fig-tree shall not blossom, neither shall fruit be in the vines, the labour of the olive shall fail and the fields shall yield no meat . . . yet I will rejoice in the Lord, I will joy in the God of my salvation.'

Timmy wanted to laugh. He knew that somehow, unexpectedly, he had stumbled upon a source of hope.

Something Different

Pete Loomis had said of his altering face: 'It's just my nose, doing what it's doing.'

What it was doing was growing a cancer.

It grew the size of a fat strawberry, then the size of a lime. Pete had always thought cancers were internal things. He thought they never showed. He thought anything that showed couldn't be a cancer, but something else of no consequence.

He was taken to hospital in Ipswich. The hospital was on a hill and looked down on the ugly town. Pete stood at the window of his ward and thought, what if this is the last view I see?

To take out the huge cancer, the surgeons had to cut away half of Pete's nose, including one nostril. They said that by doing this, they had 'contained' it. What remained of his nose was wrapped in a bag of bandages. He looked like a snowman with some white vegetable – a parsnip or a turnip – stuck into the middle of his face.

Walter and Grace came to visit him. Grace clasped her handbag on her knee. She had brought him some yellow chrysanthemums. She said: 'When you get out of here, Pete, you'd better come and live with us over the shop for a bit, till you've got your strength back. You can have Josephine's room.'

Pete didn't want to do this. He knew Grace was a good woman but she was good in ways that he found wearisome.

He said: 'That's a kind offer. But it's not as if I'd lost a leg, is it? I can manage in the bus.'

'I think I shall insist,' said Grace. 'Won't I, Walter?'

Walter had been very quiet. He had just stared sorrowfully at Pete. His eyes were wet.

'You'd better come, Pete,' he said now. 'Only for a bit. It's winter, remember.'

'What's winter?' said Pete, grinning. 'I could've woken up in my grave.'

'Ssh,' said Grace. 'No more deaths, Pete. One in the family was sufficient.'

Pete looked at her. The bandage bag made an obstacle in the middle of his vision. He looked round the obstacle at her lined white face, like a dried lily, at her neat grey hair, at her hands holding the handbag bought at Cunningham's. It's that I find repulsive, he thought, the awful precision of her, a word like 'sufficient', her mouth closing so tidily after it.

The Ward Sister had said to them: 'Don't stay too long. He's much weaker than he thinks he is.' They didn't talk about how Pete was going to look with half his nose missing. Grace talked about the battery hen house. She said bulk orders were starting to come in from lorry drivers' Pull-Ins. She said she had begun to wonder whether a second hen house shouldn't be built.

Walter said little. His bull's head seemed to droop. But he said he'd finished his song, the one he'd been struggling with for so long.

'Good,' said Pete. 'Want to sing it to cheer us all up?'

'No,' said Walter. 'Not now.'

'It wouldn't cheer us up,' said Grace. 'Walter gave me a rendition. It's a morbid song.'

'Is it?' said Pete. 'Morbid, is it, Walt?'

'Not really,' said Walter, 'not if you understand it.'

'And I don't, I suppose?' said Grace.

'No, you don't,' said Walter.

Then they left. Pete waved from his bed, but Walter followed Grace out and neither of them looked back.

While Pete was in hospital, Walter went to London. He took an early train. He told Grace that Gilbert Blakey had invited him there, to show him the Crown Jewels. He knew the Jewels would impress her. It was a Wednesday, half-day closing in the shop.

He got on a Sightseeing Bus. He sat on the top deck, in the open, with a drizzle coming down. He was given a little map of the route the bus was going to take. He saw that it passed down the King's Road, near to which he knew Gilbert to be. Part of him prayed to see Gilbert and the other part prayed not to. He didn't know which prayer was the truthful one.

He went to London because he had to get a glimpse of a new place. He had to remind himself that a world outside Swaithey existed. Swaithey had started to kiill him. He knew that if he stayed there, working in the shop, living with his mother, he would one day pick up a filleting knife and stick it into his heart. He'd known this for a while. He'd tried to recover from the loss of Gilbert by writing songs, but this hadn't been enough. He was thirty-one. Either he had to find another destination for his life or end it. He chose London because of the dark colours it was in his mind – red and black.

With Walter on the top deck of the bus was a group of Canadian women, wearing rain hats. Everything amazed them. 'My-oh-my!' they said. 'Will you look, girls!'

As the bus came down Whitehall, Walter decided that it was mainly the solidity of London that was so unfamiliar, so foreign. In Swaithey, when the October mists sat on the village and the tops of the hedgerows merged with the sky, you could imagine the whole place fading away in the dusk, never to reappear. But London felt eternal. It cast square shadows, black and wide. It felt like the capital of the world.

Walter began talking to the Canadians. The rain had stopped. They patted their permed hair. They told Walter they were from Medicine Hat, Alberta. They said Medicine Hat had no Tower and no Abbey; it had a good school and an ice rink. They told him their names: Mavis, Jane, Cecelia

Ann, Beth, Nettie and April. They said: 'This is our first trip, Walter. We didn't want to delay it any longer.'

'It's my first trip, too,' said Walter, 'but I'm thinking of coming to live here for a while.'

'You *are?*' they said. They had a habit of saying the same thing in a kind of chorus. Walter thought, they could've been backing singers when they were young.

'What's your line of country?' they asked.

Walter grinned. 'Country it is,' he said. 'Country Music.'

'My, that's interesting!' This was Nettie on her own. 'I didn't know English people sang Country Music.'

'Not many do,' said Walter.

'You shouldn't be coming to London, dear,' said Nettie. 'You should be going to Nashville, Tennessee. I have a cousin in Nashville. Married a Southern girl. They run a pharmacy. I could you give their name.'

The bus was travelling down Knightsbridge, past the Mary Quant shop, past Harrods. Walter imagined going into Harrods – and being swallowed up by an awful yearning and never coming out again. April and Jane said: 'There it is, ladies. Lit up for Christmas. Wow!' It was freezing cold on the open bus, but the fear and excitement of the Canadians kept them warm. Walter was glad he wasn't alone, especially when they reached the King's Road. He would have hated Gilbert to see the tourist bus go by and notice one lonely head sticking over the parapet: his.

He said to the Canadians: 'I have a friend living not far from here.'

'You do, Walter?'

'He's a dentist.'

'Yes?' said Beth. 'Well now, that's a thing I was once told in Medicine Hat, that the British don't care for their teeth. Is there any truth in that?'

Walter smiled. 'Yes,' he said, 'I reckon.'

'You don't floss, is that it?'

'We don't what?'

'You don't floss?'

'Make use of dental floss,' said Nettie.

Walter remembered these were words Gilbert had once used. He shook his head. Then he turned away from Nettie and Beth and looked down at the street. It was noisy and bright with people. Walter's heart began to thump. At any moment, one of them could turn into Gilbert. He might be wearing a bomber jacket or a fur. He would have changed, become more beautiful than ever. This happened in the romances his mother read: when the hero returned from his deeds on the Niger he was more handsome and irresistible than when he'd set out.

But the bus went on, past Flood Street and down towards the river and there was no sighting of Gilbert. Part of Walter felt as though he had suffered a cruel disappointment and the other part a deliverance. These feelings alternated, in waves. He held on to the seat in front of him. The sightseeing tour was nearly finished. Walter wondered whether he wouldn't stay on the bus and do the tour all over again, like he used to sit in Leiston cinema and see the feature film twice. But he knew that Nettie and Co. would be getting off and that, without them, he would feel lonely and foolish.

It was late when he got home to Swaithey. Walter expected Grace to be asleep but she was sitting in her armchair, waiting for him.

'How were the Crown Jewels?' she asked.

'Fine,' said Walter. 'Shining.'

'Did Mr Blakey show you a bit of London?'

'Yes.'

'Well, that's nice. Now you've seen it.'

Walter sat down. He felt cold and exhausted. He wanted to say to his mother, there and then, I can't go on here. I'll kill myself if you make me. I want a life of my own. But

Grace was watching him like a cat. Lately, she watched him this way from her booth in the shop, her eyes following his every movement. It was as if she knew what was in his mind.

Pete left the hospital in Ipswich. He'd grown attached to one of the nurses. He'd thought he was too old to have dreams of women, but he wasn't. He thought, perhaps one is never too old. They could cut off your nose and ears and all your limbs and your stump would still go on dreaming.

He moved into Josephine's room. He found an old Horlicks mug in the wardrobe. He looked out and saw the field with his bus in it, waiting for things to be as they were. He knew the wait was vain.

Grace fed him a lot of meat and gravy. She let him have a nip of whisky in the evening. He was in pain. He sat by the fire with his eyes closed. He thought, the only thing I'm looking forward to is hearing Walter's new song.

Walter didn't want to sing it again in front of Grace who'd called it morbid. He waited for an evening when she was out at a whist drive in the Girl Guide hut, now rebuilt in brick and used for Conservative fund-raising and meetings of the Parish Council. The story of how Mary Ward had spoiled a dancing show by appearing in wellingtons was still sometimes remembered there. But it was laughed at now. It was no longer shocking. People said: 'What a nerve that poor child always had!'

With Grace gone, Walter got his guitar and sat down in front of Pete. Before he began the song, he said: 'I've got to tell you something: one of these days, one of these years, I'm leaving. I know I'm letting down generations of Loomises, but I can't help it. I'm going to leave and that's it. It's final. I need to have a life before it's over.'

Pete nodded. He looked round the tidy front room with its chintz curtains and its shiny wooden furniture. 'I couldn't live here,' he said. 'You've done all right to stay so long.'

'I'm thirty-one,' said Walter.

'Sure,' said Pete. 'Thirty-one. Now sing.'

Walter tuned his guitar. He told Pete the song was called 'Something Different'. He said: 'I wrote it when I saw there was a lot of things I didn't understand, even at my age.'

'Your age is nothing,' said Pete. 'Now get on with it.'

Walter cleared his throat. He was proud of his song. He imagined future fans growing old and remembering it and saying: 'Wow, that was a Walter Loomis classic!' It had a wistful tune. It was in the key of B-Minor. This was how it went:

> I tried to find the answer to the earth,
>> I dug deep down to see what I could find.
> I dreamed some foolish dreams about its birth
>> And I woke up with its riddle in my mind.

> I tried to find the answer to the sky,
>> I climbed a rainbow and looked all around,
> Confusion was the thing that caught my eye
>> And mys-ter-y was what I really found.

Chorus:

Well, there's always something different hiding
There inside the something that you see!
The world is full of secrets
And I know that it won't ever
Give the secret of its secrets up to me.

> I tried to find the answer to my love,
>> I came to her and put the question, why?
> She said: 'Don't ask for what I cannot give,'
>> She said: 'Don't touch me now, don't even try.'

> I tried to find the answer to my life,

I lay alone and lonely in my bed.
I tried to paint a picture of my life
But what I painted was my death instead.

Chorus:
Well, there's always something different hiding
There inside the something that you see!
The world is full of secrets
And I know that it won't ever
Give the secret of its secrets up to me.
No, I know that it won't ever
Give the secret of its secrets up to me.

Pete was moved by Walter's song. He took a sip of whisky,
then he said: 'If my old friend, the Minister in Memphis,
could've heard that, Walter, he might've cried.'

Walter shrugged. 'Trouble is,' he said, 'my songs don't
change one single thing.'

12

1968

Revolution and Revelation

Cord was writing a letter to the Ministry of Transport. The letter would have a hundred and eighty-nine signatories. It informed the Minister that he had 'reckoned without the residents of Gresham Tears'.

They'd been told a new trunk road was planned that would slice through the water-meadows on which the villagers had gazed for four hundred and thirty-two years. The blacksmith's forge and the Gresham Cattery would go flying into history. The air would fill with a relentless thunder.

Fighting the coming of the road had cured Cord of his palsy. It had vanished. What came to him instead was rhetoric. He formed the Residents of Gresham Tears Against the Road Action Group. Its slogan was LEAVE GRESHAM ALONE, TAKE AWAY OUR TEARS. He told the assembling villagers: 'They think we're of no account. We have to prove them wrong. We may be called upon to lie down in the path of a tar-spreader. I do not rule out the all-night vigil or the long march. I, for one, am willing to contemplate the uitimate sacrifice!' The residents looked at him in alarm. They said they didn't think that it would come to that. 'This is England,' they said, 'not Hungary, Thomas.'

The campaign against the road was given, in Cord's mind,

a marvellous momentum by the events in Paris in May. He sat on his Yoga mat and talked silently to his long-dead Livia. He said: 'This is turning out to be a decade of protest and I wish you could see it. There's hope in us now. I wish you could see that. The dispossessed and the about-to-be-dispossessed (we, in Gresham) have found a voice. We're getting off our backsides. We're saying things we thought we'd never hear ourselves say. And even in Suffolk – don't laugh, Liv – we'll man the barricades if the need arises. In the absence of Parisian cobblestones we'll hurl sods . . .'

His mind was all on this, on the Road Campaign, on protest and bravery, so that the normal things of life didn't seem important any more. They seemed a bit futile, in fact. Cord sat in his garden thinking and dreaming and the summer weeds grew high everywhere and he didn't notice them.

Then Timmy came to see him and remarked on the weeds. Cord looked at Timmy and then at them. 'Oh yes,' he said. 'Well, everything in its season, that's the thing.'

Timmy seldom came. It was as if he knew Martin was the one Cord liked best. But now he had come and Cord could suddenly see that Timmy looked frightened. He stopped talking about the new season of bravery and said: 'What's up, old Tim?'

'Everything,' said Timmy.

'Everything how?' said Cord.

'The farm. It's finished.'

'Don't say that. It's your father's life.'

'Yes. But not mine.'

'It'll be yours one day.'

'I don't want it. I hate it. That's why I came to see you.'

'Hang on, Tim . . .'

'That's why I came. To tell you that I'm going to leave the farm.'

'Hang on . . .'

'Don't say I can't. You've just been talking about protest. I'm protesting, too. I loathe and detest the farm. The only thing or person or life I want is God.'

'Wait a minute . . .'

'Stop saying hang on, wait a minute. I've come to ask your help.'

'Help with what?'

'I want you to tell my mother and father.'

'Tell them what?'

'That I'm leaving. I've applied to theological college. I'm going into the Church.'

Cord took out a handkerchief and wiped his left eye. This was a habit left over from his palsy time. He stared at Timmy. The boy sat on the very edge of his chair, holding tight to its arms, blinking.

'Relax, Tim,' Cord said kindly. 'I was given a bottle of sherry by the Residents to thank me for organising the letter to the M.O.T. Let's have a sip of that and talk about it all calmly.'

'Okay,' said Timmy. 'But don't think I'm not serious. Don't think you can talk me out of it.'

'I wouldn't dream of thinking that,' said Cord. 'My respect for the individual increases day by day.'

Cord poured the sherry into two tumblers. These days, he felt reckless about almost everything. He had a sudden ache of envy at the thought of Timmy's youth and all the years lying ahead of him. He thought, if I were young I wouldn't choose the Church. Oh, no. I'd take Livia to Paris and hurl stones into the air. I'd run with her along the Quai des Invalides and watch her hair flying . . .

'All right?' said Timmy.

'All right what?'

'Are you listening?'

'Yes,' said Cord, 'I'm listening. Go ahead.'

Timmy leaned back into his chair. He didn't look at Cord,

who was taking large sips of sherry, but tilted his head back and stared at the ceiling.

He began to describe his 90° angle. He said: 'The shape of it is like the sties we make for the pigs out of corrugated iron. It's completely black and cold in there. It's mud. It's shit. And I can't stand up, even.'

'How long have you seen it all like this?' asked Cord.

Timmy explained about the two sides or arms of the angle and what they had once been. He said: 'No one can live their lives without light. Without the miraculous.'

'You'd be surprised,' said Cord.

'I can't, anyway,' said Timmy. 'I can't. I'd rather be dead. But my father won't understand. He'll think I'm letting him down. He won't understand any of it.'

'And your mother?'

'She would. She will. I don't know. But it's my father who'll stop me, not her.'

'How can he stop you, if you've made up your mind?'

'He will, somehow. Kill me, maybe.'

'Don't talk bunk, Tim.'

'He'll kill someone. One day. I've thought it for years. I never used to think it could be me.'

There was a long silence. Outside, in the weed-choked garden, all the summer birds were singing.

'Listen to that,' said Cord after a while. 'You won't hear the racket the thrushes make if we get the road.'

'No,' said Timmy.

'I hate blight,' said Cord. 'Wherever it turns up. And if you feel your life's blighted, old Tim, I'll do what I can to help you. All right?'

Caesar, Waiting

The subscriptions to *Liberty* were increasing. It had thirteen readers in Gibraltar. It ran political essays now and jokes and pen and ink drawings done by Mary to illustrate the poems; A lot of the poetry was about the Vietnam War. Mary didn't trust herself to draw faces. She drew the backs of people, running. She drew machinery and flames.

Her salary had increased. She was given a desk to replace the drinks trolley. Her drawings were signed 'Martin Ward'.

On Friday evenings, she, Tony and Rob would drink in the Drayton Arms. They would order a bottle of Bulgarian red wine and talk about foreign films and the beauty of Jeanne Moreau. Sometimes the wine made Rob think about his lost South Africa, about bioscopes and milk bars and Jacaranda trees. His sadness disgusted him. 'Sorry, Tony,' he'd say, 'sorry, Mart. Just ignore me. Talk about something else. Discuss Harold Pinter.'

Mary broke off her relationship with Georgia. She despised Georgia for desiring her. She tried to explain to her that she could only love women who loved men, not women who loved women.

Georgia threw a lamp at her. It exploded against the wall. Georgia began to scream and cry and her make-up dribbled in inky lines over her chalk-white face.

They were in Georgia's flat. It was still nicely situated but its owner was elsewhere in her mind. She swooped on things like a bat. She took her lime-green suit out of the wardrobe and tore at the seams with her teeth. She ripped it to pieces. She came from a family with strong teeth and strong hands. She even got one sleeve out of its socket. She flung the mutilated costume at Mary's chest. Then she started on her pillows. She stabbed them with scissors. She ripped open the holes and took out fistfuls of feathers and sent them flying around the room like thistledown on the wind.

Mary backed out of the room, but Georgia dived onto her. 'No one leaves!' she screamed. 'No one fucking leaves me. I'm D'Esté Defoe. I fucking leave *them*! I'm the one who does the leaving!'

Mary tried to take hold of her flying hands. She was much shorter than Georgia. One of the hands hit her face and she fell backwards into the sitting room with its pleasant south-facing view.

Being hit was the thing she feared most. It reminded her of Sonny. She had dreams about it.

She got to her feet and ran. She kicked the flat door shut in Georgia's face. She took the stairs two at a time. In a race, she knew she could outrun Georgia. She was wearing running shoes.

Letters from Georgia arrived. They were sorrowful and calm. They attempted little grieving jokes: 'I was Snow White, but I drifted.' 'You're a person of rare gifts; you never gave me any.'

Mary put them in a drawer. It seemed cruel to throw them away. Then she threw them away. They embarrassed her. She felt glad she'd never written any self-pitying letters to Mrs Ranulf Morrit.

Georgia started sending money. Mary returned it. It kept coming. It went to and fro like an unwanted thing. In the end, Mary sent ten pounds to Cord for his 'Residents Against the Road' Fund and sent a postcard of Jeanne Moreau to Georgia. On the back, she wrote: 'Your money has gone to charity. Anything more you try to give will take the same route.'

After that, there was nothing from Georgia. She was there in the magazine, of course. The advice of D'Esté Defoe poured out to her million women readers, week by week, but Mary wasn't one of them.

*

Her visits to Dr Beales continued. One day, he uncovered her first lie.

She had told him she never menstruated. He had looked at her suspiciously. He had written on his pad: never menstruated(?). But her first period had come soon after she'd thrown her skirts into the airwell, soon after she'd announced to herself that she was happy. She'd stared dumbly at the blood. She had never believed she possessed the womb from which it could come. Now it was here, a punishment. The misery of her years in Swaithey had kept it at bay. Happiness had allowed it to arrive. That was how fickle her body was.

She endured the monthly bleeding by disowning it. She never looked at it. She inserted and extracted tampons with her eyes shut. She told herself that this small flow was nothing compared to the tides that used to stream from Lindsey's body. She took aspirin round the clock for four days and nights so that no flicker of pain reached her. She pretended nothing was occurring.

Dr Beales saw it in her altered pupils.

She said: 'No, you're quite wrong. It couldn't be. There's no womb inside.'

He stood up. She had only been there for ten minutes but he told her the session was at an end.

She said: 'Dr Beales, it takes me an hour and a half to get here.'

'Good,' he said. 'Well at least you'll be spared the journey in future.'

She gaped at him. She felt sick from aspirin and now from dread.

'Since you are not telling me the truth, Marty, I am bringing this session and this whole line of enquiry to an end.'

She had to plead with him. She admitted the lie about her periods. She explained to him that it was a lie she herself still wanted to believe, that she had dreams of cutting out her womb and burying it in Antarctica. She swore it was her only lie and that all the rest was truth.

'What about your adopted parents?' said Beales. 'Have you told me the truth about them?'

'Yes,' said Mary. 'And I wrote to my father, telling him you might want to see him.'

'And your mother? The person you described as a "good woman".'

Mary took a handkerchief from her jeans and held it to her mouth. She felt icy. She could taste grey aspirin vomit in her throat. She excused herself from the room and was sick in Dr Beales's toilet. The thought of all the lies that were going to come and going to need guarding and watching made her feel so tired she wanted to lie down on the lavatory floor and sleep. But she returned to Dr Beales.

He offered her a Glacier Mint. He said: 'We'll leave it there for today. Next time, bring your father.'

Edward Harker wasn't fond of London. He believed the French understood how to set out a city and the English did not. But he came there for Mary. It was a hot June day and he arrived at Liverpool Street Station wearing his panama hat. His face was tanned from games of cricket in the back garden with Billy. He looked sprightly among the arriving passengers.

He and Mary rode the tube to Richmond. Harker gave Mary a letter from Pearl, which she put in a back pocket, to read later, when this day was safely over. She said to Harker: 'If you *had* been my father, this might not have happened.'

Harker smiled. He said: 'I'm pretty sure I know what Billy was in his previous life, did I tell you?'

'A wrestler.'

'No. An Indian princeling.'

'Why?'

'It's in his cricket. He bats with marvellous disdain. Like old Ranjitsinhji.'

They laughed. They got on a bus to Twickenham. In the sun, Twickenham seemed a nice place. The river had a shadow of blue on its surface. They were early for Beales so they sat on a bench admiring the water, pretending it was clean. After a while, Mary said: 'I hope you're not going to mind telling lies, Edward?'

Harker took off his panama and gave it a shake. He sometimes had the feeling, when he wore this hat, that there was a rodent trapped inside it that would start biting his head any minute. He examined the interior of the panama. There was nothing in it. He put it back on and said: 'I don't mind lying to your psychiatrist fellow. The thing that's going to get difficult is lying to Irene.'

'Well,' said Mary. 'Dr Beales keeps mentioning Irene. He keeps saying he will have to talk to her as well as you.'

Harker shook his head. 'I could try to explain it to her,' he said, 'but you know what she'll want to know, don't you? She'll want to know the *why* of it. And none of us really knows the why of it. Not you, not me, not the doctors. So that would be the hard bit.'

'I *will* know why. At some moment in the future. That's what I think. It'll just come into my mind in the middle of a silence. That's what I believe.'

'Maybe,' said Harker. 'Or maybe not. The world is packed with mystery, you know. We tend to forget this, but it's still packed tight with it, like water in stone.'

Dr Beales greeted Harker warmly. His secretary brought in cups of coffee. Mary didn't look at the two men, but out of the window, at the vacant blue sky.

The discussion seemed to go well for a while. Harker told Beales that, being a believer in the transmigration of souls, he had no difficulty understanding Mary's conundrum. But he was a little nervous. He embarked on an unasked-for description of one of his former lives. He told Dr Beales that as a lutenist at the court of the Danish King Christian IV he and his fellow musicians had to play by candlelight in a damp cellar underneath the state rooms. An open trap door above them allowed the King to hear the music, but when he tired of their playing he would kick the trap door shut and then the musicians' candles would blow out and they would be left in pure darkness.

Beales didn't seem interested in this story. He ignored it, in fact. He said to Harker: 'You say you understand – and I take this to mean an intellectual understanding – Marty's predicament. What I need to know is whether you are going to give your support to the journey of physical change and reconstruction she may eventually undertake.'

'Yes,' said Harker. 'I am. Mary, or Marty as you call her, had a difficult early life and I have always hoped – '

'You say she had a difficult early life. Why was it difficult?'

'For reasons she's probably outlined to you. Her belief that she wasn't, in her true essence, a girl, made everything difficult for her.'

'In what ways?'

'Well. In what ways? Well. The behaviour we expect of girls is different from the behaviour we expect of boys, and so the – '

'Describe it.'

'I beg your pardon?'

'Describe the difference between the two sets of behaviours or the two sets of expectations.'

'Well, I don't know that I can be precise, but – '

'Try to be precise.'

'Well. Take clothes, for instance.'

'Clothes?'

'Yes. Mary, always, from a young age, hated to have to wear a dress. My wife told me of one occasion, when Mary would have been six or seven, when the wearing of a smocked dress caused her great distress.'

'You weren't present on this occasion?'

'No. But – '

'Can you think of an occasion when you were present when your daughter showed similar distress?'

'Well. Many occasions. She used to say she looked ugly, felt stupid . . .'

'You used the word "behaviour". Clothes condition behaviour to some extent, but you couldn't define them as *being* behaviour. What expectations of certain behaviour in Marty's childhood caused her unease?'

'Unease? Well. Toys and games, I suppose. We expected her to play with dolls, play at being a mother . . .'

'And she refused to do this?'

'Yes. She wasn't interested in this.'

'But you insisted that she continue with this kind of play?'

'No. Not really . . .'

'Where was the unease, then?'

Mary glanced at Harker. He took one of his familiar oil-scented handkerchiefs out of his trouser pocket and wiped his face with it. It was hot in Twickenham. Mary felt guilty that he was here in this hot room.

Beales asked his question again: 'If you didn't insist that play be centred on mothering and domestic tasks, where did Marty's anxiety have its root?'

'We didn't insist. But I think we went on assuming that she would play with dolls and so forth and be interested in giving pretend tea parties and all the things which Pearl – '

'Pearl. Your real daughter?'

'Yes. Pearl loved her dolls. She had a pram for them. She tried to wash their hair . . .'

'So you never played cricket with Pearl?'

'Cricket?'

'Yes.'

'No.'

'But you did with Marty?'

Harker turned to Mary. His face looked petunia-red. 'Cricket? Did we, Mary?' he said.

'Yes,' said Mary. 'Don't you remember? In the garden. I used to mainly bowl – with that old tennis ball I had.'

'Ah, yes,' said Harker. 'So we did. So you did. So we did!'

Dr Beales was writing on his pad: Cricket(??). Harker blew his nose. Mary tried to remember what kind of bowler she'd told Dr Beales she'd been. She thought this would be his next question, but it wasn't. He put the top on his expensive pen and turned to Harker. He spoke gravely. He said: 'On Marty's first visit to me, she told me that in childhood you tried to annihilate her. What do you think she meant by that?'

Harker said: 'Do you mind if I take my jacket off?'

'Go ahead,' said Beales.

As Harker struggled out of his linen jacket, Mary struggled to remember how old she said she'd been when her real parents had died. She thought she'd probably remembered the two-minute silence and said six, but she wasn't certain. She'd forgotten she'd ever talked about Sonny, ever used the word 'annihilate'. Always, when she was with Beales, she found herself believing that Edward and Irene were her mother and father.

She stood up. 'It wasn't him, Dr Beales,' she said.

'What?' said Beales.

'It wasn't Edward. It was my real father I was talking about. He tried to annihilate me. Before he died in the Silver City crash.'

'He tried to annihilate you when you were four or five years old?'

'Yes.'

Beales turned to Harker. 'You knew about this?'

'Well . . .' said Harker.

'You didn't know about it?'

'Oh yes. I knew there'd been some trouble. Sonny was always – '

'What was meant by the word "annihilation"?'

'Well . . .'

'It's a very strong word to use, isn't it?'

'Yes, it is.'

'But not, of course, a word that a six-year-old child would be familiar with. So what incidents or feelings was Marty referring to that occurred before you became her adoptive father?'

'I don't know exactly . . .' said Harker.

'You've been her surrogate parent for fifteen years and you've never made it your business to find out what damage was done to her in early childhood?'

Harker turned to Mary. He wiped his face with his handkerchief. 'I expect you talked about this to Irene, didn't you? Not to me.'

'Yes,' said Mary. 'I don't think I ever talked about it to you.'

Dr Beales threw down his pen. He got up and crossed to the window. He stood there with his back to Mary and Harker, looking out. Harker mouthed the words: 'I'm sorry,' to Mary.

There was a fly in the room. Its mad buzzing against the window was the only sound. Mary thought, silence is all right when you know what a person is thinking in it, but not when you don't.

She stared at objects. She saw that the label on Harker's jacket read *'Milsom and Sands (Norwich)* LTD. *Men's Outfitters. Estb. 1895.'* She wished Edward was there in a Norwich clothes shop, free to saunter out into the sunshine whenever he wanted to.

She looked at the pen and ink stand on Beales's desk. It was leather and had a matching blotter. She wondered whether the ink well was made of porcelain. It was the kind of

possession Georgia might have boasted about, but it appeared
rather tarnished by lack of use.

Several minutes passed before Dr Beales came back to
the desk. He was smiling a secret smile, as if he had seen
something that amused him while looking out at the waters
of Twickenham. He looked affectionately at Harker. He rested
his elbows on the matching blotter, obscuring his notes. To
Mary's surprise, he returned to the subject of reincarnation.
The word 'annihilate' seemed to have floated out of his mind.

He let Edward Harker describe his life as a nun. He
appeared to listen attentively while Edward recounted what
he could remember of his nun's routine, his use of Coal
Tar soap, his fondness of the Psalms, the bitter cold of his
hands. Mary heard Harker's voice relax. He sat back in his
chair. He seemed to think that all the lying was over. But
Mary had seen Beales's smile. He would let Harker ramble
and then he would return to the subject of her childhood.

He didn't return to it. He continued to listen courteously
until Harker could recall nothing more of his life as a Sister
and then he got up again and thanked Harker for coming
and asked him to go back to the waiting room.

Harker looked confused. He stroked his creased linen jacket.
He started to apologise for his faulty memory, but Beales cut
him off. He wasn't smiling any more. He said: 'Wait outside,
please. Thank you.'

When he'd gone, Beales sat down. He closed his eyes.
With his eyes closed, he didn't look like a kitten or a fox
any more, but like a thin Caesar, waiting to have his head
modelled in bronze.

With his eyes still closed he said: 'By doing this, you've
set your cause back six months, maybe more, maybe for all
time.'

'By doing what?' said Mary.

Beales ignored this. He said: 'It means that all my notes
are worthless.'

He opened his eyes wearily, took some pages from Mary's file and scattered them over the desk.

'Why?' said Mary.

'Why?' said Beales. 'You know why.'

'No . . .'

'Because you've been lying, inventing, telling stories. Your parents are not dead. Your parents are John "Sonny" Ward and Estelle Maria Ward, née Cord. They live at Elm Farm, Swaithey in Suffolk. You invented their death; you invented this very likeable father. I conclude that you have therefore invented all or part of every single thing you've told me. This invalidates every session we've had. I warned you once before about lying. So there it is. You must find someone else to take your case – if you can. I have no more time for you.'

Mary felt a weight come into her chest. She thought this might be how you would feel – just for the tenth of a second – if someone had fired a bullet at you. You would stare in disbelief at your assassin, just as she was staring now at Dr Beales, and then you would fall and cease to be.

At the station, Edward said: 'I failed you. It was my fault.'

'No,' said Mary. 'He knew the truth all along. Nothing you could have said would have made any difference.'

'What are you going to do now, then?'

'Find someone else.'

'Will that be difficult?'

'It's all difficult, Edward. I wish none of it was like it is.'

Harker kissed the top of Mary's head. Then he got onto the train.

It sat waiting in dusty light and he sat inside it feeling old and a fool.

He waved at Mary, who stood on the platform, and she waved back. They waved because they thought the train was moving, but it wasn't. It was only being shunted a few yards.

They felt stupid having this waving rehearsal, so when the train did begin to move they both raised their hands very tentatively, in case this, too, was a false departure and not the real thing.

Mary went back to her room. She stood in the middle of it and stared at her possessions. For such a long time now she'd been preparing the room for Martin Ward. Her pen and ink sketches of war were taped to the walls. She'd painted the ceiling black. Above the cooker hung a photograph of Jeanne Moreau riding a bicycle.

She sat down on the bed and lit a French cigarette. She thought of the brightness on the river and the heat in Dr Beales's room. Her hope and her future had been in those places and she hadn't truly realised it until now, when they were no longer there and had no existence anywhere.

There seemed nothing to do but smoke and stare. It was Friday. She would spend the weekend staring at all her black and white things.

She had no plan. Only the eternal plan of becoming Martin.

She was in the middle of her third Gitane when she remembered the letter from Pearl. She pulled it out of her pocket and looked at Pearl's round, childlike writing on the envelope. She felt glad to be staring at something that was going to speak to her and not remain mute like the room. From some previous, dimly lit life she heard Miss McRae ask: 'What is this baby doing in my lesson, Mary?' And this made her smile.

She opened the letter. She wiped her glasses on her sleeve and read:

Dear Mary,
    I am going to send this letter with Edward. I know something is wrong, but he won't tell me

what. Please write and tell me. I've never forgotten Montgolfier and the universe. I don't want you to be unhappy.

I'm doing my exams. Biology is my best subject. English is my worst. I have no imagination. For literature we're reading a book by Joseph Conrad called *The Rover* which I don't understand. There are quite a few *sentences* I don't understand, even. One of them is 'Réal's misanthropy was getting beyond all bounds.'

Our main things in Biology are called Kingdoms. There is a Fungus Kingdom, for instance. The Animal Kingdom has a sub-kingdom called Protozoa. A fluke is one of these. A fluke leads a life inside other things, e.g. a snail, then a fish, then a human liver. I think this is more interesting than something like 'Réal's misanthropy was getting beyond all bounds.' Don't you? Think of flukes inside people!

Edward said perhaps I could come to London for the day and you could take me to the Natural History Museum. Could I? Mum has just said Pearl if you don't come down now I shall give your supper to Billy.

(Will go on later.)

Later

Here is some news for you.

I went into Swaithey church one evening to water the flowers and Timmy was there by himself. He was praying. I don't think he noticed me. (Sorry about new pen.) While I was doing the flowers he started to cry. I went and sat with him and the watering can. He just cried more and more. Then he told me the news, he's doing Theology in a Correspondence Course. He wants to become a vicar and not die working on the farm. I can't imagine him as vicar, can you. He's too small. Your father can't imagine it either. He thinks Timmy's just trying to annoy him. He's told Timmy he will never sell the farm as long as he lives. Timmy said: 'Pearl, he refuses to imagine what it's like to be me.' I said: 'I expect he wasn't good at English, like me, and has no imagination, which is why he is a farmer.' Timmy had no hankie. And I didn't. He had snot all over his hands.

I hope I could come to London and go to the N.H. Museum. And see Earl's Court, where you live.

I hope you are O.K. Do you like Brian Poole and the Tremeloes?
Please write.

love from Pearl

Mary read the letter again and then another time and then another. She didn't know why it was comforting. She read it over and over, on and on until she felt sleepy. Then she put out her cigarette and drew the curtains over what remained of evening in the lightless airwell.

She didn't undress. She got into bed still wearing her jeans. She put Pearl's letter on her pillow and placed her head on the round writing and soon slept.

13

1970

Estelle:

Nothing happens in Swaithey.

We continue. We listen out for clues to the world. The east wind blows in from Murmansk. Things pass overhead: jet planes; news from Iceland.

Then one day a tragedy takes place.

On a Friday evening, Walter Loomis took off the straw hat Grace made him wear in the shop. He hung up the hat and hung up the white meat-stained overall. He had a suitcase packed. Strapped to the case was an old guitar. Grace didn't know about the packed case and the musical instrument. She sat in her booth doing the week's sums, knowing nothing.

He came down, wearing a bomber jacket Grace had never seen. He put down the suitcase. He said: 'I'm going now. I tried to warn you about this a hundred times, but you were never listening.'

The shop was closed for just a week. Grace put up a *Notice to Customers*, apologising for the inconvenience caused.

During the week, I went on one of my walks to the river. It was a damp day. I saw Grace standing still under a black umbrella, looking at the water. She reminded me of a photograph.

I asked her into the house for tea. I sat her by the Rayburn.

Her eyes were red and dry. She said: 'Don't let me interrupt your afternoon.'

People are seldom too embarrassed to confide their misfortunes to me. It's because they think mine are worse. They think Mountview is a revolving bin like the Rotor at Battersea Funfair. They think we go flying round in it, damaging our bones, saved from death only by centrifugal force.

I made the tea. I put some flapjacks on a green plate. Grace put her hands round her teacup. She said: 'Walter's gone. My Walter.'

She described the bomber jacket, the suitcase and the guitar. She described herself inside her glass booth. She said: 'I forgot where I was with the accounts, Estelle. I had to do the accounts all again.'

She doesn't know where he is. He refused to tell her. He said he wanted to be where no one could find him. I immediately thought of a wilderness and old Walter building himself a willow cabin in it. My immediate thoughts aren't often the appropriate ones to be having at the time.

I said: 'What are you going to do, Grace?' She put her teacup down and picked up a flapjack and looked at it and then replaced it on the green plate. She said: 'I've sent for Josephine.'

She left soon after. I watched her walk over the fields and out of sight. I have never liked her. I have disliked her without knowing it for almost twenty-five years and now, at this moment of her tragedy, I see it plainly.

I watched what she did.

She hired a new butcher from Bungay, a man with a constant smile. His hands are neat and fat. She went back inside her booth as if nothing had happened. The man is called Arthur.

I moved Walter around in my mind. I put him in Africa, under a thorn tree, singing. Then I moved him to Kansas.

He and a gas station with one pump were the only upright features in the flat, yellow world.

Grace began to expand her egg empire. She built a new hen factory. She put in a thousand birds. One way of overcoming tragedy is to get rich.

Her sister Josephine moved in. Josephine kept the house. She drew the parlour curtains so that sunlight would not fade the velveteen upholstery. I met her in Cunningham's. She was buying elastic. When I asked whether there was any word from Walter, she said: 'I'm sorry, Mrs Ward, but I simply do not discuss that subject!'

The hen houses remind me of concentration camp huts. I can see them from the window of my room. England was once a beautiful place. Long ago.

Pete Loomis knows where Walter is, but Walter swore him to secrecy.

I visited Pete in his trolley bus. The air inside it smells like an old flannel.

It was evening, not quite dark, but he had his Tilley lamp going. It sighs and whistles. He said: 'Sounds can catch me off guard. Sometimes I think I'm back in Tennessee and the lamp is a lawn sprinkler.'

The wound on his face has healed. On one side, he has the profile of a monkey. He used to be large and now he seems diminished, as if he's trying to embalm himself while still alive. His neck is creased. When he pours whisky for me, his hands tremble. He said, most unexpectedly: 'You're still a lovely woman, Estelle. Does anyone ever remind you of that?'

When you've been in a place for a while, you aren't aware of the smell it had when you came in. I noticed this at Mountview. And I began to like being in the bus.

I decided to get drunk. It wasn't an unreasonable decision, considering everything.

Pete took my hand, the one not holding my glass of whisky, and stroked it. He said: 'Walter was a day-dreamer. A day-and night-dreamer. If you dream like he did, you have to get out and try things and take the consequences.'

I didn't contradict him. I used to dream of arriving at the house of Bobby Moore. It had a bell-chime. He came to the door wearing a ruffled shirt and took me into his well-exercised arms. But it was all reverie. There were no consequences except dreamed consequences of an erotic kind. And I regretted this.

Nothing happens in Swaithey.

I stayed in Pete Loomis's bus for more than two hours. Everything turned a shade of amber. I felt surprised by what I saw and said and heard.

I rolled out the comedy of my life. I said: 'We're losing Timmy. We're about to lose him. Just as Grace has lost Walter to the wilderness. We're going to have to give Timmy away.'

'To whom?' said Pete.

'To no one,' I said. 'To a vertical line.'

Pete didn't believe me. He thought I had invented this vertical line with the mad part of my mind.

'And Mary?' he said.

I said nothing.

'What's become of her, Estelle?'

'Pete,' I said, 'this isn't the subject any more. Timmy is the subject.'

'If you insist,' he said. 'But one day, Mary is going to come back. You know this, don't you?'

I said: 'All I know is that Sonny talks to nobody human now. Not to Timmy. Not to me. He talks to his dog, Wolf. He tells the dog what he wants for his supper. When he goes to the toilet, the dog sits outside the door whining with agony.'

We laughed at that point and refilled our glasses. I said: 'I told you it was comic, didn't I?'

When I left, it was dark. There was nothing amber-coloured about it. It was the deepest, softest darkness I had ever seen.

Pete didn't want me to go. He wanted to continue stroking my hand. I told him I would stay another thirty-five minutes if he told me where Walter was and then I would have to leave because it would be time for *The High Chaparral* on television. I said: 'I never miss that. I love things set in America, far away, with guns and dust.'

He said: 'Go, then. Leave an old man. I'm not breaking my promise to Walter. That's sacred.'

I waded through the darkness. There were no stars.

Earth stuck to my shoes and weighed my limbs down. I made a noise like laughter.

When the house came into view, there was one light showing in an upstairs window. Timmy's light. He sits at a desk he made out of chipboard, reading his way into a different life.

Mary:

After that letter she wrote me, Pearl got ill. She had meningitis. She was ill for a long time. She lay in her green and white room and had morphine dreams. I wanted to go and visit her, but I don't think the day will ever come when I can go back to Swaithey.

I sent her postcards of London and a record by Cat Stevens. Edward wrote me letters reporting on her progress. In one of these, he said: 'I believe that in her previous life she may have been a creature of the air – a dragonfly or a lark, she is so fragile and light.'

I remembered the day when I took her to school. I'd nearly dropped her onto my desk she felt so huge and heavy in my arms. But of course she *is* light now. She has got lighter with time.

During that winter, I told Rob and Tony about my determination to become Martin. We were in Zorba's, eating goat rissoles. They both took up their check napkins and wiped their mouths. They looked stunned. I said: 'Have a sip of Retzina before you say anything.'

Rob was the first to speak. He said: 'What's wrong with being a woman, Mart?'

I said: 'Nothing is wrong with being a woman. It's only that I'm not one. I never have been.'

Tony said: 'Heck, Mart. What a destiny! I'm flattened.'

But they grew acclimatised to it. When they did, they found me more interesting than before, as though I'd become an honorary Abo. They raised my salary. They bought me my own coffee mug with the name Martin on it. They saw me as one of the dispossessed.

And it was Tony who promised to find me a new psychiatrist to replace Dr Beales. I said: 'There is one condition: he must not live in Twickenham.'

Tony said: 'Don't be obstructive, Mart. Finding one anywhere isn't going to be a holiday.'

The one he found lived in darkness like a coelacanth. His consulting room was off Ladbroke Grove. It was full of tropical fish. This was the only illumination in it, the light from the fish tanks. In one was an axolotl. The man said, out of the green darkness: 'This is a slayer species.'

His name was Martin – a coincidence I didn't like. His second name was Sterns. He said: 'All my patients address me by my first name, but if you are uncomfortable with this, call me Sterns. It won't disconcert me.'

He was small and bearded. He had a melodic voice. He walked about while I talked, staring at the fish. The sighing and whispering of the aeration reminded me of the sea. No particle of daylight ever entered the room where we worked. This was his word – 'working'. He said: 'Martin, we are going to work on memory, on lost things, on the past. It will be the hardest work you will ever do.'

It was difficult to lie to Sterns, even in the dark. He thought my case was so interesting, he agreed to treat me without asking for money. I told him the truth about Sonny and Estelle. I described the day when Sonny cut the crepe bandages off my breasts. I told him about my mother's room at Mountview and her meaningless piece of knitting. I said: 'I'm lost to them and they to me. For ever, perhaps. Except that I still have dreams of . . . when I'm Martin, putting on armour and rescuing Estelle like Sir Lancelot and having her with me and keeping her safe.'

'And you know, of course,' said Sterns, 'that this is an unreasonable goal?'

I said: 'I know it, but I don't feel it.'

'I will help you to learn to feel it. Now I want you to start again at the beginning. I want you to describe to me everything that you felt and everything that happened on that day of the silence for the King.'

I began with that, with the sleet falling, with my prayers for the postage stamp. It seemed far away, in another country. I thought: I'm twenty-four; my life is a short one, so the telling of it will be short. But weeks passed and then months. Some of the fish died and floated upwards. Sterns's beard, lit by the aquaria, seemed to be going grey. And the repetition of my life went on and on and on. Then one day, Sterns said: 'Very well, Martin. I think it's time to take the first step. I think it is time to begin a monitored metamorphosis.'

'The male hormone, testosterone, will, when ingested into a body that is female, effect certain changes over a period of time. The most significant of these will be:

*

A loss of body fat
A reduction in breast size
An enlargement of the clitoris
The gradual appearance of facial and body hair
Cessation of the menstrual cycle.'

This was my voice describing a clinical process to Rob and Tony. We were in the office, eating our lunch of cheese sandwiches. My voice was unrecognisable to me. It was summer again. The Comme il Faut hairdressers underneath us was playing 'Pity the Poor Innocents' by Richie Havens. Tony and Rob stared at me for signs of facial hair and saw none. I said: 'It'll grow in the dark, like the greying of Sterns's beard.'

'How long is it going to take, hey?' asked Rob.

'Months,' I said. 'Or a year.'

I was afraid. I didn't tell Rob and Tony this. I was afraid that the things I had described to them so expertly wouldn't happen, that I would wait and watch and my body would stay just as it was. Every night, I took off my clothes and looked at myself. I was Mary. Older than when I threw my skirts out into the London night. Older than when I slept in Georgia's bed from Heal's. But still Mary: round face, rounded breasts, roundly hateful in her own eyes.

Yet on the very day of my first testosterone injection a letter from Cord had arrived. He had won the Battle of the Road.

'Martin,' he wrote. 'Go out into the street! Embrace the onion seller or the road sweeper! Remind them that the voice of the small man (and the small woman, come to think of it) can still make itself heard in this country. Tell them that the residents of Gresham Tears would not be moved. And now our water-meadows are safe.'

I thought, this letter on this day is a sign. Cord has got his victory and that means that I will have mine.

I waited. My veins were fed a new substance. I thought,

I must be nimble in my mind now, like the darting fish. I must be watchful and alert, but all I felt was an unreasoning terror.

Then came a day that I'd hoped for.

Pearl arrived in London. She brought a small case, so that she could stay one night with me. In the case were a white nightdress, a spongebag in the shape of a heart and a *Handbook for Dental Nurses.* She laid these things out on the floor. I said: 'Pearl, I want you to sleep in my bed and I'm going to sleep on some cushions and we can talk about Australia and the night sky.'

She is eighteen. She is studying A-level Biology. She tints her eyelashes blue. She wears her hair in two bunches tied with ribbons. Her voice has a Suffolk lilt. She hugs me and I hug her back. When I hug her, I want to cry.

She has never been to London before. She says: 'Mary, don't let me get lost, will you?'

It is Saturday. The sun is shining on the litter of the Earl's Court Road. We walk down the street arm in arm on our way to the Natural History Museum. Pearl looks all around her in wonder, as if she'd landed on the moon.

We go into the museum and stand by the plaster dinosaur skeleton, *Diplodocus carnegii.* Large things like this make me feel solemn but Pearl says: 'They were ridiculous, weren't they? One theory is they were frozen out of existence.'

I've never been in the museum before and nor has Pearl of course, but it's she who leads me around and points things out to me. There is Biology all around. Pearl's little nose gets scarlet with excitement. Heaven, for Pearl, would be full of flying frogs and milkweed butterflies.

The things we learn in a single afternoon remind me that we live on the planet of the unexpected. I now know that a centipede can run faster than a cheetah. I know that in Peru there is a snake that milks cows. I know that the Giant

Sequoia tree of California can live for fifteen hundred years. I know that the Natterjack toad and the lime tree appeared in England ten thousand years ago. I know that things believed to be extinct can suddenly reappear and that eminent biologists can die in their laboratories from surprise. I know that species can cross the world's oceans hidden in crates of bananas or bales of rubber and that such a one is the treefrog from the rainforests of Honduras which has colonised a forest near Canterbury.

I say to Pearl: 'It gives me hope, to realise all this.'

'Hope for what?' she says.

She is wearing a short pink skirt and long white socks to her knees and white shoes that fasten with a pink button. The other visitors to the museum stare at her as she passes.

'In what is possible,' I reply.

The last thing we see is a display of fishes. The living fish swim around the coral reef of Australia, but these are models, hung from the roof in a glass case on pieces of thread. You aren't meant to notice the threads, but you do.

A child wearing a plastic policeman's helmet says to his father: 'Are they puppets?' The father doesn't know how to reply. After a while he says: 'No.'

Pearl says: 'Look at their fantastic names.'

Carpet Shark. Leafy Sea Dragon. Moonish Idol. Flying Gumard . . .

We stand together and read all the names out. We sound very serious, as though we're reciting the names of the dead on the fields of France. Then we laugh and I remember Pearl's laughter in the continent of long ago and think, it crossed over to me on a ship, hidden in a fruit crate.

We have supper in Zorba's. The Greek waiters, Nico and Ari, treat Pearl as though she were Melina Mercouri. They kiss her hand.

She eats a mountain of kebabs. She doesn't seem to notice

how many. I eat some vine leaves with rice and watch over her.

Suddenly she realises how much she's eaten and stops. She says: 'Tell me about your life, Mary.'

I feel a chill coming into my arms, a kind of cramp or stiffness.

I talk about *Liberty*. I tell her that it survives because of the Vietnam War, that it sells in Amsterdam and Luxembourg and Toronto. I describe Tony and Rob and the indoor plants and my old desk, the drinks trolley. I tell her I'm lucky to be working for *Liberty* and to have the chance to draw.

After a while, when Pearl has eaten a sweetmeat full of honey, she says: 'When Edward came to see you that time, he said he was going to help you make changes in your life. Did you make them?'

I massage the tops of my arms. I say: 'Yes.'

She takes one of the bows out of her hair and it falls softly round her face. She says: 'They were secret, Edward told me. You never used to have secrets from me.'

I sigh. I call Ari and order some coffee. Ari says to me: 'Your friend, Mart. Launching a thousand ships, eh?'

'Yes,' I reply. 'At least a thousand.'

Pearl smiles, then lowers her eyes. Earlier she'd told me: 'There's only one boy I like at school. His name's Clive. He wants to be a tree surgeon.'

When the syrupy coffee arrives, I say to Pearl: 'Do you think we could always be fond of each other, no matter what?'

'You can't say "no matter what",' she replies. 'You don't know what the "what" could be.'

'You're right,' I say. 'You don't.'

There's a silence for a minute and then Pearl asks again: 'Was it a secret?'

'Yes,' I say. 'But later, I might tell you it. When we're at home. Before we go to sleep.'

'You said "home",' she says. 'Don't you still think of the farm as home?'

'No,' I say.

She gets into her white nightdress. She takes a sponge out of her heartshaped spongebag and washes the blue mascara off her eyelashes. She cleans her teeth very meticulously. I undress in stages, hiding every bit of my body.

She gets into my mahogany bed and I put some cushions on the floor and lie on them and cover myself with a blanket. Pearl says: 'Shall I read you a bit from my *Handbook for Dental Nurses*?'

It feels quiet in the building, as if everyone else were elsewhere.

I say: 'Yes. Go on.'

'I'll start at the beginning,' she says.

'Fine,' I say.

She reads: 'The dental nurse, or the dental surgery assistant as she is properly termed, is normally the first person to receive a patient. This is an important occasion, as the patient's confidence in the dentist himself will be influenced by the appearance and manner of the dental surgery assistant.

'She should therefore be smartly dressed. Attention to personal hygiene is essential, not only as it affects appearance, but also to ensure good results and prevent infection in the surgery.

'A calm, courteous and sympathetic manner, combined with a cheerful disposition, is an obvious necessity when dealing with anxious patients. The dental surgery assistant must ideally keep cool under all conditions and cope with any emergency which may arise . . .'

After a while I turn out the light.

We lie in the dark in my ship of fools. Down below in the airwell we hear someone scream.

I let time pass. My heart is beating.

Then I begin to tell Pearl about my life: about the day of the two-minute silence, about my jealousy of Timmy and my hatred of Mary. I tell her about Dr Beales and the dirty river and the lies. I don't mention Lindsey Stevens or my affair with Georgia. I pass on to describing my ally, Sterns, and his killer axolotl and his untroubled voice. Last of all, I say: 'With the injections I'm having now, my time as Mary is going to come to an end.'

Pearl is so quiet I being to wonder whether she's still there or whether I'm talking to an empty room.

Then, I hear her crying.

'Listen, Pearl,' I say. 'It's no stranger than millions of other things on earth. Don't despise me for it. You don't despise a tree for living for fifteen centuries or a treefrog for turning up in Kent. These things are just quirks of place and time, and this is what I am and have always been.'

She doesn't reply. She just goes on weeping.

'Pearl,' I say. 'Say something.'

'I can't,' she says, 'I feel so sad.'

'Listen,' I say, 'if you never want to see me again, I'll understand. I expect I've disgusted you. But even if I don't see you, even if we never eat another Greek meal together or ever again mention Montgolfier, you'll always be precious to me – my precious thing. Nothing will alter that.'

'It isn't that,' she says.

'Isn't what?'

'Isn't that I'm disgusted. Not really. It's just that . . .'

'What?'

'It was Mary I cared about. And you're killing her.'

'I know,' I say, 'but I can't not do it, Pearl. I can't. Even for you.'

The night sails on and we talk all through it. Pearl says she's too frightened to sleep. Frightened of the world.

*

The next day she goes home. Her white shoes look scuffed. There is no blue on her lashes. And when I put a kiss on her cheek in the corridor of the train, she turns away from me. She says: 'It's so sad, Mary,' and she doesn't look back.

Facing West

Two women sat alone in their houses and looked at the future. One of the women was Margaret Blakey. The other was Margaret McRae.

In the time since Gilbert's departure, the distance between Margaret Blakey's house and the Minsmere cliffs had decreased by three feet and two inches. The winters had been fierce. Hurricanes had come dangerously close. Margaret Blakey had read in the *National Geographic Magazine* that, all over the world, the edges of places were falling into the sea.

But she no longer minded. With Gilbert gone, it seemed like a thing of no significance. She sometimes thought it would be perfectly acceptable to be swept away in the middle of the night. She imagined it, in fact: the house leaning and moving in the wind, the sandstone crumbling like cake, her photographs of Gilbert falling off the walls and exploding, her bed starting to fly.

He wrote to her every week. He was making money. He sent her peculiar presents: an African mask, a coil of springs you were supposed to throw from hand to hand, a tea-towel imprinted with a picture of Hampton Court. He said in one letter: 'The nearest I will get to paradise is Flood Street,' and this, too, she considered very odd. She assumed there must be a new Gilbert replacing the one she'd known. And he inhabited a new world, a world in which people liked to spend time throwing a steel spring from hand to hand. Clearly, he preferred this kind of world to the old kind. It wasn't unreasonable. He was still young. He'd got tired of living on a precipice.

Margaret Blakey decided to stop measuring the distance between her house and the cliff edge. And she did something else. She moved out of her bedroom, which was at the front of the house, and into the back bedroom that had no view of the sea. From here, she could see fields and a wood and beyond the wood a church spire. She liked this landscape. She could imagine the rest of England spreading out and on beyond the spire. Out and on.

She said to her few friends: 'I think, as one gets older, it's perfectly all right to turn one's back on certain things.'

Miss McRae was making plans.

Her cottage was up for sale. She had finally succumbed to her homesickness for Scotland. She was going to live with her sister Dorothy near Oban. On Miss McRae's mantelpiece was a snap of Dorothy's bungalow. It was called Shepherd's Rest. It had a garden of marigolds and fruit cages. It looked out over Seal Sound, where colonies of mussels clung on at low tide. From its small patio you could watch the sun go down behind Seal Island. At night you could see the distant flash of the Oban lighthouse.

She was seventy-seven. She seldom gave death a thought. What she thought about were the walks she and her sister would take, through forests and over heather. She thought about the sound of curlews and gulls and the smell of the sea. She said, more than once: 'I have had a fortunate life.'

She had bought her cottage in Swaithey for £300. The estate agents told her it was now worth £7,000.

A young couple from London said they had fallen in love with it. They agreed to pay £6,500.

Miss McRae took up her knitting and thought about all this

money. She knew that she and Dorothy would live simply. They would make stews and eat them slowly, making them last several days. They would grow their own vegetables. She would knit them sweaters and gloves. Shepherd's Rest was a small place, not expensive to light, heated by electricity that turned itself on ,when you were asleep.

She put her knitting aside and sat down at her desk. She took up her fountain pen. She saw from the way other people wrote that fountain pens were becoming artefacts of the past. She thought, on the west coast of Scotland the gulf between past and present is not as wide as it is in England.

She wrote a letter to Mary. As she wrote, she remembered sitting by the electric fire with her and reading *King Lear* aloud. She remembered that one night a storm had rolled in over Swaithey and that Mary had said to her: 'I believe in all this. Don't you, Miss McRae?'

'All what, dear?' she'd asked.

The lightning had come in long and short flashes, like signals from a ship.

'In Lear,' said Mary. 'That all these things could happen.' Miss McRae put on her glasses.

> My dear Mary, [she wrote]
>
> I was pleased to get your last letter and to know that *Liberty* now sells in Adelaide. Thank you also for your very fine sketch of Lambeth Bridge. You draw so well now.
>
> As you know from my last of 2nd August, my plans for my return to Scotland are far advanced and despite my long years in Swaithey, I have no regrets about leaving. Am I being sentimental when I say that I think the place where one is born remains obstinately in one's heart for all time?
>
> Now, the real business of this letter. I have been very fortunate to sell this cottage for a large sum

to some nice young people from Putney. Dorothy and I will live quite happily in Shepherd's Rest on our pensions. (Dorothy, you may well recall, was a stenographer at the M.O.D. and enjoys a generous Civil Service old age stipend.) And so, dear, I am going to be in the fortunate position of being able to send you some money. I have in mind £1,000 and I would like you to know that it gives me enormous pleasure to make this gift. You are the nearest thing I have to a child of my own and your years with me in Swaithey were most happy ones for me – years I will never forget.

I know only too well that you don't like accepting presents, but I shall be very saddened if you do not accept mine. Life is a precarious business, as we understood from all our readings of Shakespeare! One does not know what the future holds. Perhaps you will never need to make use of the £1,000, but then again the day might come when it would seem like a gift from the sky. May I suggest you invest it in a Building Society so that it will be safe until such a day arrives?

I will look forward to hearing from you and to receiving what I believe is called the 'go-ahead'.

    With affectionate regards,
        Margaret McRae

She read through her letter several times and then sealed it. She went to bed. She took up a volume of Thomas Hardy's poems that she had bought at the Swaithey Bring-And-Buy for a shilling. She knew Hardy was unfashionable and that he'd treated both of his wives rather badly but this didn't prevent her admiring most of his work.

She lay in her narrow bed with the sheet very tight across her frame, memorising bits of Hardy and feeling perfectly at peace. She remembered saying to Mary: 'It is worth learning things by heart. Then they're there later, when you're ready to understand them.'

She heard an owl call out from the line of beeches that sheltered the village from the north winds. She thought of Dorothy asleep on her hillside above the sea. She thought of her beginnings in the Oban lighthouse and of her end, looking at Seal Island and at Mull beyond. She thought about the circularity of nature and the symmetry of her own life. She pitied Hardy – his head burled in one place, his heart in another. She put his body back together again and sat him down in a Dorset field to watch and listen and record:

These are brand new birds of twelvemonths' growing,
Which a year ago, or less than twain,
    No finches were, nor nightingales,
      Nor thrushes,
    But only particles of grain,
     And earth, and air, and rain.

14

1971

As Far As It Goes

Teviotts Theological College stood on windswept Sussex downland five miles from Brighton and the sea.

The Principal of Tevious, Dr David Tate, was a large man with flabby lips and a hesitant walk. He used a bitter-smelling hair oil. He was a high churchman with a distaste for the new spirit of liberalism – or what he called 'Pick 'n' Mix Theology' – afflicting Anglicanism. He was regarded as old-fashioned, eccentric and vain but his influence on the lives of the Teviotts seminarians was profound. He selected them not on their knowledge of theology but on the fierceness of their faith. He claimed to be able to discern, on the fragile basis of a half-hour interview, whether a candidate's faith was built upon granite or upon chalk. He never took his eyes from their faces. 'I excavate them,' he was fond of announcing, 'I go into their skulls and then I find it: an unshakeable thing or a thing with no real root. It's quite simple.'

In Timmy Ward, Dr Tate saw granite. To complaints from his colleagues assembled round the interview table that the applicant knew no Hebrew and only a dozen words of Latin, David Tate replied: 'These can be learned. Belief in the sacred cannot be taught. This candidate – Ward, Timothy – must come to us.'

It was fortunate for Timmy that he found himself in front of David Tate. He'd been turned down by three other colleges and had begun to hover on the edge of a vertiginous despair. He had tried to disguise it from Sonny and Estelle, but on a visit to Cord he had sat like a ghost by the fire and Cord had understood the depth of his misery. He'd handed him a tumbler of sherry. 'Tim,' he said, 'have you ever thought God might be a wrong turning?'

Timmy had looked at him in horror. His frog's eyes were filled with tears. 'No,' he replied. 'Never. Not since I gave up butterfly.'

When he was told that he had been accepted at Teviotts his mind emptied itself of his old and present life and filled up with the life to come. He thought about Teviotts for sixteen or seventeen hours out of every twenty-four. He saw the Main Building, the lonely grandeur of it out there in its treeless surroundings. He saw the ancient Chapel crouched at its back and just beside it the line of brown and white prefabricated buildings which provided living accommodation for first-year students and where, on a day in late September, he would unpack his new clothes from Cunningham's and his *Hebrew for Beginners* and look out at the clouds above Sussex.

Estelle baked a cake for him. She wrote 'Good Luck' on it in chocolate icing. It had a sag in the middle. They sat in the kitchen, the four of them, Estelle, Timmy, Sonny, and Wolf, trying to eat it. Timmy said: 'It's a good cake. It is.' Sonny took one mouthful then gave his plate to the dog who sniffed the slice of cake and walked away from it and sat down by the stove, watching.

After a while, Estelle said: 'One mustn't stand in a person's way. That's one thing I know.'

Sonny said nothing. He filled a pipe and lit it. When the pipe went out, he threw it down on the table. He stood up.

He said to Timmy: 'All I wish, son, is that those fucking Germans had shot away my heart.'

The following morning Estelle stood by the Rayburn in her frayed dressing gown with her grey hair hanging down to her waist. She was stirring porridge, opening a sliced loaf for toast. Tea had been made.

Sonny fidgeted by the kitchen door, chewing matches, wearing his farm coat. It felt cold in the house. The light on the fields could have been the light of December or January.

They ate the porridge. Sonny ate his standing up. The toast burned and filled the room with a charcoal smell. Sonny swore and went out to get the van.

The train Timmy was to catch was the same train from Saxmundham that used to take him to swimming lessons at the Marshall Street baths. In London he would get a train from Victoria to Brighton.

When it was time to leave, Estelle clutched on to the stove for warmth. Timmy kissed her cheek. Her face smelled of Pond's cream and her hair of the charcoaled toast. She said: 'Home is here, Tim. Try not to forget that, like one sometimes can.'

He went out carrying his heavy case. He wore a tweed coat, too large for him, that Cord had given him and a green scarf.

He put his case in the back of the van, where the dog travelled.

They set off. Sonny at the wheel, Sonny's cheek with a crop of white stubble growing on it, Sonny's hands red and hard, like the old weathered hands of John Wayne. The dog stood on its hind legs with its front paws on Sonny's shoulders. Timmy could smell the dog – its oily coat, its rotten breath.

A drizzle now fell. Timmy stared at early morning in Swaithey – at the awning going up over Loomis's butchers,

at the silent church – and longed for his arrival at Teviotts
where the sun would be shining.

They drove in silence. Timmy recognised it as a silence
that couldn't be broken. It was pointless to try.

They came onto the main A12 road and the drizzle turned
to rain. Lorries passed them, hurtling towards London.

Sonny slowed the van and stopped in a lay-by. They sat
there with the engine still turning. The dog started scrabbling
to get out.

'What's wrong?' asked Timmy.

'Nothing,' said Sonny.

'Why are we stopping?' said Tim.

'This is it,' said Sonny. 'This is as far as it goes.'

'What do you mean?' said Timmy.

'I mean what I say,' said Sonny. 'This is as far as the van
goes.'

They were a mile or more from the station. There was a
smile on Sonny's mouth and no smile in his eyes.

'Go on then,' said Sonny. 'Get out.'

Timmy imagined the leavetaking of the other Teviotts
entrants. He saw the tender smiles of mothers standing on
gravel driveways. He saw fathers, fighting back tears of pride,
turning the ignition keys of expensive cars.

He said: 'I'll miss the train.'

Sonny shrugged. 'Up to you,' he said.

Timmy got out. He opened the back doors of the van and
held on to the dog to stop it jumping out onto the road. He
tugged out his suitcase. He looked at the back of Sonny's
head and his shoulders inside the coat. He said: 'If I never
come home again, it will be your fault, not mine.'

He closed the van doors. Sonny drove off without looking
back, without a word.

Timmy walked through the rain, drenched by it and by the
spray from the heavy traffic. With his left hand he carried
the case. With his right he made a hitch-hiking signal. Every

thirty or forty yards he had to put the suitcase down and rest. The hour of his train neared. He asked God to give him fortitude.

No one had stopped for him and he missed the train.

He arrived at Teviotts late, in the dark, in a Brighton taxi he couldn't afford instead of in the college mini-bus.

Dr Tate was standing alone in the cold echoing hall. He held out his hand. He said: 'Welcome to Teviotts. No one else was worried but I.'

Forms of Address

Change didn't age Mary. It seemed to take her back in time.

This was the first thing she noticed – that she looked younger. Her body lost bulk. Small as she was, she began to look lanky, like a youth of thirteen or fourteen. And the hair that grew on her upper lip and in a little line around her jaw was like the hair of puberty, a faint brown fuzz.

She'd expected her breasts to shrivel. She'd imagined them looking like the breasts of an Indian woman of the Amazon forest she'd seen in a photograph at the Natural History Museum. The woman's age was thought to be ninety-nine. Instead, Mary's breasts got harder and smaller. They looked like the breasts of Lindsey Stevens three years before she had met Ranulf Morrit.

She felt light, almost weightless. She had a desire to run. The slowness of people in the street amazed her. She had dreams of her green tennis ball, how she used to hurl it away from her and run after it. In her lunch hours, she ran all the way to Hyde Park, then along the Serpentine to the boathouse. It was autumn in London. There were hardly any boaters.

One day, the boat attendant said to her: 'Want to take one out, lad?'

She went to see Sterns.

'Well?' he said.

She described her running, her feelings of weightlessness. She looked at the fish and saw them all flying and darting among their pieces of coral, as though her words had disturbed the water.

Sterns sat and smiled at her. 'Good,' he said. 'This is working benevolently. Creatively, one could say.'

'Will I grow?' said Mary. 'Boys of fourteen grow.'

Sterns tipped his head back and laughed. His voice was gentle, but his laugh was loud.

'No,' he said, 'but you may grow in spirit.'

'What do you mean?' said Mary.

'I've seen this,' said Sterns, 'in most of those I've helped – usually males who wish to become female, but one other like yourself. It has to do with being always a little outside the world. When you are apart from something it is easier to be wise about it.'

'I don't want to be "apart from the world". That's what I've felt all my life.'

'Only because you have felt divided – apart from yourself, if you like. Now, soon, your two selves will be better integrated but your status in the world will still be a special status because you will have seen the world from two different perspectives. I needn't remind you that this isn't possible for most of us.'

She told Sterns about the boat attendant. She said: 'The word "lad" stabbed me with pleasure.'

*

Irene came up to London on a Saturday Day Return. She didn't recognise Mary at the train barri'er. She said: 'I didn't recognise you, duck. I knew I wouldn't.'

She said she needed a cup of tea. She sat in the station buffet, weeping. Her hankie was too small for the size and quantity of her tears. Mary held her hand.

After a while, Irene said: 'I'm not crying because of what you've done.'

'Are you crying from shock?' asked Mary.

Irene replied that she was crying because Mary hadn't trusted her. She said: 'You trusted Edward and you trusted Pearl, but not me.'

There were paper napkins stuck into an ice-cream sundae glass on the buffet table. Mary took out one of these and handed it to Irene, who blew her nose in it.

'It isn't that I didn't trust you,' said Mary. 'I was afraid you'd be shocked, that's all.'

'Well, it is shocking,' said Irene. 'It isn't normal, is it?'

'No.'

'But what hurts is that you thought I'd be too shocked to love you any more. You didn't trust me to go on caring for you, did you?'

'I don't know, Irene,' said Mary.

'I do,' said Irene. 'You thought a person like me wouldn't be able to come to terms with it.'

Mary said: 'I hope you can forgive me.'

Irene said: 'I can forgive most things, love. You know that.'

It was a cold morning, but Irene wanted to see the Changing of the Guard. She said this would cheer her up. She said she'd been taken to see it once, long ago, before she met the printer from Dublin, and that it had given her dreams of marrying a scarlet soldier.

They arrived too soon and stood in the cold, holding on to the palace railings. Irene's nose was red from her crying and from the raw October air. Mary noticed that she looked older than when she'd last seen her and yet rather fine, as though she were at the peak of her life.

'How's Billy?' asked Mary.

'Oh,' said Irene. 'He's a Boy Scout now. He can start a fire with a magnifying glass.'

They laughed. There were French people all around them, pointing things out to each other in an animated way: 'Tu vois le drapeau? Tu vois les deux factionnaires? Ah, le soleil, tu vois?'

They were right. The sun emerged and shone on the Guards, making their swords and buckles gleam. Mary remembered Cord once saying: 'The English are damned nifty at drill. Drill is in us, like dancing is in the African. No one can say why, but it's true.'

But Irene was disappointed with the ceremony. She thought it would take longer. In her memory, there had been more Guards, more saluting, more marching as one. She said: 'I suppose everything lasts longer in the mind.'

She wanted to see where Mary was living. She stood in the lightless room and looked at Mary's drawings on the wall. She said: 'You're good at doing helicopters, love.'

She didn't like the airwell. She said: 'I'd keep wondering what was down there.'

Mary was going to make Nescafé, to show Irene some hospitality in return for all the days and nights she'd spent in Irene's cottage and all the hours she'd spent in Edward's house. But she found she was afraid. She imagined Irene stirring sugar into her mug of coffee and saying: 'What am I going to say to Estelle, Mary?' If this question had to be asked, she wanted it to be asked somewhere else. She said: 'I expect you're hungry after standing out in the cold, aren't you, Irene?'

Irene said: 'You know me, pet. Or shouldn't I call you pet any more?'

Mary said: 'None of that matters. Your being here's the thing.'

'I don't know what to call you, though. Not Mary, should I?'

'The name I've chosen is Martin.'

'But no one calls you Mary any more, do they?'

'Pearl did, when she came to see me.'

'But in time, she'll have to learn, won't she?'

Mary put on her tweed jacket. 'I've told you, Irene. That isn't the thing that matters.'

'It matters to me,' said Irene, 'but I often get upset by the wrong things, despite having Edward's brains in the house.'

'Let's go out,' said Mary. 'I'm starving. Let's talk about everything over spaghetti.'

Irene was impressed with the Italian restaurant. She liked the way they'd hung straw bottles from the ceiling and put a plaster saint up on the white wall. She said she'd never have thought of either of those things.

She ordered chicken with a surprise stuffing. She didn't want to ask what the surprise was and spoil it. Mary saw that she was trying to begin to enjoy her day.

They ate minestrone with thick white rolls. After a while, Irene said: 'Timmy's gone. I don't suppose you knew that?'

'Gone where?' said Mary.

'Left home,' said Irene. 'Gone to some Church school place in Sussex. I don't know what it's done to your mother.'

Mary stared at Irene. She felt shocked to think of Estelle on her own with Sonny.

'You see,' said Irene, 'she's got no one in the house now. Sonny's barely there. Talks to the wretched dog, not to people any more. And I'm afraid he's going to drive her back to – '

'She used to tell Cord she was happy at Mountview,' Mary said quickly.

'You went there,' said Irene. 'You saw what it's like.'

'Yes.'

'So you know. It's no place to spend half your life.'

'It's no good talking to me about it,' said Mary. 'Talk to me later. I don't know when. In a few years. Later. When something can be done.'

The surprise in Irene's chicken was garlic butter. She said she would never have thought of this either, that the day was full of things she hadn't imagined.

Mary said: 'Tell me about Pearl and Billy.' She wanted the subject of Estelle to be abandoned.

Irene smiled for the first time. She said: 'Pearl's young man is called Clive. Trees are what interests him. I said, Pearl, dove, if you marry him, you'll wind up living in a tree house most likely, but she didn't laugh and just gave me one of her stares. And as for Billy, what he'll do or be, no one can say. He says he wants to be an explorer. I said, there aren't many left, Bill. He said, no, but some. And I said what would you explore then, and he said the world. How would you travel, I said, what in? And he said, rickshaw, camel, steamer, canoe, anything. Elephant. It was when he said elephant that Edward shrieked with laughter. Shrieked and shrieked. And I was pleased really. Laughter keeps you young. That's what I think.'

In the afternoon, they went to Victoria Station and watched cartoons. They seemed to have run out of things to say. It was easier to sit in the dark and look at pigs dancing and mice scheming with human cunning.

When they came out to get the number 11 bus to Liverpool Street, Irene said: 'I've always liked it when they write "That's All Folks" in a circle. It's more friendly than "The End", isn't it?'

Mary:

After I'd received Miss McRae's £1,000, it was much easier to behave like a man.

I bought a suit and a kipper tie. I had my shoes shined. I gave tips to people.

I went into bars and bought drinks for young women and sometimes put my hand on their silky legs or touched the top of their breasts.

They expected to come home with me, but this wasn't possible except in my mind. My body had to stay inside its suit, hidden from view.

I told Sterns how much I wanted to make love to these women. He said: 'Yes. Naturally, you do. But don't run ahead of yourself. There is a long way to go yet.'

I thought, perhaps my life is like my old tennis ball I used to hurl in an arc and try to catch up with: it will always be ahead of me and never in my hand.

At least people sometimes called me 'Sir'. Barmen. Waiters. Shop assistants. I liked this. I would sit at a bar counter, smiling. But I never felt the same stupid bliss I'd experienced by the Serpentine when the boat attendant called me 'lad'. There is something about the unexpected that moves us. As if the whole of existence is paid for in some way, except for that one moment, which is free.

An unexpected thing happened to me in December.

I was at Tottenham Court Road tube station when I heard the song 'Galveston' echoing down the tunnels.

Since buying my suit, I always give a coin to the tube singers. I think of them as being between lives, like me, because to sing in the Underground couldn't be a life's goal. Sometimes you see the police asking them to move on and they look perplexed, as if they couldn't think where to move to. Pearl had said to me, eating her kebab mountain:

'Life needs a map, Mary.' I often think about this – the only little bit of wisdom to come out of Pearl in the twenty years of her existence. You can tell the tube buskers have never possessed a map or, if they once did, that it flew away in the Underground winds.

The singer of 'Galveston' was dressed as a cowboy. He had a cowboy hat on the ground, with a few pennies in it. I got out sixpence to throw to him and then I recognised him: he was Walter Loomis.

I stood a little way from him and stared at him and listened. His voice sounded beautiful to me. I thought, he must have taken a day off from the shop and started at dawn, to come and sing 'Galveston' on the Central Line. People born in Swaithey do the most unusual things.

When he finished the song, I went up to him. I said: 'You won't recognise me, Walter, but underneath everything you see, I'm Mary Ward.'

He has this heavy head that droops. It looks like it could one day fall off and roll away out of sight.

He stared at me, perplexed, as though I'd ordered him to move on.

'It's true,' I said. 'I'm Mary Ward. What are you doing in London, Walter?'

'Singing,' he said after a moment. 'Trying to stay alive with singing. You're right, I wouldn't have recognised you.'

I made him write down his address on the back of the copy of *Liberty* I was carrying. Its lead article was about the slow death from heartbreak of Lyndon Johnson on his Texas ranch. Walter said: 'It's an awful address. It's right under the power station at Battersea, but it's only till I move on.'

'Move on where?' I asked.

'America,' said Walter. 'Nashville. That's where my life's going to end up.'

*

I went to see him late one night, after the tube had closed down.

I walked over Battersea Bridge. There was a high wind and things were swirling about in the orange London sky, dead leaves and old pamphlets.

He lived in a basement in a row of little houses that were disintegrating one by one. Above the row was the power station, blotting out the moon and stars. Before he'd got up to answer the door, he'd been sitting on a hard chair, strumming. There was nothing in his room except this one chair and a bed with no cover and a juke box. Walter said: 'It works. It plays two songs, "Only You" and "You've Lost that Lovin' Feeling".'

I sat down on Walter's bed. The room smelled of unwashed clothes. He said: 'There's a kitchen as well.'

I wasn't wearing my suit. I was wearing jeans and a leather jacket. Walter said I looked more recognisable in these. He was still dressed as a cowboy. His boots had metal studs on them. His hat was hanging on the back of the door. He said there was a Country and Western Society that met once a week in a pub in the Latchmere Road and that he'd ordered these clothes from them. 'They're made in Tennessee,' he said, 'they're the genuine thing.'

He offered me some whisky. It's a drink I've tried to like and failed, but it was all Walter had, so I accepted it. When he handed me the glass, he said: 'No one else in the world knows where I am, except Pete.'

It wasn't warm in the room. Walter said he didn't mind. He was acclimatising himself. He said it fell to seventeen below in a Tennessee winter, that the trees looked as if they were made of glass.

I said: 'How will you pay to get there, Walter?' and his look became confused.

He said: 'Pete sends me dollars when he finds them. He hid them away in the bus years ago and now he can't remember where. But they turn up from time to time. I hope they're still valid. Sometimes he turns up a twenty.'

He didn't seem very interested in what or who I was becoming. His mind was on himself, on staying alive in London and getting to Nashville. I asked him whether he knew anybody there.

He said: 'You don't need to. I read this in the memoirs of a Grand Ole Opry star. If you can sing and play, you just start doing it and someone hears you sooner or later.'

I asked: 'Where do you do it, Walter?'

'Oh,' he said, 'there are some names of bars I've got. You go in there and hang around. People are kinder there.'

'Why?'

'Why are they kinder? Because they're country people.'

'Swaithey people are "country people".'

'It's not the same. Swaithey people think they know things. They think they've got everything mapped out. Country Music isn't about knowing things, it's about knowing nothing and discovering everything for the first time and then writing about it. Jimmie Rodgers, who was the first hillbilly singer I heard, used to have a thing he said to his audience. He used to say: "Hey, hey, it won't be long now," and no one really knew what he meant by that, but I know. He was talking about how he felt in his soul – that one day he'd find the answer to everything and that day wouldn't be long in coming, but at the same time it might never come, so the best thing to do while waiting was to write songs and sing them.'

'Is that how you feel, Walter?' I asked.

'Yes,' he said. 'And I'm thirty-five. I should know a lot by now and I don't, but I think the day's coming when I will. And at least I knew enough not to stay.'

'In Swaithey?'

'Yes. Except now I think of her, every morning. Getting up at five. Making tea. Going down to open the shop. It kills me. Here.'

He hit the area of his heart. It was protected by the suede fringes of his jacket.

'That's no use, Walter,' I said.

'I know. And I couldn't have stayed on. I couldn't have. I'd be dead by now.'

'I never think back,' I said.

'I don't believe that,' said Walter.

'No,' I said, 'it's true. Never.'

He asked me then what had happened to make me look like a youth that was small for his age. I thought, poor old Walter will believe anything, he hasn't got a clue about what is possible and what is not, so I said: 'This is a thing that happens to a minute percentage of people. They cross from one gender to another. It's in the Talmud. In the Bible, even. It's been known since time began. In certain African tribes such people are venerated as possessing wisdom. In the mountains of Tibet many men have ended their lives as women and they think, there, that it may have something to do with the brightness of the air.'

Walter drank his whisky. In the unshaded light of the room, I noticed a shiny bald spot on his head. I thought, he's too old to be trying to get to America.

He said: 'You expected this to happen then, did you?'

'Yes,' I said. 'Always.'

I told him about the two-minute silence. I had retold this moment so many times now – to Sterns, to Edward Harker, to Pearl – that I could see it and feel it and hear it perfectly, as if it had occurred yesterday. At the same time, I found myself thinking, did it occur at all or did I invent it?

Walter seemed quite affected by this. He said: 'I wish I'd had one moment like that. When I knew what I was.'

'You're a singer, Walter,' I said.

'Perhaps,' he said. 'That or nothing.' Then he said: 'D'you know Hank Williams?'

'No,' I said. 'I don't know any Country Music.'

He picked up his guitar. He began to sing a song called 'Alone and Forsaken'. It was one in the morning. He had no thought for all the other people asleep in the shadow of the power station. In the middle of the song, he stopped and said: 'This was the first song I found with the word "whippoorwill" in it. Nobody English even knows it's a bird.'

He resumed his singing. I'd always thought of Walter Loomis as a person who would never be good at anything and here he was singing like Glen Campbell.

> The grass in the valley is starting to die,
> And out in the darkness the whippoorwills cry.

From the Battersea darkness, a man yelled at him to shut the fuck up. He laid his guitar down with a sigh.

'London's a terrible place,' he said. 'In Tennessee, it isn't like this.'

'What *is* it like?' I said.

Walter said he didn't really know except there was a shine on everything. He started reciting the names of Tennessee trees: Live Oak, Hickory, Red-Bud, Slash Pine, Magnolia, Pecan . . .

If I'd been Rob or Tony, I would have reminded him about all the years of black slavery and segregation in the South, about freedom marchers who were killed in the middle of the road. But this was pointless. If you live in Swaithey for thirty-five years, as Walter had done, you come to believe that every bit of bad news from the rest of the world is over by the time it reaches you and so you don't have to think about it unless you're interested in History. All that concerns you is the state of your own earth: the good in it or the stones.

I asked Walter where he would live when he got to Nashville. He said he didn't know and didn't care. He said he could only imagine a small space, like a boxcar.

'This is 1971, Walter,' I said. 'The age of boxcar living is over, isn't it?'

He ignored this. He said: 'I'd like to own a dog and have it with me.'

I thought, as I left and walked back across the bridge, he hasn't got one clue about anything except his singing. He's going to an imaginary place and he'll die there.

I felt very tired. I barely knew Walter Loomis, but now he had added his name to the list of people I had to try to protect from harm.

15

1972

Transillumination

Edward Harker was inspecting wood with his illuminated magnifier. He was standing under the *Harker's Bats* sign.

Another cricket season was about to start. There was spring sunshine in the street. Upstairs, he could hear Irene hoovering. He remembered the day he'd tried to sack her while eating a Battenberg cake, and how, on his solitary holiday in France, he had thought of nothing but her.

He looked round the cellar. He wondered, without self-pity, what Irene would do with it when he'd gone. He decided that she would tidy it up a little and then leave it as it was and in time it would resemble a museum. Irene would come down the steps, once in a while, and stand at the door with her arms folded and look at it and think of him. Then she would go back up the stairs and put kettle on or water her cactus, and that would be all. Except that by then she would be growing old.

He resumed his inspection of wood grain. He thought, in my life as a nun, I used to stare at wood – at the back of a pew, at the door of the confessional box – in a concentrated way.

Pearl was sitting in a classroom at college; listening to a lecture entitled 'Caries and Civilisation'. The room was almost empty. There didn't seem to be a queue of people in the world wanting to be dental nurses.

Pearl made notes all the way through lectures because it wasn't always possible to know during a lecture what was vital and what wasn't. You only discovered the vitalness of something later on. She thought that wars might be like this for the people fighting them. They learned afterwards which battles were important and then gave the battle a name. The Americans who fought in the Battle of the Bulge, for instance. They didn't know that was what they were doing. No general came and said to them: 'Now, men, this is the Battle of the Bulge and it is going to be vital.' They just fought and died or fought and survived and later the name 'Bulge' was given to what they'd done and the word 'vital' attached to it.

This was the last lesson of the day. Pearl wrote: 'To summarise – in primitive or so-called "uncivilised" diets only raw and natural foods eaten, needing considerable amount of mastication. Mastication = secondary function = cleaning the teeth (e.g. raw carrot, a hard apple). Primitive societies = little or no food debris left on teeth. Incidence of caries is less than in civilised world.'

Pearl got on her train back to Saxmundham and thought about the word 'civilisation'. She stared at the pale green fields and the finches and sparrows flying up from them as the train passed. The thing that preoccupied her was what her contribution to civilisation was going to be. She wondered whether being a dental nurse and helping to maintain calm and order in the surgery was going to be enough, or whether something else was waiting for her. Something more vital.

Her boyfriend, Clive, was in Durham, studying tree surgery. He wrote her letters in beautiful writing like calligraphy. He told her that dreams of her hair sometimes stopped him concentrating on the trees.

Pearl liked these letters more for the handwriting than for the actual words. And she was enjoying his absence. She preferred his absence to his presence, just as she preferred thinking about him to touching him.

During her journey home, the sun went down and the green on the fields took on a peculiar whiteness, like frost. And it was during this alteration to the colour of things that Pearl decided, if he asks me, I'll say no. Because it isn't him I'm waiting for. I'm waiting for someone or something else.

Pearl wrote to Mary and asked whether she could come and stay for a night. She thought Mary might be able to help her compose a letter to Clive that would tell him she didn't love him and that she never had dreams about his hair.

In the household, Edward referred to Mary as Martin but Irene had said: 'I'm not capable of this, Edward. I'm just not.'

In Pearl's mind, Mary was between names. The old Mary, walking around in Miss McRae's clothes, was still visible to her, yet getting fainter. The new Martin, small and lean and with his soft beard, stood to one side, waiting. Pearl thought, part of me wants to keep her like this: almost invisible. Part of me doesn't want to have to see Martin close to.

But then, when she saw a sky full of stars and she remembered Montgolfier and the universe, she knew she didn't want to let Mary disappear, whoever she was trying to become. For one thing, Mary loved her. For another, she seemed to know about the world – about Greek food wrapped in leaves, about South African homesickness, about the map of South East Asia, about the sounds that came out of an airwell in the darkness, about the dances of Aboriginal tribes. She could recite The Words of Hakluyt Upon Reaching Moscow. She had spent a hundred hours in a room illuminated by fish. She knew her way to Twickenham.

Mary wrote back to Pearl very quickly. The letter was typed on *Liberty* stationery. It said: 'Bring a swimming costume. For years I've worried about you drowning so now I'm going to teach you to swim.' It was signed Mary Martin. When Irene read it, she said: 'There was an actress called that. Or still is? Sometimes you don't hear when a person's died, do you?'

They went to the baths at Marshall Street.

Pearl said: 'Timmy used to come here.'

Mary said: 'Oh yes?'

She had bought some red inflatable arm bands. She made Pearl put her arms into them. Pearl's swimming costume was turquoise, the colour of the water, and in the light of the baths her limbs looked shining white. Mary wore khaki shorts and a black T-shirt under which her breasts hardly showed now. She made Pearl sit on the side of the pool and put her legs into the water. She said: 'Almost every living thing can swim. Even an elephant. Look at the water and imagine it holding you up.'

Pearl said: 'It doesn't do any good. I'm still afraid.' At the other end of the baths, which looked a long way away to Pearl, a solitary high diver was practising.

Mary got into the water and swam a width, then came back to Pearl. She stood in front of her holding on to her hands. She said: 'Pearl, be sensible. You're my precious thing. I'm not going to let you come to any harm, am I?'

She pulled Pearl gently into the water. It came up above Pearl's waist and the ends of her hair got wet. She was trembling. Het mouth looked thin and mauve.

'Right,' said Mary, 'I'm going to keep holding your hands and I want you to lie down in the water and let your legs come up behind you. Then I'll just gently pull you around.'

'I can't,' said Pearl.

'Yes, you can,' said Mary. 'Remember the fish of the Great Coral Reef. Imagine you're one of them.'

'They were puppets,' said Pearl, 'they had strings holding them up.'

'So do you,' said Mary. 'I'm your string.'

So Pearl lay down in the water. Her hair fanned out around her head like weed. Her blue eyes looked dazzled, as though by extraordinary news. Mary walked backwards, crouching a little, pulling Pearl along.

After they'd gone round the shallow end several times, Mary put Pearl's hands onto the bar and held her feet and then made her kick her legs. She said: 'Imagine your future now: surfing, water polo!'

Pearl managed to smile. The kicking was warming her up and she felt a tiny particle of her fear fly away up into the glass roof and stay there, looking down at her.

'Now,' said Mary, 'I'm going to guide you along again, like before, but this time I'm hardly going to pull you. You're going to propel yourself with your kicking. Try to push me backwards. Imagine you're trying to push me away.'

So they progressed round and round the shallow end of the baths. A group of children arrived and stared at them: a young man wearing clothes in the water and a girl with mermaid's hair who couldn't swim.

After two hours they were tired, but they felt happy. The swimming lessons had taken Pearl's mind off the letter to Clive that still had to be composed and it had taken Mary's mind off everything in her life except Pearl. She remembered a feeling she'd sometimes had long ago in Swaithey – that she was a person sitting on her own in the dark and Pearl was a lantern slide.

That evening in Mary's room, Pearl said: 'I've got an exam at Easter. Do you mind if I read some revision notes aloud?'

Pearl was in Mary's bed and Mary was lying on the end of it, looking at their swimming clothes hanging on the fireguard and dripping onto the floor. She said: 'No.'

Pearl was wearing scarlet pyjamas. She'd tied her hair back with a white ribbon.

She said: 'Do you know what transillumination is?'

'No,' said Mary, 'but I could try to guess. It's something hidden in the past which suddenly becomes clear?'

'No,' said Pearl. 'It's a method of detecting a mesial or distal cavity. Less reliable than an x-ray but quite successful. A very bright light is placed against the crown of the tooth and the cavity is revealed as a dark shadow.'

'Oh,' said Mary. 'I see.'

She found Pearl's foot, with the blankets on top of it, and held on to it. She said: 'Tell me about Clive.'

Pearl put her revision notebook down. 'He has beautiful handwriting,' she said.

'Does he want to marry you?'

Pearl ignored this. She said: 'The thing I really love about him is his handwriting.'

They were silent for a long time. Then Mary said: 'That's one of those statements that sounds callous at first and then later not, because a person's handwriting can be the most beautiful – or the most ugly – thing about him.'

Pearl stared at Mary. She thought, I won't write the letter. Not yet. All I'll do is to remember what Mary just said in case it becomes vital in the future.

Then Pearl said: 'Changing the subject, have you ever understood what the Battle of the Bulge was?'

'Yes,' said Mary. 'I saw a film about it. Starring Robert Culp.'

'And?'

'I can't remember. I think it marked a turning point in the war.'

Later, when Mary was almost asleep on her floor cushions and the lives in the well were quietening down, Pearl said: 'Mary, I'm going to call you Martin from now on, I promise. The last time I call you Mary will turn out to be now.'

Back in '39

Sonny sat alone in the kitchen.

He was trying to remember what date it was, but he couldn't. It was April, he knew this. He just didn't know which bit of April the world was in.

He was drinking stout, as usual, but not with any enjoyment. For some time, in fact, the taste of stout had sickened him, yet he still sat there, night after night, drinking it.

The dog, Wolf, lay at Sonny's feet. It was sleeping. Human beings complained if you talked to them in their sleep. The world of their dreams was more precious to them than anything you could ever say. But dogs didn't give a damn. They woke up and maybe walked round in a circle a few times and then lay down again, listening.

Sonny rested his damaged ear on his hand. Since Timmy's leaving, it had ached more. Also, it gave him dreams about Timmy, if he slept on that side. He had to remember this and turn his head the other way, towards the blue wall.

There had been no letters from Timmy. Unless he wrote secretly to his mother and she hid the letters away. Months had passed. It was April. Each month had come and gone with no letter in it anywhere. 'It's unendurable,' Sonny said aloud to Wolf. 'It's unbearable. It's worse than the war.'

The dog got up and shook itself, then went to its bowl and lapped water. It returned to Sonny and lay down again, with its head on Sonny's feet.

Sonny reached down and stroked its head. 'I don't know why I stopped the van,' he said. 'I did it, bang, like that. I just did it and then it was done.

'I should have relented. I should've driven back and picked up the boy and said, Get in lad, go on, get in.

'I've been pig-headed from birth. Proud. No one knows why.

'I should've thought, if I do this, I won't be forgiven.

'And who can stand that – not to be forgiven by your only son? I can't. No one could.

'So what's to be done? I can't write a letter. I can't spell the word April.

'What's to be done, Wolf?'

Hearing its name, the dog gave a whine. Sometimes, late at night like this, Sonny and Wolf went for walks down to the river and Sonny would piss in the water.

Sonny refilled his glass, which was nearly full anyway. He took a disgusted sip of the beer. It was trying to kill him, but he wasn't going to let it.

'She'll have to write, that's all,' he said. 'She'll have to explain I wasn't well at that time. Disappointment can affect the things a man does. She'll have to explain that.

'And then Timmy'll write back. He'll write to say what he misses is the land – the harvest and the ditches and the whole of everything going on under the sky.'

Sonny stopped speaking. His heart felt lighter now that he'd decided what had to be done.

But he wanted it done now, tonight. He looked round the kitchen, as if he expected to find Estelle there. He knew she wasn't there and he looked round and round the room just the same.

He couldn't remember where she was. He had a feeling she wasn't in the house so he got up and whistled the dog to his side and went out into the spring night, calling Estelle's name.

She was in Pete's bus. He was playing records so old they didn't look like records; they looked like a crunchy thing you could eat. Now and then, in the conversation Pete and Estelle were having, he stopped in mid-sentence to grin at some old incomprehensible line of a song.

They were drinking whisky. They did this quite often now

because neither of them had much else to do with their time. Pete had been sacked from his job in the slaughtering yard by Grace. She paid him a little pension instead. She said: 'You forfeited your share of the business in '38, when you went slumming round America, and now your sight's faulty. We've got to call it a day.'

It was true about his sight. It was as if his wandering left eye used to be guided into alignment with the right by his nose and, after the piece of his nose was cut away, it had nothing to fix on.

He didn't care about the loss of his job. It had been a terrible job, when you thought about it. What he cared about was being alive.

He spent a lot of his time ransacking the bus to find dollar bills to send to Walter. He had moved all the furniture around. He had been through every old box and drawer and tin and jar and pot. He had made four cuts in his mattress. He had now posted to London a total of one hundred and nine dollars, thirty cents. He thought there might be more, but he didn't know where else to look.

He looked forward to Estelle's visits. He sat her down in his one comfy chair and poured her a slug of whisky and told her she still reminded him of Ava Gardner. Sometimes, he stroked her arm. Mostly, he just talked to her and played her Country songs.

She said: 'Sometimes I want to say things. Then at others I don't want to say a word. It could be determined by the moon.'

Once or twice, they danced. They held each other correctly, like old-fashioned dancers, but then they just stood in the middle of the bus, swaying.

On the night when Sonny went out into the dark calling Estelle's name, she and Pete were dancing. The song they danced to was called 'Knoxville Girl'. It was about a crime, and without meaning to Estelle found herself saying: 'There used to be rumours about you, Pete. That you'd done a criminal thing in America.'

'Yes,' he said.

'Well?' she said. 'You can tell me. I was going to commit a crime in 1966. I was going to steal a baby.'

'It was never what people imagined,' said Pete. 'Because no one in Swaithey could imagine anything like that.'

'I can imagine anything on earth. The last time I was at Mountview I shared some of my time with an air traffic controller. He wore rubber gloves. He made signals to the air.'

'I wouldn't even call it a crime really,' Pete went on. 'But I paid in away. It was 1939.'

'Tell me,' said Estelle. 'Then we could have another dance.'

The song ended, but the record still went round and round.

Pete took the needle off it. He refilled their whisky glasses. He said to Estelle: 'Telling doesn't matter now, now that I'm not part of Loomis's. I used to keep everything quiet out of respect for that.'

Then he sat on a hard chair opposite Estelle and started straight into his story. Estelle lit a cigarette. The Tilley lamp hissed like a jet of water.

Pete: 'It was when I was in Memphis, working as a church gardener. I met a girl at a honky-tonk.'

'What's a honky-tonk?' asked Estelle.

'Oh, we don't have them,' said Pete. 'Little bar kind of place where Country musicians play. You can do most things there: sing, dance, whistle, cry your eyes out, clap and scream. I loved them.

'So anyway, I met a girl there in '38. Name of Annie. Worked for this old guy, Webster Wills, who had a pawnshop. In those days, this is what Memphis had most of, after singers: pawnshops.

'She was a sweet girl. Young and sweet and poor. She worked in the backroom of the shop, cataloguing what came in and what was redeemed. Anything worth a dime came into her hands at one time or another: instruments, of course, but a lot else. Weights, radios, wedding rings, brushes and combs, lockets full of hair. You name it.

'She'd stared at me in the bar. I talked to her to stop her saying something. I thought she was going to say how ugly I looked.

'She took me home to her place, where she lived by herself with this little dog, Pixie. It was a griffon. It was the size of a squirrel. She said: "Pete, meet Pixie," and held its paws up for me to shake. Then she said: "Pixie's alone all day and he likes to be with me at night. I hope you don't mind?"

'What could I say? I said nothing. I started kissing the girl and the only thing that was on my mind was getting inside her and letting go.'

Pete took a drink of whisky. He said: 'Shall I stop? Am I shocking you?'

'No,' said Estelle. 'Nothing shocks me. What did she look like, Annie?'

'Oh, pretty and not. Mousy. Grey eyes. But lovely in all the important places. And so something started between us and I kept on seeing her. And it was all fine and sweet. Everything was fine and sweet except the dog.

'I used to say, "Annie, put the damn little dog out somewhere while we do this. Lock it in a cupboard." But she wouldn't. She liked it there, climbing all over us. She said: "Dogs are the only loyal creatures on God's earth."

'Then one night – and we were in '39 by then and war in Europe was coming – when I was in bed with Annie, I felt this awful little Pixie scrabbling onto my arse. I looked behind me to push it off and then I saw its little red thing out, the size of a beanshoot, and it was doing something against me.

'And I went crazy. It was so damn disgusting I didn't give a thought to Annie's feelings. I grabbed that disgusting

Pixie by its scrawny throat and strangled it with one hand!

'I shouldn't've done it. I should've just got angry with Annie and made her put the dog somewhere else. But I was so angry, I wasn't rational. It happens, doesn't it? I killed the dog and threw its body on the floor.'

Estelle opened her mouth and laughed. She tipped back her white throat and choked with laughter. She said: 'Oh sometimes, the world is a scream.'

Pete said: 'This wasn't a scream. I was a murderer to Annie. *And* to me, because I destroyed her and me in less than twenty seconds and I never saw her again. I used to walk past the pawnshop, but not go in. And I was sick with misery, somehow. And after a little while I thought, it's over in Memphis, Pete. It's over. And what happens to you now is the war.'

Estelle was still laughing. Then she stopped. 'Is that what happened to you?' she said. 'The war?'

'Yes. I came home and joined up. All I ever told Ernie was there'd been a bit of trouble with a girl and the word "trouble" got turned into the word "crime". I don't know how. It must have gone round Swaithey in a whisper and come out Chinese.'

Pete seemed very tired after the telling of this story. Giddy with drink and laughter, Estelle pulled him to his feet and walked him to the bed, where he lay down. She covered him with an old quilt he always claimed was his only proper souvenir of the American South; that and the hundred and nine dollars and all his memories of scarlet birds and scarlet trees.

She wandered home. She heard Sonny calling her name.

Corpus Debile

Towards the end of Timmy's first year at Teviotts, he fell ill.

The infirmary was on the top floor of the main building, right under the roof. From its windows you could see the sea. It faced south and was a bright, airy place. The founders of Teviotts had believed that most illness was caused by despair and that light had curative powers.

David Tate climbed the narrow stairs that led up to the infirmary. He was accompanied by the Matron, who led him to Timmy's bedside. In a dream, Timmy had smelled Dr Tate's hair oil and then, when he woke, there was the man sitting on a chair looking down at him. He blinked and David Tate smiled. The Matron adjusted her starched cuffs and walked away.

Timmy knew why he was ill. He was ill because he couldn't keep up with what Teviotts was trying to teach him. He was ill because Teviotts expected him to be clever. He was ill with struggling with Latin and Hebrew. The other students all seemed to be good scholars and Timmy was miles away from being a scholar at all. So he had fallen ill. 'Fallen' was the word. He had got up on a Wednesday morning and stood by his bed and fallen over. He heard someone scream and that was all that he remembered until he woke up again in the infirmary and saw a luminous brightness all around him.

When he saw David Tate sitting by him he tried to haul himself up the bed. He felt boiling hot from his sleep. His hair was damp. Dr Tate said: 'Stay still, Timothy. Stay and rest.'

His illness had been diagnosed by the doctor as a virus. Tate said: 'You have a virus. "Virus" is a useful word.'

Timmy tried to nod. He seemed to have no control over his heavy head.

'You don't have to talk,' said Tate. 'Let me talk to you for a bit, then I'll leave you in peace and you can go back to sleep.'

David Tate took off his glasses and polished them on his sleeve. Then he said: 'The curriculum at Teviotts is reasonably harsh. Men who go into the Church must at least know the Scriptures. The Church also considers a knowledge of Latin and, to a lesser extent, Hebrew to be valuable. This is rational and right. You have three years here. Two remaining. This is time enough in which to get to grips with these disciplines, as best you can.

'The Church is also at a cross-roads. It has become more secular and more liberal and this is good in many ways. It has shown itself able to resist petrification and embrace change. But.'

He stopped here. He turned slightly and stared out at the sky. He let several silent seconds pass.

'But,' he continued, 'there is a paradox at work. The Church has sought to re-define itself in order to counter the argument that it is no longer relevant to the needs of people in this very troubled century and yet in doing so it has also re-defined belief – thus undermining its primary relevance to all human existence. It has put belief on a vector. It has given belief gradations. It has made quantifiable that which cannot be quantified. And this I abhor. To me, belief *is* or it is not. You believe in Christ's resurrection or you do not. It is central to faith.

'And so I come to you, Timothy. When we had you in front of us at interview my colleagues were disposed to reject you on the grounds of academic weakness. I persuaded them to let us take you because what I saw in you was someone for whom God seemed to be as essential as air and water. I knew you would struggle with your studies. I knew you would do poorly at examinations. But I knew also, and I think I'm not wrong, that you will be a very good churchman. You will be one of the few with a vision and that *vision* will help people and bring them comfort. I'm not wrong. I know I'm not.'

Timmy turned to stare at Dr Tate. He saw him sitting there, very calmly, his head slightly raised, as though he were watching a film in broad daylight. Timmy tried to say: 'You're not wrong, Dr Tate,' but the words would let themselves only be thought and not said aloud. Nothing could be said aloud. This virus was a virus of silence.

On his last day in the infirmary, the Matron brought Timmy a letter. It was from Estelle:

Dear Tim,

Why don't you write to me? I know that letters can get to and from institutions as easily as weather.

We miss you so. I am making a flag. I will tell you about this. It is my only thing, my work of art.

Sonny has been begging me to write. For weeks and weeks, he has been begging.

He wants me to say he is sorry for what he did. He didn't mean to do it, to leave you on the road. Often we do what we don't mean. He wants me to say, please forgive him and come to see us. Even a dog in no substitute for a person.

My flag is a Union Jack. I am making it all in silk. I have to make it twice and then stitch the two sides together to make one.

It is far bigger than the table. It is a present for Colonel Bridgenorth whom I met at Mountview, of the Royal Artillery. He was once a hero and now he believes he is a Sherpa. He thinks he's on Everest. The flag is for him to plant on the summit. The Union Jack is the most complicated flag under the sun.

Must go. *Hawaii Five-O* is almost on. I love it. I love it when Jack Lord says: 'Book him, Danno!'

It sounds so final. That's why I like it. *'Book him, Danno!'*

Please write, dear Tim.

With love from your

MOTHER

Elm Farm,
Swaithey,
Suffolk.

Timmy folded the letter away. He felt weak, yet clear-headed. He thought, it's as if none of us is anchored on the earth: Livia, Estelle, me. We're genetically insubstantial. This is what Mary was fighting and fighting. She was trying to keep herself on the ground. She was fighting the air.

When the term ended, he returned to Swaithey.

Sonny met him at the station. He said: 'There you are, then,' as though he'd been looking for him in the barn and found him somewhere else.

Tim said: 'How are you?'

'Alive,' said Sonny, 'if you can call this living.'

The dog was in the van, whining. Then when Timmy got in, it began to bark.

'Shut up, Wolf,' said Sonny, but the dog kept on barking so he said to Timmy: 'You're a stranger, that's why.'

They drove the seven miles to Swaithey more or less in silence. The dog lay down and was quiet. Tim said: 'How's everything with the farm?'

Sonny took a long while to reply. Then he said: 'House is mortgaged.'

Timmy looked out of the van window that was speckled with mud. It was a dark day with low cloud. The hedgerows looked drab.

Timmy said: 'I'll help you with the harvest.'

'There isn't a harvest,' said Sonny. 'Only sugar beet.'

'Why?'

'No combine. Things have a life-span. Everything does. Even the fucking Empire had a life-span.'

Sonny laughed and the laugh turned into a cough. He slowed the van. The dog stood up and scrabbled round in a circle.

Timmy thought, something has to be said, something that will make the coming weeks bearable. I will never make a good priest if I can't console my own father.

But the thing that needed saying remained obscure. He didn't even know how to begin it. It might as well have been a piece of Latin. And now it was too late: they were at the farm.

Estelle was at the open front door. She was wearing a summer dress and a grey cardigan and when the van pulled up she drew the cardigan round herself, protecting her breasts and her sides.

Timmy got out and embraced her. Her cheek felt cold or his own lips too hot, one or the other.

'The house is mortgaged. Did Sonny tell you?' she asked.

'Yes,' said Tim.

'It wasn't our fault. Things just happen.'

'I know.'

'But your room's still there. That's still there.'

'Yes.'

'All your swimming trophies. Everything.'

'I'll take my case up, then.'

Sonny drove off in the van, Timmy didn't know where. He went up the stairs, carrying his case and Estelle followed him up and into his room which he knew was just as he'd left it and yet didn't look like his room but like a reconstruction of his room, like a film set built to deceive him. It had no smell to it, no smell of the past.

'See?' said Estelle. He begun to unpack his things. He laid his Bible and his prayer book on the table by his bed. Estelle stood against the wall, wrapped in her cardigan, watching him. She went up to him and extracted a hand from her cardigan and stroked his cheek. He smiled at her. He had no idea how the smile looked to her or what it expressed.

At supper, Sonny drank and talked. For a long time, the only creature he'd talked to was the dog. Now he seemed to be addressing the whole world.

He'd sold one field to Grace Loomis. She'd put two more hen factories on it. Nine thousand eggs a week came out of them. All sterile.

No one would take the combine away. The scrap dealers were too lazy to come and take it apart. So it sat in the bam, in its old place, still covered in sacking, rusting to pieces, slept in by birds.

Cord could have saved them from having to mortgage the house. He could have sold his house at Gresham Tears and moved into the farm, but he'd refused to do it. The old were selfish. All they thought about was saving time in which to do nothing.

The land in England was turning against the farmer. It was so tired it refused to grow anything unless you fed it with expensive chemical fertiliser. It had been on the side of the farmer for a thousand years and now it was on the side of ruin . . .

'I've told him,' whispered Estelle to Timmy. 'Sell it all, then we could rest.'

Sonny heard her. He banged the table. One of his stout bottles fell over. 'It's not mine to sell!' he shouted. 'It's Timmy's. How many hundred times do I have to remind everybody of that?'

'Sell it,' said Tim quietly. 'Sell it and save the house. You'd both be happier then and so would I.'

'*No!*' said Sonny. 'No, no, no, no, *no!*'

He raised a fist at Timmy. 'You little fucking saint!' he

shouted. 'What's wrong with you? Why do you come home and then call me a liar?'

'I didn't call you a liar.'

'Yes, you did. You said the land isn't yours.'

'It isn't mine . . .'

'Yes, it is! Every furrow of it, every stone. It's all yours. And if you walk out on me again I'll make you *eat* it. I'll make you eat up all the fucking earth!'

'Sonny,' said Estelle, 'you don't know what you're saying.'

'Don't know what I'm saying? That's good, coming from you! That's beautiful coming from where that comes! Eh, Tim? That's rich. Don't you agree, little priest?'

Timmy stood up. He said: 'Excuse me.'

He ran upstairs. The dog woke and barked. Sonny and Estelle heard Timmy being sick in the bathroom, above them.

With one movement of his arm, Sonny swept all the plates, cutlery and glasses from the table onto the tiled floor. The sound of everything breaking was like an injection of sudden pleasure into his vein. He staggered to the back door and went out into the night. Estelle covered her face with her hands inside the cardigan sleeves.

The next morning, quite late, Sonny came like a penitent to Timmy's room. His hands were shaking. He thought, I'll do anything, just as long as he stays here. I'll even kneel if he wants me to.

Timmy wasn't in his room. He was in Swaithey church. He was sitting in a front pew and staring up at the sun coming through the Sower Window. He was trying to calm his mind by remembering a Hebrew prayer. Though what he felt was horror, his face showed only an intense concentration.

He didn't hear the church door open. He was very surprised when someone said his name. He looked down from the

Sower and saw Pearl Simmonds standing by him, carrying a watering can.

She was smiling at him. Her limbs looked brown from the sun. She wore a faded blue dress. The pleasure and relief he felt when he found her there was beyond what he could describe.

He said her name.

'Tim,' she said, smiling, 'you look so different. Much older.'

'I *am* older,' he said. 'You look beautiful, Pearl.'

He stood up and put his arms round Pearl and kissed her cheek. And he thought, as he did so and smelt her hair, it reminds me of the smell of poppies in a field, in our childhoods – mine and Mary's. Pearl was one of the few amazing things. And I never saw her clearly until now.

Pearl put down her watering can. She took Timmy's hand and held it and looked down at it. She thought, he never had beautiful handwriting.

And she smiled.

Mary:

Twenty years and six months after the two-minute silence I went into hospital.

Three incisions, like a triangle, were made near to my nipples and through these wounds all the breast tissue that remained in me was taken out. The operation was called a bilateral mastectomy. The incisions were sewn up and there was my chest, neat and flat, with a bright white bandage round it.

The surgeon had good skin and eyes that were kind. He said before he cut me: 'In time, the scars will barely be visible, but the wounds will take a few months to heal.'

I lay on my back with a wire cage over my torso, to stop the sheet from pressing on me. Inside the cage I could feel nothing at first except a scalding pain. I thought I must have fallen out of my window into the airwell and broken myself in half. I couldn't imagine who had rescued me, but I remembered that, when a person falls, there is usually, by great good fortune, some other person to pick him up.

And then, in time, the pain became less.

Two faces popped up over the sides of the cage, one freckled, one tanned.

'Mart,' said Rob. 'How are you, hey?'

'Mart,' said Tony. 'We brought you a watermelon from Safeway's.'

I said: 'I'm not sure I can talk.'

Glad as I was to see them, I couldn't hold them in my vision for long. I tried to apologise for letting them slip away.

When I woke up again it was pitch dark except for a little violet-coloured bit of illumination somewhere and what had woken me was the pain returning.

I remembered how, in the past, I had imagined pain was my ally. I had imagined that if I suffered enough I would become a man, of my body's own accord.

It was so hot in the cage, I tried to move it, but raising my arm was like raising the lever on a dam and letting new pain flood through me. I lowered the lever and called out, but no one heard me.

I thought, Mary would cry now, but I refuse to. I will wait.

While I waited, I had a dream. It was of the deserted houseboat I'd seen on the river near Twickenham, with the families of ducks all round it in wire pens. In my dream, the boat broke loose from its moorings and began to float away on the current. A breeze lifted the flag and made it flutter. The boat dragged the duck pens after it, but the ducks couldn't swim fast enough and they were going to be crushed by the wire and drowned. At the thought of this, I began to cry out.

A nurse came. She said: 'All right, Martin?'

'No,' I said. 'No.'

When I next woke, it was light and there was hardly any pain at all.

Nurses have these cool, beautiful arms. They put their arms under yours and lift you up gracefully, as if you weighed nothing. They sit you on a pan. They sponge your face. They do everything smiling. I say to them: 'My special friend, Pearl, wants to be a nurse, but a dental one.'

They say: 'Here's a cup of tea, love. Drink it slowly.'

I would like to spend the rest of my life in the cool, soft arms of a nurse.

The next time Rob and Tony came, I was sitting up. They brought me a copy of the *New Statesman* and a bag of cherries.

I said: 'How many days have I been here?'

Tony said: 'Four thousand two hundred and thirty-six. It's 1984.'

Rob said: 'Three, Mart. This is your resurrection, man.'

They sat there, smiling at me. In a few weeks' time our family of three was going to break up. Tony was getting married and going back to Sydney. He had a job lined up on the *Sydney Morning Herald*. His ponytail was a thing of the past. Rob said that he and I would keep the flag of *Liberty* flying, but I wondered how long it would fly after Tony left. Georgia once screamed at me that everyone in the world is replaceable but, like much of what she said, I knew this to be untrue.

Tony's wife-to-be had wild corkscrew hair and the name of Bella. Rob and I had tried to love her, but when we realised she was going to take Tony away, we stopped trying and started sulking. Bella's father was an editor on the *Sydney*

Morning Herald. We never forgave either of them, father or daughter. I felt guilty about this, but Rob didn't. He said: 'In South Africa no one forgives anyone else anything, *ever.* And that's how it's always been.'

I felt hungry, so I started eating the cherries. I put the stones into a cluster on my night table.

Tony said: 'Tell us about it, then, Mart. Is it better without tits?'

'It will be,' I said.

'What d'you mean "will be"?' said Tony. 'What about now?'

'Now,' I said, 'it's not anything. It's just pain, then no pain, then pain again and so on. But soon – '

Tony sighed. 'With you, it's always "soon" or "later" or "next year",' he said. 'When is it going to be today?'

I stopped eating cherries. After a while, I said: 'I don't know. I'll know when it comes.'

Walter Loomis came to see me. He'd got very thin and his hair was long and shaggy. He looked as though he could be dying, but he said he wasn't, he said that on the contrary he was less than a week away from beginning his life.

He sat by me in the hospital for a long time. He ate three oranges and all the biscuits that were brought on a saucer with my tea. He wore his cowboy clothes, everything except the hat. He smelled of sweat and soot.

I asked him how he'd got enough money for his fare to Nashville.

He said: 'Do you remember Gilbert Blakey?'

I said: 'Yes. Nobody forgets their first dentist.'

He laughed. He said: 'That's a hollow laugh, Martin, not a real one.'

Then he told me about his love affair with Gilbert. He said it had happened because of the death of two world statesmen, John F. Kennedy and Anthony Eden. He described the wire wheels of Gilbert's car and the way Gilbert had tired of him for no apparent reason.

Then he said: 'I decided recently that Gilbert owed me something, so I went to see him.'

I said: 'That's brave of you Walter. I can't bear to look at the past.'

He said: 'You should see where he works now. He's got oil paintings in the waiting room and copies of the *Tatler*.

'His nurse said: "You're not in the appointment book, Mr Loomis." I said: "Yes, I am. I've been in it since 1963."

'I refused to leave. I said I'd sit there reading magazines until the Third World War arrived or until Mr Blakey agreed to see me – whichever came first. I said I was used to going without food.'

Walter was smiling his vacant smile all through this story. I kept trying to imagine whether the people of Nashville would take Walter Loomis to their hearts or laugh at him until their ribs cracked. I said: 'Go on, Walter.'

'Well,' he said, 'at about six, when his last patient had gone and I'd looked all through *Country Life* and *Harper's Bazaar* Gilbert came in. He looked peculiar. His hair looked dyed. He looked far older. His voice had changed. It was all blah-blah-blah now.

'I explained about getting to Nashville. He said in his blah-blah, Why on earth d'you want to go *there*? So I tried to explain that and how I had to have a life before it was over and I hadn't had one.

'I started to threaten him. I said I'd tell all his posh patients what he was and what he did. He looked exhausted by now, Martin. I was going to say, This is Suez, don't bungle it; but then I couldn't remember exactly what had happened at Suez and what had been bungled. I didn't want him to catch me out. He's far cleverer than me.'

Walter got the money he asked for. A hundred and fifty pounds wasn't much to Gilbert Blakey with his smart practice in Chelsea and I expect the news that Walter was leaving England was news he'd wanted to hear for years and years, Just In Case. He knew that Just In Case sometimes arrives, like Just Until.

Walter had bought his ticket. The idea of flying frightened him, he told me, but he expected somebody would look after him and tell him where the toilets were and how to change planes at New York. The date of his departure was four days away. He had written to Pete and Grace, telling them he was leaving, but only Pete had replied. The members of the Latchmere Country Music Association had given him an old map of Nashville and taught him the first lines of the Declaration of Independence. He said: 'I wish I'd known years ago that the Pursuit of Happiness was a right. In Swaithey it wasn't, was it?'

'No,' I said. 'It was a wrong.'

When Walter got up to leave, he looked all round my hospital room. I thought he was searching for something else edible but he said he'd got into the habit of staring at places, saying goodbye to little bits of England. Then he said: 'I'd like to wish you good luck in your life as Martin.'

'Thanks, Walter,' I said.

'I don't suppose we'll ever see each other again, will we?'

'No,' I said, 'but send me a postcard. Tell me how you get on in Music City.'

He grinned.

I remembered him in the Loomis slaughtering yard, grinning at the sky.

'Just that *name* makes me shiver,' he said.

Then he was gone. Only the smell of him remained. An Indian nurse came in and opened my window.

I'd informed Pearl about my operation. She didn't seem shocked or sad. She wrote me a letter saying: 'When you get out of hospital I'll come for a week and care for you. You can have the bed and I'll sleep on the floor. On our course we have to learn about first aid and resuscitation. I'm the perfect person to help you.'

I went home in a taxi. I felt weak. When I lifted anything, the pain came back to my wounds. I imagined all the other operations waiting for me in the future and the pain still to come; and I had a thought that I hardly ever allow myself to think: why couldn't it have been simple? Why couldn't I have just accepted being Mary Ward?

The answers are: because it wasn't. Because I couldn't. Because I am *not* Mary Ward. And no one – not Harker, not Sterns, not I – can explain it better than that. All we have are theories. It remains one of all the million mysteries left in the world.

When I got home to my room, Pearl was there. She was wearing a white overall, belted at the waist. She had stuck some cornflowers into a glass vase. She said: 'This is Emergency Ward 10.'

I kissed her hair. If I hadn't been in pain, I think I would have put my arm round Pearl's waist and we would have stood like dancers, cheek-to-cheek, letting time pass.

'How do you feel, Martin?' she said.

This was the first time she'd ever called me Martin.

'I'm glad you're here,' I said. 'I haven't got any strength.'

She'd tidied everything in my room. She'd put all my inks in a line and my sketches in neat piles. My little cooker was shining.

I sat down on the bed. Standing, I felt insubstantial. An icy sweat began to break out on my head.

I let Pearl undress me. I was too weak to feel shy. She folded up my clothes and put them on a chair. She helped me into my pyjamas and I got into bed. It was about mid-day but to me it felt like the other side of next week. Pearl said: 'Shall I read to you or would you like to watch Fanny Cradock?'

But I couldn't answer. A little rhyme my mother had taught me when I lay between her and Sonny in the sagging middle of their bed came back to me and the words settled on my brain like snow:

> Winking, Blinking and Nod one night
> Sailed out in a wooden shoe
> Into a land of misty light
> Into a sea of blue.

I had a dream about Pearl. We were lying together on a raft made of logs. The sea under us was calm and blue, but in the distance we could see a storm coming towards us.

I was wearing a life jacket and Pearl was wearing nothing. I took my life jacket off and put it on Pearl because I knew that she still hadn't learned to swim. I cradled her in my arms and stroked the hollow of her back. I knew that all my life had been a preparation for the moment when I would steer this raft safely through the storm. Then Pearl would settle down beside me and touch my lips with her soft fingers and say: 'It's all right, Martin. It's over now.'

I woke up and stared at the cornflowers. I couldn't seem to move my head or my eyes to see what was beyond them. I said: 'Pearl, are you there?'

No one answered.

The pain in my chest was very bad. I thought, I don't know what date it is. It could be the date on which Walter Loomis flies to Nashville and is never seen again. To keep the pain steady so that it could be borne, I tried to remember the names of Tennessee trees, starting with Hickory.

I seemed to wait a long time for Pearl to return. I could hear life going on in the airwell but my life felt as if it couldn't be resumed until Pearl got back.

She came in, carrying a bag of groceries. She said: 'I hope you like Mulligatawny soup. It reminds Edward of India.'

She put on her white overall and stood at the stove boiling the soup and smiling into it. I wanted her to turn and smile at me but she didn't and it was then that I guessed she had a secret she was keeping from me.

This secret was the storm on the horizon I'd seen in my beautiful dream of the raft and I sat up and stared all around my room looking for a life jacket and not finding one.

People think of the night as a time when nothing's going to happen to them unless death happens. They say 'Goodnight, see you in the morning.'

I knew something was going to happen that night. I knew that what was going to happen was the telling of Pearl's secret, but I didn't know what the secret was or what it was going to do to me.

We ate the Mulligatawny soup with bread and butter. I took some pills and the pain went away but I knew that it was in me, lying in wait. We played Beggar My Neighbour but my mind wasn't on the game; it was on the night, coming closer.

Pearl helped me get up to wash. Then she straightened my bedcovers and got into her white nightdress and we lay down, me in the bed, Pearl on the sofa cushions on the floor. I turned out the light. I did not say: 'Goodnight, Pearl, see you in the morning.' I waited, hardly breathing.

When it came, it was like a rat, this secret. It sprang into the room and terrorised me. I lunged out for a weapon. I felt the stitches in my chest tear.

I grabbed everything that was near me: my book, my lamp, my invalid pillows, the vase of cornflowers. I hurled them all, one by one, at the rat. And I screamed. Louder than any of those other night-screamers out there in the black well. Louder than on the day when Sonny tore off my bandages.

The word I screamed was *NO!*

Part Four

16

1973

Doodle-ei-dip

In the fall of '72 Walter Loomis arrived in the town they call Music City USA.

The word 'fall' had haunted him since the age of sixteen. A season to dream in, Pete had said. Autumn-known-as-fall.

He wasn't dreaming. He'd had his boots re-heeled. The Tennessee ground was solid underneath him. But he felt stunned by the brightness of the air. He found it difficult to look at the sky.

A bus had taken him from the airport to downtown Nashville. The bus sounded strange, as if it had an engine room in it somewhere and should be travelling on water. He was the only white person on it except for the driver. The black passengers fussed and fidgeted. They put things into their old pieces of luggage and took them out again. They talked in low voices, like people complaining about the price of bread. One of them whistled.

The bus stopped a few times on its way to downtown. Some of the black passengers got off and walked towards a line of little low houses. The houses were made of planks and every one had a plank verandah and a swing seat and a yard full of junk, as though junk were what grew here beside the highway instead of flowers. Walter remembered that the American word for earth was dirt.

It was early afternoon. In England this particular day had already come and gone and turned into silence. Walter imagined the Suffolk winds rocking Pete's bus and Grace in her upstairs room wearing her Viyella nightdress, sleeping without moving. The distance between himself and these imaginings felt very large.

He was very tired but couldn't allow himself to feel it. He had a schedule of things to do. This schedule had been worked out for him by the members of the Latchmere Country Music Association. Only one of them had been to Nashville but all the rest had read about it and heard about it and dreamed about it so often that they believed they knew their way around. They told Walter: 'What you do when you arrive, duck, is the following: Number one, buy a local paper and find a room. There are places called rooming houses, run by families or widows and all the rooms in rooming houses are cheap.

'Number Two, head for Lower Broadway known as Lower Broad. This is the street where all the little bars and honkytonks are and people are kind to would-be singers here because would-be singers make up about one half of the population, so they know the kinds of things and the kind of help you'll need.

'Number three, introduce yourself to people all the time. Say, Hello, my name's Walter Loomis and I'm from England and I'm hoping to get a break here in Nashville. Remember to say *here* in Nashville, not just in Nashville because "here" is what everyone likes to add in there, pet. They like to emphasise the now. It's as if they're in Heaven and they want you to marvel at it so they say, *here* in Heaven. You see what we mean, Walter?'

He saw. He felt he *was* in a kind of heaven because of the colossal shine on things and the flame colours of the trees.

When the bus arrived at the depot, he carried his guitar and his suitcase to a bench and sat there, blinking. He thought, I will follow the schedule, but it's going to take time. First, I have to acclimatise my eyes.

He found a room in a big house on Greenwood Avenue. It was known by its number, 767. The owners were called Mr and Mrs Pike. When he'd been there a month and the dry fall was over and gone, Mrs Pike said to him: 'I expect you noticed, Walter, we're formal in the South, but Mr Pike and I have taken to you, dear, and we'd be happy for you to call us by our first names which are Audrey and Bill C.'

'Oh,' said Walter. 'Are you sure?'

'Certainly. We talked it over.'

'Audrey and Bill C.'

'That's it.'

'What does C. stand for, Mrs Pike?'

'Audrey, Walter.'

'Oh yes. Audrey.'

'Well C. stands for Clement, dear. William Clement Pike. But those names never set right with Mr Pike. He was always Bill C., ever since he could talk.'

Walter's room was on the ground floor at the back of the house. It looked out onto a vegetable garden where Audrey Pike grew watermelons and peas. Beyond the peas were three chestnuts always referred to as the shade trees. Walter formed the habit of sitting at the small table in front of his window thinking up songs and staring at the shade trees. Sometimes he saw scarlet birds flying into them. The first time he caught sight of one, he thought it must have escaped from a theme park.

'Why no, dear!' laughed Audrey Pike. 'That's a cardinal. You can see them 'most every place you go. You keep a watch out, Walter.'

He kept a watch out. Not just for cardinals. He watched

everything that moved, everything there was. He knew that his life had begun, years too late, but at least it had started before it had ended. So he had to notice things. He went to sleep late and woke early. He couldn't afford to miss too much time.

Bill C. was a roofer. His favourite season was winter when the storms and gales arrived. He told Walter: 'You can make a good living out of roofs in Nashville, son, and we don't need to let out rooms. But Miz Pike likes to do that. She takes a pride in the quality of room we offer and she likes the company, since the Lord didn't bless us with children of our own. And you, Walter, being from England, that's made her happy. She never went to England, but those Jeeves stories made her die laughing. And she wants to help any way she can.'

'I appreciate that,' said Walter.

'See, in Nashville,' explained Bill C., "most everything is done word of mouth. This town is a small big town. You know?'

Audrey found Walter a job in the neighbourhood, raking leaves. He worked the mornings only. When the leaves were all raked and burned the neighbourhood women discovered other tasks for him. He chopped wood and mended fencing. He cleared garages of their old plastic trash. The women brought him coffee and slices of pineapple upside-down cake. Some of them wore their hair in curlers all day long. Some were older than all their lifetime's trash, but still feisty, with their feet in rubber overshoes and their fists gnarled and clenched.

In December, it sometimes snowed in the night, a soft dusting. Then the mornings would be bright and the sky a monumental blue and Walter's eyes, still not acclimatised, would water as he began work. On this kind of day, he could no longer see Swaithey in his mind. It was as if a winter fog had come down and covered it. Now and again, however, while he was tearing down creeper from walls or taping leaky hoses or standing still on the snow drinking sweet coffee, he was visited by the image of his father, Ernie, wearing his white butcher's coat and his jaunty hat and smiling as though his face were going to burst.

He mentioned this to Pete in the first airmail letter he had ever sent in his life. He wrote: 'I now and then see Dad in my mind. He looks very happy. Like I remember him looking when I was a boy.'

Of the ghost of Arthur Loomis there was no sign.

About Walter's dream of becoming a singer, Audrey had said: 'We're with you, Walter. Only don't forget you can die from a dream. Remember the forty-niners? We'd be sad if y'all died.'

Bill C. hadn't mentioned death. He mentioned a person called Fay May. He said: 'Listen, Walt. I know Fay May. I did her roof for just about nothing 'cept plates of lunch. You go talk to her and mention you're a friend of mine. And you hang around her place and listen and talk and watch out and something'll turn up. She turns no one away.'

It was a small, grimy bar with oilcloth covers on the tables and sawdust on the floor. In neon was written *Fay May's Lounge*. On the walls were thousands of signed photographs of the stars of the Grand Ole Opry, half of them dead. There was a poster advertising Hank Williams's last concert, the one he never lived to give. It told his fans he would be there to sing for them 'if the Good Lord's willing and the creek don't rise'. A blackboard over the bar listed ten different types of beer. Above this hung a threadbare confederate flag. The place smelled of spilt beer and cigars. Fay May herself stood behind the bar, smiling.

She had fleshy arms and dyed brown hair piled up on her head. Walter guessed she might be the same age as Grace, but Grace was growing old watchfully, and this woman looked as

though the passing of days was of no concern to her. Walter
sat down on a bar stool. He had never heard of any of the
ten types of beer advertised. He chose one at random and
Fay May opened a bottle and set it in front of him next to
a heavy glass.

'Here y'are, Sir,' she said, 'and welcome to the Lounge.'

Walter decided to wait awhile before mentioning Bill C. Pike.
He looked along the bar. It was two-thirty in the afternoon.
He saw a line of men smoking and chewing and passing a
bottle of Jack Daniels back and forth. They talked in slow
voices. One of them wore a spotted scarf over his head like
a pirate. The others were dressed as cowpokes. They looked
past their prime, sad around the eyes, as if there had never
been a prime to be past.

The one closest to Walter who looked younger than the
rest turned towards him and looked him over and asked:
'Tourist, is ya? Canadian?'

Walter shook his head. He wasn't wearing his fringed leather
coat or his stetson; he was wearing a tartan work jacket with
a fleece lining belonging to Bill C.

'Alaskan?' said the man. 'I went to Alaska one time. Nearly
died.'

'English,' said Walter.

The man's features settled into a freeze-dried smile and
stayed that way. He shook his head from side to side.

'England!' he said through the smile. 'You mean to tell
me England's still *there*?'

'Yes,' said Walter. 'It's still there.'

The man slapped his thin thigh. 'Well I'll be darned!' he
said.

Walter couldn't decide what to say. Part of him wanted
to tell the man that for him, too, England – or the only bit
of it that he really felt was his, Swaithey – had disappeared
from sight. In the end, he said nothing. He shrugged and
smiled.

'Have another beer?' offered the man.

Walter wasn't enjoying the beer but he remembered one of the Latchmere people saying to him: 'Accept hospitality whenever it's offered. Southerners love to give. It's their pastime. We make tea. They make friends. Unless you happen to be black.'

'Okay,' said Walter, 'thanks.'

'And by the way,' said the man, 'I didn't mean no disrespect. I laugh easily. Most every darn thing under the sun makes me smile. I'm made that way.'

'It's a good way to be,' said Walter.

'Don't know 'bout that. But let me introduce myself: Bentwater Bliss. Born Illinois 1920. Named for my home town of Bentwater. Still alive, just. Still solvent. Still singing!'

Bentwater stuck out the hand that had been holding on to the bottle of Jack Daniels and Walter shook it.

'My name's Walter,' he said, 'Walter Loomis. And I'm hoping to –'

'Welcome to Nashville, Walter. And what's your line of business?'

Walter cleared his throat. 'I was in the meat trade,' he said.

'In the meat? Well, there's a coincidence. There's nothin' I don't know 'bout meat. Worked in a stockyard from the age of twelve to the age of thirty-two. My name was Bentwater LeQuaide back then and when I got over here to Nashville I done changed it. I chose "bliss" 'cause that was the word I was in the minute I sat me down here at Fay's an' someone started singing. I ain't joking. I was purely in bliss from that day!'

He laughed the laugh that had been coming on ever since the mention of England. When he recovered from the laugh he called Fay May and ordered Walter's beer. He said to Fay: 'This is Walter from England, Fay. And he was in the meat like me once upon a time. You take care a him while I go and sing now, okay?'

'Okay, Bent,' said Fay May. She smiled at Walter and shook his hand. 'You're welcome to the Lounge,' she said again.

'Thank you,' said Walter.

She winked at Bentwater, who was climbing down from his bar stool. 'You don't gotta listen to Bent singing if you don't want to. He sings like a live hog boilin'!'

'How come I make me a living, then?' said Bentwater.

'Heaven knows!' said Fay May. ''Less it's only from kind hearts.'

There was a chair and a microphone in the window of Fay May's Lounge. Walter had noticed these. Bentwater picked up a guitar and sat down on the chair. He coughed a bit, tuning the guitar. The talking and laughing in the Lounge faded like sound turned down. The line of drinkers at the bar refilled their glasses and sat still. Walter noticed that on a little table near Bentwater's chair was a sweet jar half-filled with dollar bills. A sign propped against the jar read: SINGERS SING FOR TIPS. THANK YOU.

Bentwater had one long pointed fingernail. He used it like a plectrum.

'He picks good, whatever you say,' said Fay May.

He had a high, nasal kind of voice. He started with a Louvin Brothers' number, 'If Only I Could Win Your Love'. Beyond him and beyond the window, the afternoon was fading to blue. Then he introduced a song he'd written himself. It was an old sad ditty about the poor of the fields and hills, the kind of song that used to squeeze tears out of Pete Loomis's meandering eyes. The Lounge fell quiet. Bentwater sang on:

Ask me where my hope and fortune lie;
They lie below me in the rushy river
And above me in the bright blue sky . . .

Walter went home to 767 and told Audrey and Bill C. that he'd met Bentwater Bliss. In the evenings, Audrey and Bill C. sat in front of a wood-burning stove playing Pinochle.

'Oh my!' said Audrey. 'Tell 'im, Bill C.'

'That one,' said Bill C. 'He's been around a long time.'

The Pikes had been playing Pinochle together for so many years, they could play and carry on a conversation at the same time. Bill C. told Walter that Bentwater had come to Nashville in 1959 in a stolen meat truck. He resprayed the truck purple and parked it by the river and lived in it for a year. Then he had to sell the truck just to live and he slept in a pile of sand. They said: 'He paid his dues all right – and how – and now they have him on the Opry 'bout three times a year. He had a good voice when he came here but just gently he drank it to almost nothing.'

'Don't hang around with Bentwater, Walter,' said Audrey. 'He'll wind you up drinking.'

'Well,' said Walter. 'He said he'd introduce me to some people.'

'That's true, Bill C., isn't it?' said Audrey. 'He knows just about everyone on Music Row.'

'He *knows* 'em,' said Bill C., 'but that don't help him none. They know he ain't reliable. They know he's reliable as the wind.'

Walter went to his room and sat down at his table in front of the window. It was pitch black. He couldn't see the silhouette of the shade trees. It felt so quiet, he thought it might be starting to snow.

He remembered his afternoon. He and Bentwater had walked down Lower Broad past the bars and the clothes stores and the pawnshops to the river and watched a riverboat full of tourists dock below them.

Bentwater had said: 'The founders of Nashville came in two parties. One came overland and the other came hundreds of miles up the Cumberland River, all the whole way pushing against the current. And that's how it is in the music business,

Walter. Every man starting out's got the current against him and what that current is, is all the people who made it already who either want to keep ya out or else steal your songs or do you down somehow.'

'I knew it wasn't going to be easy,' said Walter.

'Not only is it not easy, pal,' said Bentwater, 'it's also friggin' hard. And there's another thing.'

Walter could smell salt coming off the river, like the sea. He thought, everything here is different from how it is in other places. 'What other thing?' he asked.

Bentwater turned towards him and gave his arm a squeeze. 'Well,' he said, 'the thing is, Walter, in your case you're an innocent, right? You don't know First Avenue from the First Commandment, right? You're a country boy, but from the wrong country. To summarise, you know d-e-d about it.'

Walter looked up at the sky, fading to mauve. 'What's d-e-d?' he asked.

Bentwater laughed. His laugh turned quickly to a wheeze. 'Doodle-ei-dip!' he said. 'Or in other words, *nothing*! See what I mean?'

Walter had felt foolish. He'd felt foolish for a good few minutes. Then he'd remembered an extraordinary thing and he'd told this to Bentwater while the riverboat tourists tramped past them and at their backs the neon signs of Lower Broadway came on.

He said: 'Years ago, I went to a fair and had my hand read. By a woman named Cleo. She had plastic teeth. There were spangles on her spectacle frames. I got to know her quite well before she died.

'And she told me something I never understood till now. Or rather, I misinterpreted it. She said: "I see a river." She was positive about this. She said a river would definitely be part of my future. I always thought it was a river in England called the Alde, but I was wrong. It's this river. The Cumberland. And she said everything in my life would lead me here.'

Bentwater had listened attentively, then rubbed his eyes with his hands, like a man suddenly dog-tired. 'Could be,' he said. 'Or could be not. I never believed I got my life written down on my hand. My life's inside me, waiting. It ain't no place else.'

Walter liked this. He thought about it now in his room at 767, staring at the empty window. Bentwater Bliss was fifty-three but he could still feel his grand future in his heart, waiting its time.

Mary:

I went back to see Sterns. He was in mourning for his axolotl which had died unexpectedly. The name of the axolotl had been Ken. Sterns said: 'We shouldn't give creatures names. It's the name that breaks your heart.'

I told him about my guineafowl, Marguerite, taken away in a sack. He said: 'You might have considered replacing her, or you might still consider it.' He said: 'Newts are good company.'

I was grateful for the dark and the sighing of the fish tanks. I sat there for a while, not speaking. I could feel my wounds aching and my head filling with a black sea.

'Well,' said Sterns, 'you have something to tell me. What is it?'

I said: 'I want to die.'

Sterns got up and walked around in the room with his face turned away. Then he sat down again. 'Go on,' he said.

I didn't want to say anything more. I just wanted to sit there and not move.

Sterns waited. He is a person who can hold himself so

completely still you can't even see him breathing. He is like Ken in this respect.

I closed my eyes. I was remembering how my father's faulty hearing used to be cured by the sound of my crying. I said aloud: 'My whole life has been absurd.'

People say things like this to Sterns all the time. That's what his job is – to listen to the absurdity of everything. He's so used to it, he doesn't even look startled. He just watches the fish, their colours and their graceful swimming, and nods his head.

He got me to speak by getting up and going out of the room, leaving me alone. The moment he'd gone, I felt lost and abandoned. I felt as if I were in a pot-hole, beyond reach of every human thing. I imagined Sterns letting himself out of the house and walking away down Ladbroke Grove. I wanted to call out to him but the feeling of being in a hole was so intense that I knew I wouldn't be heard.

He hadn't abandoned me. He'd just gone to the lavatory. When he returned, he sat down on the far side of the room and blew his nose on some apricot-coloured toilet paper. He said: 'Why do you want to die?'

I told him about Pearl.

I described what happened. I said: 'I knew she had a secret but I didn't know what it was going to be.

'The secret was Timmy. My brother. He took everything of mine when I was a girl. Everything. Except Pearl.'

So I told him everything I felt about Pearl, my precious thing. I told him how much I wanted to protect her from drowning. I told him that I'd always loved every single thing about her, including her snoring and her ambition to be a dental nurse. I said: 'In the future that I'd imagined she was going to be there. As Martin I was going to love her properly and protect her from other men. And she would love me back. That's what I'd always planned.'

'And now?' said Sterns.

'There is no now,' I said. 'I'll never see her again. Or her family, who were kind to me. Never. I can never see her or want to see her. Ever. Because she's engaged to Timmy. This was her secret. Timmy's going to go into the Church. He'll be a curate somewhere and Pearl will be his wife. She won't even get to be a dental nurse. She'll have a lost life.'

Once I'd started talking I didn't want to stop. I kept remembering things: Montgolfier and the universe, the Flying Gumards of the coral reef, the definition of transillumination.

And I saw that these things were the highlights of my life, like my life was the room we were in and these times with Pearl were the fish tanks, illuminating the empty space. And so I said: 'When I see it like this, it's not surprising I did what I did.'

When I left Sterns, I found it terrible to walk in daylight. The air hurt me. I thought, I'll go to where I can be killed by light alone.

It was a March day. You could smell breaths of spring. You'd turn a corner and suddenly get a waft of something beautiful and fierce.

I walked to the Serpentine. I found the boat attendant who had called me 'lad', the very same one. I said: 'I'd like to take a boat out, please.'

The wind was buffeting everything. The trees looked startled. They would have liked to flee.

My boat wouldn't stay still. Swans bumped by, regarding me. They seemed to have purpose and a destination in mind.

I lay down in the boat. I examined the sky. It was empty of everything but atoms of blue expanding out and up into meaningless space. Then I saw a white shape floating, miles high. I thought, it could be a seagull or it could be Livia turning and turning in her glider, looking for the one living or inert thing she hadn't wearied of. Turning and turning and not finding it. Finding nothing.

I've never tired of Pearl. I would never have tired of her. Even her round writing I love and her white plimsolls. Every hair on her body. Her amazement at treefrogs. Her terror of water. Everything. And I know this – know it without knowing it: that for one person to love every last and least thing about another isn't as rare as you might believe. What is rare is for all that to bring the person happiness. What it brings is exhaustion.

I didn't see this till the night of Pearl's secret. I deluded myself that my life as Martin, holding Pearl in my arms, was going to come one day. I'd always believed it without once saying it. This was the name of my future, *Martin and Pearl, Estb. c. 1976.*

It wasn't surprising then – not to me – that when she told me about Timmy I flung a lamp at her and then a book and the vase of cornflowers and all my invalid's pillows. And then I flung another much more terrible thing: I flung myself.

The lamp knocked Pearl over and she fell onto the floor. Then the vase landed by her head and broke into fragments and the water spilled into her hair.

She tried to get up. She kept saying: 'Don't, Martin! Don't!' but I told her to shut up. I said I didn't want to hear any words from her mouth ever again unless they were words of love for me.

I knelt over her. Using all my strength, I took her thin wrists in my hands and pinned them down behind her head, among the pieces of broken glass.

I could feel my two triangles of wounds tearing and starting to bleed into my bandages, but I thought, mouths are wounds worse than these, the pain of what mouths say is worse.

I opened my mouth and put it on Pearl's. She tried to twist her head away from me but where her head moved, mine followed. My head is as heavy as stone. It's so full of longed-for things.

I kissed her. I put my tongue into her mouth and sucked an her sweetness. I drank her. My head grew light with the sweetness of my precious thing. And I laid my pain on her breasts. My blood came through the gauze and stained her.

She was weeping. Her face was hot with sorrow. And gradually I felt it transferred to me, her burning misery. One moment I was giddy with the sweetness of Pearl and the next I was heavy and inert and on fire with shame.

I stopped kissing her. I knelt between her legs. She was sobbing. She put her hands over her face, blocking me from her view.

'Pearl,' I said. 'I'm sorry. I'm *sorry*. Forgive me. You're my precious thing . . .'

She got to her feet. She began putting all her belongings into her suitcase. It was night. I tried to warn her not to go anywhere but she paid no attention. All she kept saying was: 'I am not a *thing*. I am not a *thing*. I am not a *thing*!'

Thing. Person. Beloved. What matters is that she was precious to me. It's not only the naming of something that makes us love. It's everything entire.

Now, she's gone. I lie in my boat and ask the universe to fall on me and crush me in its freezing glitter. But there's no sign of the universe. It has moved on.

My life is lived from hour to hour: an hour with Sterns, an hour out here on the water. My boat's number is one. When my hour ends, the attendant hails me through a megaphone: 'You in Number One, Sir, come in.'

I didn't want summer to arrive. Or autumn. I tried to slow down time. In summer or in autumn – I didn't know which – my brother was going to marry Pearl. I wanted to be dead by then.

I sat in the *Liberty* office doing drawings of rice fields and grazing oxen with napalm bombs about to fall on them. I put myself anonymously into every picture.

Tony was gone. Rob was in love with a girl called Electra. I told him: 'I feel as if we're all in a Greek tragedy.' He said: 'Mart, keep a hold on what you still have, hey?'

Zorba's closed. I don't know where everyone went, Nico and Ari and so on. I just arrived there one evening and the restaurant was gone and the front was covered with fliers for demos and rock concerts. I stood and stared at it for about ten minutes and then I went home and ate a marmalade sandwich and remembered Irene. I said to Rob the next day: 'There's not a lot to keep a hold on, you know.'

I started counting the things I had left. One of them was Cord. I hadn't written to him for a long time. I'd been too cowardly to tell him what I'd done to myself. I thought, the sight of me with a wispy beard would be more wounding than the sight of some geese making an arrow in the sky.

But now I wanted to see Cord. He was seventy-eight. I wanted to sit in an armchair opposite him and drink Wincarnis and talk about history. Not the Hakluyt kind of history but my own. I wanted to know the minute-by-minute truth about Livia's death, where and how she went and why. Because I'd been thinking, it's not too late to take glider lessons; I still have most of Miss McRae's money; she may even have known I'd need to get out of this world.

I wrote to Cord. I described myself. I said: 'I'm more Martin than when you last saw me. I wear horn-rimmed glasses, like Ringo Starr. The hair on my face is brownish. My chest is flat but scarred. The next operation will be to remove my womb.'

He wrote back straight away, using the old green ink. He said: 'Is it a sad business or is it a happy thing? That's all I care about. Which is it, bad or good?'

I didn't write an answer to this. I got on a train to Norwich and Cord met me in his new car which was called an Austin Allegro. He said: 'I drive it so slowly, I call it the Andante.'

He didn't comment on my appearance. I expected him to faint when he saw me or run away, as if I were a trunk road arriving to obliterate the water-meadows of Gresham Tears, but he didn't. All he said was: 'Martin Ward, I presume?'

During the drive in the Andante, he asked: 'Is it for the better, then? That's the thing.'

I looked out at the hedgerows of south Norfolk here and there green, here and there not. I said: 'Yes. Except that it isn't finished and never can be, really.'

'No,' said Cord. 'That stands to reason.'

Then a little further on, as we were going through the town of Bungay, he said: 'We're all something else inside. Old Varindra explained that to me. But he said it's a mistake to think the inner thing is fully formed. It can't possibly be. Nothing grows properly in the dark.'

When we arrived at Gresham Tears, we had a meal of boiled beef, followed by mandarin oranges from a little tin. Cord was addicted to mandarin oranges. He said: 'When you grow old you need sweetness in things, heaven knows why. As that Dylan chap used to say, the answer's blowing about somewhere but nobody finds it.'

After supper we sat by the fire, drinking. I'd brought something to give Cord. It was Livia's silver locket with a piece of her hair inside. I said: 'I kept it for all the years I was a girl. Now I want you to have it.'

He put it down on the frayed arm of his chair and stared at it.

'I remember this,' he said. 'It's not Livia's hair, you know.'

'Oh?' I said. 'My mother used to tell me it was Livia's hair.'

'No. It's Sophia's hair, Livia's mother. Your great-grandmother. Liv had it since she was a child.'

'Why didn't my mother know that?' I asked.

'I expect she forgot,' said Cord. 'What belongs to whom gets obscured by time.'

I was silent for a minute, drinking my drink, warming my feet. Then I said: 'Livia's dying has always been obscured by time. I've never known about it properly, like where was she going in the glider?'

'Nowhere,' said Cord.

'What d'you mean?'

'She wasn't going anywhere. She was just circling. She took off from the field and – '

'Which field? Where?'

'Place called Ashby Cross. Ashby Cross Glider Club. Not far from here.'

'And?'

'She was doing a circuit, that's all. Floating on thermals. Turning.'

'And then?'

'She was on her second circuit. She lost height very suddenly. I wasn't watching, thank God. I wasn't there. But she lost her thermal and she started to come down and down. People at the club said she could've made it in except for the wires.'

'What wires?'

'Pylon wires. Electric. I mean, that's why I said to those chaps at Mountview, don't do this electric stuff to my daughter. Once was enough.'

'She flew into the electric cables?'

'Yes.'

'She was *electrocuted*?'

'Yes, old chap.'

'Why wasn't I ever told that?'

'Don't know.'

'I imagined it all wrongly.'

'Did you? What did you imagine?'

'An impossible thing: that she just floated into the sky and disappeared.'

'Well,' said Cord, 'there you are. What we dream up is invariably better, eh?'

We had a game of Scrabble. Cord made the word 'quietude' on a triple, using all his letters, and scored a hundred and thirty-three in one go. We carried on drinking. I had the letters y, a, a, x, t, l, l, in my tray and was praying to be able to make the word 'axolotl' by some miracle when Cord suddenly looked at me and said: 'Now that you're here, Martin, I think it's time for you to go and sort things out with Estelle.'

I didn't look up. I moved my letters around. 'Is she at Mountview?' I asked.

'No,' said Cord.

I gave up on 'axolotl'. I put down 'tilly'.

'What's that when it's at home?' said Cord.

'A lamp,' I said. 'A gas lamp.'

'It's got an e,' said Cord. 'T-i-l-l-e-y.'

'Not always,' I said. 'That's an alternative spelling. I can't see my mother, Cord. Don't ask me to.'

'When, then?'

'I don't know. Never, probably. Everybody in Swaithey is in the past. That was another life and it's finished.'

'No, it isn't,' said Cord. 'Est isn't in the past. She's sitting in the dark, watching television and waiting.'

'I don't want to talk about it,' I said.

'She won't say what she's waiting for. Perhaps it's for you. For your forgiveness.'

'*Don't*, Cord,' I said. 'Don't say anything more. Quietude, please.'

An awful thing happened then. Cord began to cry. He looked exactly like he'd looked at Mountview, when my mother had wiped her face with her hair.

I wanted to put my arm round him, but I just sat there. I removed 'tilly' from the board. I let him cry on.

'Listen, Cord,' I said after a while. 'Tell her I died. Then she won't wait.'

I went back to Sterns.

I told him that in my dreams I made identity parades of everyone I'd once loved and shot them to pieces with an automatic rifle. Pearl became a thousand particles of matter.

He said: 'Consider this, Martin. The mind can get tired of both the internal and external landscape. And I believe yours is exhausted with both. I want to recommend that you leave England for a while.'

'To go where?' I said.

'It probably doesn't matter where.'

'Do you mean a holiday? Mine isn't the kind of life you have holidays from.'

'No,' said Sterns, 'I don't mean a holiday. I mean a long period of time away. I can get you in to have the hysterectomy done as soon as you feel up to it and once you've recovered from that I believe you should go and look at another place, another bit of the world. All you've ever experienced is England. Buy a globe and look at it, Martin. Remind yourself how small England is and how vast all the rest.'

I didn't say anything. I felt astonished.

'Well?' said Sterns.

'I don't know,' I said. 'I've never thought about it.'

'Think about it now. You say you want to die because there's nothing left in England that's precious to you any more. You're twenty-seven. Go and find something new.'

I said: 'The problem is the summer. I don't want to live through that.'

Sterns made a note on his pad. Beales used to write everything down; Sterns only wrote things down now and then.

'You can have your surgery in the summer,' he said. 'We

can cradle you through it in that way. As you know already, surgery alters time.'

That evening I borrowed an atlas from Rob. We knelt on the floor with our bottoms in the air, turning the pages.

'Trouble is, Mart,' he said, 'you know no one anywhere, except Tony in Sydney and he betrayed us for that bleddy Bella and her crazy hair.'

'Knowing people doesn't matter,' I said.

'Yes, it does,' he said. 'You've never been an exile. I have. I know what matters and what's of no consequence.'

Estelle:

We're having a wedding in Swaithey. It's going to be on the Fourth of July, Independence Day. I find that ironic. No one else does. They say: 'Estelle, you see some difficulty in everything.'

There *is* some difficulty in everything. There is difficulty in waking up in the morning. There is difficulty in remembering why you're alive.

Weddings make me constipated. I have to hold on to myself, hold everything in. But this is the last wedding of any importance: Timmy's to Pearl. It's the one we'll remember till we fade away.

I made it my business to go round to the parties concerned and to try to find out what they were hoping for.

Irene was sewing day and night. She'd bought twenty-one yards of white satin from Cunningham's. She looked as though a parachute had landed in her lap. In a box were seven hundred tiny pearls, not real but lifelike. Irene said: 'When I named her Pearl, I imagined this, a bodice encrusted with these.'

I helped her stitch the train. Pearl came and stood on a stool in her bra and knickers while Irene pinned bits of the dress onto her. She stood on her stool and stared out of the window at people passing in the street. She seemed preoccupied, as though she were working out a long and complicated sum.

When Pearl went out I said to Irene: 'Is it what you want?'

'Is what what I want?' she said.

Billy came in. 'Billy, mind out,' Irene said before he'd opened the door. Billy is a teenager. He is like Irene, fat and sweet.

He looked down at all the furls of satin. 'Mum,' he said. 'Me and Dad are going fishing.'

'All right,' said Irene. 'Remember the big umbrella.'

It was a scorching day outside. Irene has stopped noticing weather. Her mind is in a new landscape, the landscape of Pearl's wedding dress. This is all she can see. She talks with pins held between her teeth. She strokes the satin like a lover's skin. She holds it against her face. She has forgotten my question. She says, still biting the pins: 'I never had a white wedding of my own.'

I invited Pearl out to the farm. I wore lipstick and put my hair in a French pleat. I provided a lunch of Findus smoked-haddock pancakes served with broccoli. Sonny was away in the barn keeping cool in the dusty shade.

I said to Pearl: 'You and Timmy, you seem like babes to me. Are you ready for all this?'

'How does anyone know when they're "ready"?' she said.

I thought about Sonny and me; the touching and wanting that went on and on, filling up every minute of time. I said: 'Could you live without him?'

'Yes, I could,' said Pearl, 'but I don't want to.'

'Has he made love to you?'

Pearl blushed. Then she looked at me coldly. She was

thinking this was none of my business and she was right. She said: 'Timmy's a Christian. He's going to be a vicar.'

'I know that,' I said.

'But we want children,' said Pearl. 'We both do. We've talked about it. That's the day I long for.'

She was sitting opposite me at the kitchen table. A slab of sunlight lay on her shoulder and made her hair shine like spun glass.

I said: 'You're so beautiful, Pearl. You could have any man you chose.'

'I'm tired of being beautiful,' she said. 'I've been told that all my life. All I want to be now is me, with Timmy. And then a mother.'

'What about your ambition?' I asked.

'What ambition?' she said.

'To be a dental nurse. I remember, when we did *What's My Line* at Mountview, there was one. Or I think that was what she was. Her name was Anthea. Her mime was leaning over and staring down at something. The something was a mouth, but we never guessed it. We thought the something could be the Grand Canyon or a butterfly alighting on a window sill.'

Pearl stared at me. I didn't like to imagine what she was thinking.

After a moment, she said: 'As you know, we're going to get digs in Brighton. I'll do dental work there until Timmy finishes at Teviotts.'

'And then what?' I said.

'Then, we'll see,' she said. 'Cleaning up people and helping them to stay calm is a good training for motherhood.'

'Biology was what you used to love,' I said.

'Yes,' said Pearl. 'I still do. I've told Timmy, I'd like to keep fish.'

On the subject of a wedding, nobody tells the whole truth.

There *is* no whole truth, just as there is no heart of the onion; there are only the dreams of individual minds.

I tried to find out what Timmy was dreaming of. He said: 'Peace.'

He's grown since he was at Teviotts. He's worked so hard, it's elongated his bones.

'Do you mean peace of mind?' I asked.

'Just peace,' he said. 'I didn't believe I'd find it in a human being. I used to think it was only in things you couldn't define.'

'And?'

'The minute I put my arms round Pearl, that day, I felt it: absolute, perfect calm.'

I smiled at him. He so seldom tells me things. It was my father who came and told me Timmy wanted to go into the Church. Tim didn't have the courage.

We were sitting in front of the television. A film was on with the sound turned down low. Doris Day began singing almost silently through layers of gauze. Sonny was out in the night walking the dog.

'Are you a virgin, Tim?' I said.

He looked away from me. 'Why are you so interested in other people's lives?' he said. 'Why don't you get more interested in your own?'

I ignored this. I moved my eyes back to the television. Rock Hudson arrived at the end of Doris's quiet little song and held out a bunch of roses. I said: 'You both seem like babes to me, Tim. I don't want you to get lost, that's all.'

'It's you who are lost,' he said.

Then he left me to watch the rest of the movie alone. I adore films. Ninety-nine per cent of them end with the future all nicely arranged.

Sonny is trying to rearrange the future. He believes he can.

346

I told him: 'If you were at Mountview, Sonny, they'd explain to you about Delusion.'

He said: 'I'm not at Mountview. So don't say another fucking word.'

He's dreaming all right. He's told himself Timmy's going to change his mind about the farm. He believes that when Teviotts is over Timmy and Pearl will come back to Suffolk and take on the farm.

I don't know where we'll live, Sonny and I.

I think he may be building a nuclear fallout shelter for us in his head, connected to an electricity cable and a sewage pipe. We'll sleep in bunks: Sonny and Wolf underneath, me above.

I say nothing more about Delusion. Sonny says: 'It's obvious. Work it out. He'll want a proper home for his bride. And this is where her roots are, too. She'll need to be near Swaithey. Think about it. It's the only logical course for them to take.'

I remind him the world isn't logical. That's the insurmountable object in the way of human happiness.

Sonny doesn't reply. He stares at me, looking me over. He says: 'Are you going to get something done about your hair before the wedding? You can't go looking like that.'

I had it cut and permed. I thought, as it was all being rolled up on hard curlers like bones, Ava Gardner never had a perm. Not that I recall. Did she?

I looked neat and old. I looked a generation older than I was.

On The Day, the Fourth of July, in the very early hours, before Irene was up and ironing the dress one last time, before Timmy was awake and saying his prayers, I had an orgasm.

Nothing and no one touched me, except in a dream. But the orgasm was real and I woke up in the middle of it and cried with pleasure.

I couldn't remember the dream. And I couldn't remember when I'd last had an orgasm. It might have been in 1966 when I was in love with Bobby Moore, Captain of England.

We had a Teviotts student staying with us. His name was Julian. He was very tall, with white knuckles. He reminded me of a bamboo. He was going to be Timmy's best man.

There were no bridesmaids. Just Billy, dressed as a page in breeches, carrying the train, smiling. The only woman taking part in the ceremony was Pearl. And when we heard the rustle of the twenty-one yards of satin we all turned and stared and an absolute hush fell on us as we recognised the most beautiful bride this side of every ocean.

She was on Edward's arm. She smiled up at him. I heard the squeak of taffeta as Irene searched for a hankie.

But it didn't go as planned.

Half-way down the aisle, Edward collapsed. He fell sideways, tugging Pearl with him. He hit his head on a pew. Pearl fell on top of him, almost obliterating him with her dress. She screamed. Billy turned pale and covered his mouth with the train.

I stayed where I was, staring. Irene and Sonny and Timmy went running back. I thought, I saw this once before: something terrible happen among satin and net. It was in the Girl Guide hut.

The wedding march went on for a few bars, then stopped. My father was standing next to me, wearing a white peony in his button hole. He took my arm. He said: 'Hold on, Est.'

Edward was carried out into the porch. Pearl was crying. The bamboo stood by the altar, swaying.

I sat down. I felt worn out. I thought, that orgasm wore me out before this day even began.

'Is he dead?' I said to Cord.

'Almost certainly not,' Cord replied.

The vicar walked past us, his head high. He's a proud man with no grace. Timmy is all humility and gentleness compared to him. It could be that only one of them believes in Jesus.

'I'd better go and see,' I said.

Cord and I held on to each other. The smell of the perming solution is still on my hair and makes people close to me gag.

We found Edward alive and sitting up on astone bench.

Irene and Billy had their arms round him. Pearl was kneeling by him wiping her tears with her veil. Timmy and Sonny looked on gravely. The vicar stood by, clasping and unclasping his hands. Beyond the porch the July sun shone on the grass and on all the old tilting tombstones.

Edward was apologising. He said: 'I only fainted once before and that was on the cricket field. Only once before . . .'

'Don't try to talk, Edward,' said Irene.

'No. Don't try to talk, Dad,' said Billy.

'Don't talk,' said Pearl, weeping.

'It was the heat,' said Edward, disobeying his whole family, 'that's all it was. That and nerves. I'll be fine in a moment, Pearl, and we'll have another run at it.'

'No,' said Irene. She stroked Edward's wild white hair. There was a cut on his forehead where it had hit the pew.

Cord said: 'I'd take it easy, old chap.'

I said nothing. I felt too tired to speak. But I was glad Edward was alive. He's one of the few people in this place we would all mourn.

'I'll stand in for you, Dad,' said Billy. 'I've always wanted to give Pearl away.'

We all smiled.

Pearl got up off her knees. Her dress with the seven hundred tiny pearls was marked and dusty.

Irene said: 'We've got to get this cut seen to.'

Edward was driven home. Irene, Pearl and Billy went with him. I felt sorry for Tim.

We all sat in the cool church waiting. The organist played us some Bach.

Tim and the bamboo knelt together, praying.

I thought, it's a good thing it's summer and not likely to get dark. I closed my eyes. I heard a voice near me and it said: 'Mother . . .'

I opened my eyes immediately. I looked all around. But she wasn't there, of course. She is in the past. It's only in rare moments like these, when you have to wait for the present to carry on, that she slips into my mind . . .

It carried on eventually.

Billy led Pearl down the aisle. Her train followed, dragging on the floor. Edward sat in the pew with Irene, wearing a bandage round his head.

You could see Billy Harker grinning through the back of his head. He gave Pearl to my son and the vicar pronounced them man and wife.

I choked on the smell of my perm and on the sweet singing of the choir.

'They're babes,' I said to Cord. 'Lost in a wood.'

'Hush, Stelle,' he said. 'Give them a chance.'

17

1974

Hallowed Ground

Bentwater Bliss lived in a motor home. He told Walter: 'I long ago sold the motor, but that's what I still call it.' It had its own mail-box on a birchwood post. It was number 315 in a trailer park. The trailer park was situated between a drive-in bank and a Garden of Rest. Bentwater said: 'You cash in your chips; then you call it quits!'

The motor home reminded Walter of Pete Loomis's bus. He thought it remarkable that the two people who believed in his singing both lived in motor vehicles that couldn't move. He described the trolley bus to Bentwater, how it had no electricity and how, at dusk, the heifers clustered round it. Bentwater shook his head. 'Goddamned England!' he said.

Bentwater had a plan. When he heard Walter sing he knew he was hearing something good, so the plan came into his head straight away: he would make himself Walter's agent. Walter had the voice but he, Bentwater, knew the town. Together they would get rich.

He waited and listened and let time pass. Then he said to Walter: 'Okay, Walt. This is the darn plan. We write songs till they're coming out of our bones. We hire some pickers. We cut a demo tape. Then it's Vietnam: saturation bombing. We knock on every door on Sixteenth Avenue.

We napalm the record companies and the radio stations. We wake up the whole of Nashville. And all I'll take is twenty per cent.'

Walter went home to 767. He thought of it as home now. It was spring and the shade trees were coming into leaf. In front of 767 were two redbuds. In a single weekend they'd exploded into flower, just like Pete had said they would. The flowers were bright raspberry pink, the colour of Cleo's rayon bedsheets.

He told Audrey and Bill C. that Bentwater Bliss was going to be his agent. Audrey said: 'There are genuine real agents in Nashville, dear. Why don't we get a name and have you go on over and see one of them?'

'They don't know me,' said Walter. 'They won't work for me. Bentwater will work for me.'

'He'll work for you,' said Bill C., 'then he'll cheat ya. Simple as that.'

Walter wrote regularly to Pete. He tried to give him a picture of his new life. He described his yard work, the bonfires of the fall, the mending and clearing of winter, the digging and sowing of spring. He listed the things he was given by the women he worked for: jars of pickled beets, slices of pie, watermelons, home-made candy, tins of tobacco, hand-me-down shirts, a putting iron and a box of old fireworks. He said: 'I've felt since I got here that I was in the right place. And now, with the help of Bentwater, whom I trust even though Bill C. doesn't, I think I shall get to stand up and sing at long last. I shall dedicate my first song to you. I haven't forgotten Jimmie Rodgers, the Singing Brakeman or writing "Oh, Sandra" when I thought I was in love. If it comes right, I'll owe it all to you.'

He didn't write to Grace.

He thought about her. He was glad that every one of her days was safely ended soon after his had begun. He let her birthday pass. When he became a singer he'd send her his news. He would write: 'You have a famous son.'

The first time he sang to an audience was at a funeral.

The deceased was a woman of sixty-two named Mrs Riveaux. She wasn't going to be buried in any Garden of Rest but under a giant magnolia tree on her farm near Franklin. Bentwater explained: 'She loved that 'ere land and she liked the music of the country. She was a pure Tennessee woman. She could even dance.'

Her husband was a circuit judge, to whom Bentwater owed his life. This was why Bent and Walter were going to sing at Mrs Riveaux's funeral, because the Judge never forgot the people he'd saved. He knew that a person who needs saving once may need saving over and over.

'How did he save you, Bent?' asked Walter.

They were in the motor home, drinking beer. The little electric refrigerator kept kicking in and making a vibrato humming.

'He saved me by having me work for him on the farm,' said Bentwater. 'I was up before him on a vagrancy charge. I'd been sleeping in a pile of sand. Living off garbage. Stealing tobacco. He could have sent me down but he didn't. He had me come out to the farm and work there for bed and board. I slept in what once was the slaves' cabin. I think my mattress still had the body fluids of slaves steeped into it 'cause it smelled like it was a person. But it was better than sand.

'And Miz Riveaux, she was kind to me. She give me clothes to wear. I never knew whose they'd been. She give me a razor and soap and one-day-old newspapers. And I used to sing for her and the Judge. In summer. We used to sit out on the porch with no light 'cept the mosquito flares, singing.'

'How long did you stay there?' asked Walter.

'Oh, a year maybe. Till I got sick of the sight of the sky. I'm not cut out for living on a farm.'

'Nor was I,' said Walter.

'I mean, it's okay for a while and then you just mainly tire of it.'

'Yes. You do.'

'I knew Fay May by that time. She gave me a break in the Lounge, singing for the jar money. I bought me an old car and lived in that. Parked it near the heap of sand, so as I could see where I'd once been. I ain't no Nietzsche nor Wittgenstein, Walter, but one thing I do think and that's this, if you don't know the place where y'all been you could wind up back there and not recognise it and when that happens you are purely in shit creek. You are going round in a friggin' circle, an' that's tragic.'

The Riveaux were Baptist. The funeral was in a small white church standing on its own in the middle of Riveaux land.

Walter wrote to Pete:

> It had a garden – lawns and beds – and I said to Bent: 'My uncle was once a church gardener in Memphis,' and he said: 'No kiddin', Walt?'
>
> Mrs Riveaux's coffin was ebony. It looked large to me so I think she must have been tall. There was a ton of flowers.
>
> I had to go and buy a suit for the funeral and I bought a black leather tie on a string. Bentwater wore lizard boots but I just wore some plain shoes.
>
> The Reverend talked about the good woman Mrs Riveaux had been while she was alive and how she and the Judge loved all living creatures, including the negroes and the poor and the hogs in the field. He made her sound like a female Jesus. He said the Riveaux farm was a place of beauty in a devastated world.

Bent introduced me as his new singing partner. He wasn't going to mention the agent business in front of a funeral congregation. He said I'd come all the way from Suffolk, England, because of my love of song.

I played the guitar and Bent played the mandolin. We led the hymns. The mourners sang loud, as if they all belonged to the Sally Ann.

Then we did two songs composed by Bent that were Mrs Riveaux's favourites. We'd worked out some lovely harmonies. And I could see lots of the mourners crying. The titles of Bent's numbers were 'Bird in the Sky' and 'Down in My Yard There's a Creek that Flows to Heaven'.

We didn't go to the burial. That was a private thing, under a magnolia. But before we left, the Judge came and shook my hand. He said: 'Welcome to Tennessee. I'll say prayers for your success in your chosen task.' I thought the word 'task' was a bit peculiar, but I expect you remember that lots of words here have different meanings from the ones we're used to giving them.

By the time of Mrs Riveaux's funeral, Walter's repertory of songs for the demo tape was almost complete. He saved every cent he could save from his yard work for the day when he and Bent would hire session musicians and studio time and cut the tape. He thought of this day as a boulder. He was in a cave (quite an enjoyable cave where it was warm in winter) and the boulder was lying across the exit. It didn't fit exactly. You could see light around it and weather. You could hear storms.

He described the boulder to Audrey Pike. He said: 'I've got my eye on it most of the time.'

She said: 'All I wish is, Walter, that you weren't putting your trust in Bentwater Bliss.'

He had to shrug this off. No one had trusted Pete Loomis except him. And Bentwater had become his mentor and guide. Without him and all the hours spent in the motor home he could have lost direction by now. He could have resigned himself to a life spent raking leaves.

And then Bentwater made something else happen. It happened in one afternoon, a Friday. After it, Walter's eye was only on the boulder some of the time and all the rest of the time it was elsewhere and blinking with fright and joy.

They were backstage at the Ryman Auditorium, among the ropes and pulleys and sandbags that raised and lowered the advertising hoardings, behind the ragged blue and gold curtains.

Bentwater had a single slot in the Grand Ole Opry line-up that night and he was here to rehearse. He was describing the origins of the Ryman to Walter. He said: 'This is hallowed ground, Walt. In more ways than one. It was once a Gospel tabernacle where all the travelling evangelists came and preached. Now it's the Mecca of Country Music. It's where stars are made: Roy Acuff, Loretta Lynn, Patsy Cline, Bill Monroe, Hank Snow, Hank Williams, Minnie Pearl, Johnny Cash . . . you name it. Elvis sang on this stage in '54. The temperature here can go as high as 101 degrees. It's holy air. Can you feel it? And these are its last days. The whole shooting match is moving to a new concert hall called Opryland.'

Walter stared up at the advertisements for 'Union 76 Gas' and 'Goo-Goo Clusters' and the 'National Life and Accident Insurance Company', then out at the wooden seats like pews and the stained-glass windows above. He was about to say that he could definitely feel the holiness of the air when a thin girl in a skimpy sweater and skirt and high-heeled shoes came up to Bentwater and took his arm and said: 'Hi, Bent. How y'all doing?'

Bentwater gave the girl a kiss. She wore dark lipstick. Her brown hair was tied up in a bundle on the top of her head. Her face was long and pale. Walter stared at her and thought, she looks tired; she looks in need of someone.

'I was tellin' Walter about the history of this place,' said Bentwater. 'Walter's from England.'

'Well,' said the girl, 'I declare.'

Walter held out his hand. The girl shook it lightly, hardly touching it.

'This is Skippy Jean Maguire,' said Bentwater. 'She's been a backup singer on the Opry for a few years now. You can sing any darn song you like, Walter, and Skippy Jean will find the harmony to it. And she's self-taught. Can't read a note-a music!'

'That's right,' said Skippy Jean. 'Music sheets, they might as well be in Japanese. You a singer then, Walter?'

'Trying to be one,' said Walter. 'Going to be one.'

'He *is* a singer,' said Bentwater. 'He sang with me at Miz Riveaux's funeral and we had all the whole church weepin'. And now we're going to cut a demo. Yore looking at a future star, Skippy Jean.'

'That right?' she said. This was a kind of question but the way she said it made it sound like an answer to something.

Walter said: 'Bent's going to be my agent.'

Skippy Jean dug Bentwater in his gut. 'Sweet Jesus!' she said, 'you mean you *trust* him?'

'Yes,' said Walter.

'Hell,' she said, 'I wouldn't trust Bentwater Bliss further'n I could spit. You better get someone to watch over you, honey. Or you'll be sleepin' on First Avenue.'

Walter took out a packet of chewing gum from his jacket pocket and offered Skippy Jean a piece. 'You can watch over me,' he said, 'if you like.'

She stared at him. Bentwater stared at him. The thing he'd just said had sounded like a declaration of love. He should have felt embarrassed but he didn't. Skippy Jean took the piece of gum.

He watched her all evening.

There were three backup singers – two girls and one man. They sat on high stools near the microphones, waiting for their moments. They sang as if singing were breathing, as if they did it in their sleep. They put their three heads in a cluster. Walter kept thinking, I wish my head was part of the cluster, close to hers.

Bentwater sang 'Bird in the Sky'. Skippy Jean and the other backers sang a better, sweeter harmony than Walter had achieved at the funeral.

At the end of the night, late, they went with a crowd to Fay May's and Bentwater and Walter went with them. It was then that Walter realised he hadn't had his eyes on the boulder for hours.

He sat next to Skippy Jean. She chain-smoked. He breathed in her perfume and her smoke.

He reminded himself how hopeless the passions of his past had been. Then he told himself that his particular past was further away than most people's. He'd cut it adrift by coming to America. It was a speck on the horizon, receding and receding. Soon, it would plummet out of sight and out of mind.

He bought drinks for her. She held her glass in both hands, like a child.

He said: 'Are you married to anybody?'

She didn't answer this. She put down her drink and smiled at him. One of her false eyelashes had come unstuck at its corner.

She said: 'The way you make the language sound, Walter, that sheerly mesmerises me.'

Heartless River

Timmy graduated from Teviotts College. He could feel the Hebrew that he'd struggled with for so long already leaving his mind. His head ached, trying to retrieve it. Then he let it go.

He asked himself and he asked Pearl where lost knowledge went. Did it hang in the air, like a cloud of flies, waiting to be rediscovered?

Pearl said: 'Tim, your head's full of unverifiable things. It's lucky my field is Biology, isn't it?'

David Tate was moved by the sight of Timmy in his curate's black. He put both his hands on Timmy's head and said a blessing. Privately, he asked God to protect Timothy from malice.

Timmy's curateship was in Shropshire, not far from the Welsh border. Pearl and Timmy would live in a slate-roofed bungalow. It had a garden of cabbages. There were two bedrooms in it, one for them and one for the baby Pearl was expecting in the winter. The names they'd chosen for the child were David and Sophie.

The church was called St Swithin's. It shared a valley with three sheep farms and two hundred houses and a municipal swimming pool. When Timmy saw that a pool was right there at the foot of the grassy hills he thought, the 90° angle is now a 180° angle. The horizontal line is the earth, the perfect dome is the sky.

They came to Swaithey for a few days, to say goodbye. They didn't stay at the farm. Pearl wanted to sit with Irene, arm in arm and warm and cosy and talk about the baby. Billy knelt at Pearl's feet and laid his head on her abdomen, listening for signs of life. Edward went to the attic and brought down the crib that he'd made for Billy and gave it to Timmy. Everybody in the house felt comfortable and at peace.

Timmy and Pearl went to the farm for one day.

'*One* day,' said Sonny. 'One solitary fucking day.'

They sat in the living room with the TV turned down. The perm was growing out of Estelle's hair. Half of it was straight again and half curly. Ava Gardner had never looked like this.

It was harvest time, except that there was no harvest. In four fields there was the beet crop. What grew in all the rest were thistles and dock and ground elder and sweetbriar and horseradish and grass.

'It's still yours,' said Sonny to Timmy. 'You've neglected it and it's all gone downhill, but it's still yours. You and Pearl and the baby could live here. You could have our old room. We wouldn't mind. We'd stay out of your way. You could have the run of the place . . .'

'No,' said Timmy.

'This is your last chance,' said Sonny.

'You know we can't,' said Timmy.

'*What?*' said Sonny. 'Speak up.'

'We're going to Shropshire. It's all arranged.'

'I'm telling you, this is your last chance. It's good land underneath. Fewer stones than in the days of my father. This has been Ward land since before the first war.'

'Don't go on, Sonny,' said Estelle.

'I'm not going on. I'm just telling him this is his last chance.'

Estelle said: 'Lunch is ready.'

They went into the kitchen. The dog lay under the table. It rested its head on Pearl's white shoes.

Estelle had cooked a frozen chicken, bought ready-dressed in a plastic bag from Grace Loomis's 'Frozen Convenience Meats' counter. Estelle knew the chicken tasted of nothing. She preferred things to taste of nothing than to taste like they once had long ago. She said: 'Convenience Meats may not have got as far as Shropshire yet, but they'll get there in time, I expect.'

Pearl said: 'Shropshire's a very beautiful county, did you know?'

'Yes,' said Estelle, 'but it's on the other side of England. When will I get to see my grandson?'

'I don't know,' said Timmy.

'As often as possible,' said Pearl.

'What does that mean?' said Estelle.

'It means as often as we can,' said Timmy. 'We can't be more precise about it than that.'

'Nothing is precise,' said Estelle. 'That is what you can be precise about: nothing.'

A silence fell. Pearl thought, this is how it always was here, how it always must have been, for Timmy and for Mary. It was always filled with this unendurable silence. All they could do was leave . . .

Timmy and Pearl left soon after lunch. They drove away in Edward's car.

Estelle kissed them both and said goodbye. She said: 'Look after each other, that's the thing.'

Sonny was silent. He just stared at them and nodded. Then, as they were getting into the car he said: 'The room I sleep in would do as the baby's room.'

They didn't hear this. They waved and smiled as they drove away.

Estelle refused to remember the date of the thing that occurred next. She'd say: 'I can't be precise. Who *can* be?'

It was after Timmy and Pearl had gone to Shropshire. Estelle was watching tennis the day it happened. She could have memorised the date from Wimbledon, but she refused to. She said to Sonny before he went out: 'The American players never give up. They're not like us. Billie Jean's not going to give up, I can tell.'

Sonny walked in the direction of the river. The dog, Wolf.

was with him. He carried the small gun, a four-ten shotgun he used for shooting rabbits. Rabbits had been almost wiped out by man's ingenuity once; then they returned. Men went on and on believing they were ahead of nature and nature outwitted them, on and on, over and over.

It was a humid, sunless day. The cloud was like a suffocating rug thrown between the earth and the sky.

Sonny didn't know why he'd chosen the river, but when he got there he knew. Memory was in the river. And resolution.

He squatted down. Squatting was uncomfortable at the age of fifty-six. He wished there was a stone to sit on. After squatting for a while, he let himself fall onto his knees.

He was in the place where his father had made a willow plantation. There had been money in it then. You stuck in sticks of willow. You made sure the water was channelled to their feet. And the sticks took root and grew into little saplings that sprouted a head of willow wands. The wands were stripped and sold to thatchers and basket-makers. It was money from nothing.

Everything in Sonny's father's life happened late, except death which happened early. He was already old when Sonny was a boy: an old man making his willow beds by the river and laughing and saying: 'Money from nothing!' But it wasn't nothing. Gangs of boys had to strip the willow wands, using an awkward implement like a pair of blunt scissors, called a Brake. Sonny was part of the gang. They squatted in the field beside the heap of wands. The heap rose above their heads. Their task seemed to have no end. And Sonny's father stood near them, gleeful and proud, with his back turned. He never understood how terrible their work was. 'Money from nothing.'

Sonny thought, what am I waiting for? What have I been waiting for all this time? Waiting for someone to say: 'You worked hard with the Willow Brake, here is your reward and your rest.' Waiting for someone to say: 'You were saved from death on the Rhine to cultivate your land and now you can lie down and be at peace.'

He was as still as stone, listening. In his father's day, in his mother's day, they used to speak about the music of the river. His mother came from a family of craftsmen. They made merry-go-rounds. They heard music where there was none. They were oblivious to the heartlessness of water and sky. They were fools.

Sonny didn't know how long he'd been kneeling there. His knees felt sucked into the earth. He thought, I'd better get on with it before my fucking knees start growing roots like the willow.

He put a cartridge into the single-barrelled gun. He snapped it shut and took off the safety catch.

He felt all around him for a stick or a twig to throw for the dog.

He found something. It was a rusted piece of tin. It could have been the handle of an old bucket.

Wolf sat at his side, scratching. He'd scratched a part of his flank raw.

Sonny whistled. The dog's ears went up. 'Fetch!' said Sonny and threw the bucket handle into the river.

The dog went running after the thrown object. At the water's edge he hesitated, as Sonny knew he would. Wolf wasn't fond of the river.

Sonny lifted the gun. He'd always liked this particular gun, its lightness and accuracy. He aimed at Wolf's head, just above his leather collar. He fired and the dog fell. The body lay half in and half out of the river. Later, the force of the current would draw it down and in.

Sonny could hear himself wheezing and gasping, even muttering or jabbering like an idiot. In the still and silent day the shot had been deafening.

His hands shook. He knew he had to hurry. If he didn't

hurry the thing wouldn't be done. The pointless waiting would resume; the waiting that killed you in the end . . .

He re-loaded the gun. He held it down at his side, pointing towards his head. He stuck the barrel in his coral ear and pulled the trigger.

Pete Loomis found Sonny's body.

He'd gone to the river to get watercress for Estelle. She used to gather it herself; now she barely went out of the house except, once in a while, to get drunk with Pete and to dance.

Pete returned to the bus. He poured himself a slug of whisky and drank it down. He found a blanket. He returned to the river and covered Sonny's dead body with this. He walked very slowly and carefully up to the farmhouse. As he approached, he could hear applause coming from the TV.

He went into the sitting room. Estelle was kneeling in front of the television smiling. As soon as she saw Pete she said: 'Billie Jean won! She was a set and a half down but she never gave up. We should be more like the Americans.'

Pete said: 'Yes.'

Then he came and sat down clumsily by her on the floor and took her hand.

18

1975

Martin:

Every morning, when I wake up, I forget where I am. I have to stare at the furniture until I remember.

Coming here was Rob's idea. He said: 'Mart, I just thought of someone you know in a far-away place – that boy who went to Tennessee.'

'Walter?'

'Yes. Go there. He'll need rescuing by now. And the American South still thinks it's a country on its own. It's one of the last imaginary places on earth.'

I had the next bit of surgery, the hysterectomy. I lay in the hospital and wondered about the cost of moving from the known to the unknown. Sterns came to see me. I said: 'Would Tennessee be an appropriate place?' He said: 'Anywhere is appropriate. Leaving England is what matters. Use the money you got from Miss McRae.'

My address is 767 Greenwood Avenue, Nashville TN, 37212. I have Walter's old room. Walter lives in a downtown apartment now and wears a rhinestone jacket, but that is a long sweet story . . .

Audrey and Bill C. Pike believe I'm an ordinary man, not an imaginary one. Their black maid, Lois, cleans my room. I have none of Mary's possessions left. My underwear comes from Burton's. I wear a silk scarf, folded into a pad, inside my blue Y-fronts. I own seven of these scarves, some spotted, some paisley. The feel of silk in the groin is civilised.

Bill C. found me a job in a supermarket. I pack groceries into brown paper bags for the customers and carry the bags out to their cars. Some of the cars are pink, with white steering wheels.

I earn a very small wage. I rely on free food and on tips. It's January. The cars slither about on the parking lot. When the rain falls, it turns to glass. Sometimes the customers' hands are too frozen to give me the tip. But I'm always polite. I wear a Russian fur hat, with the flaps down over my ears. I touch the hat in a kind of salute. The people here like things to be formal. They like everyone to know his place and to stay in it.

I take the food back to Audrey and she makes peculiar meals with it: Black Eye Bean Soup and Corn Bread and meat in oyster sauce. She says: 'In my mind, Martin, I sometimes cook for the boys I never had. That's how crazy I can get.'

She isn't crazy at all. She sews normally. She doesn't caress the sewing machine. Her hair is brown and neat. She's the kind of woman anyone would like to have as a mother. Even Lois loves her. She brings her paintings of dinosaurs her children have made at school and Audrey says: 'Why, how enchanting, Lois, and how kind.' She tapes them to the side of the refrigerator so that Bill C. and I can admire them.

My own drawing has ceased. I drew Vietnam for such a long time that I can't remember how to do ordinary things. And the war's over at last. A nation can get so tired of something that it wants to drown in the Sea of Forgetfulness and be reborn pink and innocent like a car. I can understand that.

The second thing I remember when I wake, after I've looked at the furniture, is that my father is no longer alive.

I get up then. I take a shower. I start my day. I listen out for sounds of life: for Lois arriving, for Bill C. singing in the bath, for Audrey switching on the radio in the kitchen. I draw back my curtains and look out at the morning. I feel a kind of happiness coming on.

When the news came, I memorised the words. I locked them into my mind for ever. I felt a quickening inside me.

It was Cord who wrote. The letter was in green ink and free of Wincarnis stains. The words I memorised were these: 'It seems it wasn't an accident. He shot the dog first. Then he blew his head away.'

'He blew his head away.' Safe in my memory now, for always.

So then I get on a bus and go to work. It's nearly always the same bus driver. He says: 'Mornin', Sir. How y'all today?' And every morning, without fail, I am moved by this and I say: 'Fine.'

At the supermarket, people are less friendly. It's cold in there. The checkout women wear mittens. They don't think of the grocery packers as being part of the staff. We're invisible to them. They gossip to each other. They discuss TV programs and nail hardening products and men. They leave us out.

I don't mind. I'm not in search of friends and confidences. I'm concentrating on being. I live each hour, one by one. My mind is quiet and still. I'm no longer waiting for time to pass.

The only person I've got to know at the supermarket is called Les Chesney. He's in charge of in-store hygiene. His job is to wander about, looking for cockroaches and inspecting the fingernails of the counter staff. Everybody loathes him except me. He has the power to fire a meat packer for not wearing a hairnet. He has fat, clean hands and a weight problem. He's referred to as 'Les Ches'. I don't know why I like him, except that when I heard him called 'Les Ches' I remembered Sterns saying: 'It's the name that breaks your heart.'

Sometimes I go to a bar with Les Ches after work and drink

Mexican beer. He says: 'I used to play ice-hockey, Martin. Then my left tibia got smashed and that was it.'

I say: 'I'm sorry, Les.'

He says: 'I had a wife back then and a leatherette suite. I was thin.'

I say: 'The past is another country. The past is Atlantis.'

He says: 'Excuse me, Mart, Atlantis was a city not a country.'

'Whatever,' I say, 'it doesn't matter. The point is, it's no longer there.'

'I dunno,' he says. 'I refuse to give up on it. I do crash diets from time to time. I write letters to my ex. I even get dreams about furniture.'

'Well,' I say, 'I don't think it's wise, Les.'

'Why not? I had a nice life then. I knew who I was. Don't you sometimes want your past back?'

'No,' I say. 'Never.'

Les's eyes are small and tucked deep into his face. He has trouble staring.

'I guess,' he says, 'if you're from England you got so much darn past all around ya, you just can't face adding to it. That right?'

I smile. I say: 'That's one way of seeing it.' I buy Les another beer and he says: 'You're a nice person, Martin. You're like people used to be.'

Then I go back to one of Audrey's meals. The only thing she makes that I can't stand is turnip greens. They have a sour taste. Everything we eat is dead but turnip greens are the only food I can think of that tastes of death. I apologise to Audrey. She says: 'No need to 'pologise. We all have our likes and dislikes. Walter, now, he *loved* my greens. Didn't he, Bill C.? Remember that?'

Walter loved this room. He wrote me a letter describing it and its view of the vegetable garden and the shade trees. He told me about the scarlet birds.

Then he didn't write again and I thought it's all starting now, the disappointment, the failed hopes. But I was wrong. He was too busy to write, that's all. He was too busy writing songs in Bentwater's motor home and falling in love and saving for his rhinestone jacket. He was walking round second-hand car lots, stroking Chevrolets. By the time I arrived at 767 he was out of here and living where he lives now, on First Avenue, with Skippy Jean Maguire.

I didn't recognise him. I saw this tall man dressed in snakeskin and glitter. His hair was going grey. He came to the door whistling. Behind him in the living room was a thin girl in a tight dress lying on the floor, smoking.

I said: 'Walter?'

He gaped at me. Gaping, he looked more like his former self.

He said: 'Jesus! Mary?'

'Martin,' I said.

He turned and called out to the thin girl. 'Sky!' he called. 'Come here! We've got a visitor from the old country.'

He calls her 'Sky'. Whenever they're together, which is nearly all the time, his big hands are caressing some part of her – her ear, her neck, her hair, her foot. She leans against him, smiling. She rests her body on his, like he was a chair. Sometimes she looks as though she could drop off into a beautiful sleep.

She told me how they met. She said: 'It was in Fay May's. After the Friday night Opry, 'fore the Opry moved out to Opryland. It was love at first glance, wasn't it, Walter?'

'Yes,' said Walter. 'I'd been watching you all evening.'

'Oh that's right,' she said. 'He'd been watching me. So you can't say "first glance" can you, 'cause he glanced at me before I glanced at him, okay?'

'And then?' I said.

'Well,' said Sky. 'You ever been in love, Martin?'

'Yes,' I said.

'Then you know how it is, okay? I don't have to describe it. But I will go right ahead and describe it anyway, right?

'We were just drinkin' an' all and Walter, he comes and sits by me and the darn near-first thing he says to me is: "Are you right now married to anybody?" I didn't answer. I didn't say yes or no. I told him he had a speaking voice like no other I'd ever heard 'cept in the movies when you get an English sea-captain or spy or somethin'. I said I was mesmerised by his voice. That's the word I used: "mesmerised". And that was it then, wasn't it, Walter? That was the beginning of everything right bang there and then.'

I spend time with them on Sundays. Sky cooks brown shrimp in butter in a skillet and we eat the shrimp with bread and beer. It's a delicious meal. Sometimes Bentwater Bliss is there. When I met him, he said: 'I quit singing, now, Martin. I'm too old to sing. I'm an agent now and, I tell ya, the sound that Walter and Sky make together is the prettiest sound I ever had the good fortune to hear. And now it's all starting to happen for them here in Nashville.'

They've formed themselves into a singing duo. The first name Walter thought up was 'Earth and Sky'. Bentwater said: 'You can't do that, Walt. 'Less you want the whole world to think Earth's your name.'

'I don't mind,' said Walter.

'You gotta practise minding, then,' said Bentwater. 'Earth just ain't a thing you can call yourself.'

So this is what they chose: 'Swaithey and Sky'.

I said nothing.

Walter looked at me. He knew what my thoughts were. He said: 'It's just a name, Martin. It begins with S.'

When spring comes I stare at all the blossom along Twenty-First Avenue and get a longing for something I can't name. Then I do name it. As I walk through the empty parking lot, I name it. It's a longing to be out of the city. It's a longing to hear a river or hear silence. Only that.

At the weekend I say to Audrey: 'Is Tennessee a beautiful state?'

'Beautiful state?' she says. 'Let me tell you, Martin, this is one of the loveliest states in the Union. You get on a bus headed south toward Franklin an' you'll see.'

I get on a coach like a Greyhound Bus. The coach radio is playing the kind of songs Walter used to live for before he started living for Skippy Jean Maguire.

I'd bought a ticket to Franklin, but I ask the driver to tell me when we're in the middle of nowhere and to set me down there.

'Okay,' he says. 'What kinda nowhere do you want, Sir? Fields? Woods? Parkland? I gotta know what kind.'

'Fields,' I say.

'Not a suicide, are ya?'

'No.'

'Okay,' he says. 'I got it. I know the place.'

The place is a valley. On either side of the road are poplars. Beyond the poplars are fields of green corn and beyond them, sloping grasslands fanning out and up in a bowl towards a rim of forest. There's a track running by the side of the maize field. On the verge, pecking by a poplar root, is a solitary hen.

I set off along the track. The hen follows me. I see it running along, trying to catch me up. It thinks I'm going to lead it home.

The day is what Les Chesney would call 'pretty'. He means fair, beautiful, cloudless. He said: 'When I was married, Martin, it's like all the days were pretty then.'

I'm wearing the high boots made of tough hide Walter helped me choose. In them I feel tall. I swagger.

I swagger on up the track with my companion, the hen. It's a Rhode Island Red. I recognise its scarlet comb.

The track turns left where the grasslands begin. I stop. The hen turns left and runs faster. I can hear a dog barking so I know that eventually the track leads to a farm.

I go on up the grass slopes. I can see the house now, in the distance, sheltered by trees. It's the only house in the valley and I suspect that whoever owns it owns all the land as far as anyone can see. He is in paradise; only, his TV reception is poor.

I sit down on the springy grass. I light a cigarette and look around at all the beauty there. I think to myself, in the summer there'll be work on the farms, picking fruit. That kind of work makes you strong.

I stare at the roof of the house.

Some time after the important letter, the one I'd memorised and locked inside me, Cord had written with some more news. He said: 'The farm has gone. The house went to people from London. They're tearing it down. They're going to put some other version of it there. The mortgage is paid off.

'Grace Loomis bought the land. She's farming turkeys on it. She's building a meat factory. She has a ruddy great fleet of lorries delivering to supermarkets all over the country.

'Your mother's here, in Gresham Tears, with me. Hard to say who's taking care of whom. The thing is, Martin, I'm getting so bloody old.'

So I let myself think of her, sometimes. Now that my father's dead; now that she's with Cord; now that Timmy and Pearl are a long way away.

When things are slack at the store or when I'm alone in my room at 767 watching the birds flying in and out of the shade trees, I imagine her. And now, here in this valley, smoking a Marlboro, I think of her sitting by the fire, or out by the porch helping Cord to prune the Albertine.

She is young, in my mind. Her hair is still black and long, falling thickly round her face.

19

1976

Martin:

Walter and Sky are trying to get married, or rather, what they're trying to do is locate Sky's first husband so that she can divorce him and marry Walter. She says to me: 'He was always elusive, Martin. He was always slithering away someplace.'

Now he's slithered away into the blue. He used to work on the river boats and he's probably on a river somewhere but they've no idea which one. They're sending letters to river boat companies all over the South. There are more rivers in the United States than in any other continent on earth.

Happiness is making Walter fat. He can't fasten his rhinestone jacket, but he doesn't care. 'Swaithey and Sky' have been signed up by a record company called TMS Records. I'd never heard of it. It's not exactly Decca. I say to Walter: 'What does TMS stand for?'

'Oh,' he says, 'I dunno.'

Sky says: 'What it stands for doesn't matter. It's like WSM 650, the radio station. That got started by an insurance company an' their slogan was "We Shield Millions" so they decided their call-sign would be WSM. Now, hardly anyone remembers the "We Shield Millions" thing. You see what I'm saying? WSM has become a kind of *word*.'

'But it stood for something once,' I say. Sky thinks I'm a pedantic person, needing everything explained. She says: 'TMS could be anything. It could be Tuna Mayonnaise Sandwich. It could be To-Morrow is Sunday. The point is, it doesn't matter. What matters is they've signed us.'

Bentwater has got his hair blowdried. He's cut down on the whiskey. He's fumigated his motor home. He says to me: 'We're hitting it now, Mart. Success. We're kickin' down the door. And all of us gotta stay sharp.'

I tell Audrey and Bill C. what's going on. They've never heard of TMS Records. Bill C. says: 'Tell Walter to watch his back. Leopards don't change their spots.'

But Walter pays no attention. The only thing that can make him depressed is thinking about Pete.

Pete told him in a letter that his bus is surrounded by wire fencing on three sides. Beyond the wire are turkeys. There are more than a thousand of them. Pete is hemmed in with their gobble-gabbling noise and their stench. He put: 'I'm going mad. If the bus could still move, I'd just drive away.'

'What can I do?' Walter asks me.

'I don't know,' I reply.

'I've got to do something but I can't think what. I owe my life to Pete.'

I tell him I'll think about it. I say: 'Out where I am now, I do a hell of a lot of thinking.'

Where I am is on Judge Riveaux's farm.

It's a farm given over to three things: to hogs, to summer fruit and to birds. The birds are: peacocks, guineafowl, turkeys, pheasants, chickens, geese and doves. They run and flap and fly all over everything, everywhere. The peacocks live on the roof. Sometimes they walk into the kitchen. The thing the late Mrs Riveaux loved most was all these living and wandering birds.

Bentwater Bliss found me my job. I told him I wanted

to leave the grocery store and work in the country, picking fruit or beans. He said straight away: 'I'll call the Judge. He's lookin' for someone. Miz Riveaux, she used to run that place singlehanded with just that old Jeremiah Hill to help her. The Judge thought he could do what she did. He figured, *Hell,* she was a *woman*! I can do whatever she did and in half the time. But he can't. It's got him baffled why, but he can't.'

So Bent drove me out here. The house is white board with a shingled roof. It has four wood-burning stoves to warm it. There's no garden, just as there was no real garden at Swaithey. The farm starts at the back door. There are barns for the hogs in winter and right by the barns the low brick house where Jeremiah Hill lives with his family. Beyond the bean fields is a creek, with an old canoe tied up. On the other side of the creek is a wood full of beeches, chestnuts, hickories and live oaks. The doves are pinkish-grey. They live in a white dovecot on a pole.

Judge Riveaux speaks so softly you can hardly hear what he says. You wonder how he used to make himself understood in court.

When I arrived with Bent, Jeremiah's wife, Beulah, had made tea and a pineapple cake. Jeremiah and Beulah are black. They have twins, aged seven, called Lettie and Glorie, short for Violette and Gloria. Jeremiah is fifty-five and Beulah is thirty-one. He had another wife in the past, from whom he slithered away.

We sat down with the tea and cake. The Judge looked at me with quiet brown eyes. He said: 'You were born on a farm, Martin. That it?'

'Yes,' I said. 'In Suffolk, England. It's stony soil. The first thing I can remember is picking stones.'

'Most of Tennessee is red clay. Good and rich. You can grow 'most anything in the Tennessee earth. But my wife, she used to have a gift for makin' things grow and I don't have that. You either have that or you don't have it. One or the other.'

'We used to keep birds,' I said suddenly.

'You did?'

'Yes. Hens. Guineafowl. I had a pet guineafowl I named Marguerite.'

'Well, now. Mrs Riveaux, she thought birds were just the finest thing, didn't she, Bent?'

'Yes, Sir,' said Bentwater. 'She did.'

'Now the peacocks, they screech sometimes. And to my ears that is one purely dreadful sound. But my wife, she didn't even mind that. You ever heard that, Martin?'

'No,' I said.

'Well you will, if you come to work here. You strong, though? You don't look strong. But nor did my wife. And she was. She could hold a hog down.'

'I'm stronger than I look,' I said. 'And I don't tire.'

The Judge smiled. He was dropping cake crumbs all down his shirt. 'Bentwater worked for me once, didn't you Bent?' he said. 'He used to tire. He could sleep anywhere. He could lie down on the bare dirt and start dreaming. Right?'

I moved out of 767. It was summer. Outside my window were watermelons and sugar snap peas. The shade made by the shade trees was black.

Bill C. and Audrey cooked me a farewell meal. It was Shrimp Creole. They said: 'We know Judge Riveaux. He's a good man. He treats the world right.'

I said goodbye to Les Ches. He said: 'Goddammit, Martin. You were the long-sufferingest friend I ever had.'

I don't live in the Judge's house. I live in what he calls 'the studio'. The studio was once a barn. The Riveaux converted it into a separate living space for their daughter, Suzanne, when she grew up and wanted to be an artist. Then she moved away. She married a Claims Adjuster from Florida. She lives in Boca Raton with three children. She never paints now and she never comes back to the farm.

Some of her possessions are here. There's an album full of photographs. There are books on Klimt and Picasso and Edward Hopper. There's a pile of records and a love letter from a boy called Irwin. There's a photograph of Mrs Riveaux when she was young. The bed is wide. It has a heavy quilt over it that hangs to the floor.

At night, cockroaches come out from under it and do figure skating in the moonlight.

I get up at six. I put on my overalls and my boots. There is no planning done on this farm. I walk down to Jeremiah's house and he says: 'Okay. What we do this mornin', we hoe the beans,' or sometimes: 'What the hell we gonna do today? Mend the post fence? What we do?'

Sometimes, Beulah calls out: 'Come in, Mister Martin. Have some coffee. Ain't no hurry this mornin'.'

So I go into their house, which is always dark, winter and summer. Lettie and Glorie sit side by side drinking milk, with their school lunch boxes packed and ready on the table. The colour of their eyes is amber. One morning, I said to them: 'Do they teach you about the universe at school?'

'No,' said Lettie.

'We don't know,' said Glorie.

'Well,' I said. 'I used to make up stories about the universe you know, about the stars? I could tell you one some time if you wanted.'

'Mamma tells us stories,' said Lettie.

'She tells us real stories,' said Glorie.

'That's good,' I said. 'Mine aren't real.'

While we sit there, drinking Beulah's coffee, Jeremiah decides what we're going to do. In winter, he sits there a long time, near the woodstove, deciding.

Then we go out and start our task, whatever it may be:

making a ditch, chopping wood, mending a fruit cage, burning bean stalks, mucking out the hogs' barn. He and Mrs Riveaux used to work together. They did everything side by side except the tractor work. And this is how Jeremiah likes to work with me. He says he can't concentrate if he isn't talking. He says: 'Miz Riveaux, by the time she died, she knew my whole life. I told her it in 'bout one million sections. She knew my life better 'an I know it myself.'

Now, he's telling it over again, to me. He says: 'The thing 'bout my life, Mister Martin, is this. What I don't have, an' what I never done had, is the gift of contentment.

'Now Beulah, she says to me: "Look at you' life, Jeremiah Hill, and then look back at the life of you' ancestors who were slaves down in Georgia." She says: "You look at that an' see if you don't got a reason to be happy."

'An' she' right. I got some reasons. One reason I got is her. And Lettie and Glorie. An' Mrs Riveaux, Miz Judge, she always did every way treat me fair.

'So I got reasons. I know that. An' once in a while it can come at me, like a breeze in August, a little sudden breeze of happiness. You know? But it don't last. I don't know why. I was always that way, all my life. Little breeze. Feel it right here, on my face. Then it goes.'

We're cleaning a ditch. We're not far from the creek. It's a hot day but we're down in the deep ditch and it's cool here.

I say: 'In the times when you're not happy, Jeremiah, are you *unhappy*?'

He stops work and considers this. He wipes his face on his overall sleeve.

'Unhappy?' he says. 'No. It ain't that. It ain't that. It's just, I keep on thinkin' there's somethin' more. I keep on and on believing there's somethin' *more* gonna come an' then I'll be happy. After that new thing done come. After that *more* thing done show itself to me. Then I'll be a happy man.'

*

Some evenings, I have supper with Judge Riveaux. He can't cook. Beulah makes all his meals and sends Lettie and Glorie over with them. But he's fond of carving. He likes it when Beulah roasts a hen or cooks a ham. He takes a very long time sharpening the knife.

He doesn't talk much. He stares at his food with his kind eyes. He says one evening: 'I never went to England. My wife and her friend Kathleen, they used to go. To see Shakespeare. You can see Shakespeare in Nashville. I guess you can see Shakespeare in Alaska. But that wasn't good enough for Mrs Riveaux; she liked a thing to be authentic.'

Then he says: 'Mrs Riveaux was an anglophile. We got a larder full of Cooper's Oxford Marmalade. I tell her in my prayers that you're working here and I can feel her smile.'

I say: 'I'm sorry I couldn't have met Mrs Riveaux.'

'Yes,' says the Judge, 'yes.' Then he changes the subject. He says: 'Tell me about that farm in England. Still there, is it?'

'It was sold,' I say. 'When my father died. The land's still there. But I left it a long time ago.'

'Can't remember it, can you?'

'No,' I say. 'I can remember it.'

The Judge is sitting very still. He doesn't want the conversation to go back to the subject of Mrs Riveaux. He wishes he hadn't mentioned her. And so, to comfort him, I start describing Elm Farm, I take myself on an imaginary walk, out of the back door round the farmyard where Marguerite used to peck, into the barn where I tried to turn mower blades into swords, down the lane to the field where the hen houses used to be, where Timmy threw grain up into the air. I describe the Scots pine and the tyre swing. I walk on down to the river and the watercress beds . . .

The Judge folds up his napkin. He rests his hands neatly on the folded square.

I say: 'There were two acres of forest not very far from

the house. When I was a child I got lost there. The night fell and I couldn't see my way out. I held on to a tree and waited. I was found in the end. But I don't love woods and trees the way most people do. What I love here is the silence and the sky.'

It has started to get dark while I've been talking. It's a summer darkness, mauve and soft.

'Go on,' says the Judge.

'There's nothing more,' I say. 'That's it.'

Sterns sends me a command. He says: 'It's time to come home. It's time to go on with your life.'

He believes I should have what he calls 'reconstructive surgery'. He thinks I am one of the few female-to-male transsexuals for whom the creation of a penis is of critical importance.

This penis is real flesh, my flesh, moved and sculpted.

A pedicle or barrel of tissue would be raised on my abdomen. Operation by operation, it is moved downwards till it hangs where it should. The urethra is re-routed into it. A synthetic stiffening rod of the same kind that is inserted into the penises of impotent men is sewn inside it.

With this, I could be a woman's lover. She would know no difference. Almost none.

Sterns believes that I will never be happy until I am capable of this. He thinks this is what I keep dreaming about.

I don't dream about this. I don't dream about anything. Days unfold. Martin lives them. He works through the hot afternoons. He drinks lemonade made by Beulah. He listens to Jeremiah's life. He strokes the necks of the peacocks. He sleeps soundly in the big bed. I am him and he is me and that's all. That's enough.

The woman I wanted was Pearl. I wanted to be Pearl's universe. For her, I would have re-made myself as often and as completely as she demanded. She could have gone on inventing me until death parted us.

Sterns knows this. Knowing it, you'd think he'd have a better understanding of my everyday dreams. But then he is a long way away from me and sitting in the dark. He has fish as companions. He's never seen the sun on the creek. He's never heard Walter Loomis sing.

I tell Sterns in a letter that I have no desire to return to England. I tell him I have reached a plateau, a level place. I say to him: 'Something or someone would have to *call* me back for me to give up the life that I have. The idea of more surgery doesn't call me.'

I remind him and I remind myself that I am thirty years old.

And out in the fields I say to Jeremiah: 'Age isn't the only thing to creep up on us. Sometimes it's happiness.'

Walter has bought a car. It's a second-hand blue Chevvy with patched leather upholstery.

He folds the roof down and drives around in the sunshine with his rhinestone elbow leaning out into the breeze. Sky sits beside him with a chiffon scarf tied round her hair. When the fall comes, they're going to go on a trip in search of Sky's husband. They say: 'We want to be married before the cold weather blows in.'

Their record is out. TMS Records gave a little party for them. Everyone drank and danced. I thought it was going to be an LP containing all the songs Walter's been writing since the beginning of time, but it isn't. It's a single. And it isn't often played anywhere. But no one is downhearted. Walter and Skippy Jean and Bentwater all say: 'That was just a start. A single is a toe in the lake.' The lake they're dreaming of is where the sword Excalibur lies, jammed into a rock.

They live on what Sky earns as a backup singer and on

Walter's yard work. The last gift he had from one of his women employers was a baseball bat.

Sometimes, he sings for tips at Fay May's. He's earned more than two hundred dollars in tips and he tells me: 'I'm sending these to Pete. I've told him to save for an engine to put in the bus. Then he can drive it away. He can convert it into a proper motor home. He could go somewhere where he can get electricity in through the window.'

One Sunday, Walter and Sky and I drive out to Opryland. Sky says: 'This isn't just a concert hall, it's a complex. When they finish it, it's gonna be like a village. That's why they call it Opryland. You could live here and not move and have everything you need.'

It has the biggest parking lot in the world.

The blue Chevvy is the only car on it. We sit and stare at all the flat space round us.

Bentwater is with us. He's showing no sign of betraying Walter. Sometimes, what the world predicts doesn't occur. He looks at the enormous car park and says: 'This moves me somehow. Hell knows why.'

And then something beautiful happens . . . Sky has brought her roller skates. She tells us these are the same skates she's had since she was thirteen. She puts them on. She hitches up her skirt and unties her scarf and climbs out of the Chevvy. She clomps a few yards and then turns round and smiles at us.

'Go on,' says Walter. 'Let's see you!'

So she starts skating. With the thin legs she has, the skates look enormous. I expect her to fall and bruise herself. But she doesn't fall. She lifts her arms like a dancer and glides cleanly away. She does circles and figures. Her hair flies out as she goes faster. She's as graceful as a swallow. We sit absolutely still, with the sun burning down on us, gazing at her.

A girl on a parking lot roller skating. You wouldn't necessarily have thought of that as a wonderful thing.

'Darn *me*!' says Bent.

Walter hears nothing, sees nothing, except Sky. He gets slowly out of the car and walks towards her. He takes off his rhinestone jacket and lets it drop. He holds out his arms.

I have bought a Roach Motel. Now, in the bright nights, there's no sign of my cockroaches. They've waltzed into the motel and died. Les Ches had Roach Motels on his brain, along with his leatherette lounger and his lost wife.

Our minds are like women at a jumble sale, sifting and searching, moving things around.

Mine still moves one piece of the past around:

Estelle. My mother. Est.

Sometimes – most of the time – she's with Cord at Gresham Tears. Sometimes, she's at Mountview. She's never with Timmy and Pearl. Sometimes, she's walking along, in no place that I recognise.

Wherever I move her, she is beautiful. Even when she's knitting a grey square. Her skin is white and clear and she's wearing her old beautiful smile.

Sometimes she's at a window. It might be a window at Gresham Tears, or it might not. All I see is that the window is half-open and that there is sunlight falling onto my mother who stands there, waiting.

20

1980

Estelle:

A new decade.

But.

These days, you have to put 'but' after everything. 'I am alive. But.'

Too much has happened to me. These happenings crowded together so densely in my mind that I had to find some rest here, at Mountview.

But.

Mountview is closing down.

This is what they tell us. They say: 'It is new government policy.'

I never used to notice what governments did. I should have paid closer attention.

It's going to become a hotel. There's going to be a swimming pool, underground. I say to them: 'That's perfectly all right. I'll stay on and become a hotel resident. I'll buy a swimming costume.' They say: 'Stop turning things into jokes, Estelle. Concentrate on getting well.' I say: 'In the old days, if you made a joke here, it was considered as a sign of recovery.' They say: 'The staff are more adequately trained in this modern day and age.'

These new, more adequately trained staff believe they

can make you well by asking you questions. I have my own personal questioner. She is called Linda. She's young enough to be my daughter. I go to what is called a Counselling Room and sit opposite Linda and she interrogates me. She smiles as I come in and then she always says the same thing. She says: 'Right, Estelle. Where *were* we?'

Where were we?

I don't know.

That's why I came here. To remember whereabouts I was in my life.

But Linda's in a hurry. She has six weeks in which to cure me. Then we all have to walk out of here, carrying our overnight bags.

I say to Linda: 'The government has overlooked a simple thing: you cannot mime tap dancing.'

The things that overcrowded my mind were deaths.

Sonny's. I forget when.

Then after that there was a period of respite when I lived with Cord at Gresham Tears. He said: 'What's happened to your cooking, Est? It's gone off.'

So I started to make the old kind of food. I made oxtail stews and shepherds' pies and Summer Pudding. And Cord and I began to thrive and get fat. In the mornings I'd hear him whistling in his room. In the afternoons we went for walks. He said: 'It's good to see you well again.' I made a wild-flower collection and bought a flower press. We spent some of our evenings making greeting cards.

But then the other deaths came.

Pete Loomis died in a hospital in Ipswich. No one went to see him except me. The cancer he'd had in his nose reappeared in his lung. He told me the turkeys were the cause. He said: 'If I were a younger man, I'd sue.'

I said: 'Listen, Pete, when you get out of here, come and stay with me and Cord. It's quiet there.'

He never got out of the hospital.

We buried him in Swaithey churchyard.

Grace Loomis said: 'If ever there was a wasted life, Estelle, this was it.'

I said: 'Your son wouldn't agree,' and I walked away from her.

Walter sent a guitar-shaped wreath made of carnations.

Pete left me his wind-up gramophone and his record collection.

Cord said: 'The things we treasure, honestly!'

The trolley bus was removed by the council, on Grace's orders. She said it was a health hazard.

We went on with our life at G. Tears, as Cord often called it. It was during that time that Cord said: 'There's something I want to tell you before I go, Stelle.'

'Go where?' I said.

'Pay attention,' said Cord. 'Listen, for once.'

I said: 'I'm listening. This is all I ever do: listen out for clues to the meaning of the world.'

We sat in deckchairs in the garden. We were getting so fat, the chairs creaked.

Cord said: 'Remember Mary?'

I said: 'It's history. It became history years and years ago.'

'All right,' he said. 'It's history. But you might as well get the history right. We've all protected you from it – Irene, Pearl, Timmy, me – but it's time you knew.'

So he told me the story of Martin.

When he'd finished, I had to go in search of something sweet to sustain me. I opened a packet of Cadbury's Orange Creams. I brought it out to the garden and put it near me, under my deckchair, in the shade.

I didn't speak. Cord was never like Linda. He didn't make you talk when you didn't want to.

I sat there, eating chocolate biscuits. After a long time, I said: 'Were we the cause? Sonny and me?'

Cord shook his head. He said: 'You, of all people, know that certain things appear to have no cause. They just *are* and that's it. And the answer's blowing in the wind.'

Where was I?

Where were we?

'Talking about your father's death,' says Linda.

'Was I?' I say.

'Yes,' says Linda.

'Well,' I say, 'I don't want to talk about that.'

And I don't. It was the saddest death of all.

It was after that that I had to come here because all I was doing was eating and staring out of the window. There was no room in my mind for anything except those two activities. I ate and looked out at the garden and when the darkness covered everything, I looked at that.

I say to Linda: 'One can endure it when certain things are in the past, but when almost everything is in the past, the present is too lonely.'

'Very well,' she says. 'Let's talk about the present. Who is in the present?'

'I am,' I say. 'But not for long. I'm being closed down. I'm not allowed to buy a swimming costume . . .'

'Estelle,' she says, 'we're not talking about this.'

'Why not?' I say. 'We should be. Where will I go when I leave here?'

'That's what I'm asking you. Who is there? Who is still part of your life?'

'I don't know,' I say. 'I have no idea. I can't think of anyone.'

'Timmy?' she says.

'Tim?'

'Yes.'

'Well,' I say, 'the part of my life that he's in takes place in Shropshire, but I hardly go there at all.'

'Why not?' she says.

I don't know how anyone can imagine this kind of interrogation can make a person well. My mother used to say: 'Try not to *quiz* people, Estelle. It's very rude, darling.'

'Why not?' says Linda again.

I say: 'Well, Shropshire's a long way from Suffolk. But that's not the point. The point is, in the old days here at Mountview, we were just allowed to *be*. We watched football. We played panel games. We walked in the gardens . . .'

'These are not the "old days",' she says.

'I know,' I say, 'but what *are* they? What kind of days are they?'

She looks confused for a moment, like some participants look on *Question Time*. Then she says: 'This is a new decade.'

I'm trying to remember all the new things.

There is going to be a new President of the USA. He was once married to Jane Wyman, friend of Ava Gardner.

There is a new kind of murderer in Yorkshire, in the area round Leeds.

There has been a new earthquake in Algeria.

We have a new Olympic gold medallist. He is a swimmer, younger than Timmy.

Japan has been given a new panda by China. Its name is Wong-Wong. Someone tells us that pandas encourage better relations between nations. Japanese children sing a song of welcome: 'Oh Wong-Wong, we've been waiting for you so long,/Let's play together amicably . . .'

Japanese songs do not have to rhyme.

In my next interrogation session, I say to Linda: 'What else is new?'

She says: 'There's going to be a new postage stamp, in honour of the Queen Mother's eightieth birthday.'

I say: 'I remember when her husband died. King George

VI. On the day of the funeral we stood in a potato field, trying to have a silence.'

'Yes?' says Linda. 'Tell me about that. Who was there?'

'Well,' I say, 'the four of us. Sonny and me. Timmy and . . .'

'And who?'

'And Martin,' I say.

'I don't know anything about Martin. Who is Martin?'

'My other child,' I say. 'He lives in America. He's not in my life. I haven't seen him for twenty years.'

'Why?' says Linda.

I say, 'God, you're tiring us out with all this questioning. We won't be able to stand, let alone walk out of here and back into the community.'

'When you've answered this, you can go,' she says.

'I don't *know* the answer,' I say.

'Then we have to find it,' she says, 'don't we, Estelle?'

When a questioner says 'we', he or she means 'you'.

How can anyone amass all the knowledge we need to stay alive in the world?

I get up out of my chair and lie down on the floor of the Counselling Room.

Linda orders me to get up. She says I am one of the most obstructive people she has ever met.

When she says 'met', she means 'questioned'.

She is tired of me.

I am tired of everything.

But she lets me go to my room. It's the same room I've always had here, and I've grown attached to it.

It's like a train compartment. When I'm in it, I'm always trying to travel somewhere in my mind.

It's not time for supper. I think I will go down and watch the new earthquake on television. Except that now that I'm up in my room alone I start wishing I was back with Linda.

I lied when I said that all I could see out of the window

after my father died was the garden and then the night. I saw Mary in the garden. When the night came, I still saw her there. She stared back at me. She threw a tennis ball at the glass.

I would like to tell Linda this.

I *have* to tell her.

I go running down the corridor. I hate running. I've never liked it.

I push my way past a man on the stairs. He's an out-and-out lunatic. He sings, 'Goodnight, Campers,' all day long. His vocal chords are breaking.

I go rushing to the Counselling Room, calling Linda's name. I open the door. There's another woman in there, being interrogated. I say: 'Linda, there's something I have to say!'

'You've had your hour, Estelle,' she says.

'I know,' I say, 'but I have to tell you this one thing. Please!'

'No,' she says. 'This is Marjorie's hour. I'll see you tomorrow.'

Tomorrow was the word I kept using.

I'd say: 'Tomorrow, I will do something about Mary.'

I'm fifty-five.

I sit down at the table in my room.

It's a September evening, getting dark.

In front of me is one of the home-made greetings cards I made with Cord. We never sent them to anyone. I brought them here to distribute among the sherpas and the air traffic controllers.

This card has scabious on it and poppies and lucerne and grass.

It's easier to write a greetings card in the mind than it is to actually write it. The message in the mind can always be altered. It can go through any number of invisible revisions. It could be metaphorical or fantastical. It could mention the heart of the onion, the explosion in the sky. It could be poetic or ironic. It could describe the search by torchlight, by tilleylight in the forest, the success of a conjuring trick in mid-afternoon in summer . . .

But once the message is there, written down with the green-ink pen, it has the appearance of something a bit lame, a bit pathetic. The act of writing it has changed it. It isn't really what you meant to say. It isn't even a greeting.

I stare at it. I read it again and again and again, until the words have no meaning at all:

> Dear Martin,
> Please forgive me. I hope you can.
> From your mother, Estelle.

It gets so dark, I can hardly see it, but still I go on staring at it.

At least the writing is quite neat.

That's something.

It doesn't look as though it's been written by a mad person but only by a woman with no imagination.

ACKNOWLEDGEMENTS

I would like to thank the following people, without whose knowledge, assistance and generosity this novel could not have been written:

Joan Bakewell, Janine Jacono, Victor Morris, Marc Larousse, Don Morant, Prebend Hertoft, Lee Goerner, Liz Hodgkinson, Ann Cook, Carolyn Dobbins, Ray Wix, Jeannie Sealey, John Lewis, Robert Dudley, Anita Cook.

The author and publishers are grateful to Faber & Faber Ltd for permission to quote from *The Hollow Men* by T. S. Eliot.

The author and publishers are grateful for permission to reproduce words from songs as follows:

The Yodelling Cowboy, words and music by Jimmy Rodgers, *Frankie and Johnny*, sung by Jimmy Rodgers, and *I'm working on the building*, words by A. P. Carter: used by kind permission of Peermusic (UK) Ltd, London.

Rose Marie, *Early Morning Rain* and *Alone and Forsaken*: reproduced by kind permission of Warner Chappell Music Ltd.

Every effort has been made to trace the holders of copyrights. Any inadvertent omissions of acknowledgement or permission can be rectified in future editions.

Rose Tremain

The Gustav Sonata

The *Sunday Times* Top Ten Bestseller

What is the difference between friendship and love?

Gustav grows up in a small town in Switzerland, where the horrors of the Second World War seem a distant echo. But Gustav's father has mysteriously died, and his adored mother Emilie is strangely cold and indifferent to him. Gustav's life is a lonely one until he meets Anton. An intense lifelong friendship develops but Anton fails to understand how deeply and irrevocably his life and Gustav's are entwined until it is almost too late...

'This is a perfect novel about life's imperfection... Tremain is writing at the height of her inimitable powers... Remarkable and moving'
Observer

'A magnificent novel, heartbreaking, unsentimental and beautifully written'
John Boyne, *Irish Times*

'Beautifully tender and brilliantly written... A tale of the most powerful part of any friendship: love'
Stylist

'A perfect gem of a novel'
Mail on Sunday

VINTAGE

Rose Tremain

Restoration

When a twist of fate delivers an ambitious young medical student to the court of King Charles II, he is suddenly thrust into a vibrant world of luxury and opulence. Blessed with a quick wit and sparkling charm, Robert Merivel rises quickly, soon finding favour with the King, and privileged with a position as 'paper groom' to the youngest of the King's mistresses. But by falling in love with her, Merivel transgresses the one rule that will cast him out from his new-found paradise...

'Triumphant'
Sunday Telegraph

'To be moved and impressed by a novel and yet so entertained, is rare'
Fay Weldon

'A dazzling triumph... It is nothing less than superb'
New York Times Book Review

'A most beautiful and original novel'
Independent

'Gripping'
Herald

VINTAGE

Rose Tremain

Merivel

The gaudy years of the Restoration are long gone and Robert Merivel, physician and courtier to King Charles II, sets off for the French court in search of a fresh start. But royal life at the Palace of Versailles – all glitter in front and squalor behind – leaves him in despair, until a chance encounter with the seductive Madame de Flamanville allows him to dream of a different future.

But will that future ever be his? Summoned home urgently to attend to the ailing King, Merivel finds his loyalty and skill tested to their limits.

'One of the great imaginative creations in English literature'
Daily Telegraph

'An unadulterated delight'
Independent

'Rich and satisfying'
Sunday Times

'A tour de force of literary technique, a treasure house of diligent research and imaginative ingenuity'
Daily Telegraph

'Wonderfully entertaining'
Guardian Books of the Year

VINTAGE

Rose Tremain

The Road Home

Lev is on his way from Eastern Europe to Britain, seeking work. Behind him loom the figures of his dead wife, his beloved young daugher and his outrageous friend Rudi who – dreaming of the wealthy West – lives largely for his battered Chevrolet. Ahead of Lev lies the deep strangeness of the British: their hostile streets, their clannish pubs, their obsession with celebrity. London holds out the alluring possibility of friendship, sex, money and a new career and, if Lev is lucky, a new sense of belonging...

'A novel of urgent humanity'
Sunday Telegraph

'A classic work by the gifted Tremain'
Guardian

'Rose Tremain does not disappoint. *The Road Home* is thematically rich, dealing with loss and separation, mourning and melancholia... As always her writing has a delicious, crunchy precision'
Observer

'Filled with emotional richness, complex sensibility and a passionate insistence on the humanity of the poor'
Sunday Times

'Tremain is a magnificent story-teller'
Independent on Sunday

VINTAGE

Rose Tremain

Trespass

In a silent valley in southern France stands an isolated stone farmhouse, the Mas Lunel. Its owner is Aramon Lunel, an alcoholic haunted by his violent past. His sister, Audrun, alone in her bungalow within sight of the Mas Lunel, dreams of exacting retribution for the unspoken betrayals that have blighted her life.

Into this closed world comes Anthony Verey, a wealthy but disillusioned antiques dealer from London seeking to remake his life in France. From the moment he arrives at the Mas Lunel, a frightening and unstoppable series of consequences is set in motion...

'Taut...full of suspense...bewitching'
Observer

'Thrilling...a terrific book, accomplished in its poised, imaginative storytelling and its vivid, sensual rendering of landscape and character, emotion and memory'
The Times

'An intelligent and terrifyingly plausible meditation'
Sunday Telegraph

'A sumptuously shaded portrait of a private, lonely place and its stranded people'
Independent

'A truly wonderful, disturbing and thrilling story'
Sunday Express

VINTAGE

Rose Tremain

Music & Silence

Winner of the Whitbread Novel Award

In the year 1629, a young English lutenist named Peter Claire
arrives at the Danish Court to join King Christian IV's Royal
Orchestra. From the moment when he realises that the
musicians perform in a freezing cellar underneath the royal
apartments, Peter Claire understands that he's come to a place
where the opposing states of light and dark, good and evil, are
waging war to the death.

Designated the King's 'Angel' because of his good looks, he
finds himself falling in love with the young woman who is the
companion of the King's adulterous and estranged wife,
Kirsten. With his loyalties fatally divided between duty and
passion, how can Peter Claire find the path that will realise his
hopes and save his soul?

'A magnificent novel...a brilliant book which will
repay many readings'
The Times

'Tremain's achievement in *Music & Silence* is extraordinary...
A narrative as funny as it is compelling'
Daily Telegraph

'Intricate and sparkling... Ingenious, amusing and beautifully written'
Observer

'A superb novel... A wonderful, joyously noisy book'
Guardian

'Lyrical, voluptuous...splendid... A sumptuous drama lit
by the glamorous torchlight of the courtly past'
Sunday Times

VINTAGE